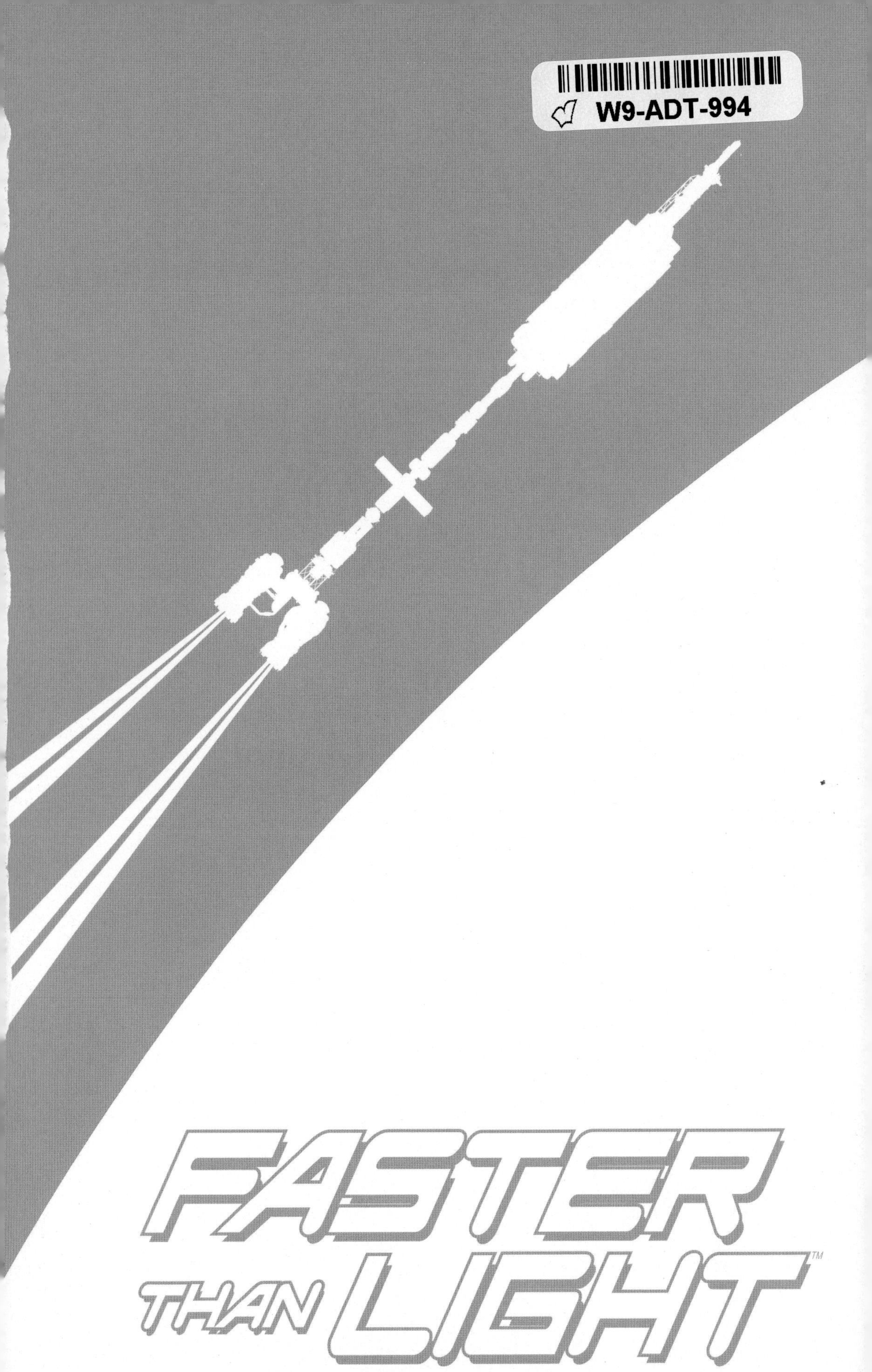

FASTER THAN LIGHT™

Visit
EXPERIENCEANOMALY.COM/FTL
on your Apple or Android device
to get the free companion app.

- Watch the captain's log
- Read the backstory in the encyclopedia
- Interact with Augmented Reality aliens,
  ships, weapons, and more

First Printing: March, 2016   **ISBN: 978-1-63215-684-6**

FASTER THAN LIGHT, VOL. 1. MARCH, 2016. Published by Image Comics, Inc. Office of publication: 2001 Center Street, Sixth Floor, Berkeley, California 94704. Copyright © & ™ 2016 ANOMALY PRODUCTIONS. All rights reserved. FASTER THAN LIGHT™ (including all prominent characters featured herein), its logo and all character likenesses are trademarks of Anomaly Productions, unless otherwise noted. Image Comics® and its logos are registered trademarks of Image Comics, Inc. Shadowline ® and its logos are registered trademarks of Jim Valentino. No part of this publication may be reproduced or transmitted, in any form or by any means (except for short excerpts for review purposes) without the express written permission of Anomaly Productions. All names, characters, events and locales in this publication are entirely fictional. Any resemblance to actual persons (living or dead), events or places, without satiric intent, is coincidental. For information regarding the CPSIA on this printed material call: 203-595-3636 and provide reference #RICH-671147. Printed in the USA. For international rights, contact: foreignlicensing@imagecomics.com. ISBN: 978-1-63215-684-6

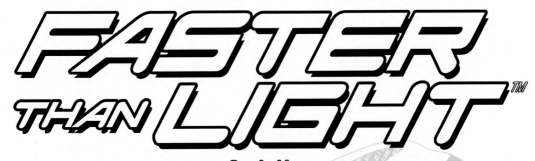

image® COMICS PRESENTS A Shadowline® PRODUCTION

FASTER THAN LIGHT™

Created by

BRIAN HABERLIN & SKIP BRITTENHAM

for ANOMALY™ PRODUCTIONS

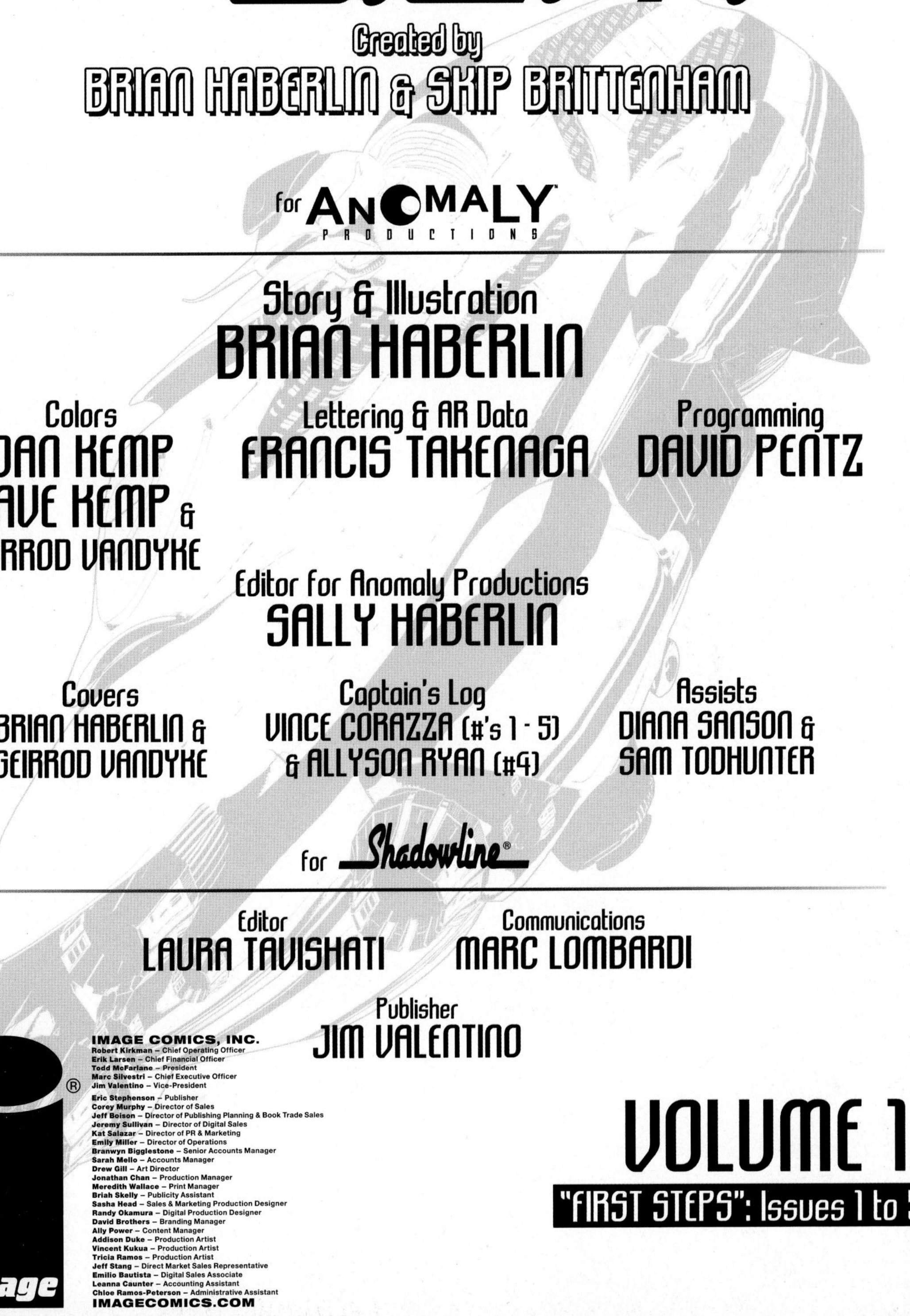

Story & Illustration
BRIAN HABERLIN

Colors
DAN KEMP
DAVE KEMP &
GEIRROD VANDYKE

Lettering & AR Data
FRANCIS TAKENAGA

Programming
DAVID PENTZ

Editor for Anomaly Productions
SALLY HABERLIN

Covers
BRIAN HABERLIN &
GEIRROD VANDYKE

Captain's Log
VINCE CORAZZA (#'s 1 - 5)
& ALLYSON RYAN (#4)

Assists
DIANA SANSON &
SAM TODHUNTER

for Shadowline®

Editor
LAURA TAVISHATI

Communications
MARC LOMBARDI

Publisher
JIM VALENTINO

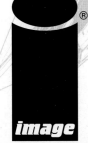

IMAGE COMICS, INC.
Robert Kirkman – Chief Operating Officer
Erik Larsen – Chief Financial Officer
Todd McFarlane – President
Marc Silvestri – Chief Executive Officer
Jim Valentino – Vice-President

Eric Stephenson – Publisher
Corey Murphy – Director of Sales
Jeff Boison – Director of Publishing Planning & Book Trade Sales
Jeremy Sullivan – Director of Digital Sales
Kat Salazar – Director of PR & Marketing
Emily Miller – Director of Operations
Branwyn Bigglestone – Senior Accounts Manager
Sarah Mello – Accounts Manager
Drew Gill – Art Director
Jonathan Chan – Production Manager
Meredith Wallace – Print Manager
Briah Skelly – Publicity Assistant
Sasha Head – Sales & Marketing Production Designer
Randy Okamura – Digital Production Designer
David Brothers – Branding Manager
Ally Power – Content Manager
Addison Duke – Production Artist
Vincent Kukua – Production Artist
Tricia Ramos – Production Artist
Jeff Stang – Direct Market Sales Representative
Emilio Bautista – Digital Sales Associate
Leanna Caunter – Accounting Assistant
Chloe Ramos-Peterson – Administrative Assistant
IMAGECOMICS.COM

VOLUME 1.

"FIRST STEPS": Issues 1 to 5

Man is an artifact designed for space travel. He is not designed to remain in his present biologic state any more than a tadpole is designed to remain a tadpole.

William S. Burroughs

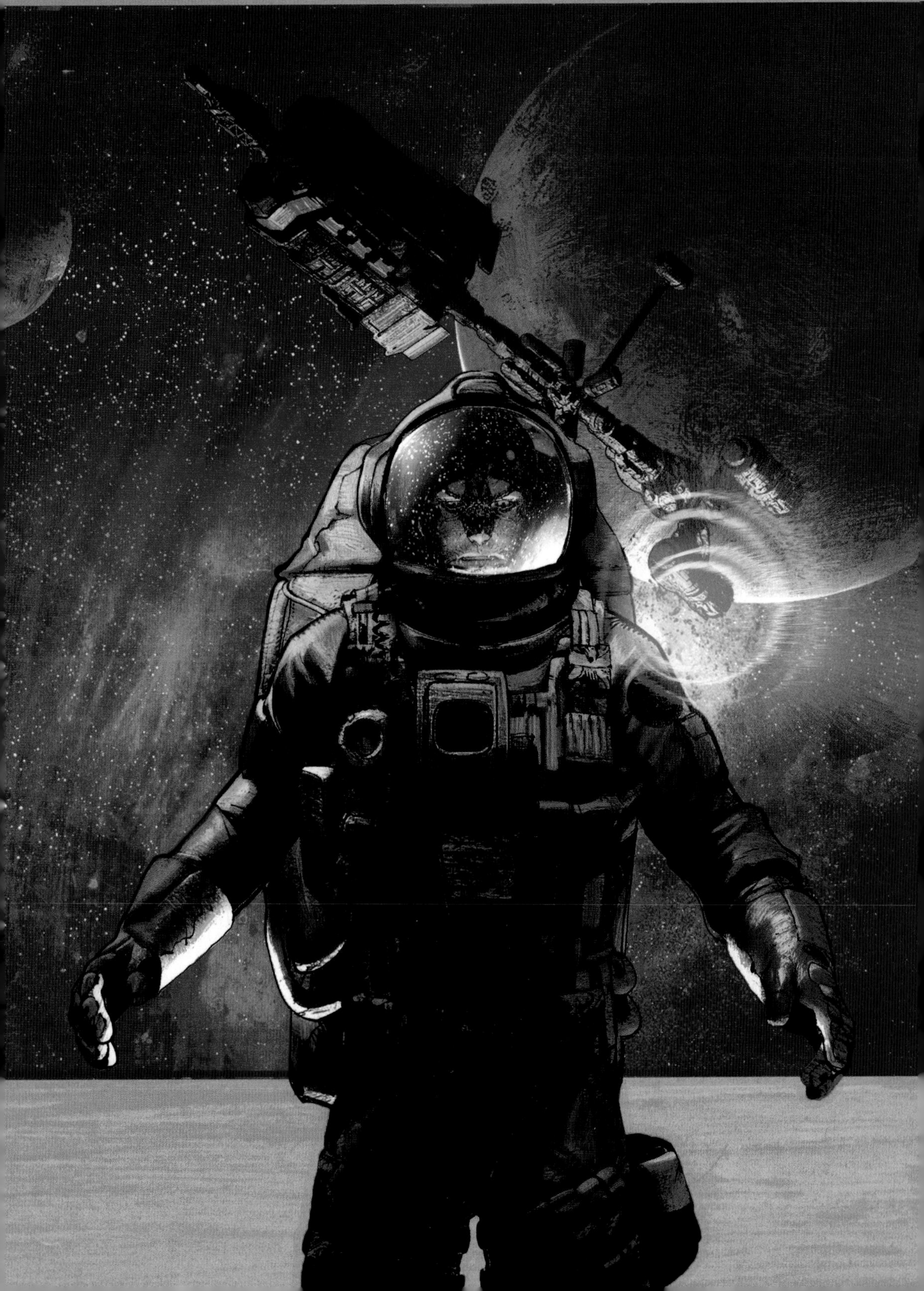

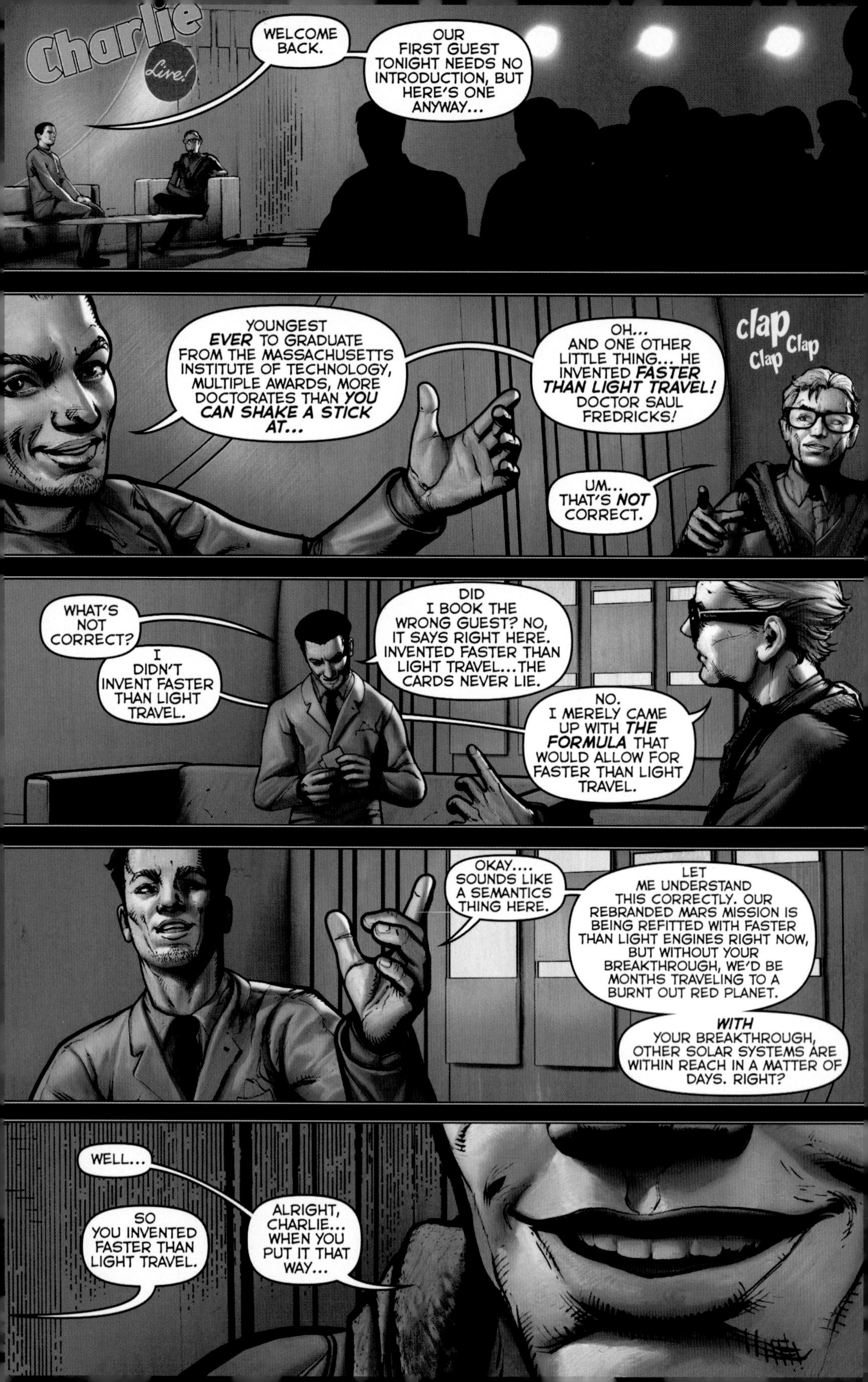
Charlie Live!
WELCOME BACK.
OUR FIRST GUEST TONIGHT NEEDS NO INTRODUCTION, BUT HERE'S ONE ANYWAY...
YOUNGEST EVER TO GRADUATE FROM THE MASSACHUSETTS INSTITUTE OF TECHNOLOGY, MULTIPLE AWARDS, MORE DOCTORATES THAN YOU CAN SHAKE A STICK AT...
OH... AND ONE OTHER LITTLE THING... HE INVENTED FASTER THAN LIGHT TRAVEL! DOCTOR SAUL FREDRICKS!
clap Clap Clap
UM... THAT'S NOT CORRECT.
WHAT'S NOT CORRECT?
I DIDN'T INVENT FASTER THAN LIGHT TRAVEL.
DID I BOOK THE WRONG GUEST? NO, IT SAYS RIGHT HERE. INVENTED FASTER THAN LIGHT TRAVEL...THE CARDS NEVER LIE.
NO. I MERELY CAME UP WITH THE FORMULA THAT WOULD ALLOW FOR FASTER THAN LIGHT TRAVEL.
OKAY.... SOUNDS LIKE A SEMANTICS THING HERE.
LET ME UNDERSTAND THIS CORRECTLY. OUR REBRANDED MARS MISSION IS BEING REFITTED WITH FASTER THAN LIGHT ENGINES RIGHT NOW, BUT WITHOUT YOUR BREAKTHROUGH, WE'D BE MONTHS TRAVELING TO A BURNT OUT RED PLANET.
WITH YOUR BREAKTHROUGH, OTHER SOLAR SYSTEMS ARE WITHIN REACH IN A MATTER OF DAYS. RIGHT?
WELL...
SO YOU INVENTED FASTER THAN LIGHT TRAVEL.
ALRIGHT, CHARLIE... WHEN YOU PUT IT THAT WAY...

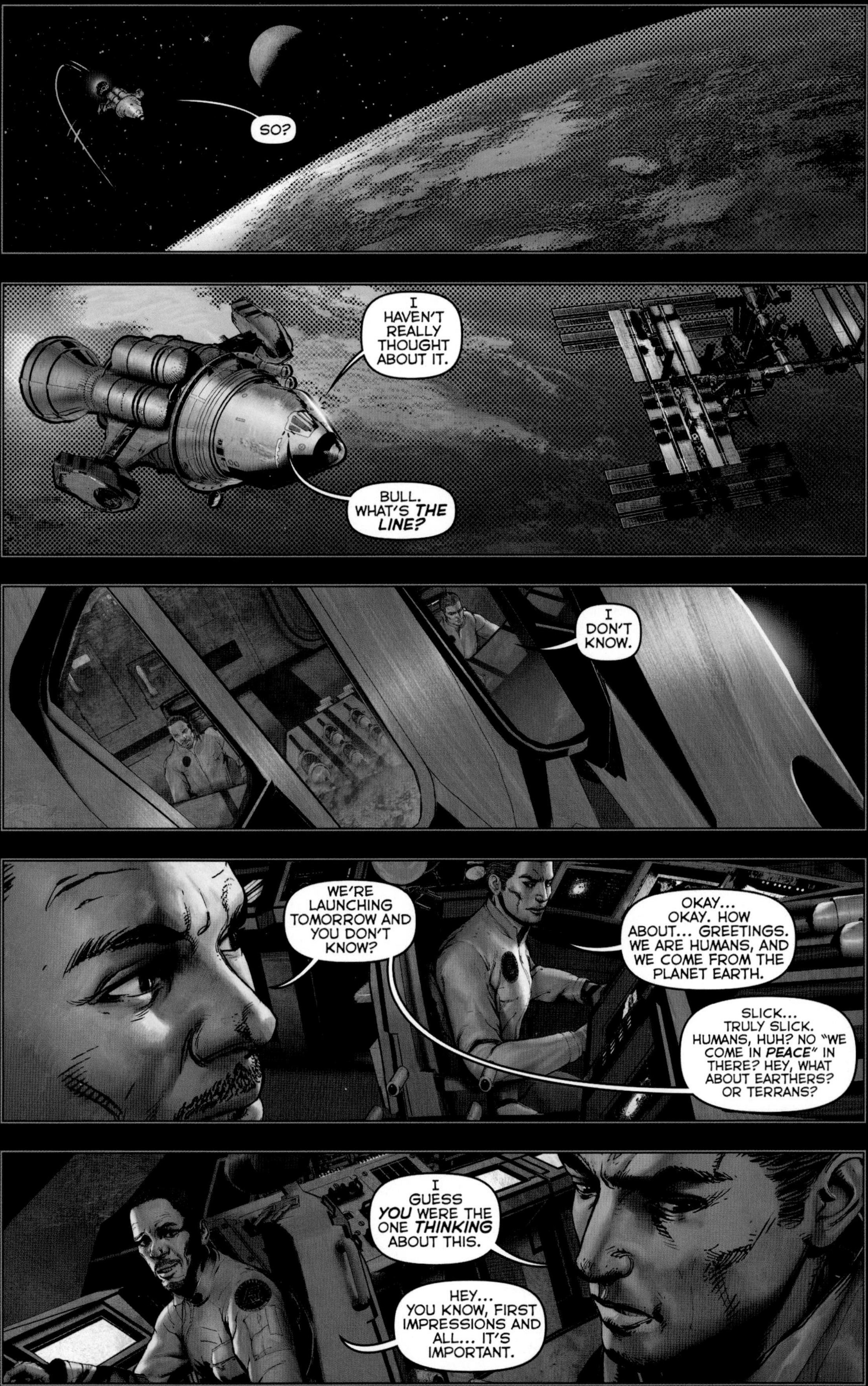
SO?
I HAVEN'T REALLY THOUGHT ABOUT IT.
BULL. WHAT'S *THE LINE?*
I DON'T KNOW.
WE'RE LAUNCHING TOMORROW AND YOU DON'T KNOW?
OKAY... OKAY. HOW ABOUT... GREETINGS. WE ARE HUMANS, AND WE COME FROM THE PLANET EARTH.
SLICK... TRULY SLICK. HUMANS, HUH? NO "WE COME IN *PEACE*" IN THERE? HEY, WHAT ABOUT EARTHERS? OR TERRANS?
I GUESS *YOU* WERE THE ONE *THINKING* ABOUT THIS.
HEY... YOU KNOW, FIRST IMPRESSIONS AND ALL... IT'S IMPORTANT.

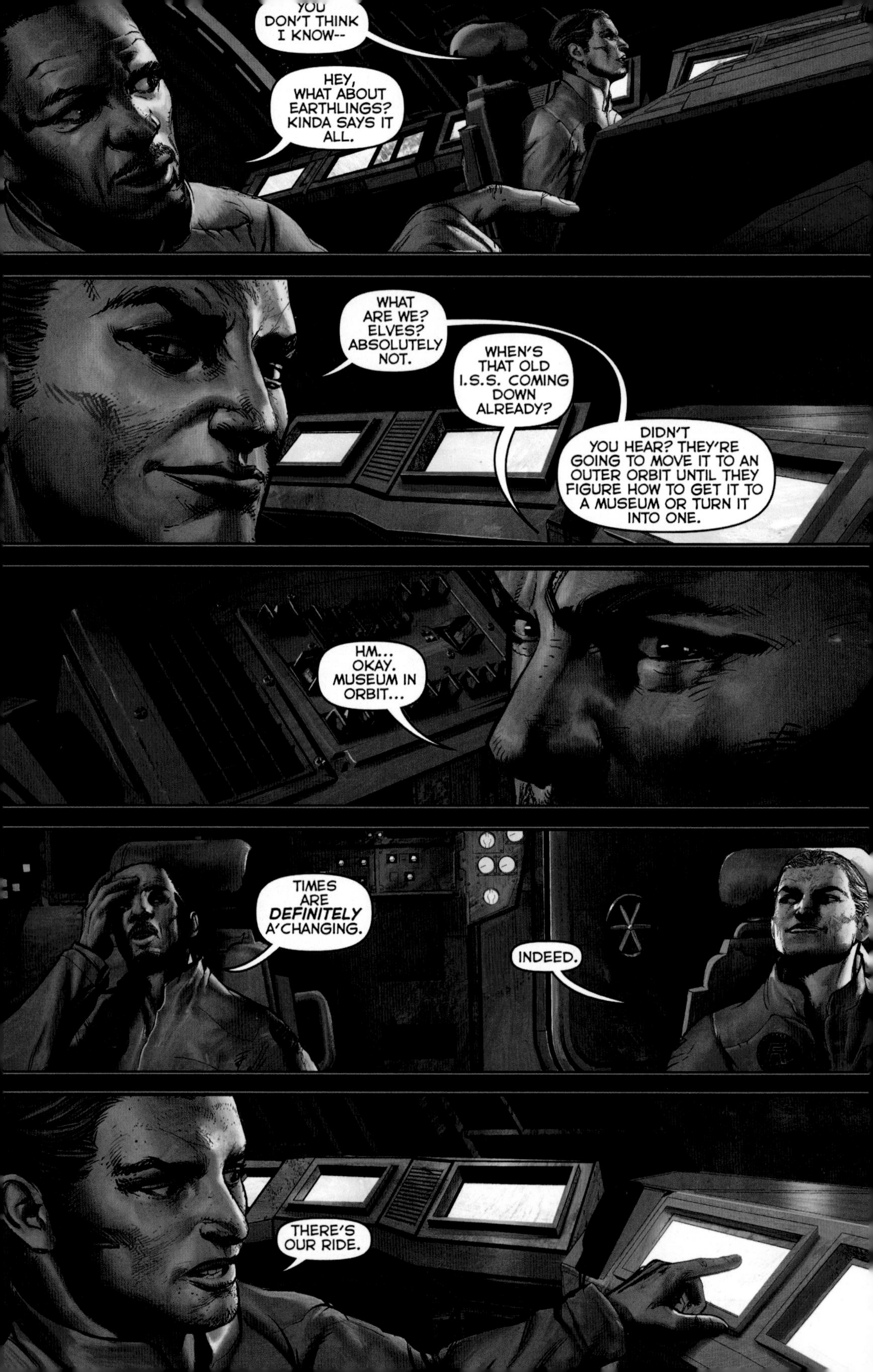
YOU DON'T THINK I KNOW--
HEY, WHAT ABOUT EARTHLINGS? KINDA SAYS IT ALL.
WHAT ARE WE? ELVES? ABSOLUTELY NOT.
WHEN'S THAT OLD I.S.S. COMING DOWN ALREADY?
DIDN'T YOU HEAR? THEY'RE GOING TO MOVE IT TO AN OUTER ORBIT UNTIL THEY FIGURE HOW TO GET IT TO A MUSEUM OR TURN IT INTO ONE.
HM... OKAY. MUSEUM IN ORBIT...
TIMES ARE *DEFINITELY* A'CHANGING.
INDEED.
THERE'S OUR RIDE.

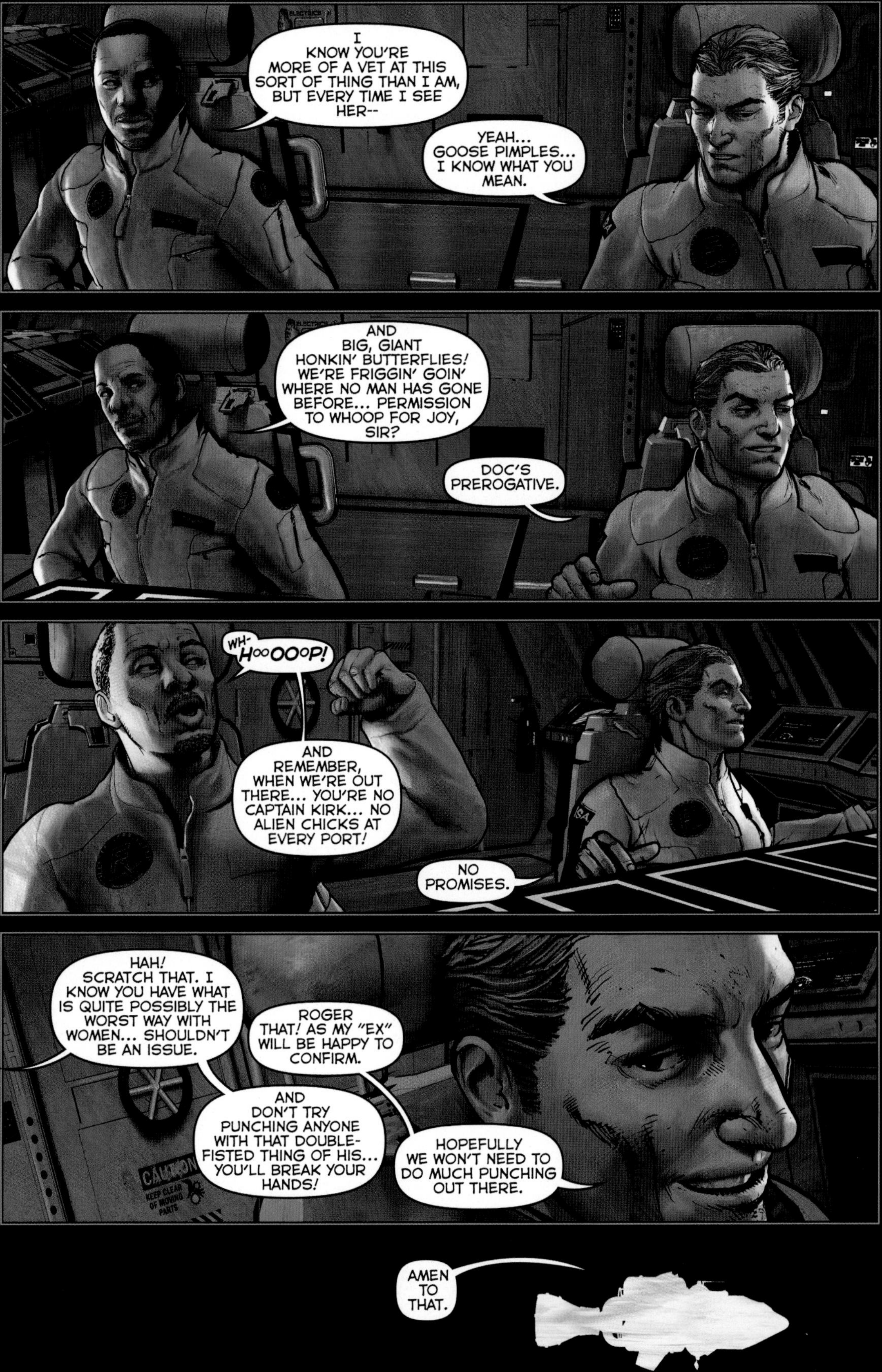
I KNOW YOU'RE MORE OF A VET AT THIS SORT OF THING THAN I AM, BUT EVERY TIME I SEE HER--
YEAH... GOOSE PIMPLES... I KNOW WHAT YOU MEAN.
AND BIG, GIANT HONKIN' BUTTERFLIES! WE'RE FRIGGIN' GOIN' WHERE NO MAN HAS GONE BEFORE... PERMISSION TO WHOOP FOR JOY, SIR?
DOC'S PREROGATIVE.
WH-HOOOOP!
AND REMEMBER, WHEN WE'RE OUT THERE... YOU'RE NO CAPTAIN KIRK... NO ALIEN CHICKS AT EVERY PORT!
NO PROMISES.
HAH! SCRATCH THAT. I KNOW YOU HAVE WHAT IS QUITE POSSIBLY THE WORST WAY WITH WOMEN... SHOULDN'T BE AN ISSUE.
ROGER THAT! AS MY "EX" WILL BE HAPPY TO CONFIRM.
AND DON'T TRY PUNCHING ANYONE WITH THAT DOUBLE-FISTED THING OF HIS... YOU'LL BREAK YOUR HANDS!
HOPEFULLY WE WON'T NEED TO DO MUCH PUNCHING OUT THERE.
AMEN TO THAT.

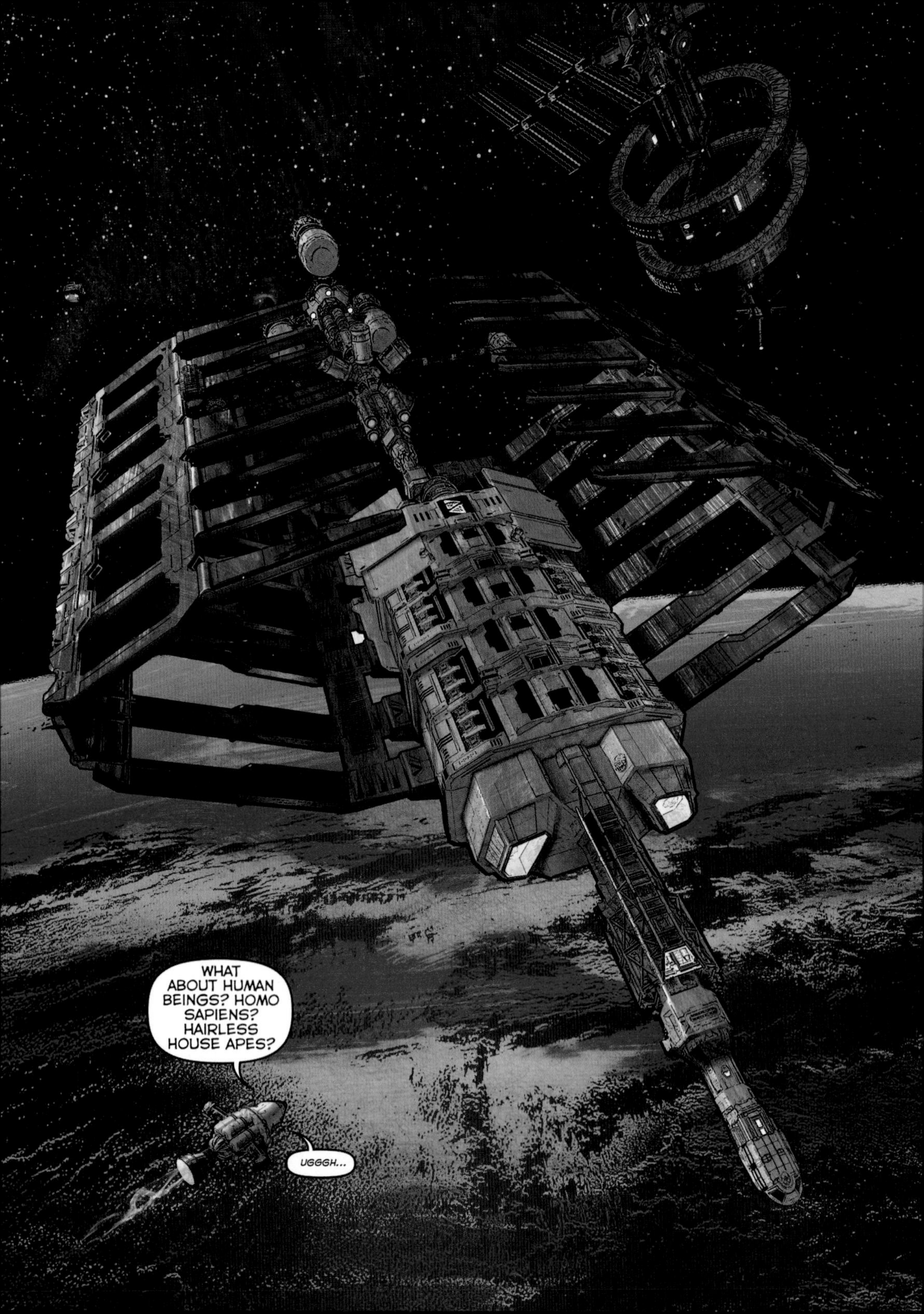
WHAT ABOUT HUMAN BEINGS? HOMO SAPIENS? HAIRLESS HOUSE APES?
UGGGH...

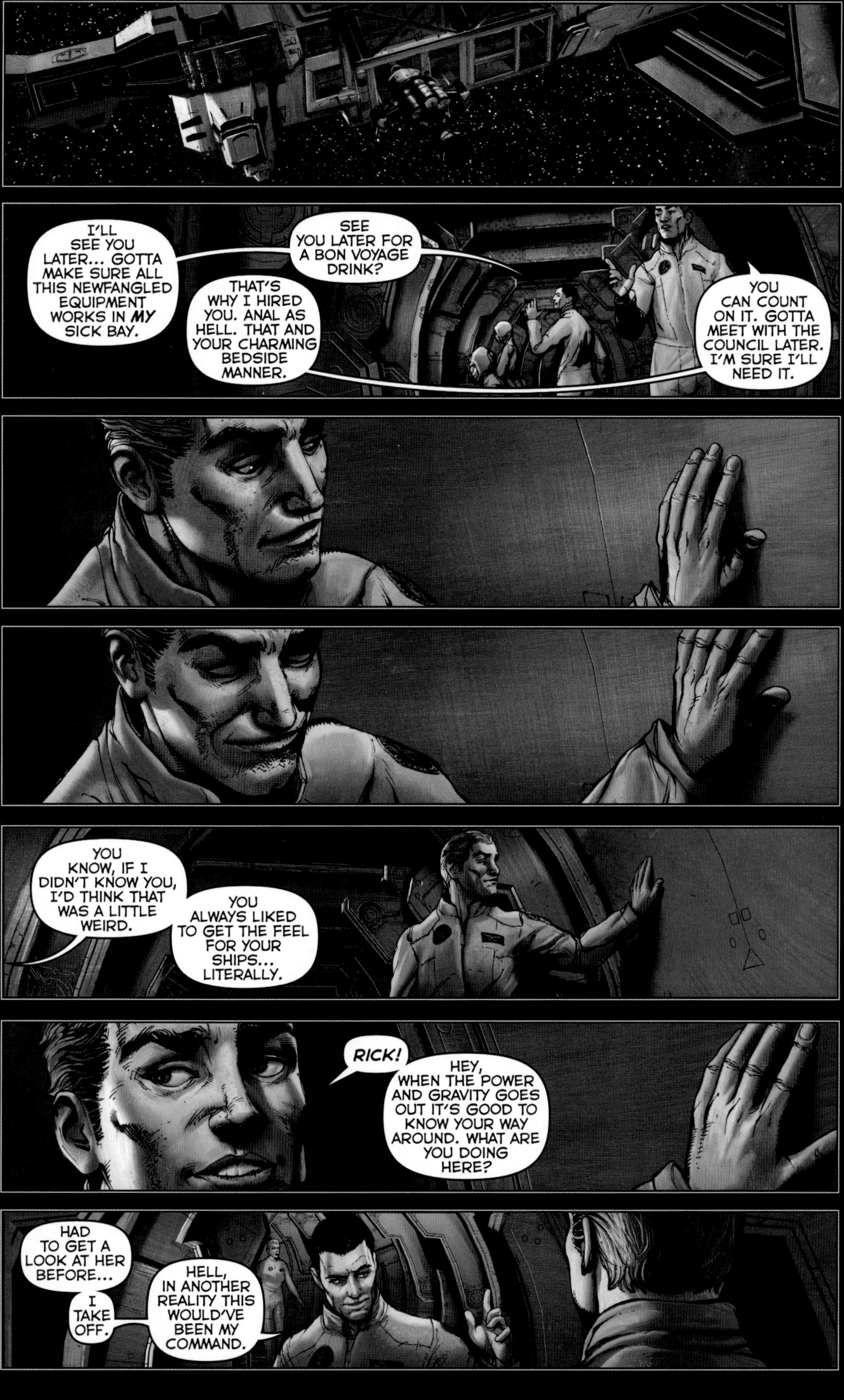
I'LL SEE YOU LATER... GOTTA MAKE SURE ALL THIS NEWFANGLED EQUIPMENT WORKS IN *MY* SICK BAY.
SEE YOU LATER FOR A BON VOYAGE DRINK?
THAT'S WHY I HIRED YOU. ANAL AS HELL. THAT AND YOUR CHARMING BEDSIDE MANNER.
YOU CAN COUNT ON IT. GOTTA MEET WITH THE COUNCIL LATER. I'M SURE I'LL NEED IT.
YOU KNOW, IF I DIDN'T KNOW YOU, I'D THINK THAT WAS A LITTLE WEIRD.
YOU ALWAYS LIKED TO GET THE FEEL FOR YOUR SHIPS... LITERALLY.
RICK!
HEY, WHEN THE POWER AND GRAVITY GOES OUT IT'S GOOD TO KNOW YOUR WAY AROUND. WHAT ARE YOU DOING HERE?
HAD TO GET A LOOK AT HER BEFORE...
I TAKE OFF.
HELL, IN ANOTHER REALITY THIS WOULD'VE BEEN MY COMMAND.

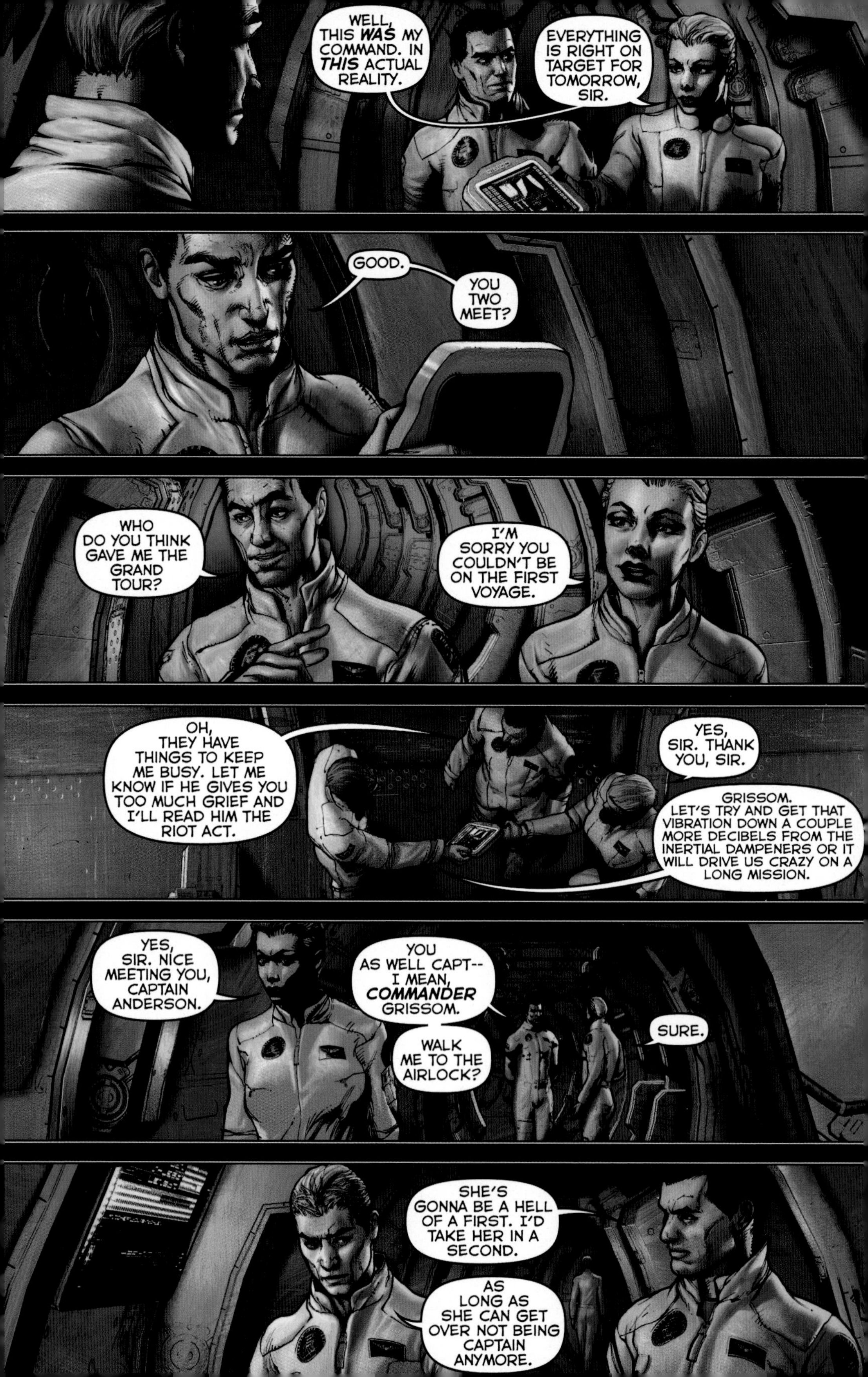
WELL, THIS WAS MY COMMAND. IN THIS ACTUAL REALITY.
EVERYTHING IS RIGHT ON TARGET FOR TOMORROW, SIR.
GOOD.
YOU TWO MEET?
WHO DO YOU THINK GAVE ME THE GRAND TOUR?
I'M SORRY YOU COULDN'T BE ON THE FIRST VOYAGE.
OH, THEY HAVE THINGS TO KEEP ME BUSY. LET ME KNOW IF HE GIVES YOU TOO MUCH GRIEF AND I'LL READ HIM THE RIOT ACT.
YES, SIR. THANK YOU, SIR.
GRISSOM. LET'S TRY AND GET THAT VIBRATION DOWN A COUPLE MORE DECIBELS FROM THE INERTIAL DAMPENERS OR IT WILL DRIVE US CRAZY ON A LONG MISSION.
YES, SIR. NICE MEETING YOU, CAPTAIN ANDERSON.
YOU AS WELL CAPT-- I MEAN, COMMANDER GRISSOM.
WALK ME TO THE AIRLOCK?
SURE.
SHE'S GONNA BE A HELL OF A FIRST. I'D TAKE HER IN A SECOND.
AS LONG AS SHE CAN GET OVER NOT BEING CAPTAIN ANYMORE.

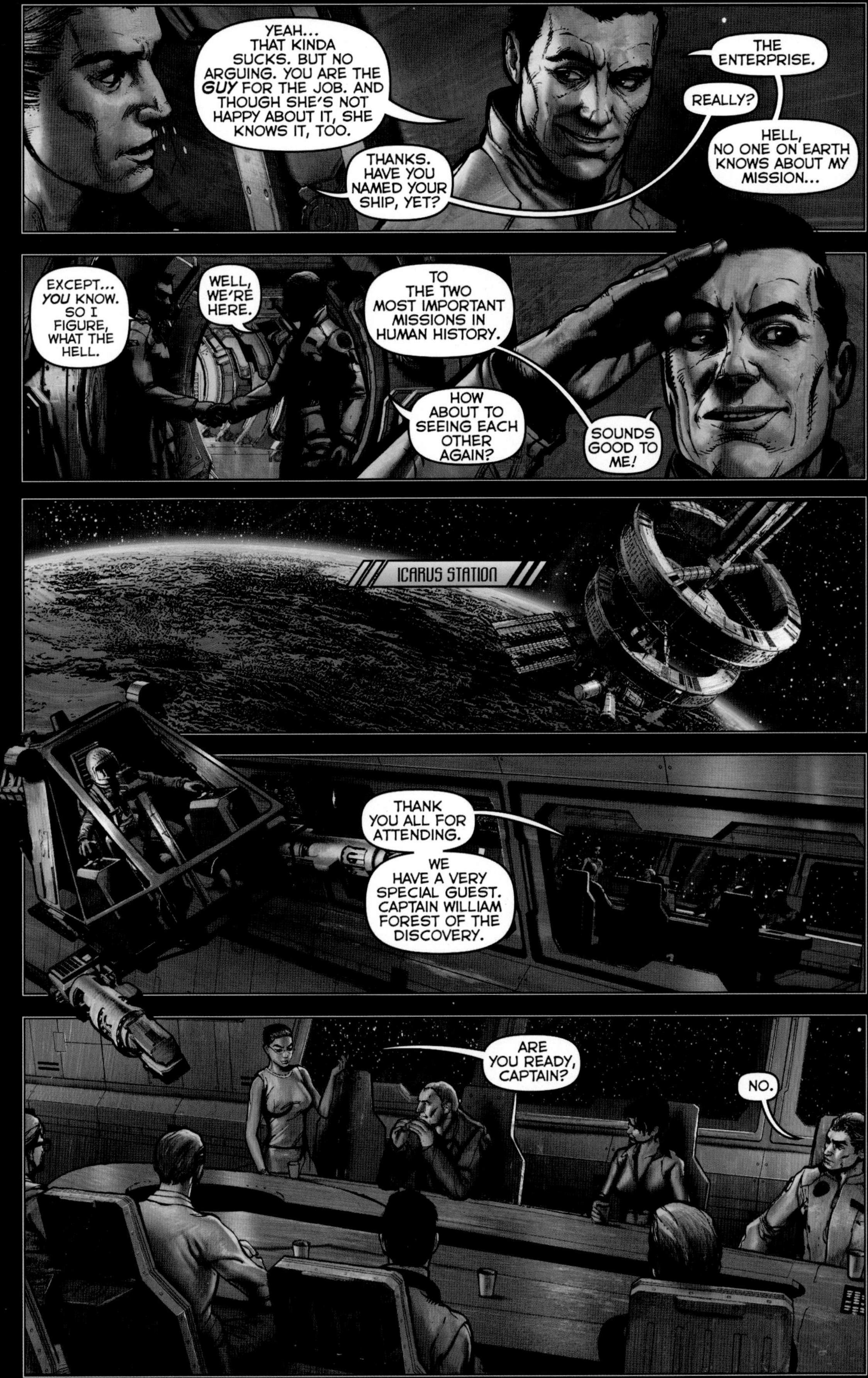
YEAH... THAT KINDA SUCKS. BUT NO ARGUING. YOU ARE THE GUY FOR THE JOB. AND THOUGH SHE'S NOT HAPPY ABOUT IT, SHE KNOWS IT, TOO.
THANKS. HAVE YOU NAMED YOUR SHIP, YET?
THE ENTERPRISE.
REALLY?
HELL, NO ONE ON EARTH KNOWS ABOUT MY MISSION...
EXCEPT... YOU KNOW. SO I FIGURE, WHAT THE HELL.
WELL, WE'RE HERE.
TO THE TWO MOST IMPORTANT MISSIONS IN HUMAN HISTORY.
HOW ABOUT TO SEEING EACH OTHER AGAIN?
SOUNDS GOOD TO ME!
ICARUS STATION
THANK YOU ALL FOR ATTENDING.
WE HAVE A VERY SPECIAL GUEST. CAPTAIN WILLIAM FOREST OF THE DISCOVERY.
ARE YOU READY, CAPTAIN?
NO.

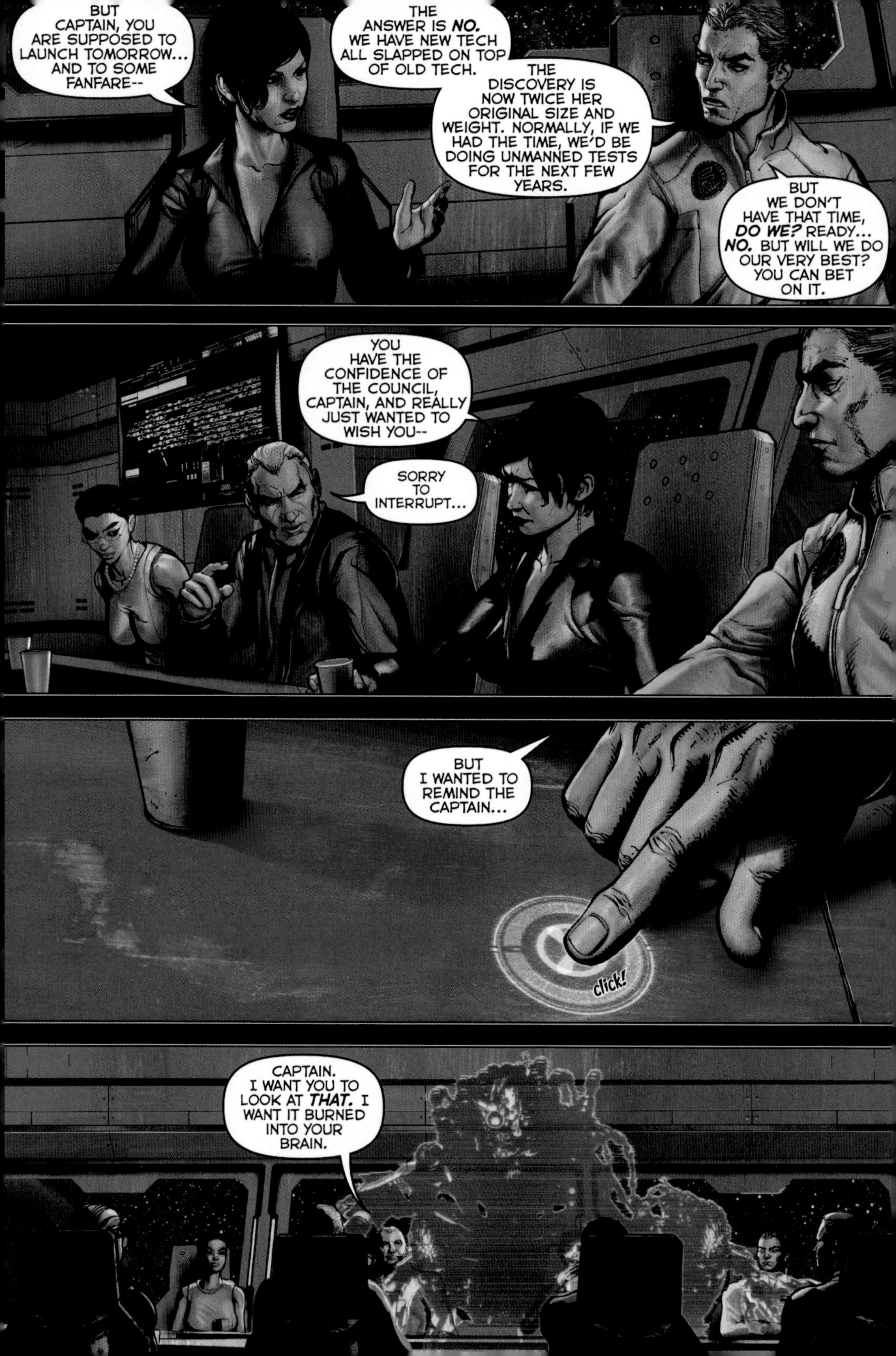
BUT CAPTAIN, YOU ARE SUPPOSED TO LAUNCH TOMORROW... AND TO SOME FANFARE--
THE ANSWER IS **NO.** WE HAVE NEW TECH ALL SLAPPED ON TOP OF OLD TECH.
THE DISCOVERY IS NOW TWICE HER ORIGINAL SIZE AND WEIGHT. NORMALLY, IF WE HAD THE TIME, WE'D BE DOING UNMANNED TESTS FOR THE NEXT FEW YEARS.
BUT WE DON'T HAVE THAT TIME, **DO WE?** READY... **NO.** BUT WILL WE DO OUR VERY BEST? YOU CAN BET ON IT.
YOU HAVE THE CONFIDENCE OF THE COUNCIL, CAPTAIN, AND REALLY JUST WANTED TO WISH YOU--
SORRY TO INTERRUPT...
BUT I WANTED TO REMIND THE CAPTAIN...
click!
CAPTAIN. I WANT YOU TO LOOK AT **THAT.** I WANT IT BURNED INTO YOUR BRAIN.

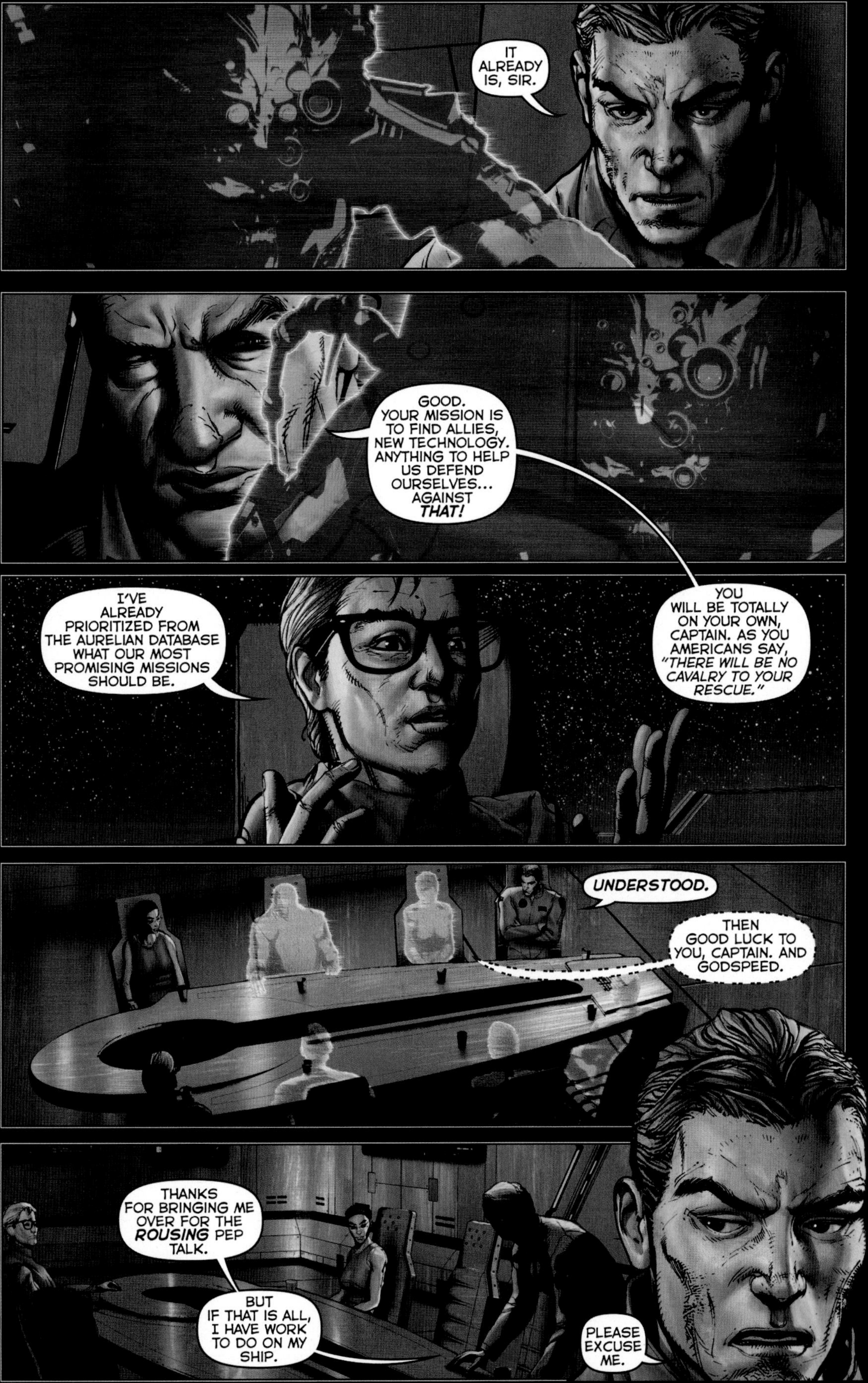
IT ALREADY IS, SIR.
GOOD. YOUR MISSION IS TO FIND ALLIES, NEW TECHNOLOGY. ANYTHING TO HELP US DEFEND OURSELVES... AGAINST *THAT!*
YOU WILL BE TOTALLY ON YOUR OWN, CAPTAIN. AS YOU AMERICANS SAY, *"THERE WILL BE NO CAVALRY TO YOUR RESCUE."*
I'VE ALREADY PRIORITIZED FROM THE AURELIAN DATABASE WHAT OUR MOST PROMISING MISSIONS SHOULD BE.
UNDERSTOOD.
THEN GOOD LUCK TO YOU, CAPTAIN. AND GODSPEED.
THANKS FOR BRINGING ME OVER FOR THE ***ROUSING*** PEP TALK.
BUT IF THAT IS ALL, I HAVE WORK TO DO ON MY SHIP.
PLEASE EXCUSE ME.

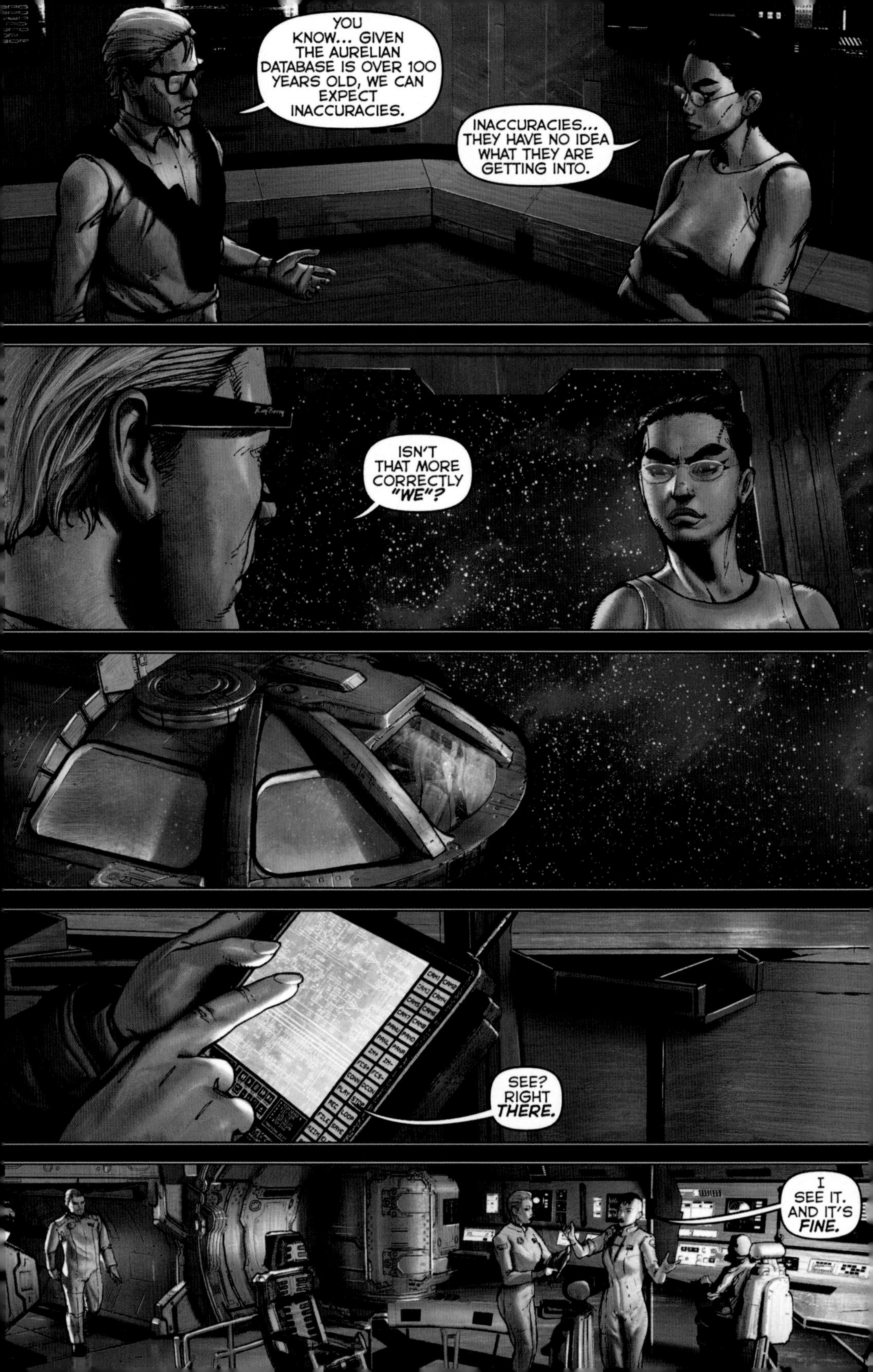
YOU KNOW... GIVEN THE AURELIAN DATABASE IS OVER 100 YEARS OLD, WE CAN EXPECT INACCURACIES.
INACCURACIES... THEY HAVE NO IDEA WHAT THEY ARE GETTING INTO.
ISN'T THAT MORE CORRECTLY *"WE"*?
SEE? RIGHT *THERE.*
I SEE IT. AND IT'S *FINE.*

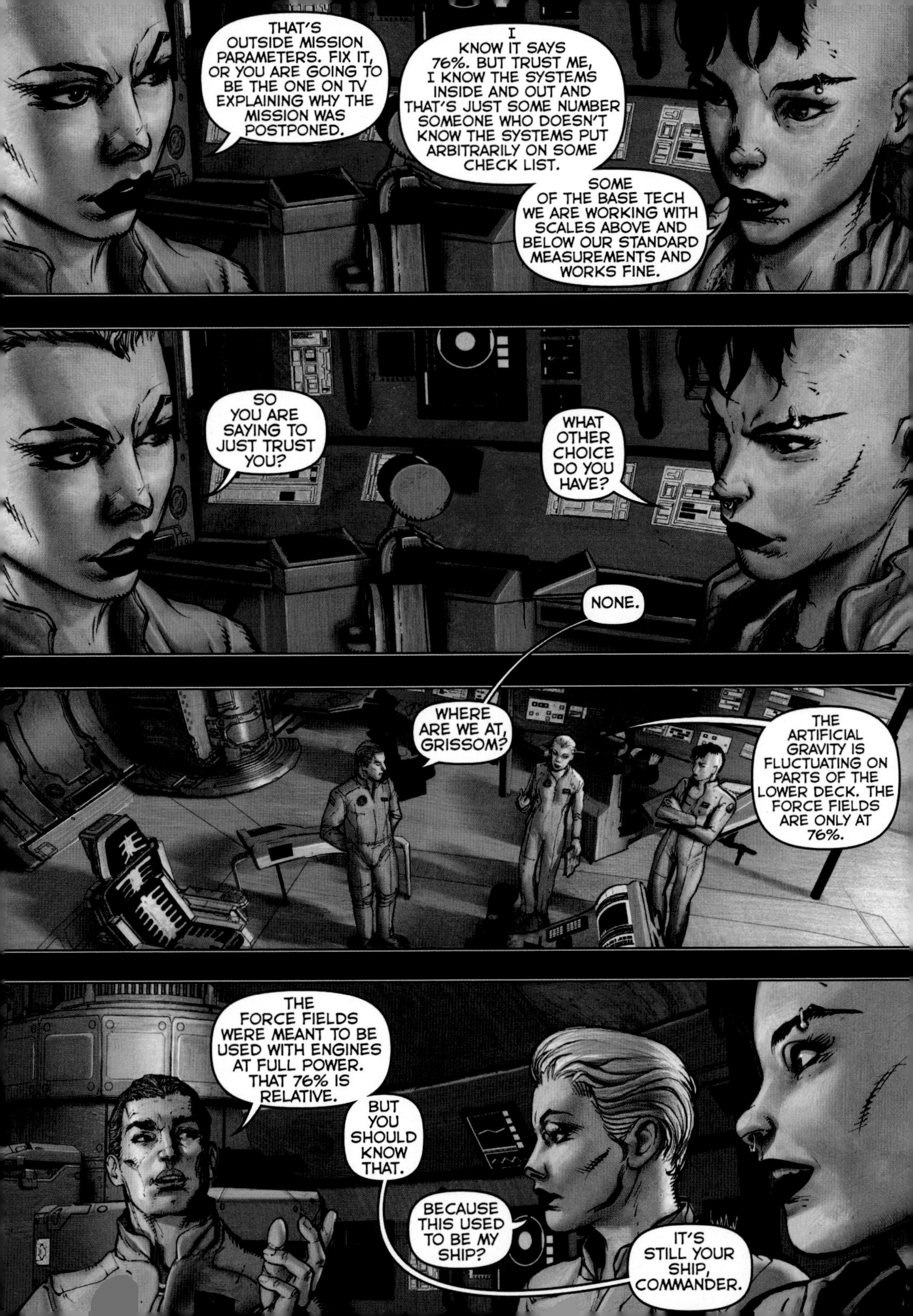
THAT'S OUTSIDE MISSION PARAMETERS. FIX IT, OR YOU ARE GOING TO BE THE ONE ON TV EXPLAINING WHY THE MISSION WAS POSTPONED.
I KNOW IT SAYS 76%. BUT TRUST ME, I KNOW THE SYSTEMS INSIDE AND OUT AND THAT'S JUST SOME NUMBER SOMEONE WHO DOESN'T KNOW THE SYSTEMS PUT ARBITRARILY ON SOME CHECK LIST.
SOME OF THE BASE TECH WE ARE WORKING WITH SCALES ABOVE AND BELOW OUR STANDARD MEASUREMENTS AND WORKS FINE.
SO YOU ARE SAYING TO JUST TRUST YOU?
WHAT OTHER CHOICE DO YOU HAVE?
NONE.
WHERE ARE WE AT, GRISSOM?
THE ARTIFICIAL GRAVITY IS FLUCTUATING ON PARTS OF THE LOWER DECK. THE FORCE FIELDS ARE ONLY AT 76%.
THE FORCE FIELDS WERE MEANT TO BE USED WITH ENGINES AT FULL POWER. THAT 76% IS RELATIVE.
BUT YOU SHOULD KNOW THAT.
BECAUSE THIS USED TO BE MY SHIP?
IT'S STILL YOUR SHIP, COMMANDER.

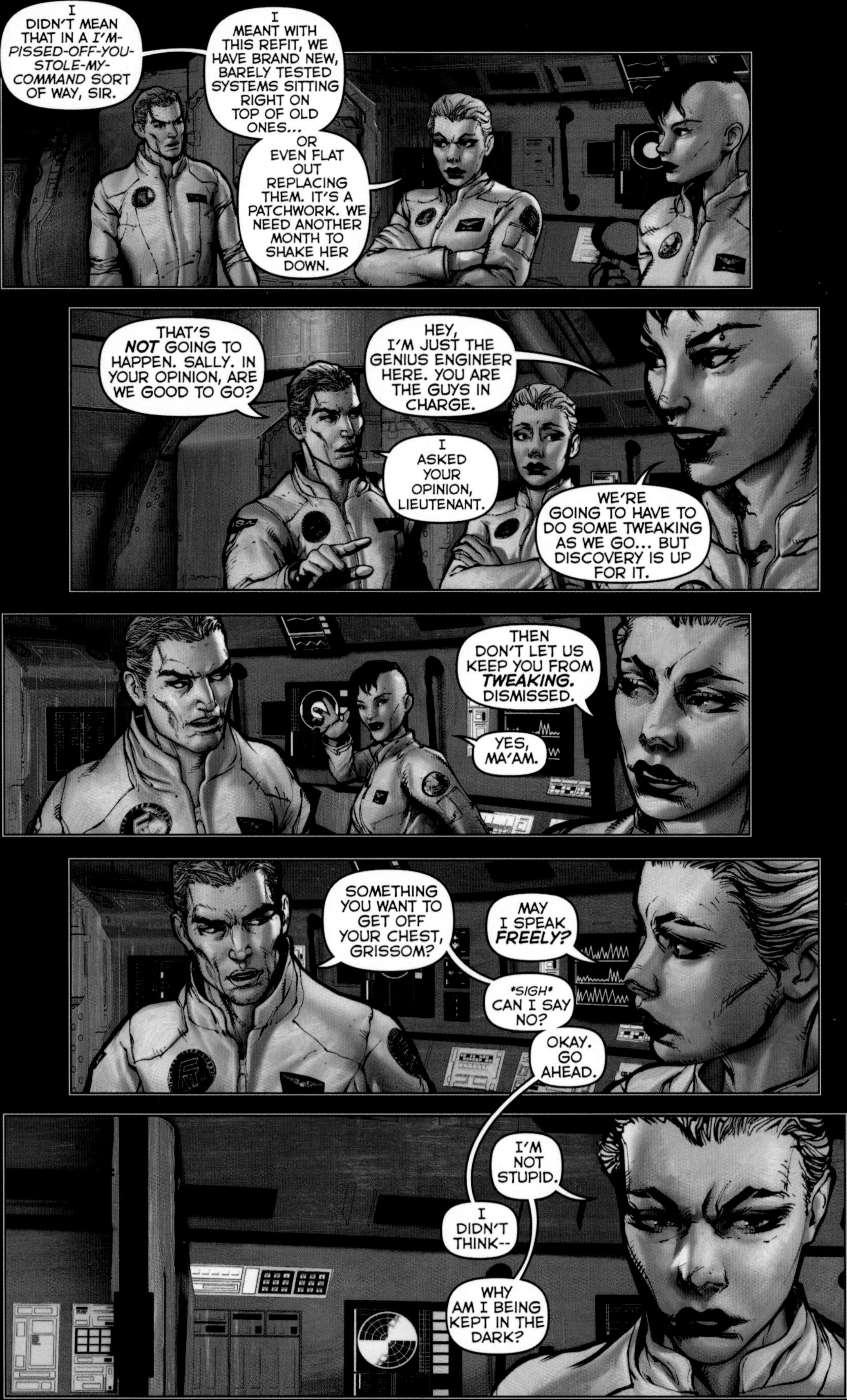
I DIDN'T MEAN THAT IN A *I'M-PISSED-OFF-YOU-STOLE-MY-COMMAND* SORT OF WAY, SIR.
I MEANT WITH THIS REFIT, WE HAVE BRAND NEW, BARELY TESTED SYSTEMS SITTING RIGHT ON TOP OF OLD ONES...
OR EVEN FLAT OUT REPLACING THEM. IT'S A PATCHWORK. WE NEED ANOTHER MONTH TO SHAKE HER DOWN.
THAT'S **NOT** GOING TO HAPPEN. SALLY. IN YOUR OPINION, ARE WE GOOD TO GO?
HEY, I'M JUST THE GENIUS ENGINEER HERE. YOU ARE THE GUYS IN CHARGE.
I ASKED YOUR OPINION, LIEUTENANT.
WE'RE GOING TO HAVE TO DO SOME TWEAKING AS WE GO... BUT DISCOVERY IS UP FOR IT.
THEN DON'T LET US KEEP YOU FROM ***TWEAKING.*** DISMISSED.
YES, MA'AM.
SOMETHING YOU WANT TO GET OFF YOUR CHEST, GRISSOM?
MAY I SPEAK ***FREELY?***
SIGH CAN I SAY NO?
OKAY. GO AHEAD.
I'M NOT STUPID.
I DIDN'T THINK--
WHY AM I BEING KEPT IN THE DARK?

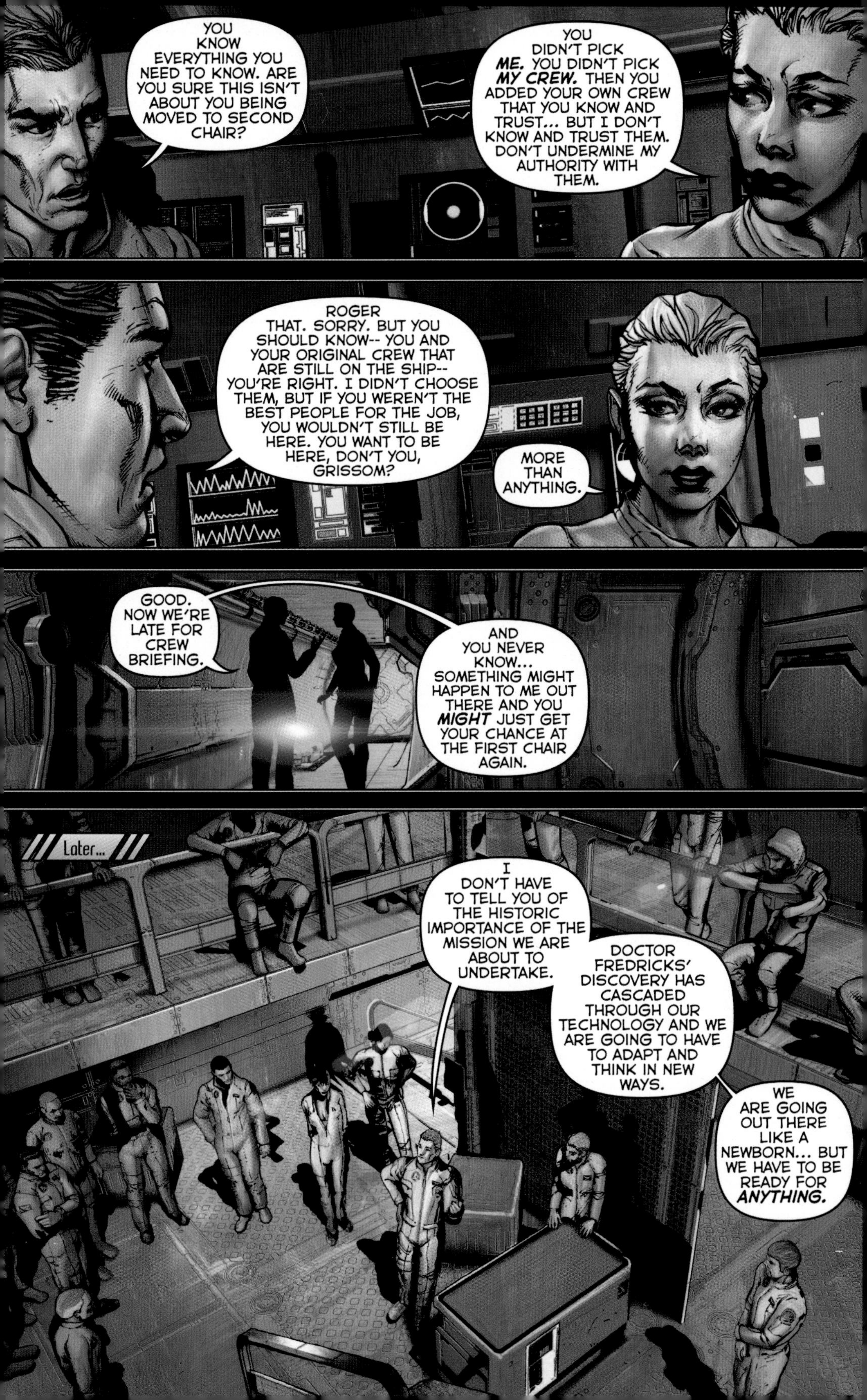
YOU KNOW EVERYTHING YOU NEED TO KNOW. ARE YOU SURE THIS ISN'T ABOUT YOU BEING MOVED TO SECOND CHAIR?
YOU DIDN'T PICK ME. YOU DIDN'T PICK MY CREW. THEN YOU ADDED YOUR OWN CREW THAT YOU KNOW AND TRUST... BUT I DON'T KNOW AND TRUST THEM. DON'T UNDERMINE MY AUTHORITY WITH THEM.
ROGER THAT. SORRY. BUT YOU SHOULD KNOW-- YOU AND YOUR ORIGINAL CREW THAT ARE STILL ON THE SHIP-- YOU'RE RIGHT. I DIDN'T CHOOSE THEM, BUT IF YOU WEREN'T THE BEST PEOPLE FOR THE JOB, YOU WOULDN'T STILL BE HERE. YOU WANT TO BE HERE, DON'T YOU, GRISSOM?
MORE THAN ANYTHING.
GOOD. NOW WE'RE LATE FOR CREW BRIEFING.
AND YOU NEVER KNOW... SOMETHING MIGHT HAPPEN TO ME OUT THERE AND YOU MIGHT JUST GET YOUR CHANCE AT THE FIRST CHAIR AGAIN.
Later...
I DON'T HAVE TO TELL YOU OF THE HISTORIC IMPORTANCE OF THE MISSION WE ARE ABOUT TO UNDERTAKE.
DOCTOR FREDRICKS' DISCOVERY HAS CASCADED THROUGH OUR TECHNOLOGY AND WE ARE GOING TO HAVE TO ADAPT AND THINK IN NEW WAYS.
WE ARE GOING OUT THERE LIKE A NEWBORN... BUT WE HAVE TO BE READY FOR ANYTHING.

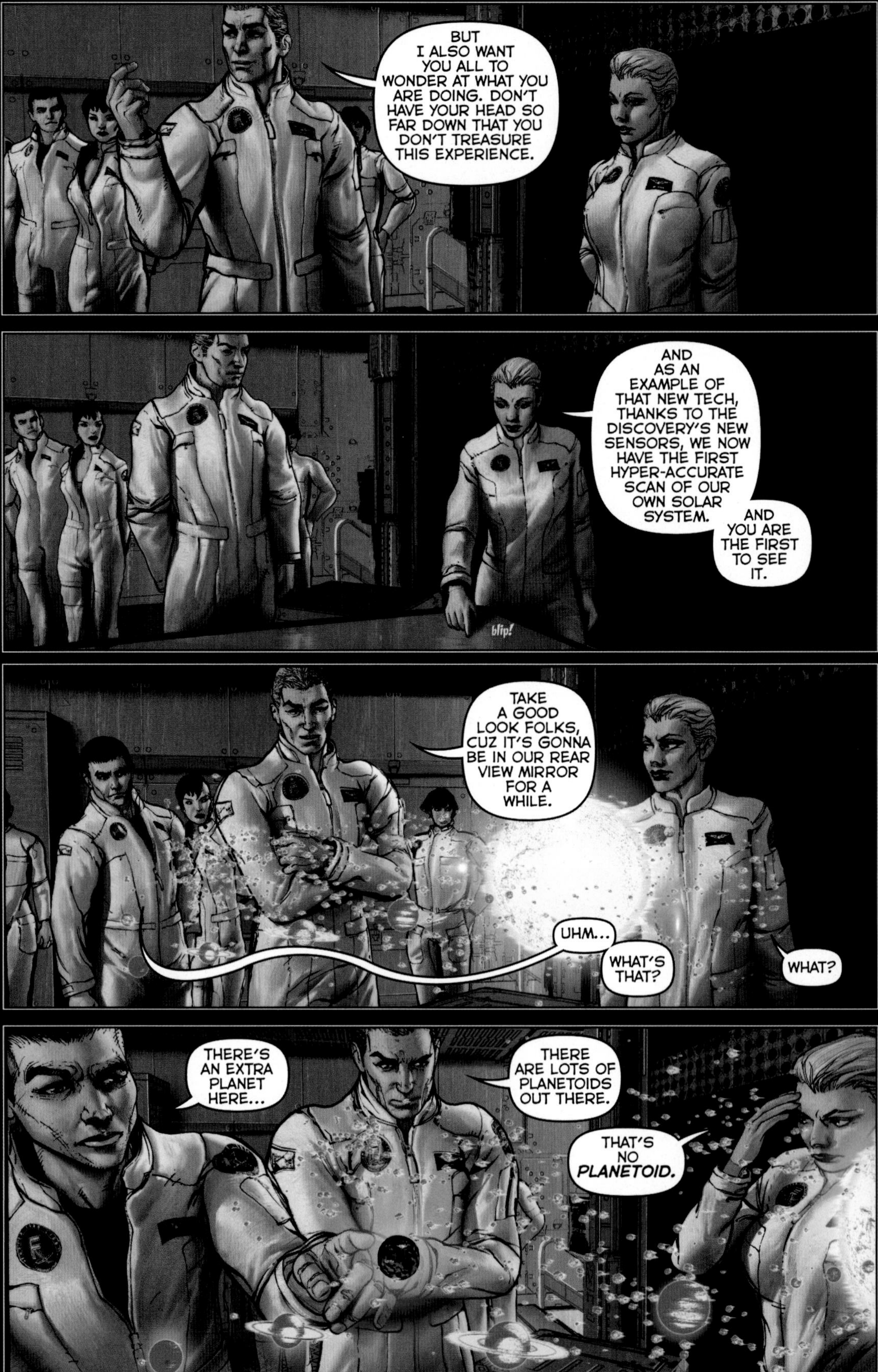
BUT I ALSO WANT YOU ALL TO WONDER AT WHAT YOU ARE DOING. DON'T HAVE YOUR HEAD SO FAR DOWN THAT YOU DON'T TREASURE THIS EXPERIENCE.
AND AS AN EXAMPLE OF THAT NEW TECH, THANKS TO THE DISCOVERY'S NEW SENSORS, WE NOW HAVE THE FIRST HYPER-ACCURATE SCAN OF OUR OWN SOLAR SYSTEM.
AND YOU ARE THE FIRST TO SEE IT.
blip!
TAKE A GOOD LOOK FOLKS, CUZ IT'S GONNA BE IN OUR REAR VIEW MIRROR FOR A WHILE.
UHM...
WHAT'S THAT?
WHAT?
THERE'S AN EXTRA PLANET HERE...
THERE ARE LOTS OF PLANETOIDS OUT THERE.
THAT'S NO PLANETOID.

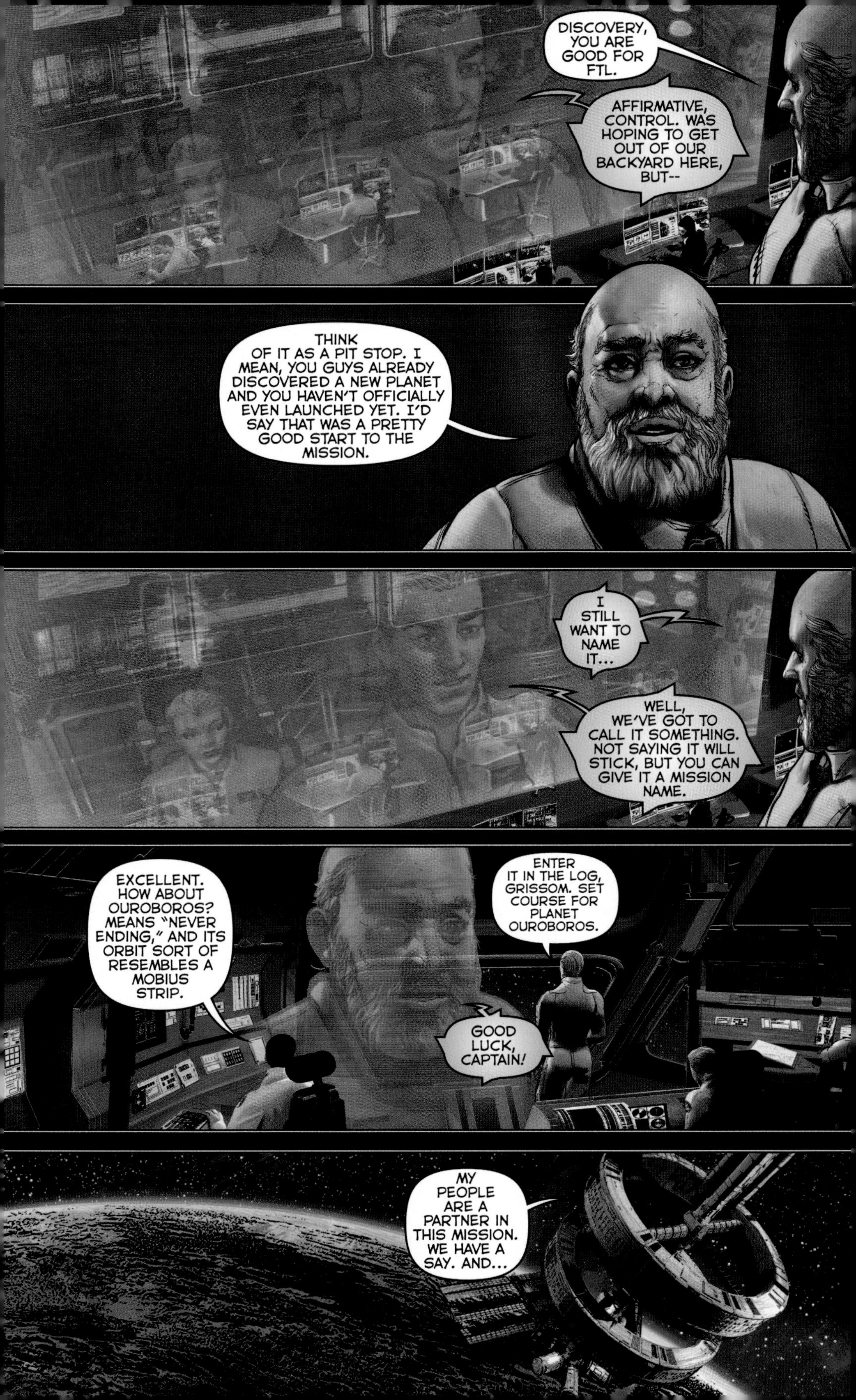
DISCOVERY, YOU ARE GOOD FOR FTL.
AFFIRMATIVE, CONTROL. WAS HOPING TO GET OUT OF OUR BACKYARD HERE, BUT--
THINK OF IT AS A PIT STOP. I MEAN, YOU GUYS ALREADY DISCOVERED A NEW PLANET AND YOU HAVEN'T OFFICIALLY EVEN LAUNCHED YET. I'D SAY THAT WAS A PRETTY GOOD START TO THE MISSION.
I STILL WANT TO NAME IT...
WELL, WE'VE GOT TO CALL IT SOMETHING. NOT SAYING IT WILL STICK, BUT YOU CAN GIVE IT A MISSION NAME.
EXCELLENT. HOW ABOUT OUROBOROS? MEANS "NEVER ENDING," AND ITS ORBIT SORT OF RESEMBLES A MOBIUS STRIP.
ENTER IT IN THE LOG, GRISSOM. SET COURSE FOR PLANET OUROBOROS.
GOOD LUCK, CAPTAIN!
MY PEOPLE ARE A PARTNER IN THIS MISSION. WE HAVE A SAY. AND...

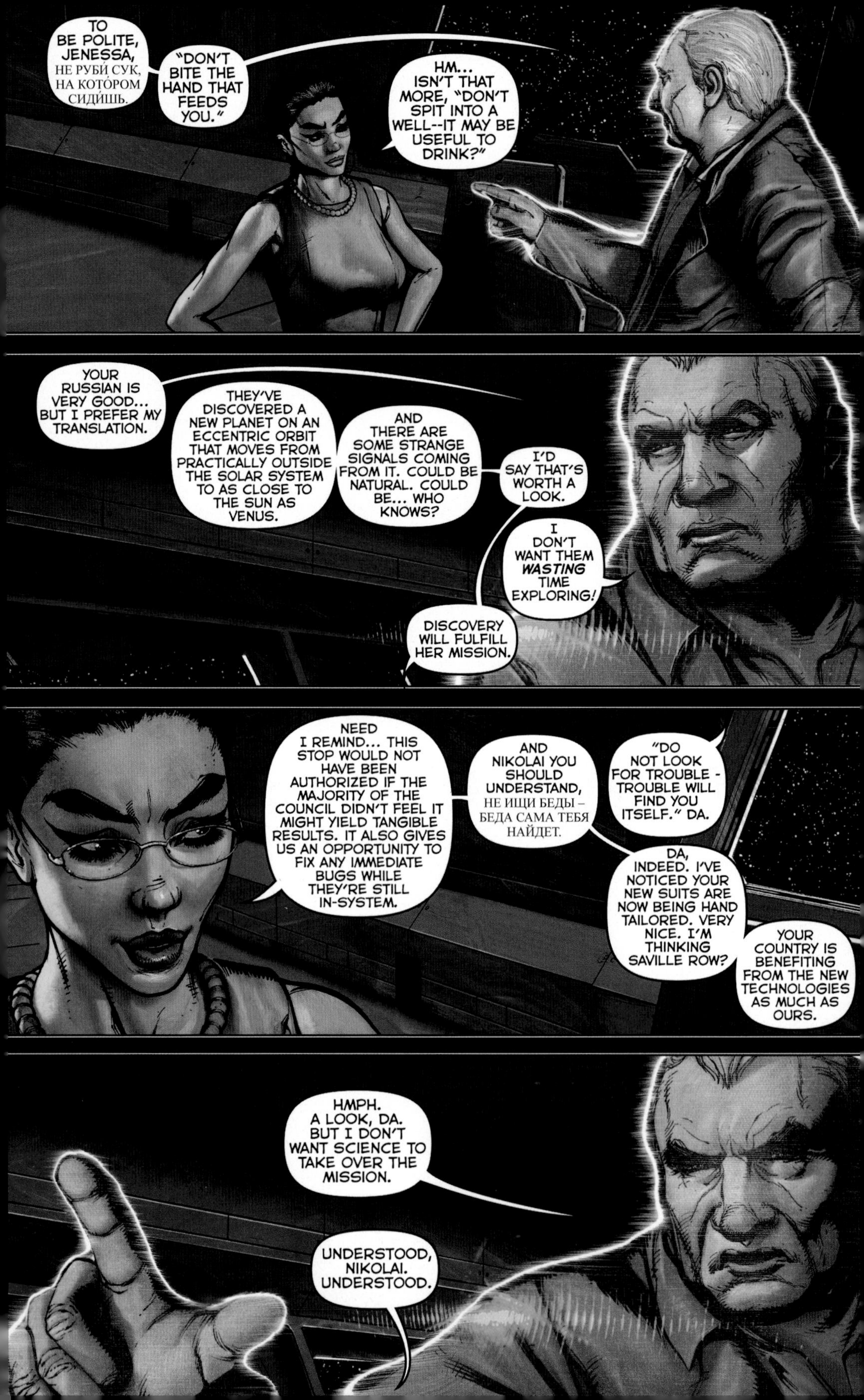
TO BE POLITE, JENESSA, НЕ РУБИ́ СУК, НА КОТО́РОМ СИДИ́ШЬ.
"DON'T BITE THE HAND THAT FEEDS YOU."
HM... ISN'T THAT MORE, "DON'T SPIT INTO A WELL--IT MAY BE USEFUL TO DRINK?"
YOUR RUSSIAN IS VERY GOOD... BUT I PREFER MY TRANSLATION.
THEY'VE DISCOVERED A NEW PLANET ON AN ECCENTRIC ORBIT THAT MOVES FROM PRACTICALLY OUTSIDE THE SOLAR SYSTEM TO AS CLOSE TO THE SUN AS VENUS.
AND THERE ARE SOME STRANGE SIGNALS COMING FROM IT. COULD BE NATURAL. COULD BE... WHO KNOWS?
I'D SAY THAT'S WORTH A LOOK.
I DON'T WANT THEM *WASTING* TIME EXPLORING!
DISCOVERY WILL FULFILL HER MISSION.
NEED I REMIND... THIS STOP WOULD NOT HAVE BEEN AUTHORIZED IF THE MAJORITY OF THE COUNCIL DIDN'T FEEL IT MIGHT YIELD TANGIBLE RESULTS. IT ALSO GIVES US AN OPPORTUNITY TO FIX ANY IMMEDIATE BUGS WHILE THEY'RE STILL IN-SYSTEM.
AND NIKOLAI YOU SHOULD UNDERSTAND, НЕ ИЩИ БЕДЫ – БЕДА САМА ТЕБЯ НАЙДЕТ.
"DO NOT LOOK FOR TROUBLE - TROUBLE WILL FIND YOU ITSELF." DA.
DA, INDEED. I'VE NOTICED YOUR NEW SUITS ARE NOW BEING HAND TAILORED. VERY NICE. I'M THINKING SAVILLE ROW?
YOUR COUNTRY IS BENEFITING FROM THE NEW TECHNOLOGIES AS MUCH AS OURS.
HMPH. A LOOK, DA. BUT I DON'T WANT SCIENCE TO TAKE OVER THE MISSION.
UNDERSTOOD, NIKOLAI. UNDERSTOOD.

SO...

...AND TELL THE TRUTH... OR OUR AUDIENCE WILL *KNOW*...

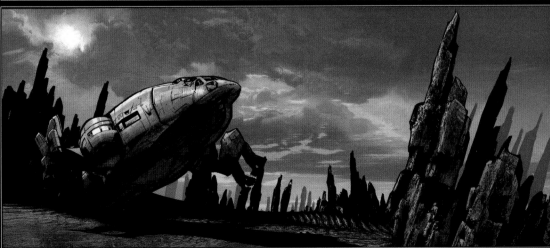

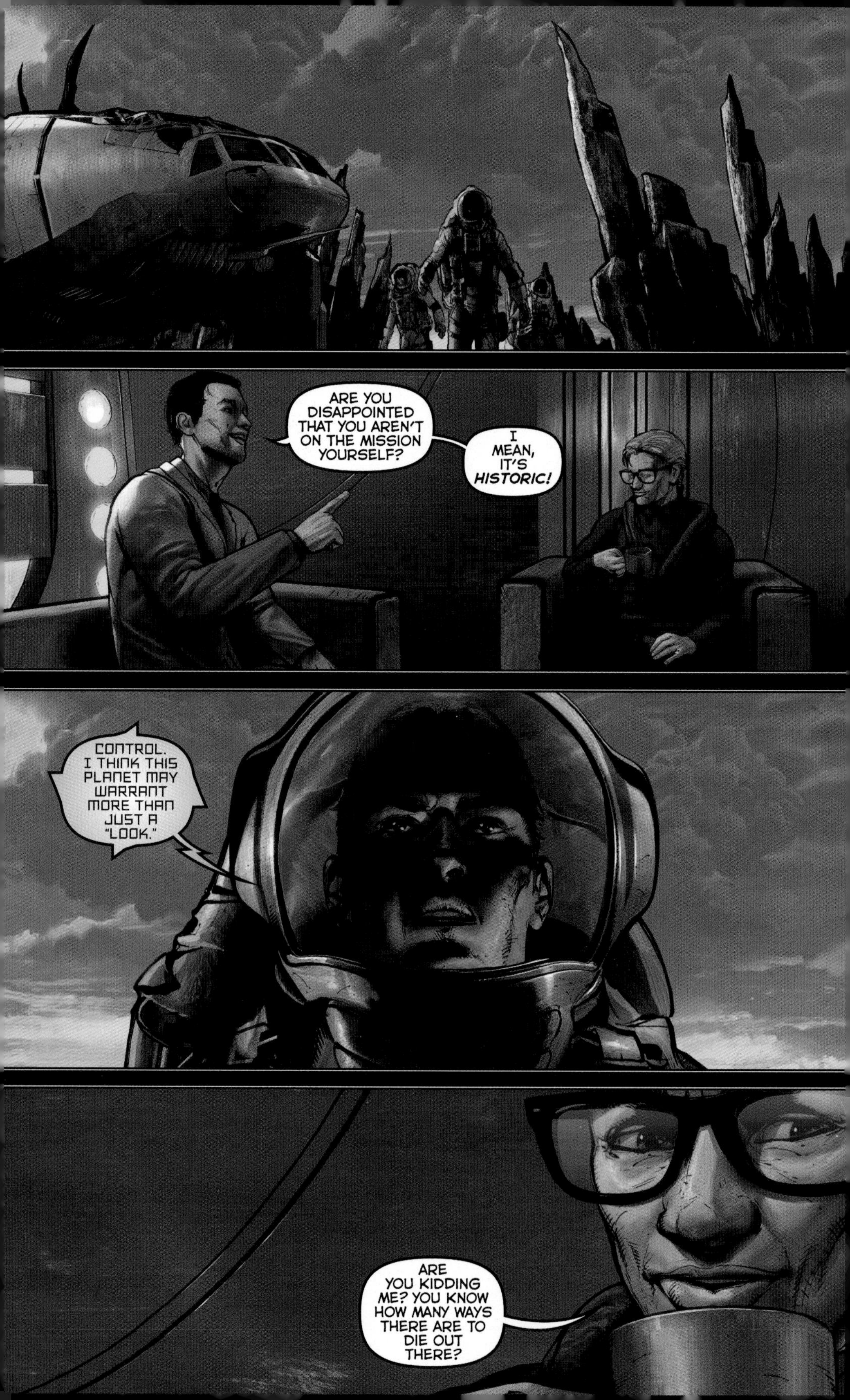
ARE YOU DISAPPOINTED THAT YOU AREN'T ON THE MISSION YOURSELF?
I MEAN, IT'S *HISTORIC!*
CONTROL. I THINK THIS PLANET MAY WARRANT MORE THAN JUST A "LOOK."
ARE YOU KIDDING ME? YOU KNOW HOW MANY WAYS THERE ARE TO DIE OUT THERE?

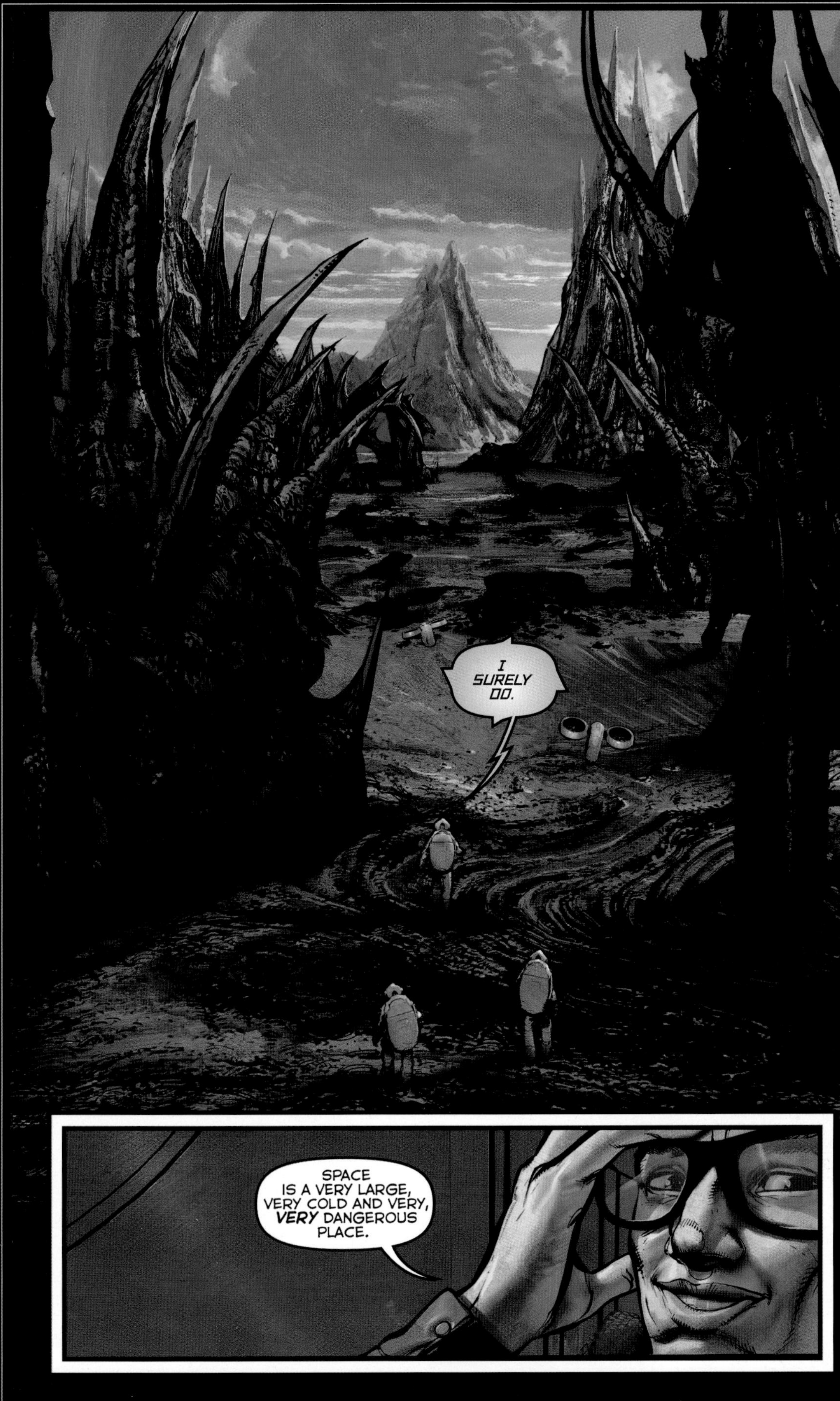
I SURELY DO.
SPACE IS A VERY LARGE, VERY COLD AND VERY, VERY DANGEROUS PLACE.

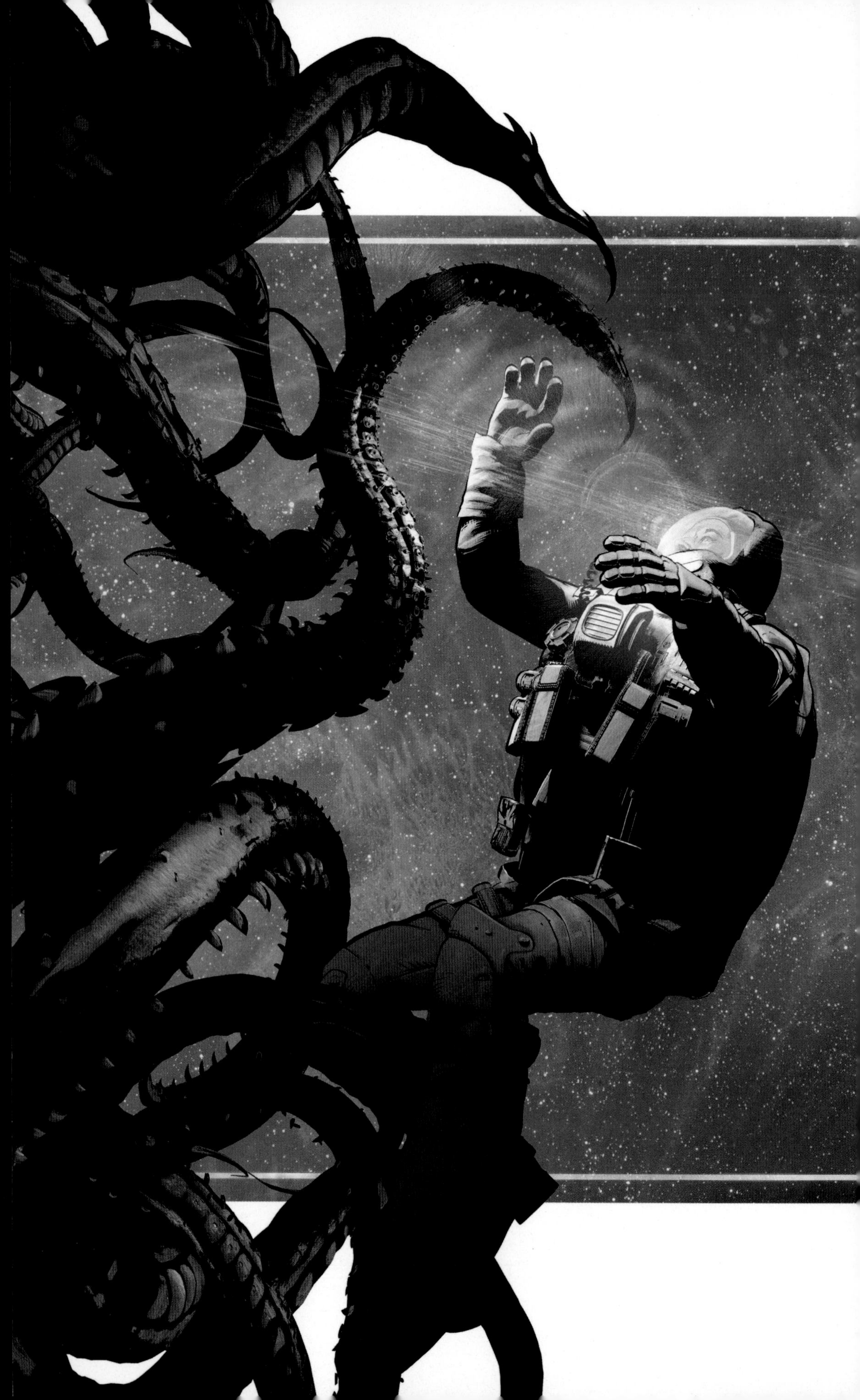

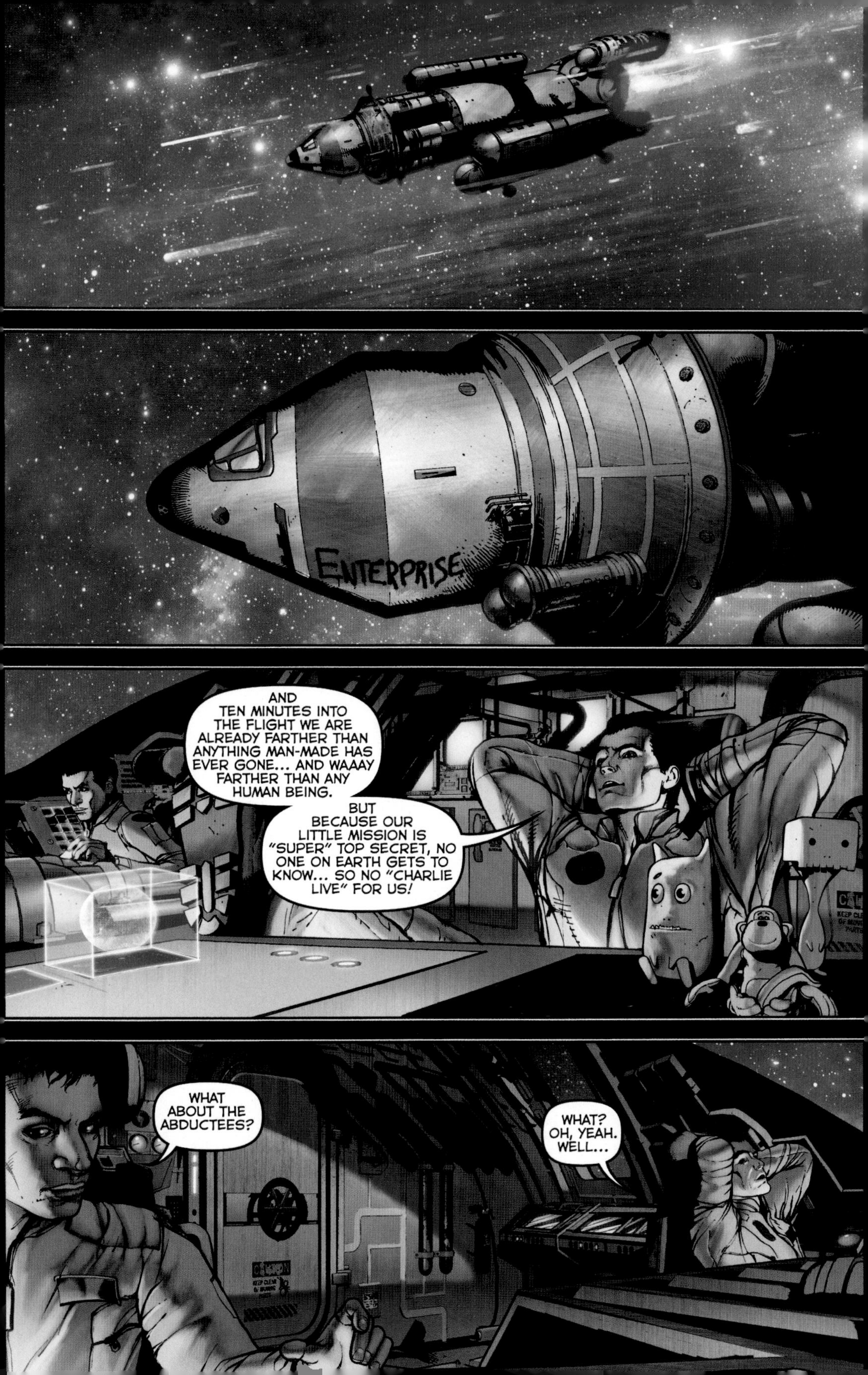
ENTERPRISE
AND TEN MINUTES INTO THE FLIGHT WE ARE ALREADY FARTHER THAN ANYTHING MAN-MADE HAS EVER GONE... AND WAAAY FARTHER THAN ANY HUMAN BEING.
BUT BECAUSE OUR LITTLE MISSION IS "SUPER" TOP SECRET, NO ONE ON EARTH GETS TO KNOW... SO NO "CHARLIE LIVE" FOR US!
WHAT ABOUT THE ABDUCTEES?
WHAT? OH, YEAH. WELL...

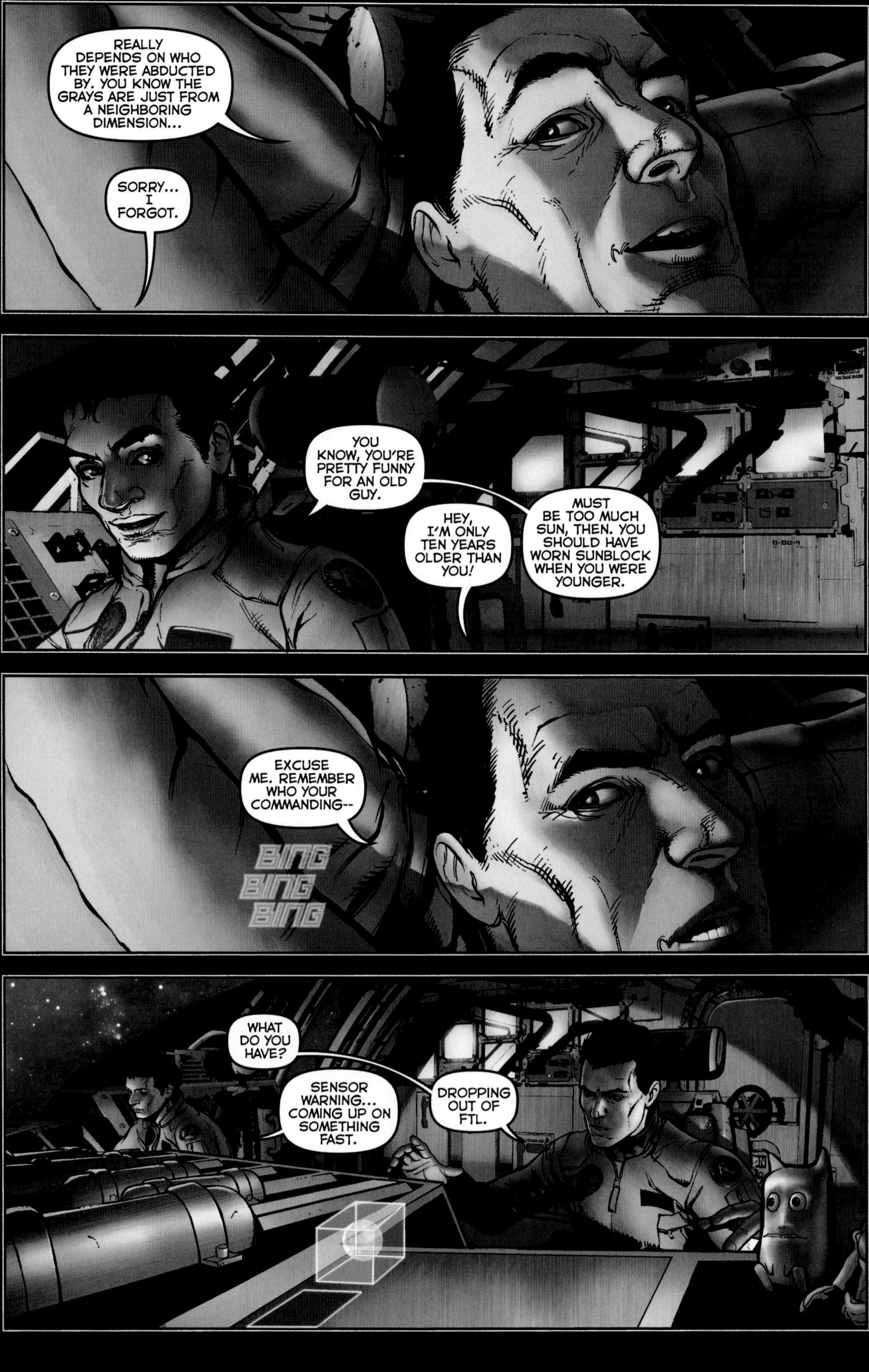
REALLY DEPENDS ON WHO THEY WERE ABDUCTED BY. YOU KNOW THE GRAYS ARE JUST FROM A NEIGHBORING DIMENSION...
SORRY... I FORGOT.
YOU KNOW, YOU'RE PRETTY FUNNY FOR AN OLD GUY.
HEY, I'M ONLY TEN YEARS OLDER THAN YOU!
MUST BE TOO MUCH SUN, THEN. YOU SHOULD HAVE WORN SUNBLOCK WHEN YOU WERE YOUNGER.
EXCUSE ME. REMEMBER WHO YOUR COMMANDING--
BING BING BING
WHAT DO YOU HAVE?
SENSOR WARNING... COMING UP ON SOMETHING FAST.
DROPPING OUT OF FTL.

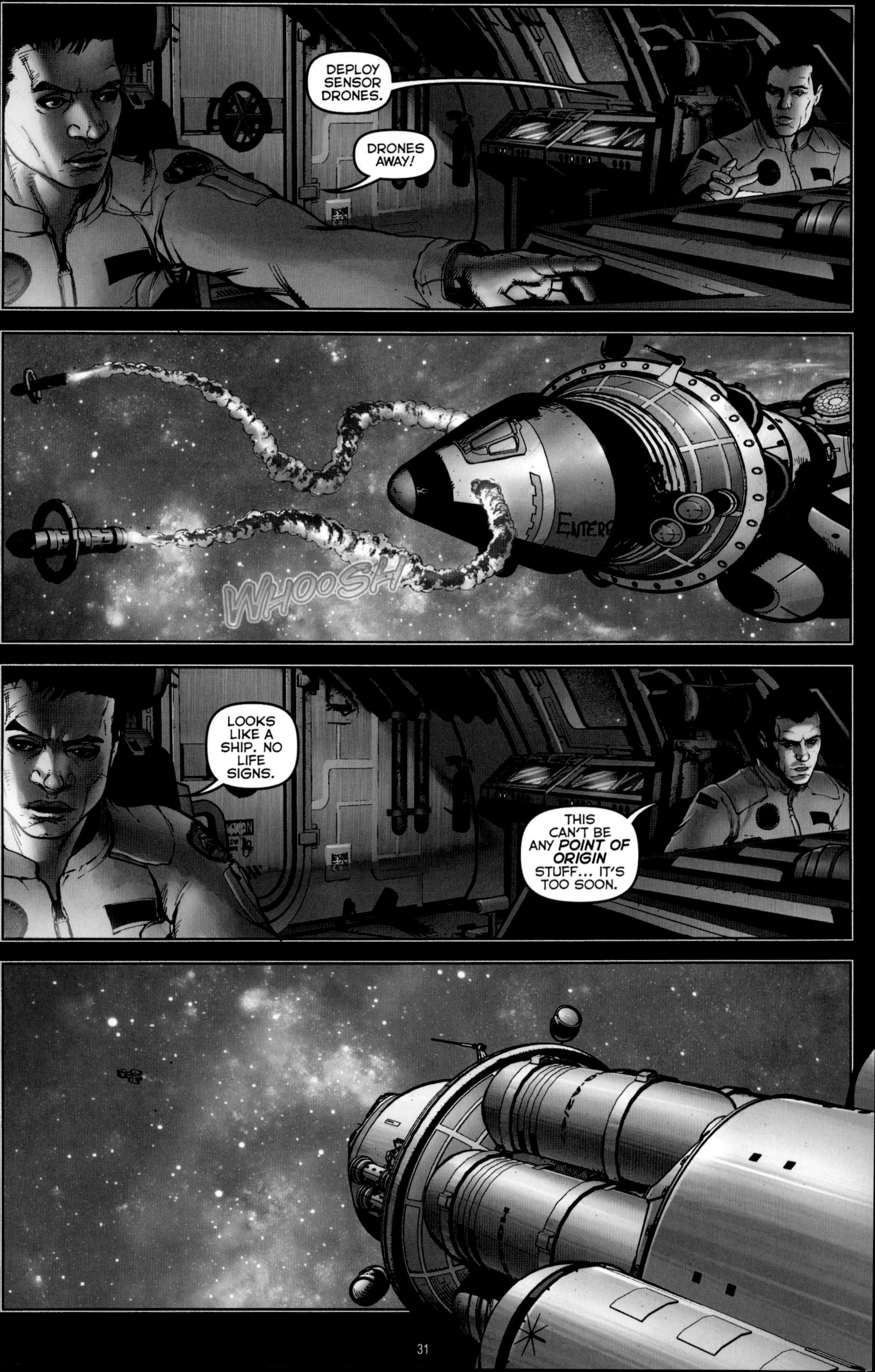
DEPLOY SENSOR DRONES.
DRONES AWAY!
ENTER
WHOOSH
LOOKS LIKE A SHIP. NO LIFE SIGNS.
THIS CAN'T BE ANY POINT OF ORIGIN STUFF... IT'S TOO SOON.

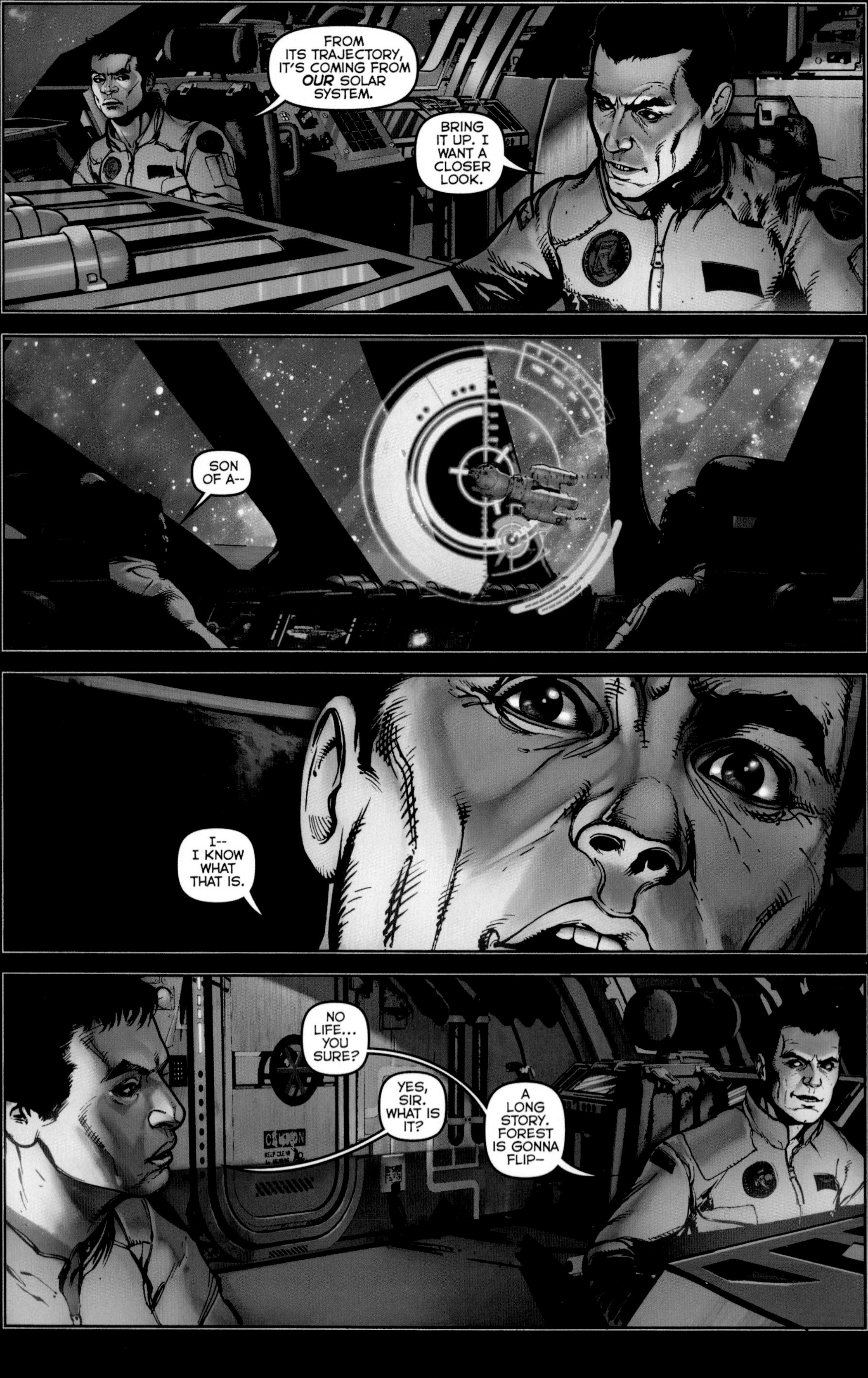
FROM ITS TRAJECTORY, IT'S COMING FROM **OUR** SOLAR SYSTEM.
BRING IT UP. I WANT A CLOSER LOOK.
SON OF A--
I-- I KNOW WHAT THAT IS.
NO LIFE... YOU SURE?
YES, SIR. WHAT IS IT?
A LONG STORY. FOREST IS GONNA FLIP-

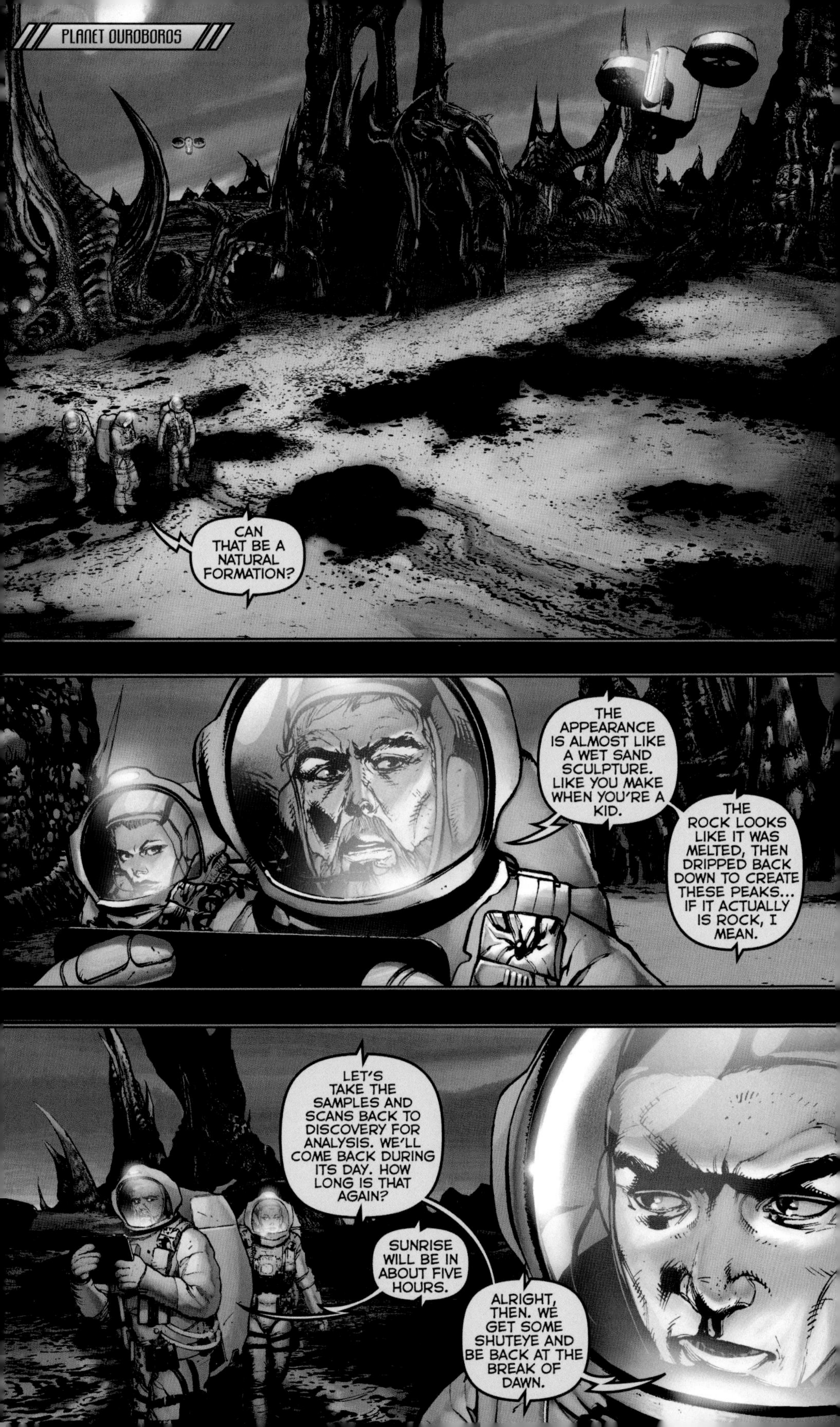
PLANET OUROBOROS
CAN THAT BE A NATURAL FORMATION?
THE APPEARANCE IS ALMOST LIKE A WET SAND SCULPTURE. LIKE YOU MAKE WHEN YOU'RE A KID.
THE ROCK LOOKS LIKE IT WAS MELTED, THEN DRIPPED BACK DOWN TO CREATE THESE PEAKS... IF IT ACTUALLY IS ROCK, I MEAN.
LET'S TAKE THE SAMPLES AND SCANS BACK TO DISCOVERY FOR ANALYSIS. WE'LL COME BACK DURING ITS DAY. HOW LONG IS THAT AGAIN?
SUNRISE WILL BE IN ABOUT FIVE HOURS.
ALRIGHT, THEN. WE GET SOME SHUTEYE AND BE BACK AT THE BREAK OF DAWN.

CAPTAIN? I HAVE A MESSAGE FORWARDED TO YOU FROM CAPTAIN ANDERSON. LOOKS LIKE IT'S JUST AN IMAGE.
ROGER THAT. GO AHEAD AND SEND TO THE SUIT.
00:10:46:02
LOOK FAMILIAR? :0
00:10:46:02

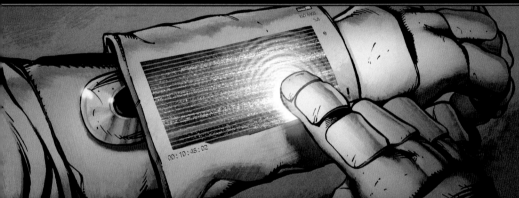

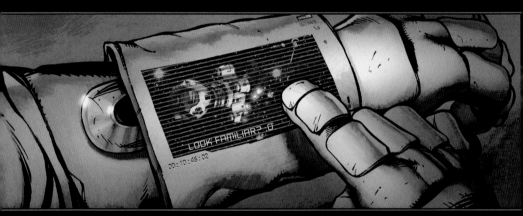

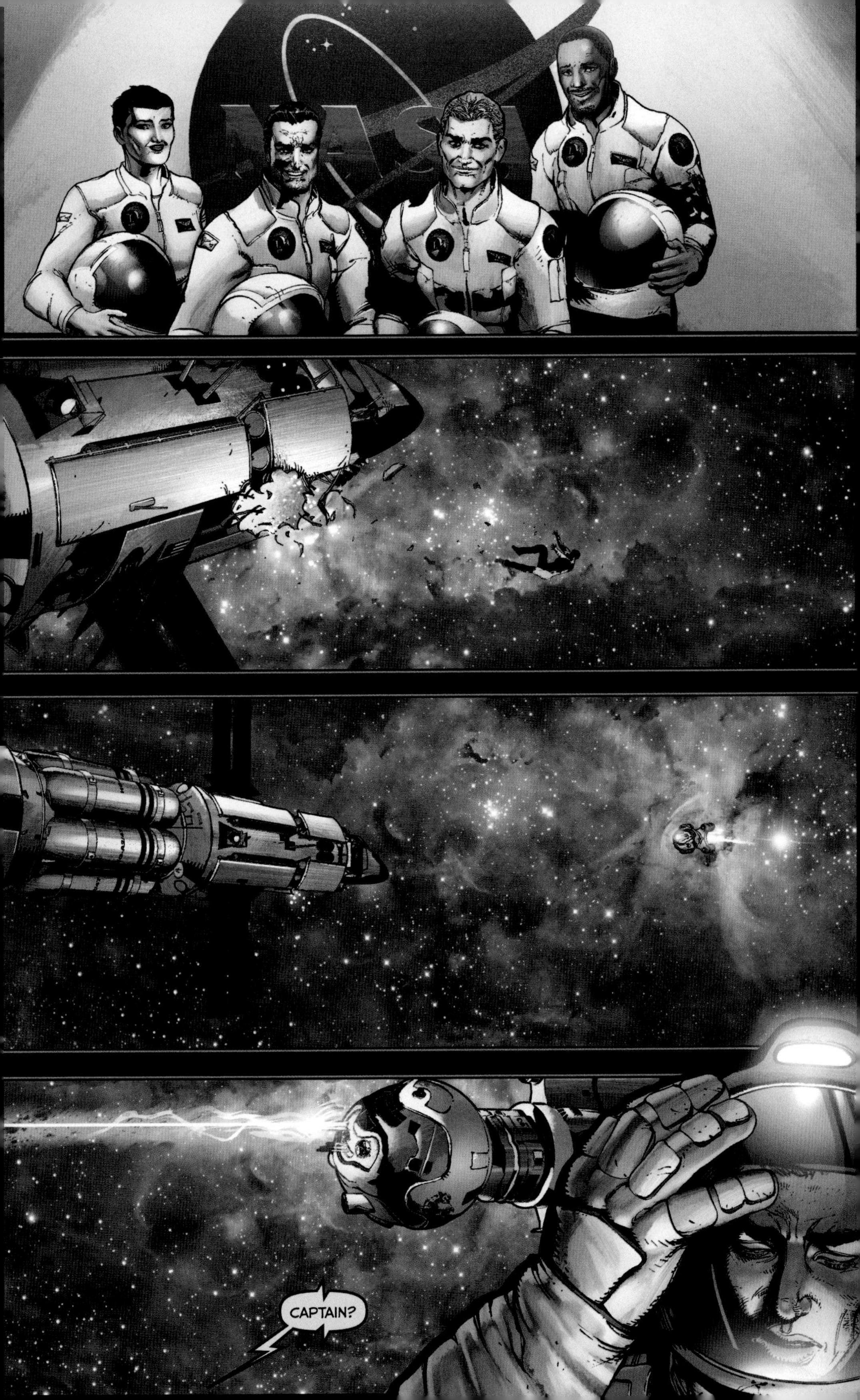
CAPTAIN?

CAPTAIN!

SIR? EVERYTHING OKAY? YOU LOOK LIKE YOU'VE SEEN A GHOST.

MORE LIKE SOMEONE WALKED ON MY GRAVE. I'LL FILL YOU IN LATER. LET'S GET OFF THIS ROCK.

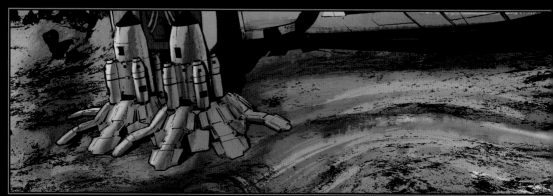

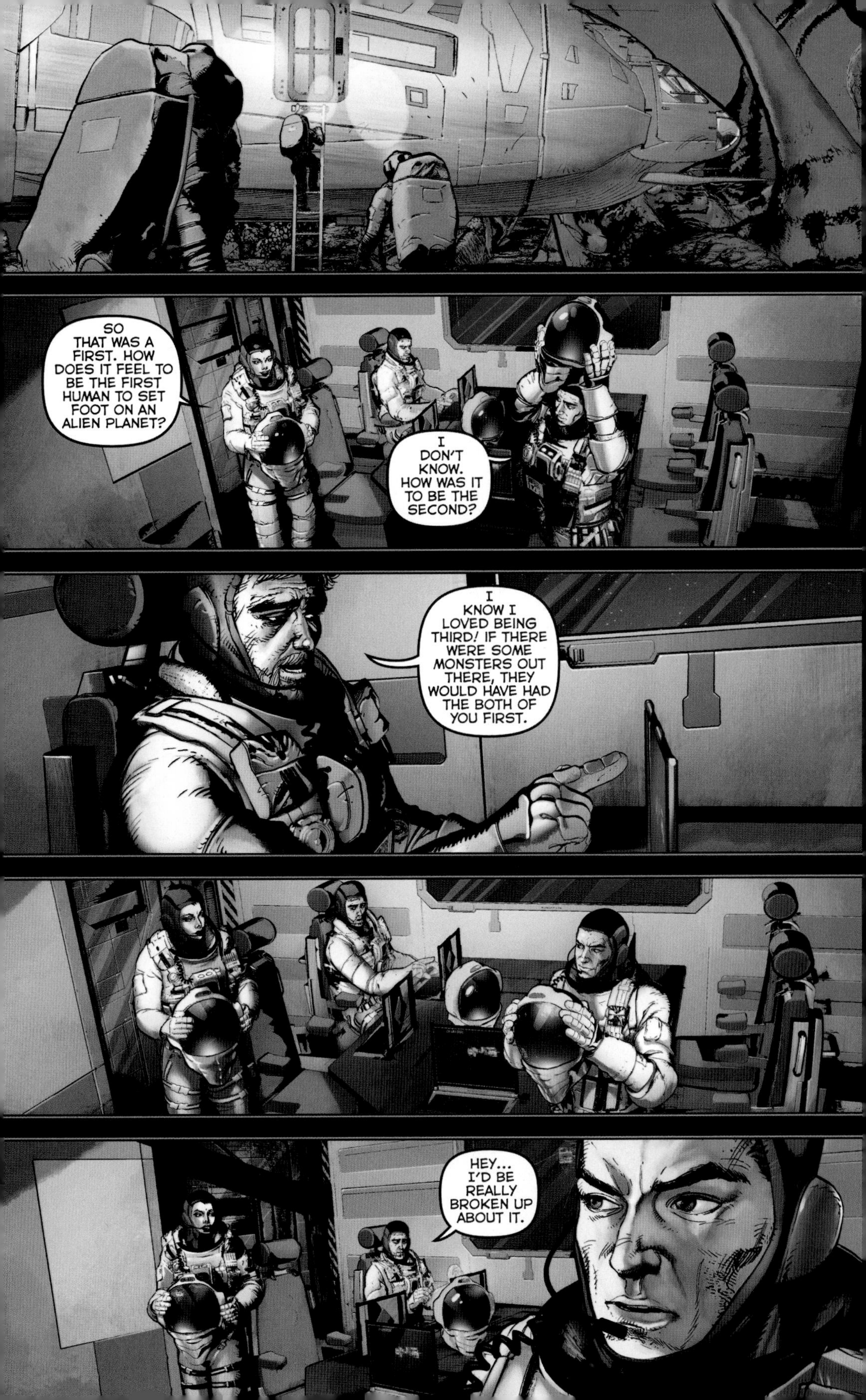
SO THAT WAS A FIRST. HOW DOES IT FEEL TO BE THE FIRST HUMAN TO SET FOOT ON AN ALIEN PLANET?
I DON'T KNOW. HOW WAS IT TO BE THE SECOND?
I KNOW I LOVED BEING THIRD! IF THERE WERE SOME MONSTERS OUT THERE, THEY WOULD HAVE HAD THE BOTH OF YOU FIRST.
HEY... I'D BE REALLY BROKEN UP ABOUT IT.

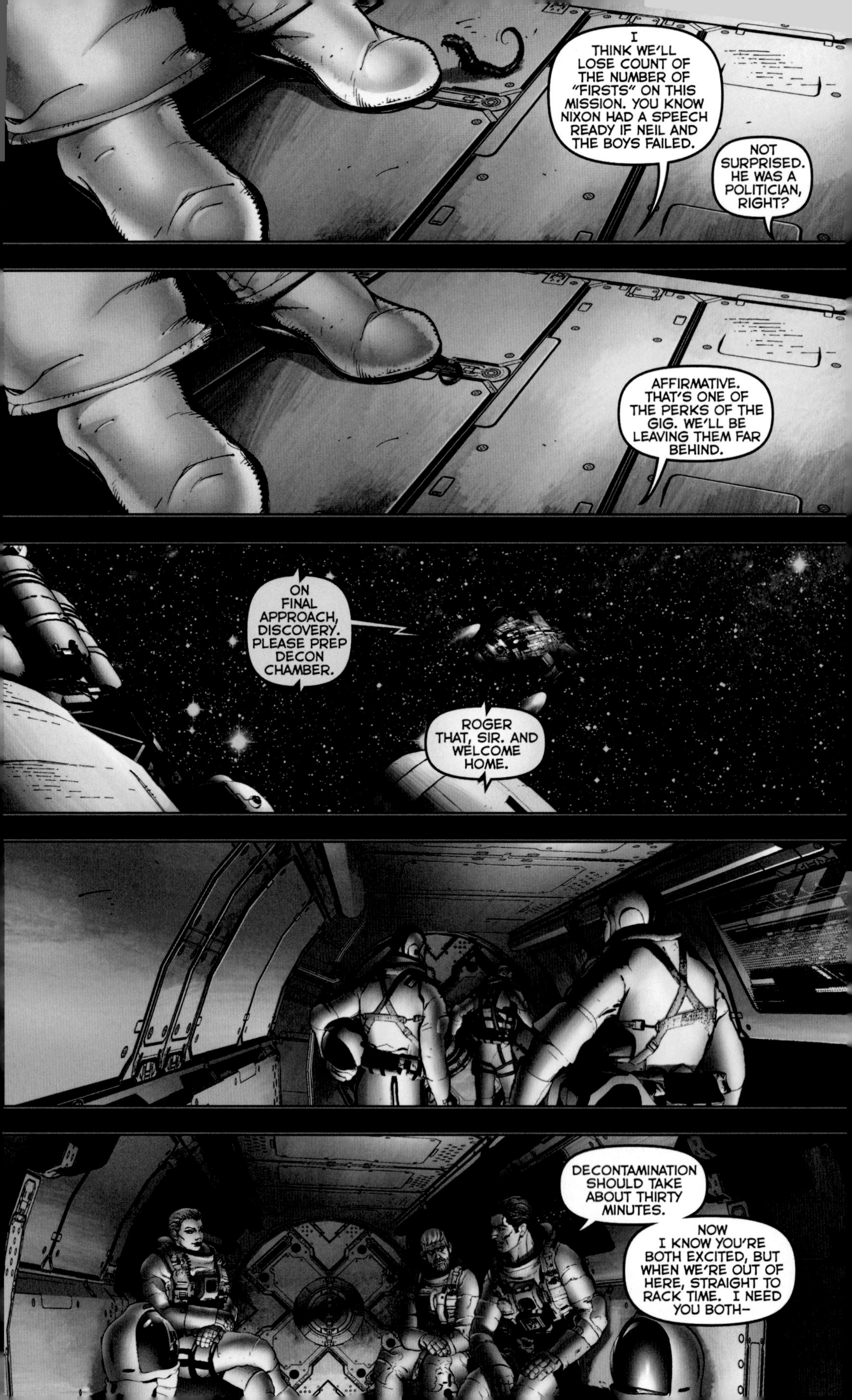

I THINK WE'LL LOSE COUNT OF THE NUMBER OF "FIRSTS" ON THIS MISSION. YOU KNOW NIXON HAD A SPEECH READY IF NEIL AND THE BOYS FAILED.
NOT SURPRISED. HE WAS A POLITICIAN, RIGHT?
AFFIRMATIVE. THAT'S ONE OF THE PERKS OF THE GIG. WE'LL BE LEAVING THEM FAR BEHIND.
ON FINAL APPROACH, DISCOVERY. PLEASE PREP DECON CHAMBER.
ROGER THAT, SIR. AND WELCOME HOME.
DECONTAMINATION SHOULD TAKE ABOUT THIRTY MINUTES.
NOW I KNOW YOU'RE BOTH EXCITED, BUT WHEN WE'RE OUT OF HERE, STRAIGHT TO RACK TIME. I NEED YOU BOTH–

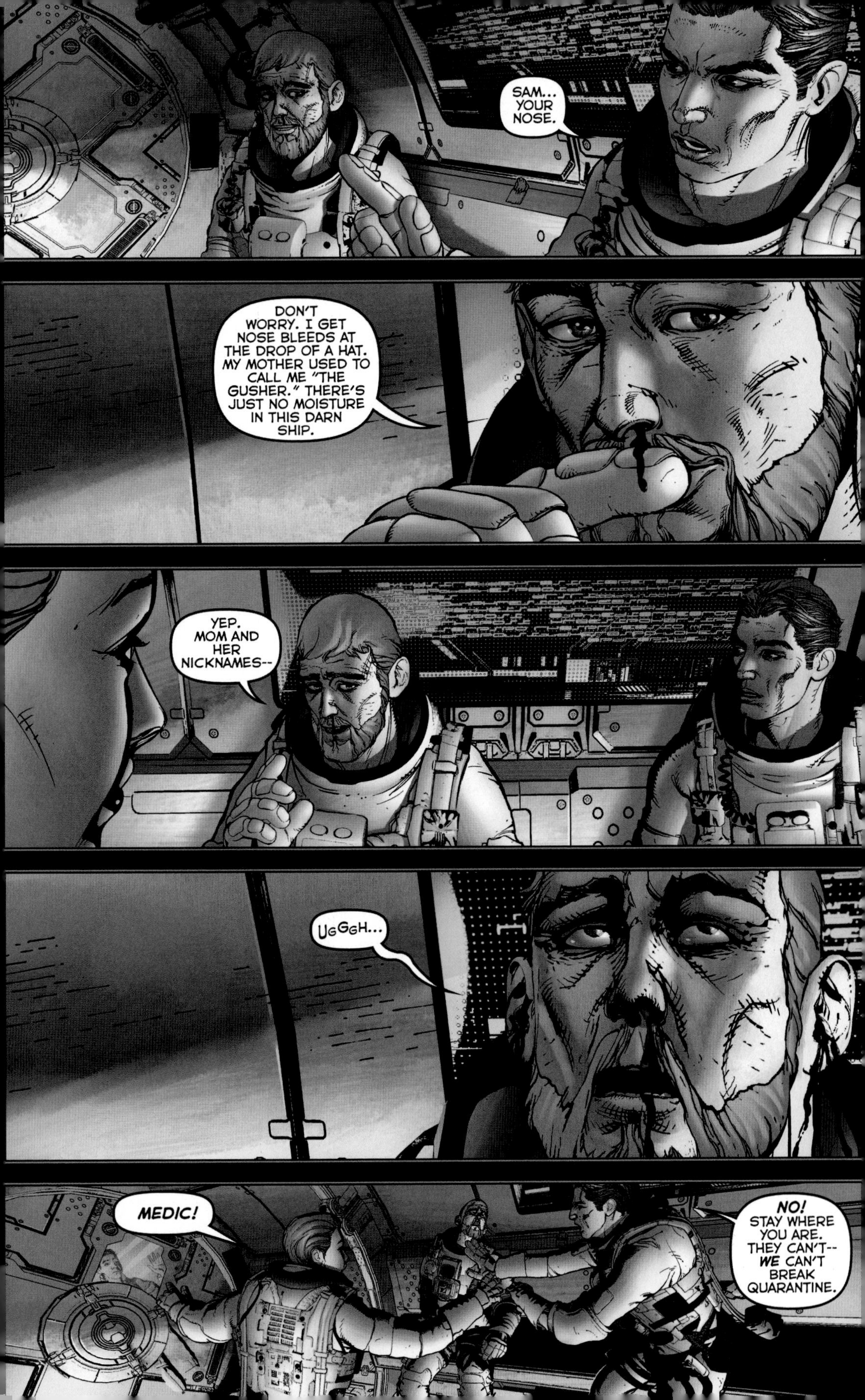
SAM... YOUR NOSE.
DON'T WORRY. I GET NOSE BLEEDS AT THE DROP OF A HAT. MY MOTHER USED TO CALL ME "THE GUSHER." THERE'S JUST NO MOISTURE IN THIS DARN SHIP.
YEP. MOM AND HER NICKNAMES--
UGGGH...
MEDIC!
NO! STAY WHERE YOU ARE. THEY CAN'T-- WE CAN'T BREAK QUARANTINE.

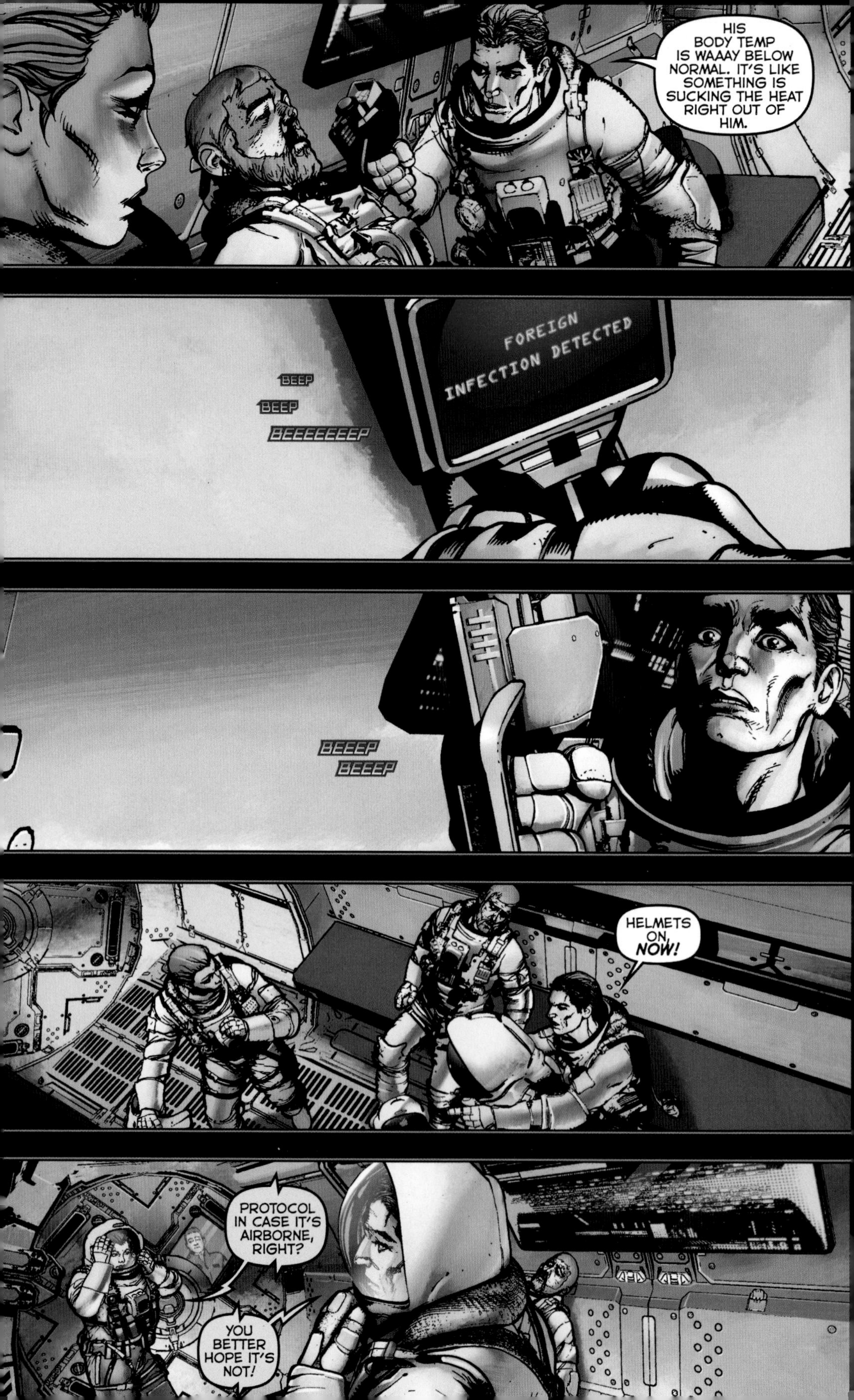
HIS BODY TEMP IS WAAAY BELOW NORMAL. IT'S LIKE SOMETHING IS SUCKING THE HEAT RIGHT OUT OF HIM.
FOREIGN INFECTION DETECTED
BEEP
BEEP
BEEEEEEEP
BEEEP
BEEEP
HELMETS ON, NOW!
PROTOCOL IN CASE IT'S AIRBORNE, RIGHT?
YOU BETTER HOPE IT'S NOT!

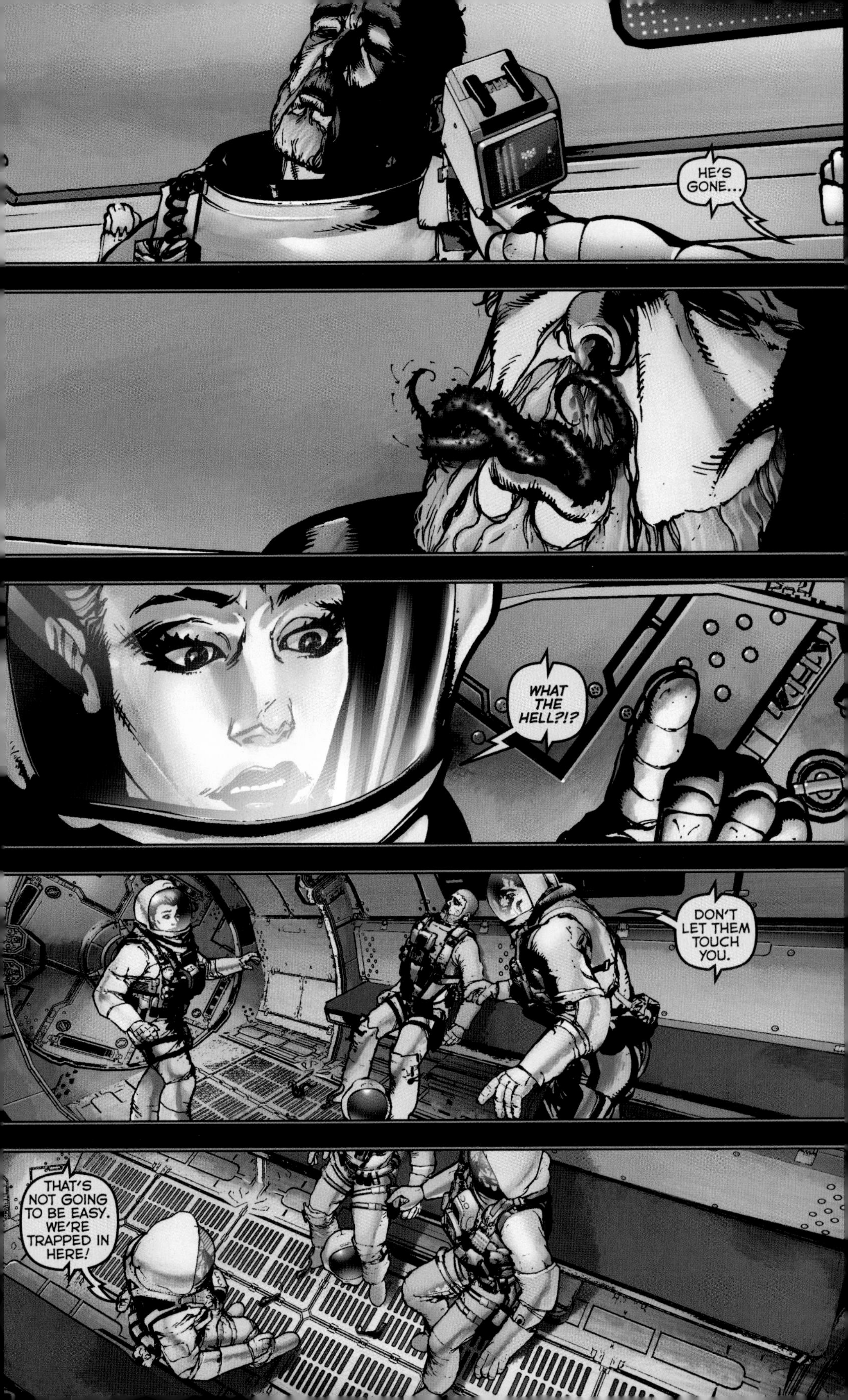
HE'S GONE...
WHAT THE HELL?!?
DON'T LET THEM TOUCH YOU.
THAT'S NOT GOING TO BE EASY. WE'RE TRAPPED IN HERE!

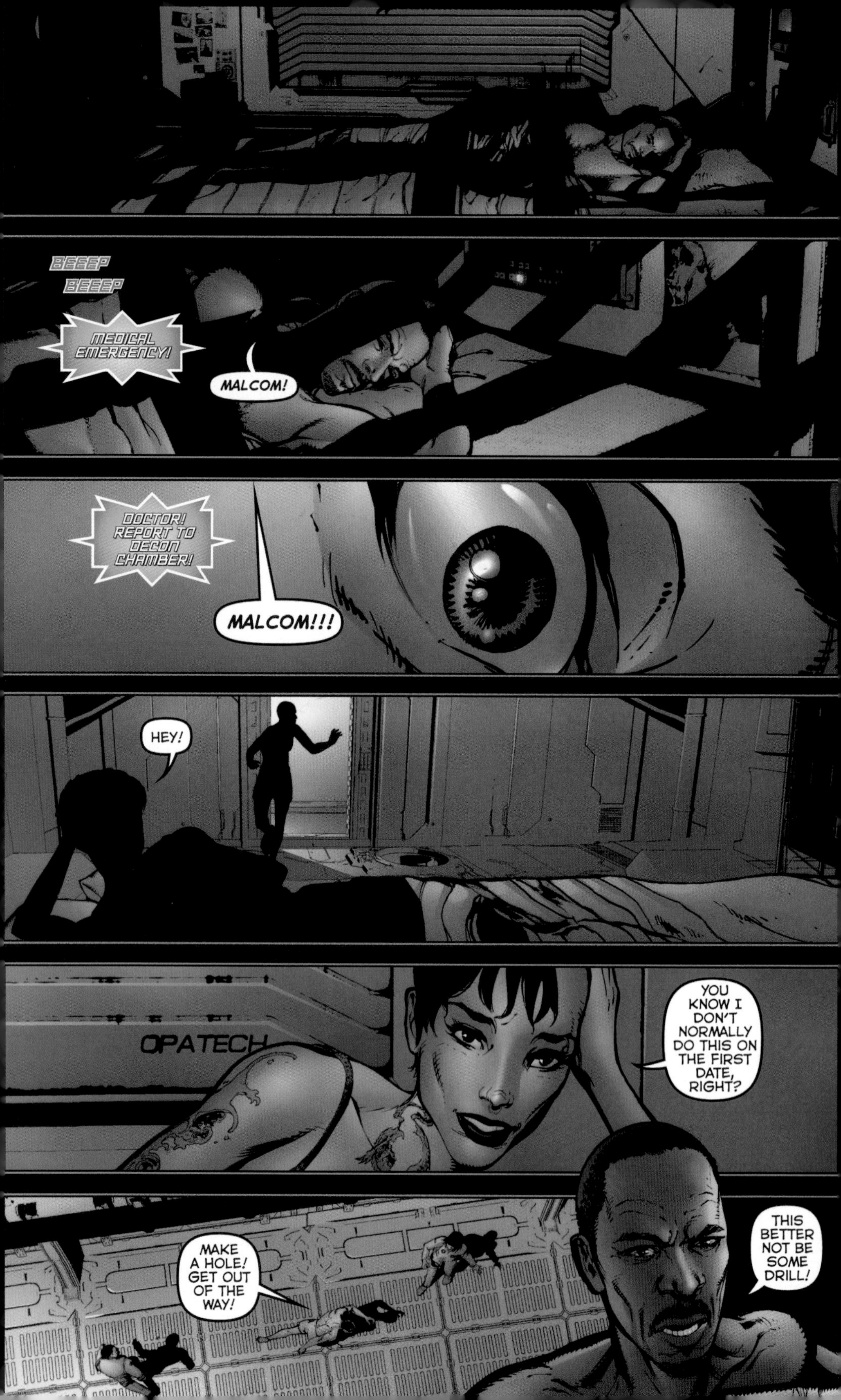
BEEEP
BEEEP
MEDICAL EMERGENCY!
MALCOM!
DOCTOR! REPORT TO DECON CHAMBER!
MALCOM!!!
HEY!
OPATECH
YOU KNOW I DON'T NORMALLY DO THIS ON THE FIRST DATE, RIGHT?
MAKE A HOLE! GET OUT OF THE WAY!
THIS BETTER NOT BE SOME DRILL!

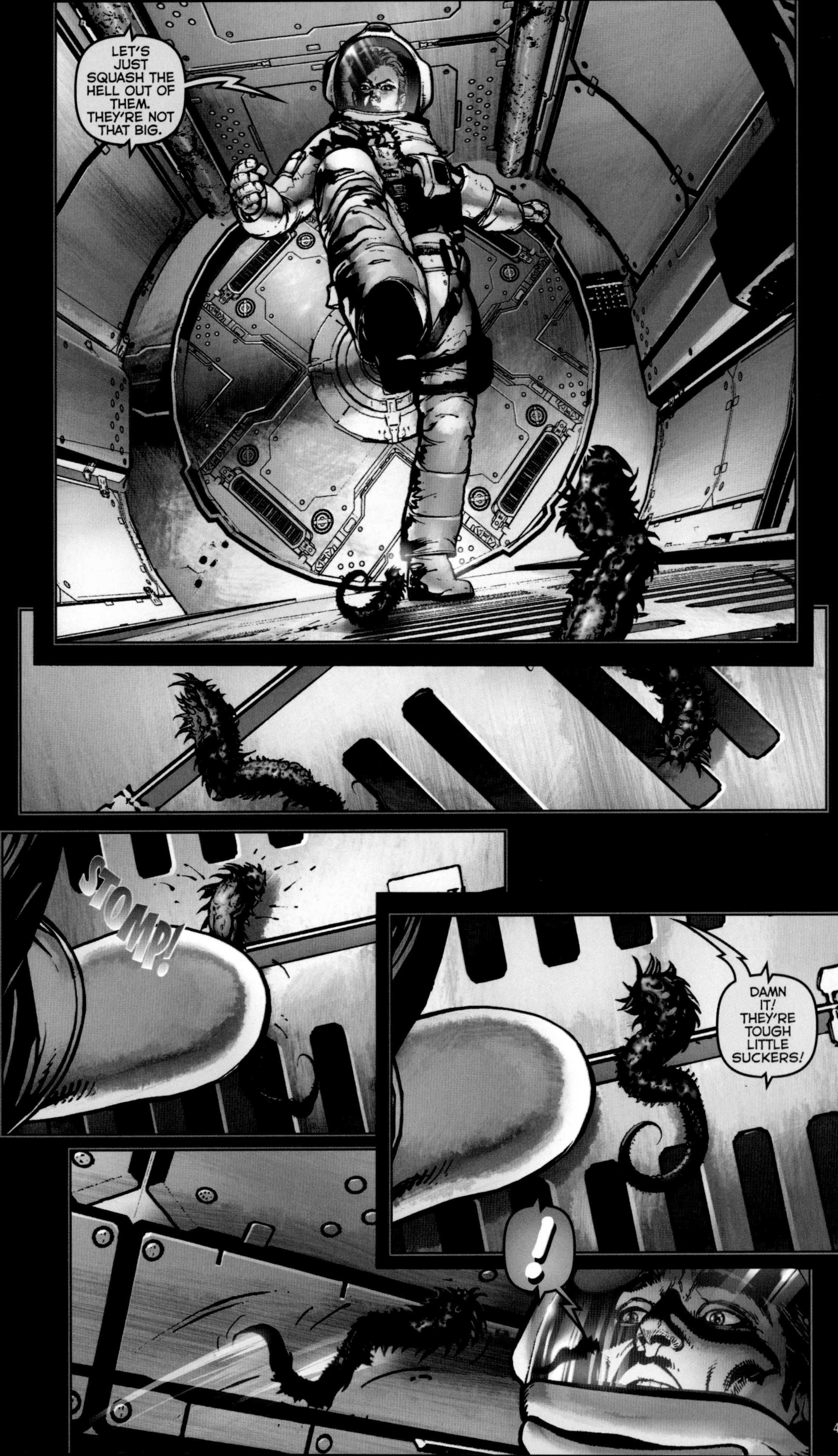
LET'S JUST SQUASH THE HELL OUT OF THEM. THEY'RE NOT THAT BIG.
STOMP!
DAMN IT! THEY'RE TOUGH LITTLE SUCKERS!
!

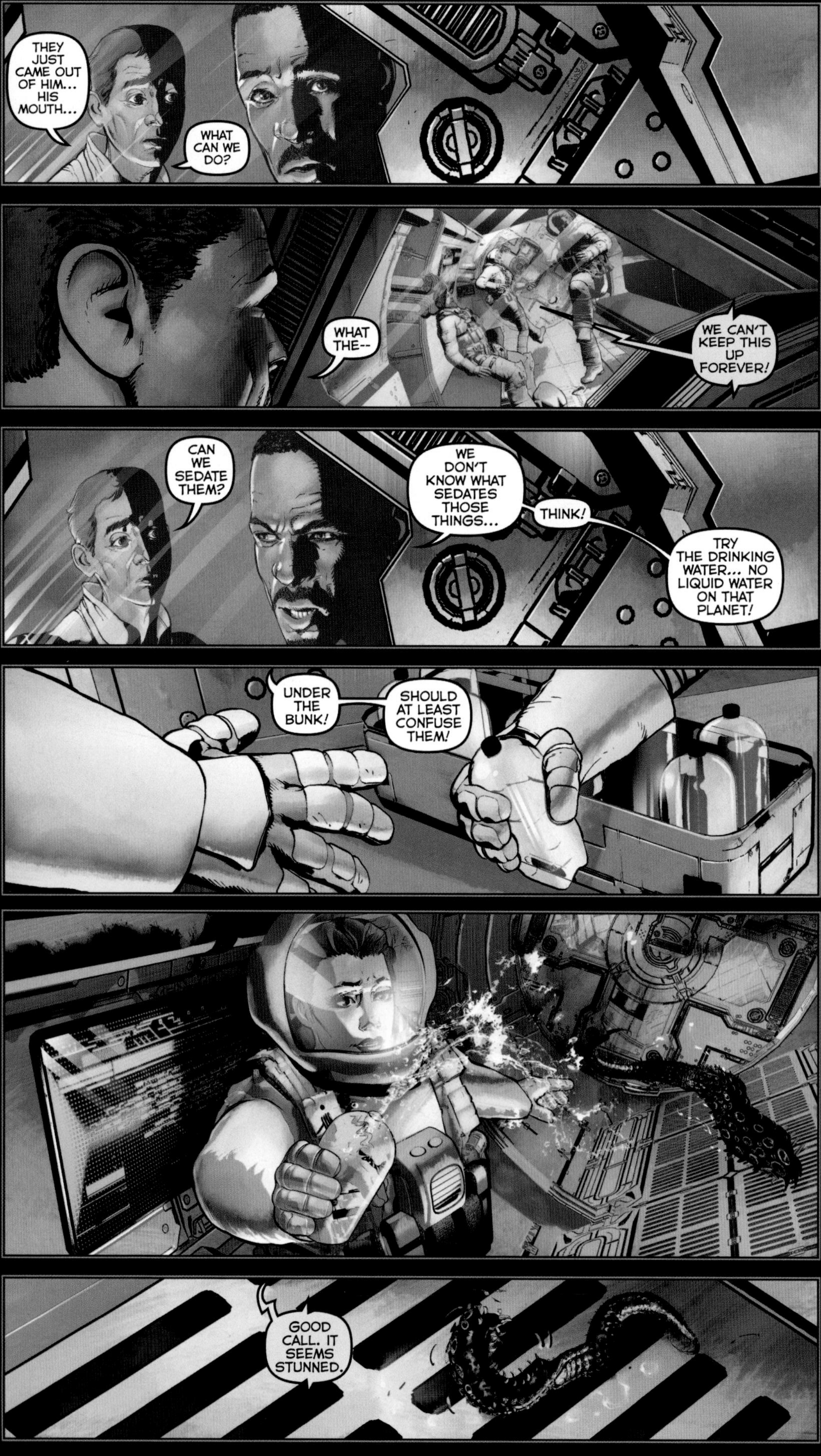
THEY JUST CAME OUT OF HIM... HIS MOUTH...
WHAT CAN WE DO?
WHAT THE--
WE CAN'T KEEP THIS UP FOREVER!
CAN WE SEDATE THEM?
WE DON'T KNOW WHAT SEDATES THOSE THINGS...
THINK!
TRY THE DRINKING WATER... NO LIQUID WATER ON THAT PLANET!
UNDER THE BUNK!
SHOULD AT LEAST CONFUSE THEM!
GOOD CALL. IT SEEMS STUNNED.

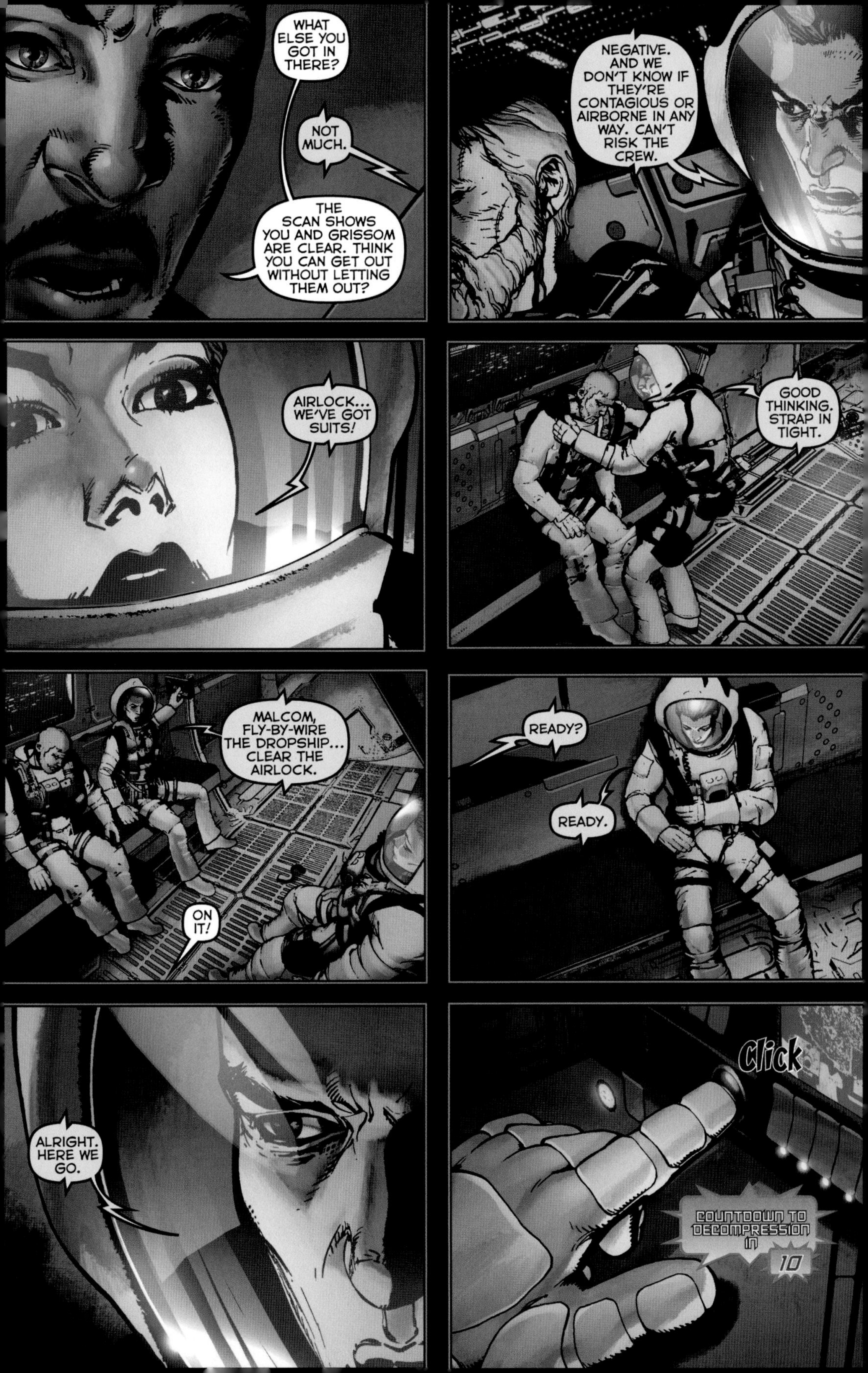
WHAT ELSE YOU GOT IN THERE?
NOT MUCH.
THE SCAN SHOWS YOU AND GRISSOM ARE CLEAR. THINK YOU CAN GET OUT WITHOUT LETTING THEM OUT?
NEGATIVE. AND WE DON'T KNOW IF THEY'RE CONTAGIOUS OR AIRBORNE IN ANY WAY. CAN'T RISK THE CREW.
AIRLOCK... WE'VE GOT SUITS!
GOOD THINKING. STRAP IN TIGHT.
MALCOM, FLY-BY-WIRE THE DROPSHIP... CLEAR THE AIRLOCK.
ON IT!
READY?
READY.
ALRIGHT. HERE WE GO.
Click
COUNTDOWN TO DECOMPRESSION IN
10

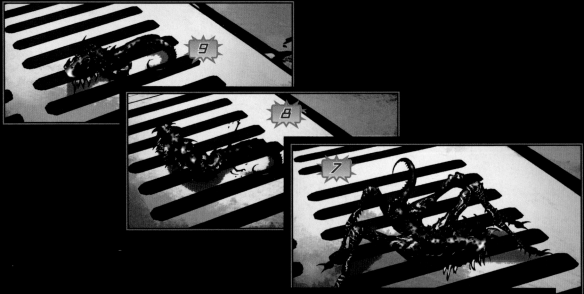

DAMN IT! THAT THING *CRACKED* MY HELMET!

YOUR STRAP! IT *TORE*--

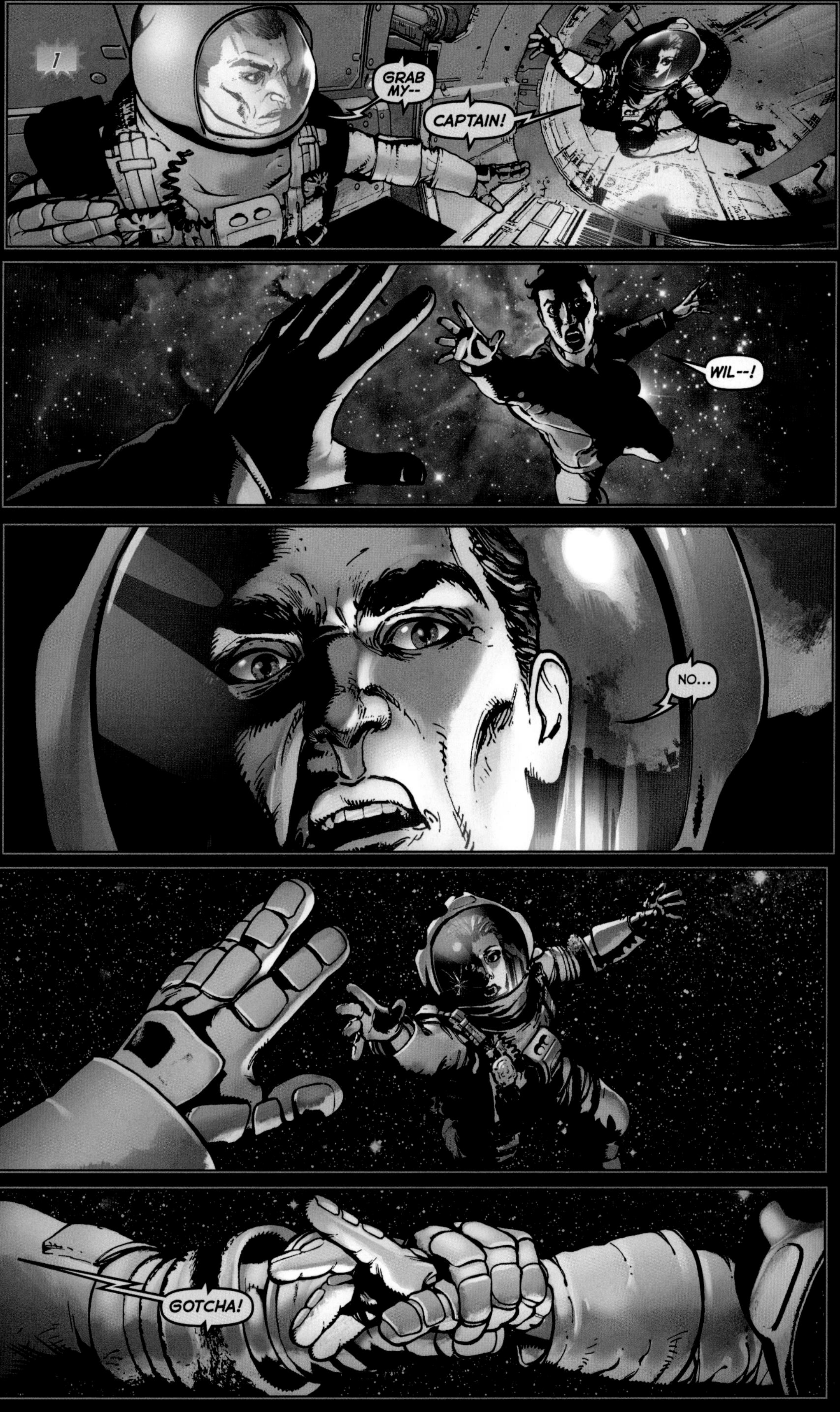
1
GRAB MY--
CAPTAIN!
WIL--!
NO...
GOTCHA!

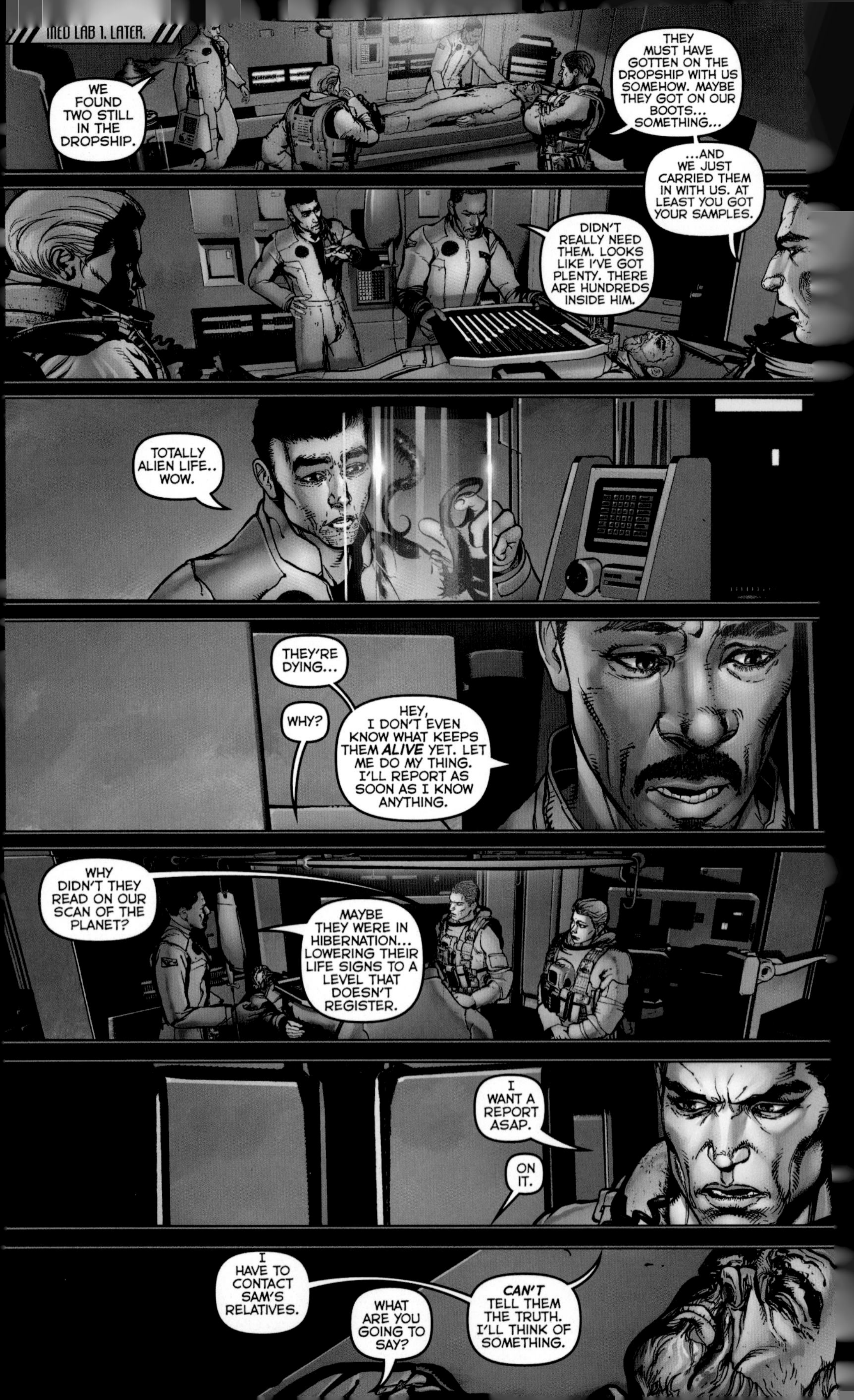
MED LAB 1. LATER.
WE FOUND TWO STILL IN THE DROPSHIP.
THEY MUST HAVE GOTTEN ON THE DROPSHIP WITH US SOMEHOW. MAYBE THEY GOT ON OUR BOOTS... SOMETHING...
...AND WE JUST CARRIED THEM IN WITH US. AT LEAST YOU GOT YOUR SAMPLES.
DIDN'T REALLY NEED THEM. LOOKS LIKE I'VE GOT PLENTY. THERE ARE HUNDREDS INSIDE HIM.
TOTALLY ALIEN LIFE.. WOW.
THEY'RE DYING...
WHY?
HEY, I DON'T EVEN KNOW WHAT KEEPS THEM *ALIVE* YET. LET ME DO MY THING. I'LL REPORT AS SOON AS I KNOW ANYTHING.
WHY DIDN'T THEY READ ON OUR SCAN OF THE PLANET?
MAYBE THEY WERE IN HIBERNATION... LOWERING THEIR LIFE SIGNS TO A LEVEL THAT DOESN'T REGISTER.
I WANT A REPORT ASAP.
ON IT.
I HAVE TO CONTACT SAM'S RELATIVES.
WHAT ARE YOU GOING TO SAY?
CAN'T TELL THEM THE TRUTH. I'LL THINK OF SOMETHING.

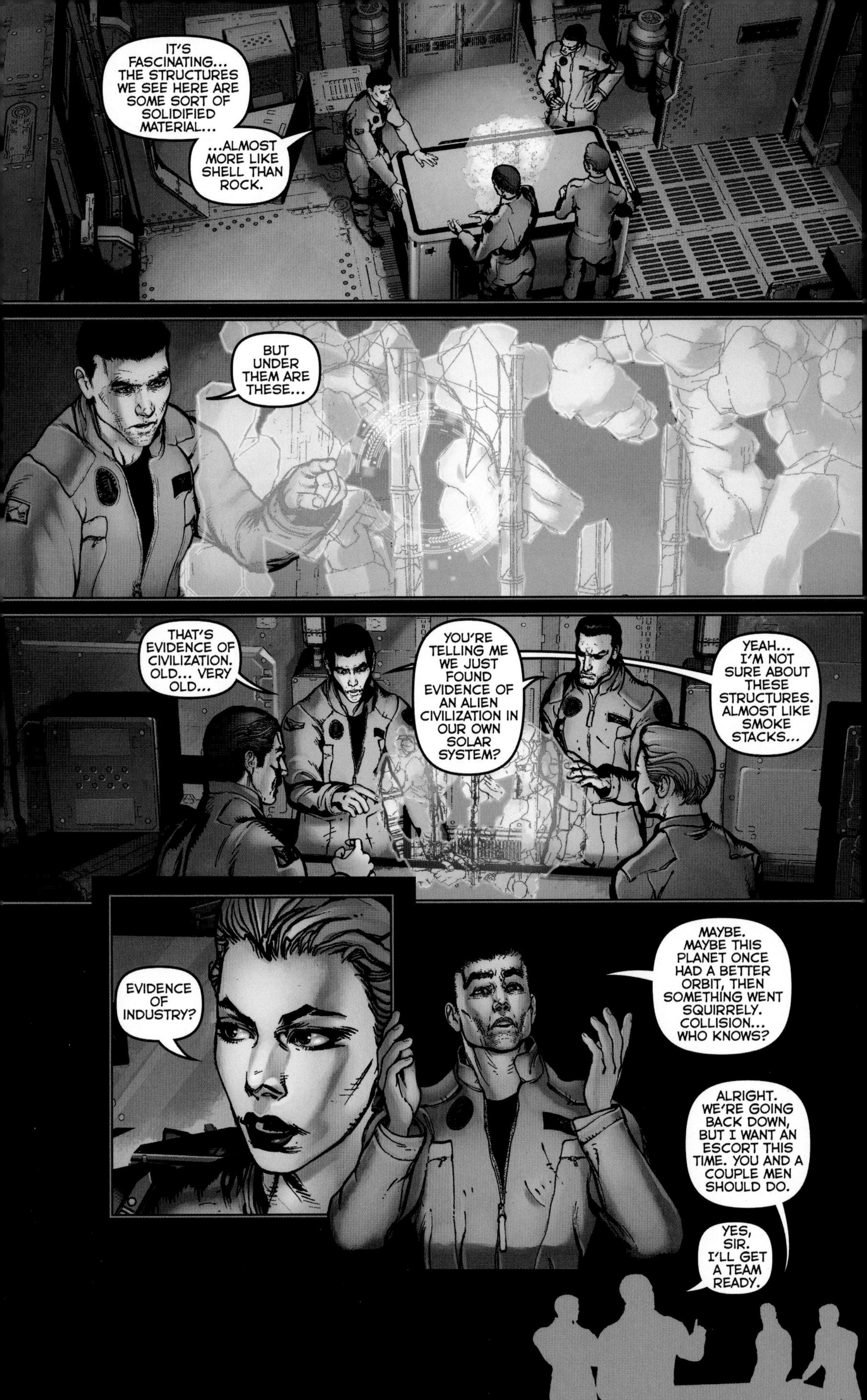
IT'S FASCINATING... THE STRUCTURES WE SEE HERE ARE SOME SORT OF SOLIDIFIED MATERIAL...
...ALMOST MORE LIKE SHELL THAN ROCK.
BUT UNDER THEM ARE THESE...
THAT'S EVIDENCE OF CIVILIZATION. OLD... VERY OLD...
YOU'RE TELLING ME WE JUST FOUND EVIDENCE OF AN ALIEN CIVILIZATION IN OUR OWN SOLAR SYSTEM?
YEAH... I'M NOT SURE ABOUT THESE STRUCTURES. ALMOST LIKE SMOKE STACKS...
EVIDENCE OF INDUSTRY?
MAYBE. MAYBE THIS PLANET ONCE HAD A BETTER ORBIT, THEN SOMETHING WENT SQUIRRELY. COLLISION... WHO KNOWS?
ALRIGHT. WE'RE GOING BACK DOWN, BUT I WANT AN ESCORT THIS TIME. YOU AND A COUPLE MEN SHOULD DO.
YES, SIR. I'LL GET A TEAM READY.

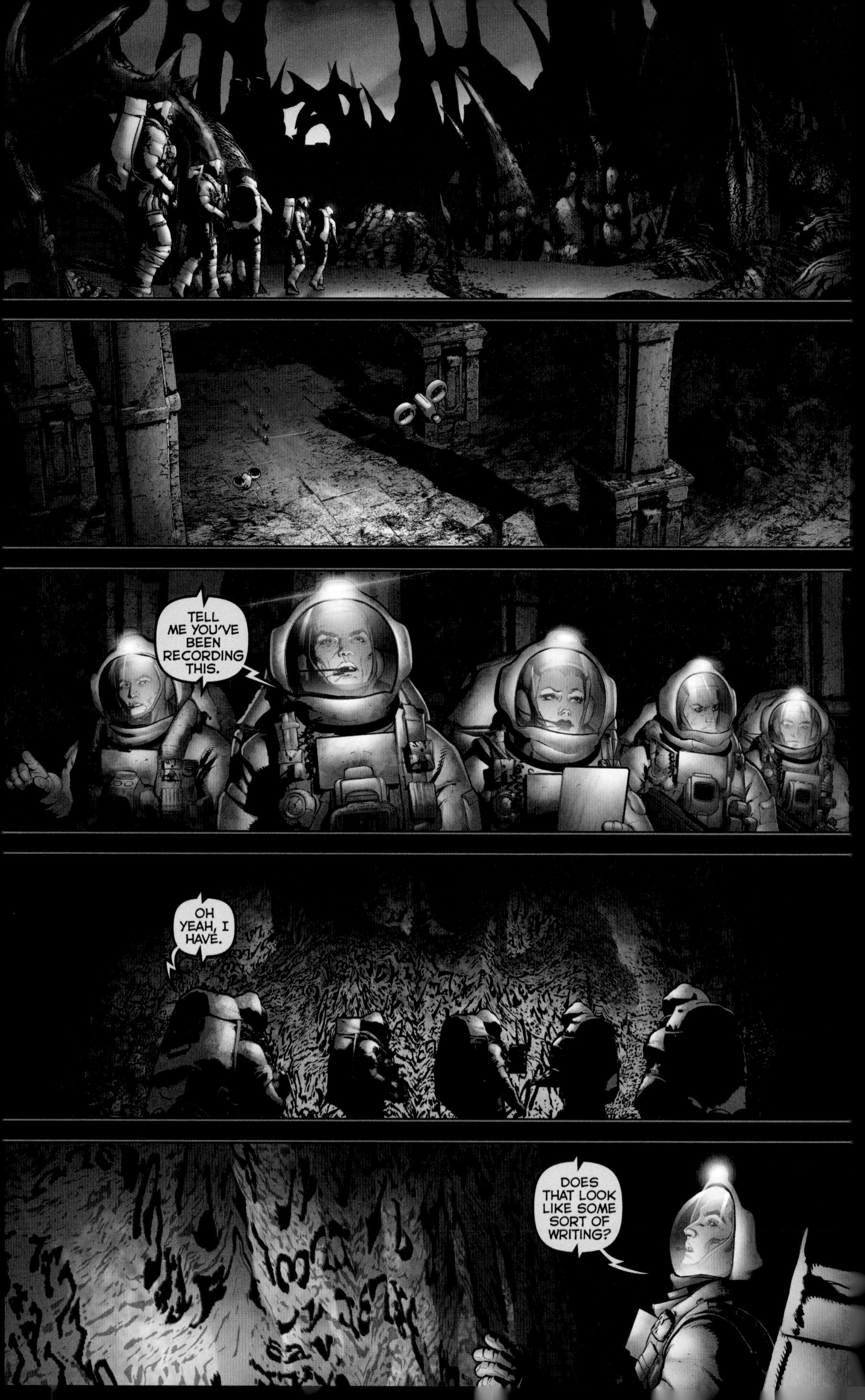
TELL ME YOU'VE BEEN RECORDING THIS.
OH YEAH, I HAVE.
DOES THAT LOOK LIKE SOME SORT OF WRITING?

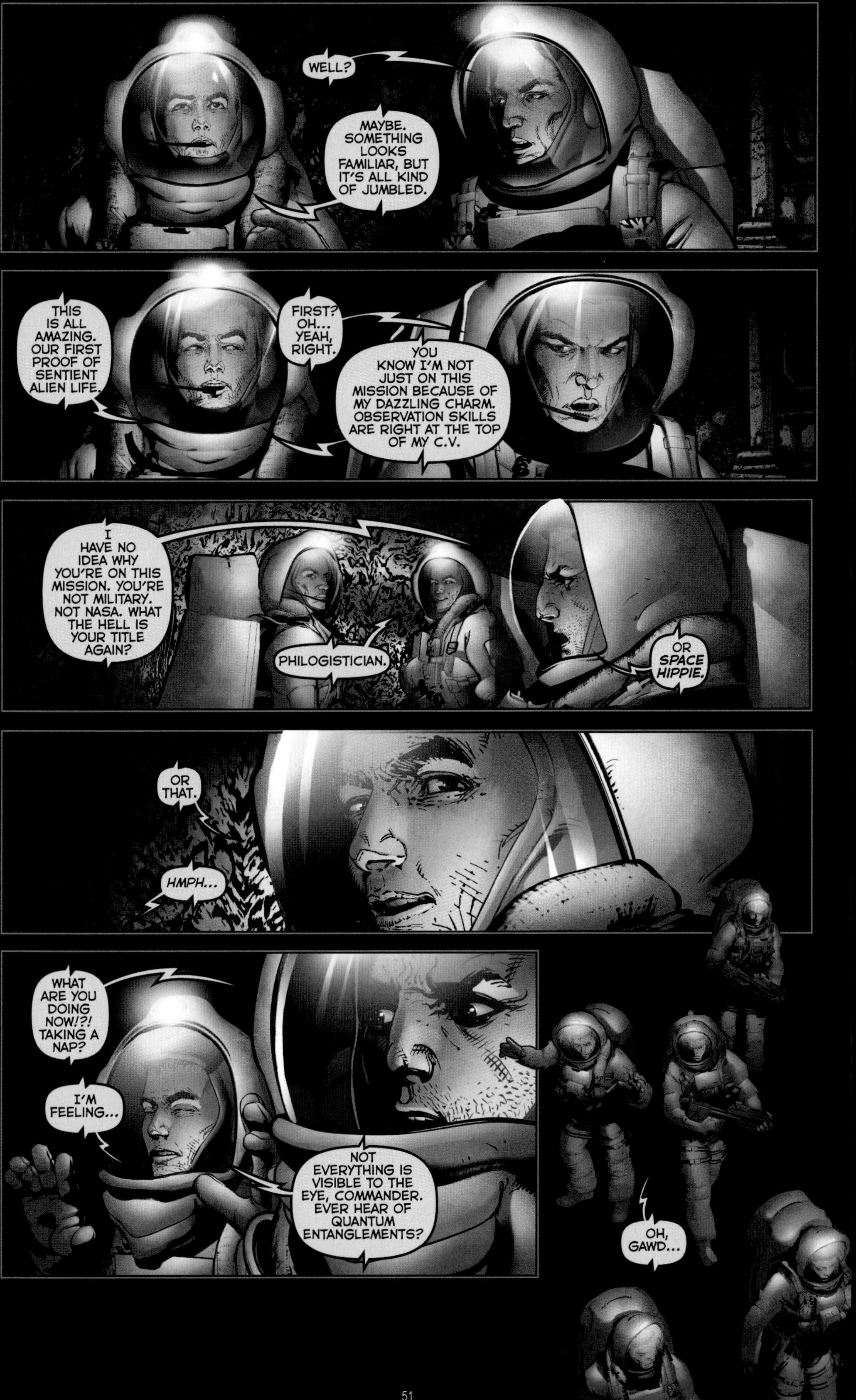

WELL?
MAYBE. SOMETHING LOOKS FAMILIAR, BUT IT'S ALL KIND OF JUMBLED.
THIS IS ALL AMAZING. OUR FIRST PROOF OF SENTIENT ALIEN LIFE.
FIRST? OH... YEAH, RIGHT.
YOU KNOW I'M NOT JUST ON THIS MISSION BECAUSE OF MY DAZZLING CHARM. OBSERVATION SKILLS ARE RIGHT AT THE TOP OF MY C.V.
I HAVE NO IDEA WHY YOU'RE ON THIS MISSION. YOU'RE NOT MILITARY. NOT NASA. WHAT THE HELL IS YOUR TITLE AGAIN?
PHILOGISTICIAN.
OR SPACE HIPPIE.
OR THAT.
HMPH...
WHAT ARE YOU DOING NOW!?! TAKING A NAP?
I'M FEELING...
NOT EVERYTHING IS VISIBLE TO THE EYE, COMMANDER. EVER HEAR OF QUANTUM ENTANGLEMENTS?
OH, GAWD...

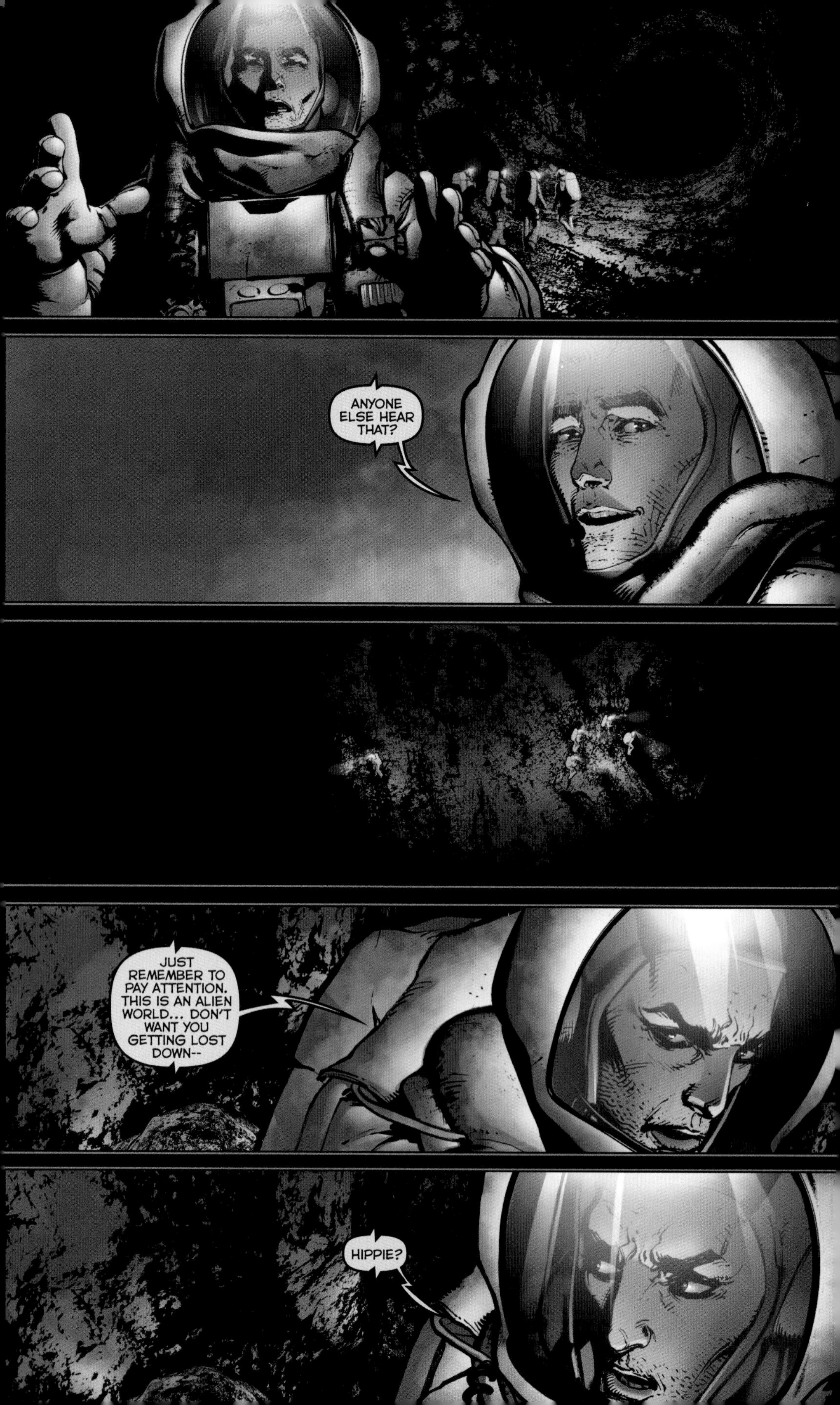
ANYONE ELSE HEAR THAT?
JUST REMEMBER TO PAY ATTENTION. THIS IS AN ALIEN WORLD... DON'T WANT YOU GETTING LOST DOWN--
HIPPIE?

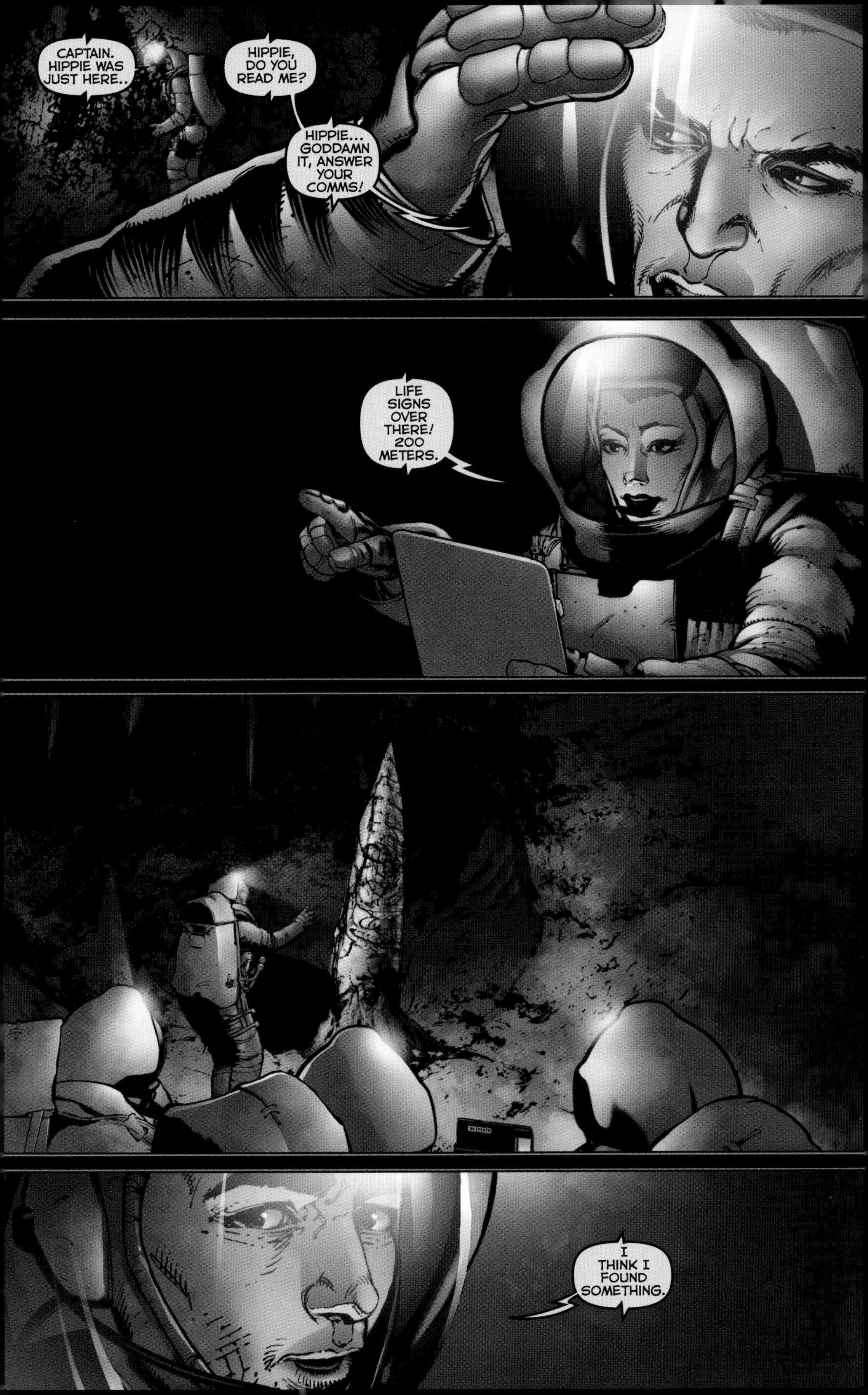
CAPTAIN. HIPPIE WAS JUST HERE..
HIPPIE, DO YOU READ ME?
HIPPIE... GODDAMN IT, ANSWER YOUR COMMS!
LIFE SIGNS OVER THERE! 200 METERS.
I THINK I FOUND SOMETHING.

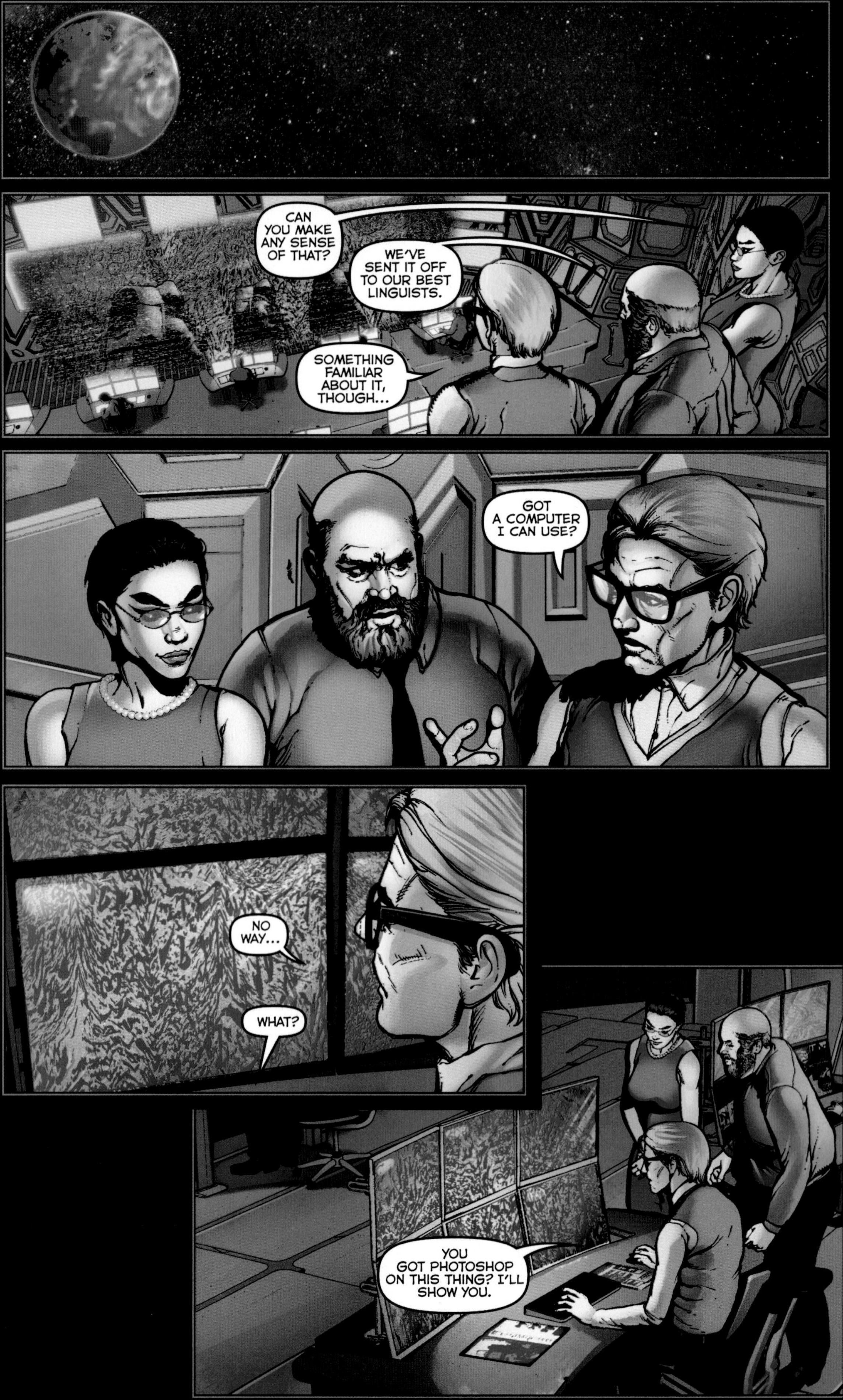
CAN YOU MAKE ANY SENSE OF THAT?
WE'VE SENT IT OFF TO OUR BEST LINGUISTS.
SOMETHING FAMILIAR ABOUT IT, THOUGH...
GOT A COMPUTER I CAN USE?
NO WAY...
WHAT?
YOU GOT PHOTOSHOP ON THIS THING? I'LL SHOW YOU.

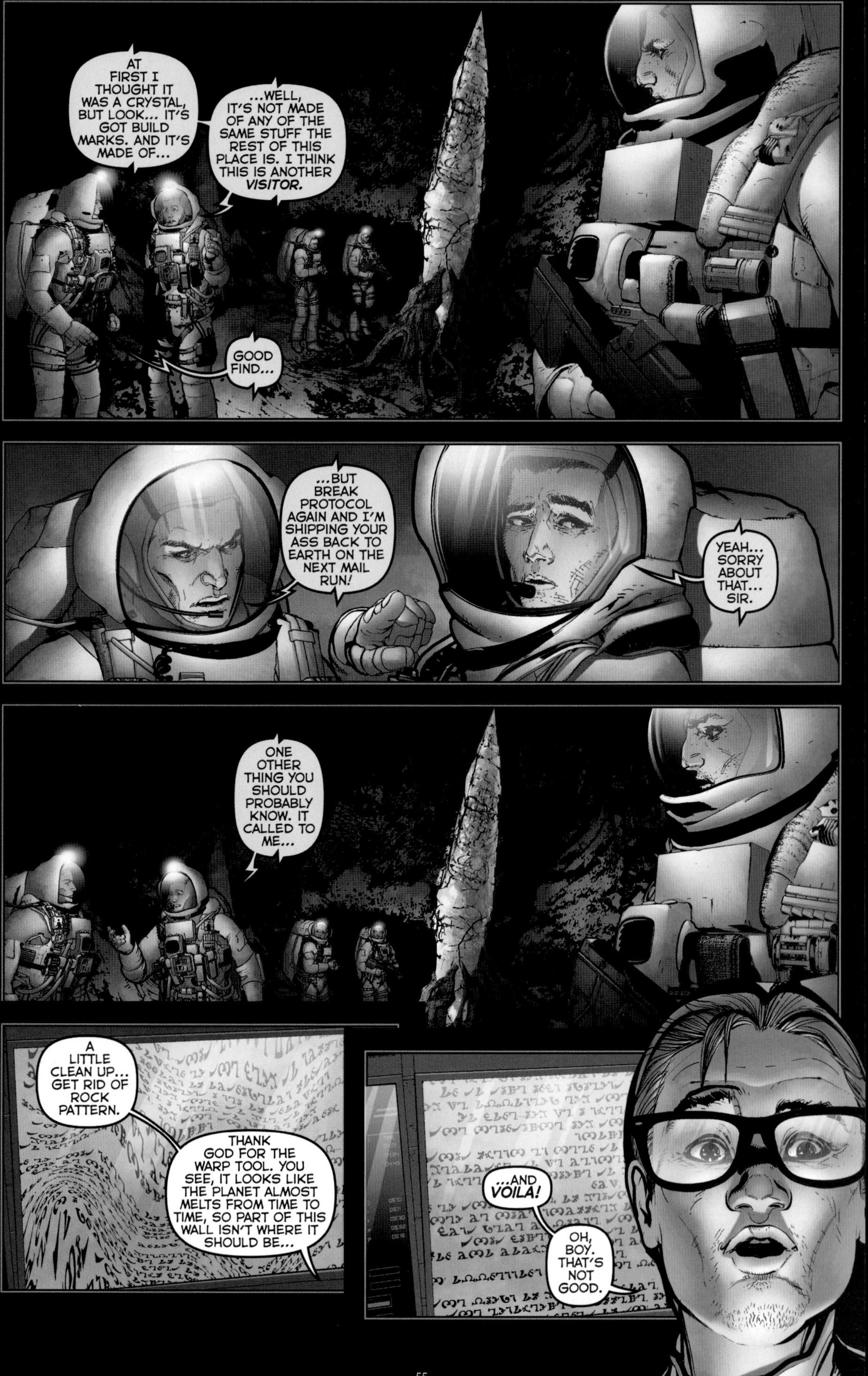
AT FIRST I THOUGHT IT WAS A CRYSTAL, BUT LOOK... IT'S GOT BUILD MARKS. AND IT'S MADE OF...
...WELL, IT'S NOT MADE OF ANY OF THE SAME STUFF THE REST OF THIS PLACE IS. I THINK THIS IS ANOTHER VISITOR.
GOOD FIND...
...BUT BREAK PROTOCOL AGAIN AND I'M SHIPPING YOUR ASS BACK TO EARTH ON THE NEXT MAIL RUN!
YEAH... SORRY ABOUT THAT... SIR.
ONE OTHER THING YOU SHOULD PROBABLY KNOW. IT CALLED TO ME...
A LITTLE CLEAN UP... GET RID OF ROCK PATTERN.
THANK GOD FOR THE WARP TOOL. YOU SEE, IT LOOKS LIKE THE PLANET ALMOST MELTS FROM TIME TO TIME, SO PART OF THIS WALL ISN'T WHERE IT SHOULD BE...
...AND VOILA!
OH, BOY. THAT'S NOT GOOD.

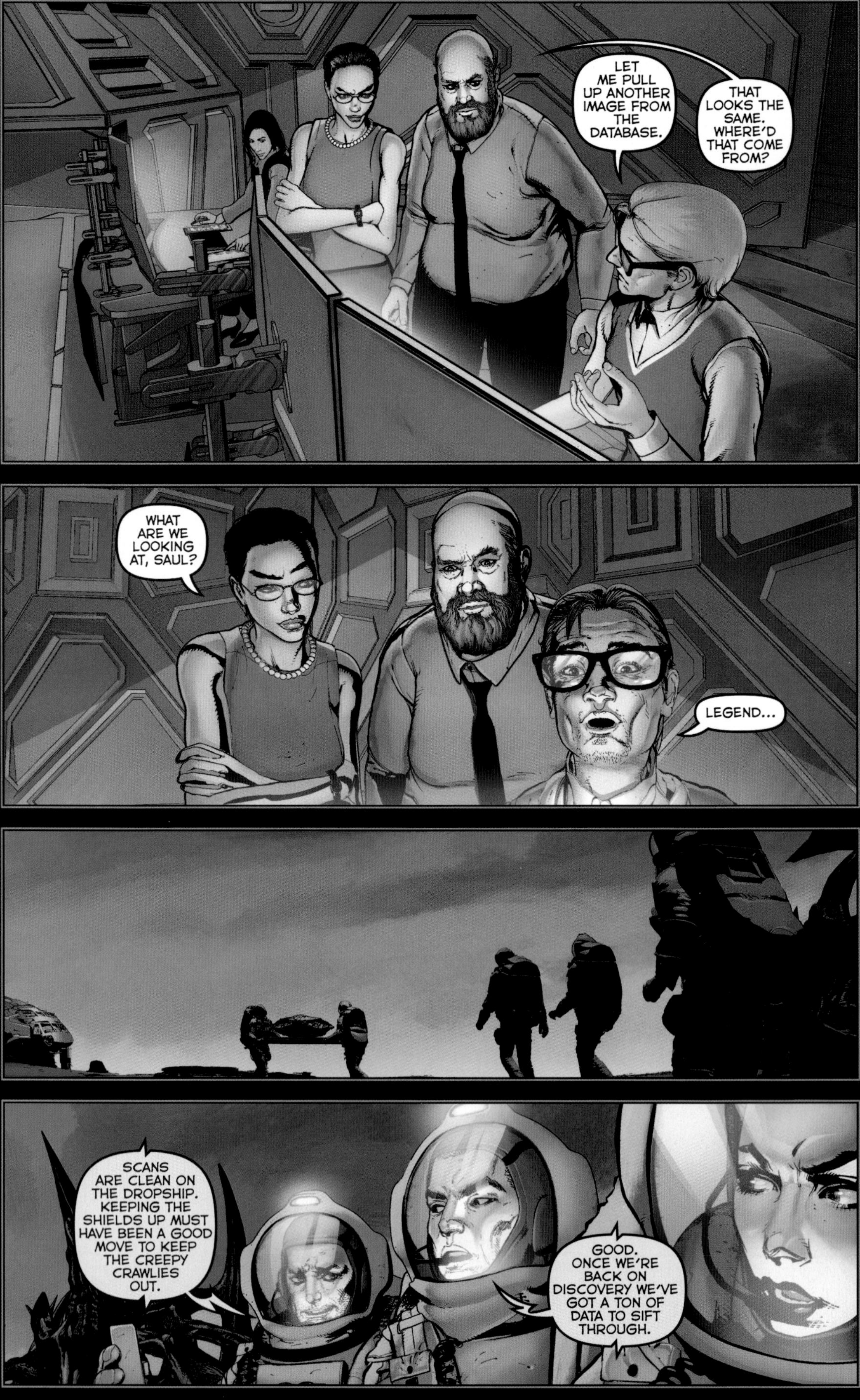
LET ME PULL UP ANOTHER IMAGE FROM THE DATABASE.
THAT LOOKS THE SAME. WHERE'D THAT COME FROM?
WHAT ARE WE LOOKING AT, SAUL?
LEGEND...
SCANS ARE CLEAN ON THE DROPSHIP. KEEPING THE SHIELDS UP MUST HAVE BEEN A GOOD MOVE TO KEEP THE CREEPY CRAWLIES OUT.
GOOD. ONCE WE'RE BACK ON DISCOVERY WE'VE GOT A TON OF DATA TO SIFT THROUGH.

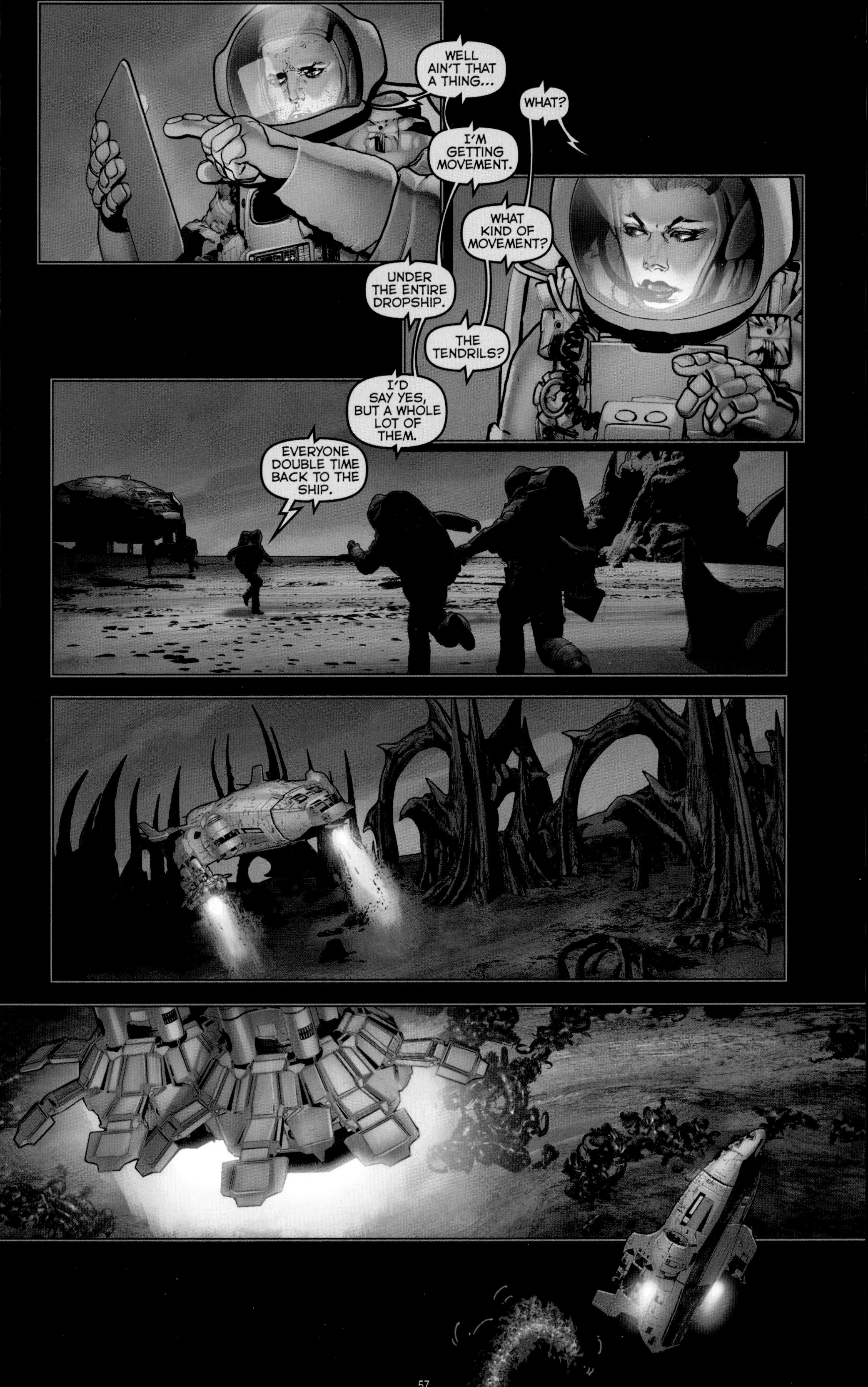
WELL AIN'T THAT A THING...
WHAT?
I'M GETTING MOVEMENT.
WHAT KIND OF MOVEMENT?
UNDER THE ENTIRE DROPSHIP.
THE TENDRILS?
I'D SAY YES, BUT A WHOLE LOT OF THEM.
EVERYONE DOUBLE TIME BACK TO THE SHIP.

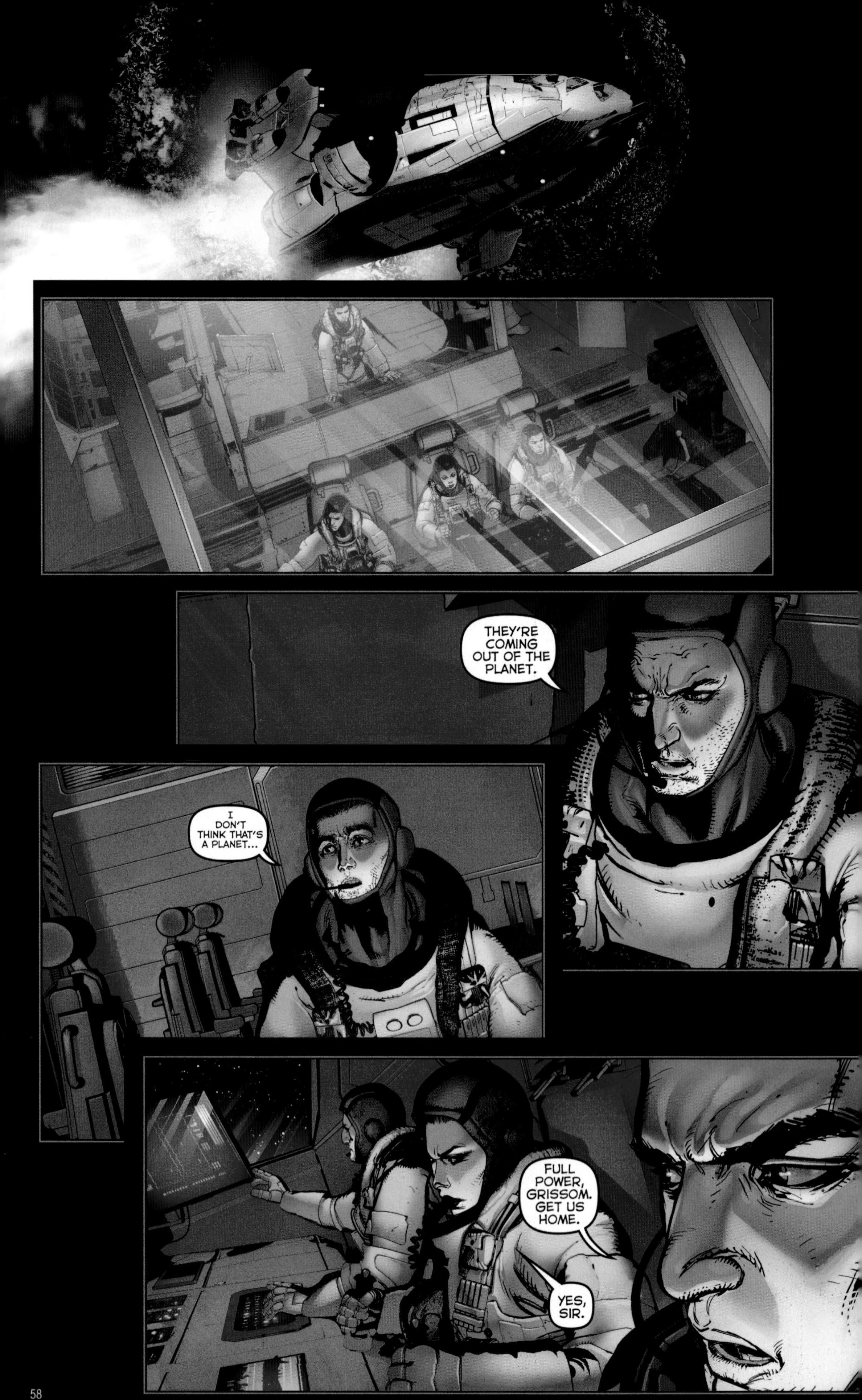
THEY'RE COMING OUT OF THE PLANET.
I DON'T THINK THAT'S A PLANET...
FULL POWER, GRISSOM. GET US HOME.
YES, SIR.

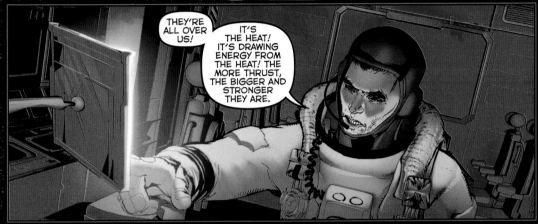

THEY'RE ALL OVER US!

IT'S THE HEAT! IT'S DRAWING ENERGY FROM THE HEAT! THE MORE THRUST, THE BIGGER AND STRONGER THEY ARE.

YOU SAID THE SHIELDS KEPT THEM OUT, RIGHT?

LOOKED LIKE IT.

THEN PUT ALL YOU HAVE IN THE SHIELDS. I'M HOPING IT WILL LET US SLIP THEIR GRIP.

YES, SIR!

WE'RE FREE!

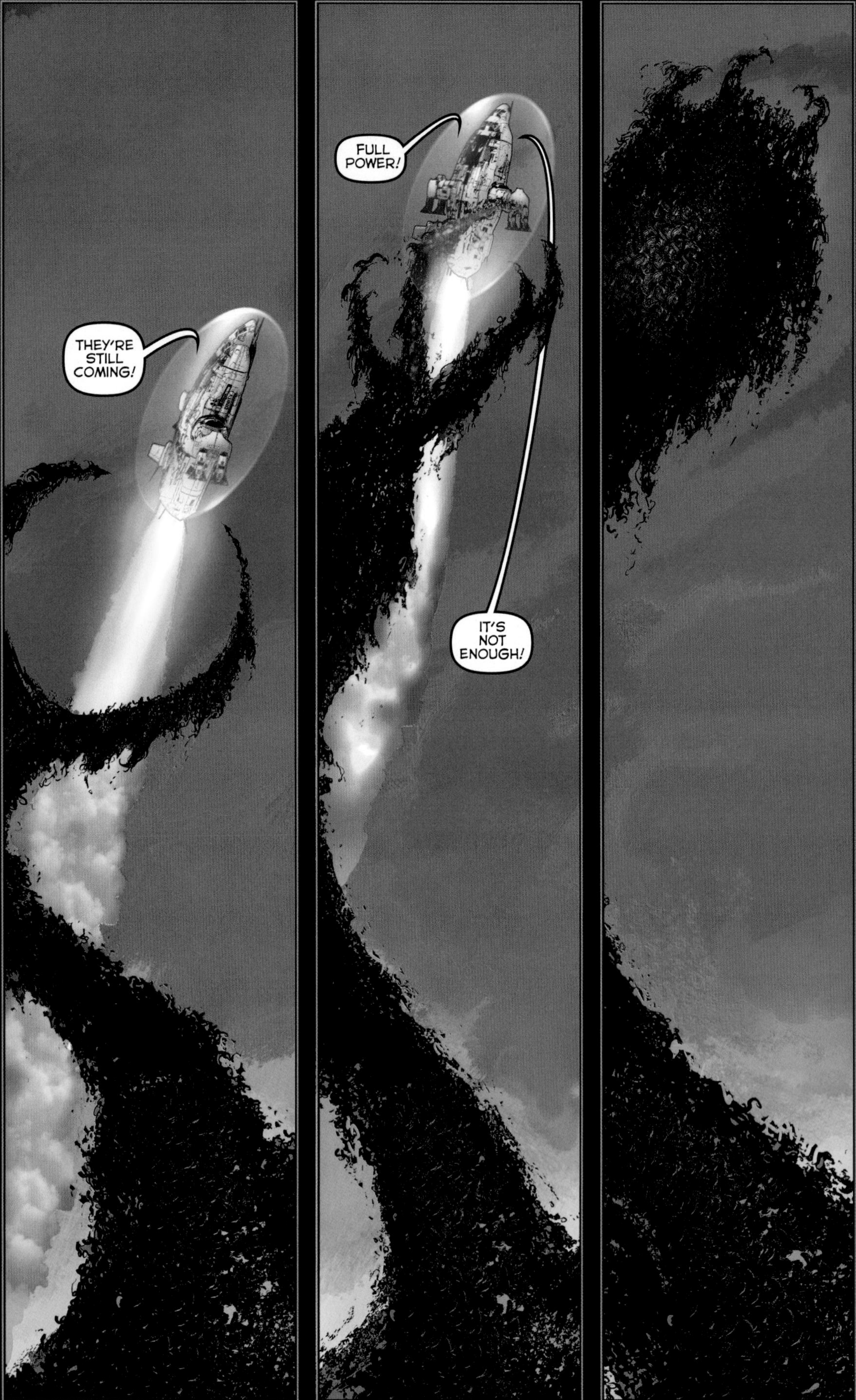
THEY'RE STILL COMING!
FULL POWER!
IT'S NOT ENOUGH!

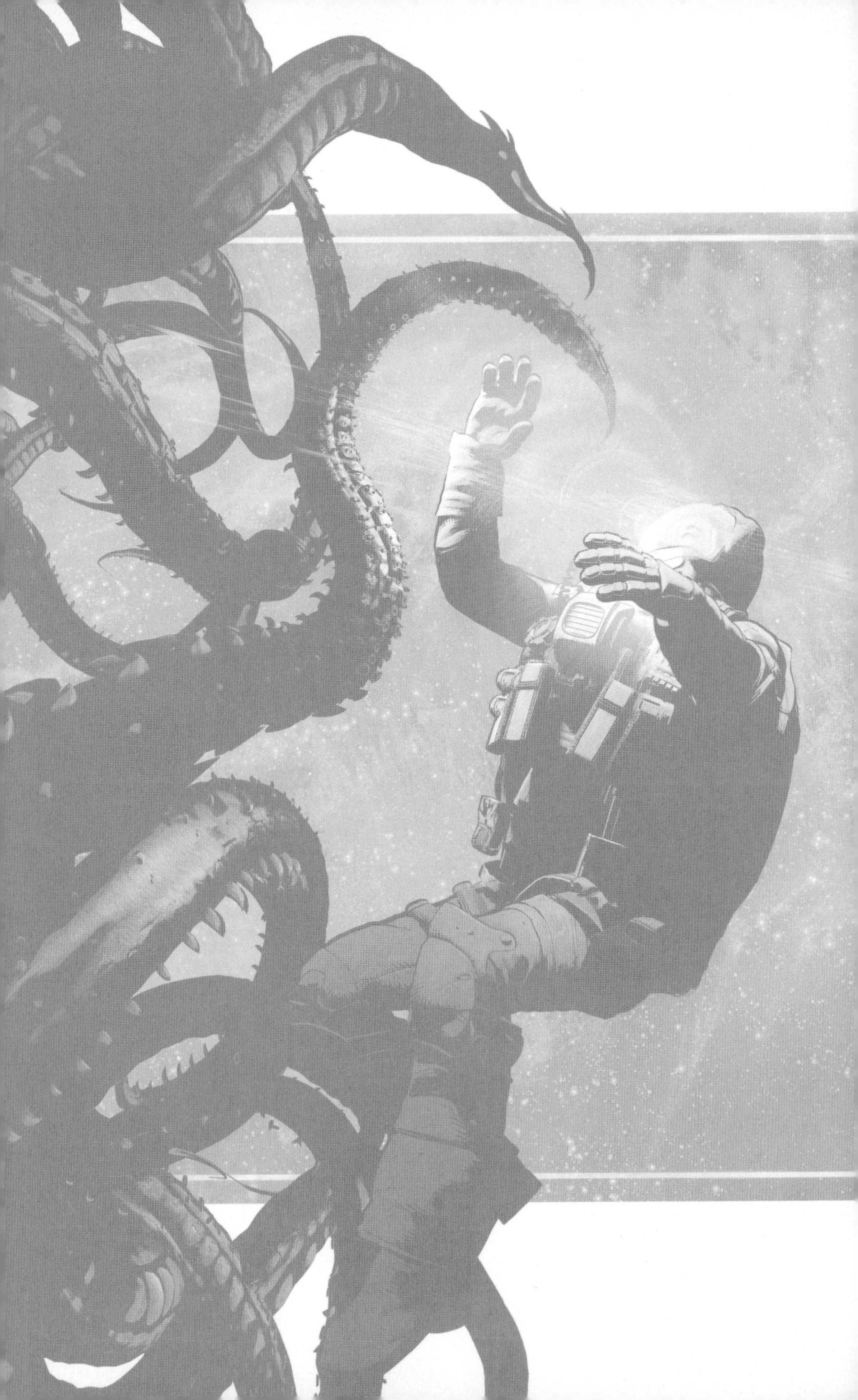

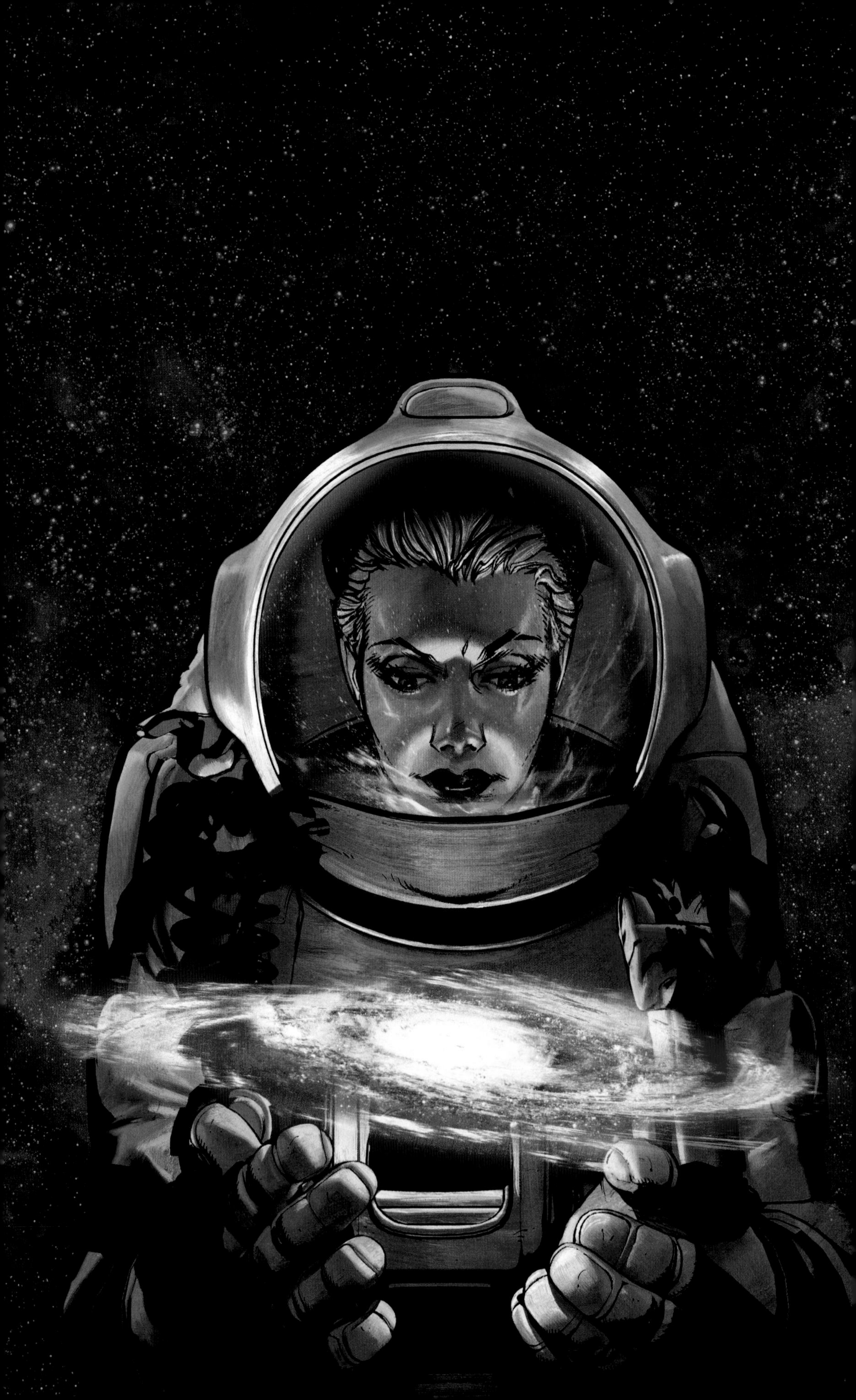

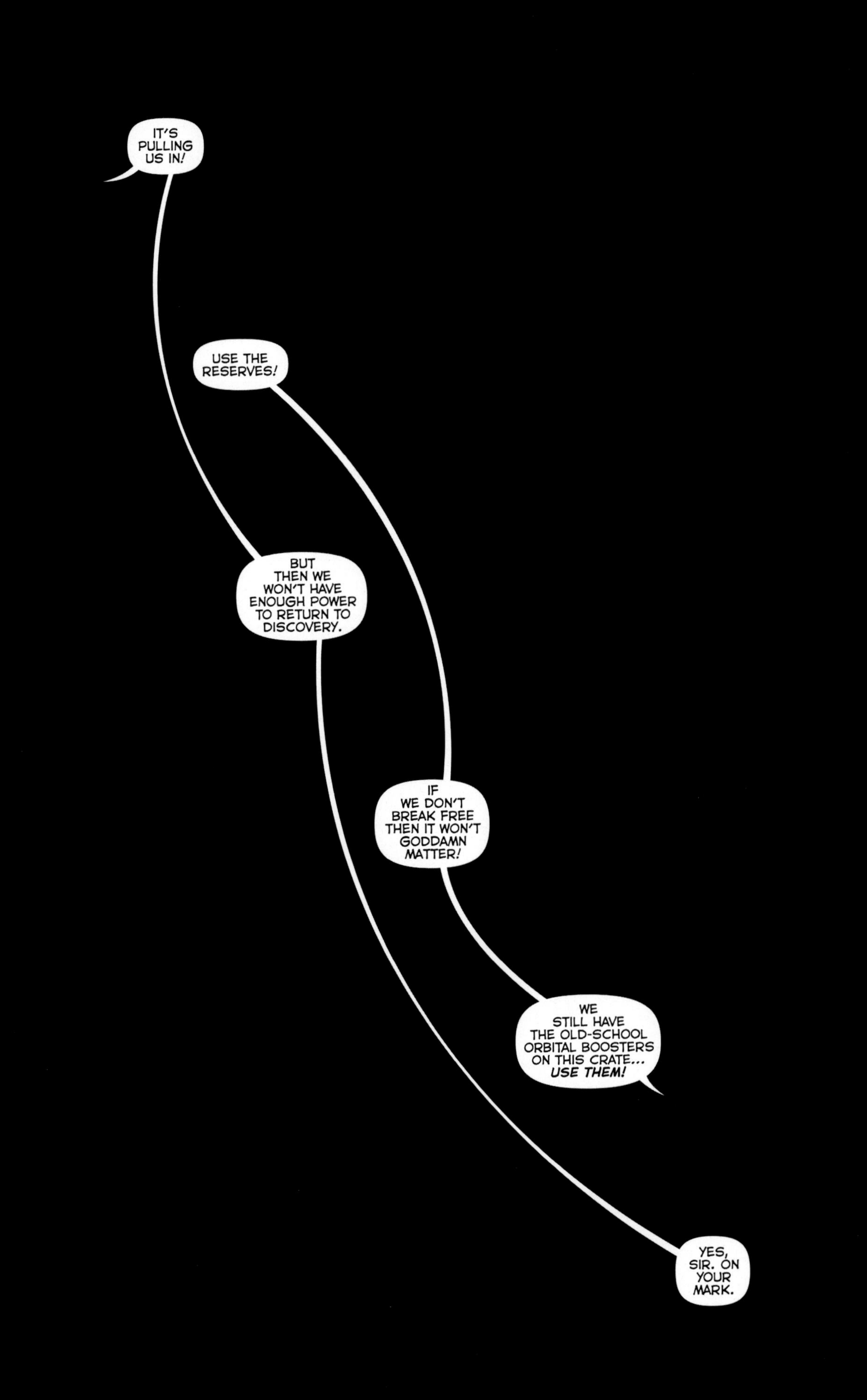
IT'S PULLING US IN!
USE THE RESERVES!
BUT THEN WE WON'T HAVE ENOUGH POWER TO RETURN TO DISCOVERY.
IF WE DON'T BREAK FREE THEN IT WON'T GODDAMN MATTER!
WE STILL HAVE THE OLD-SCHOOL ORBITAL BOOSTERS ON THIS CRATE... *USE THEM!*
YES, SIR. ON YOUR MARK.

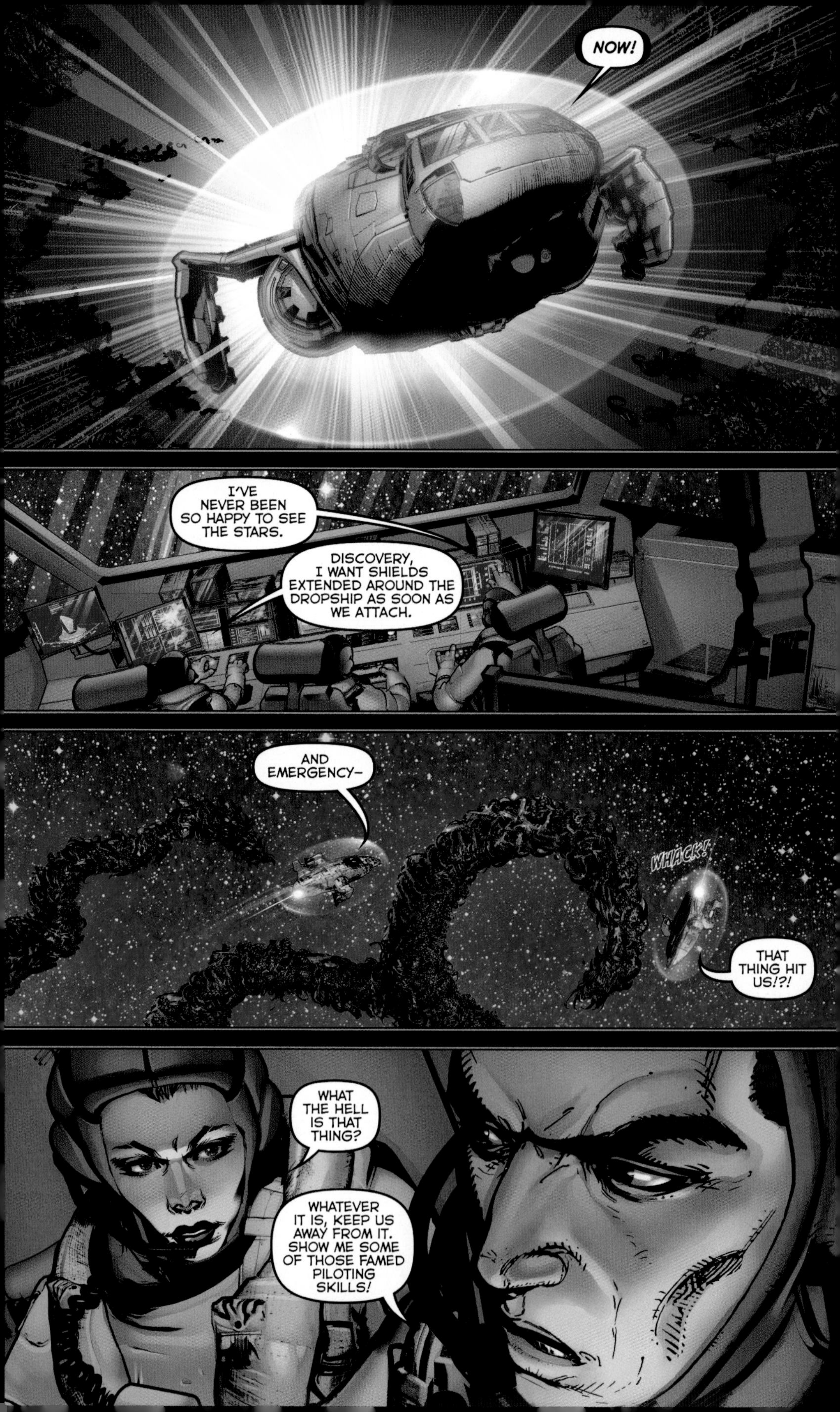
NOW!
I'VE NEVER BEEN SO HAPPY TO SEE THE STARS.
DISCOVERY, I WANT SHIELDS EXTENDED AROUND THE DROPSHIP AS SOON AS WE ATTACH.
AND EMERGENCY–
WHACK!
THAT THING HIT US!?!
WHAT THE HELL IS THAT THING?
WHATEVER IT IS, KEEP US AWAY FROM IT. SHOW ME SOME OF THOSE FAMED PILOTING SKILLS!

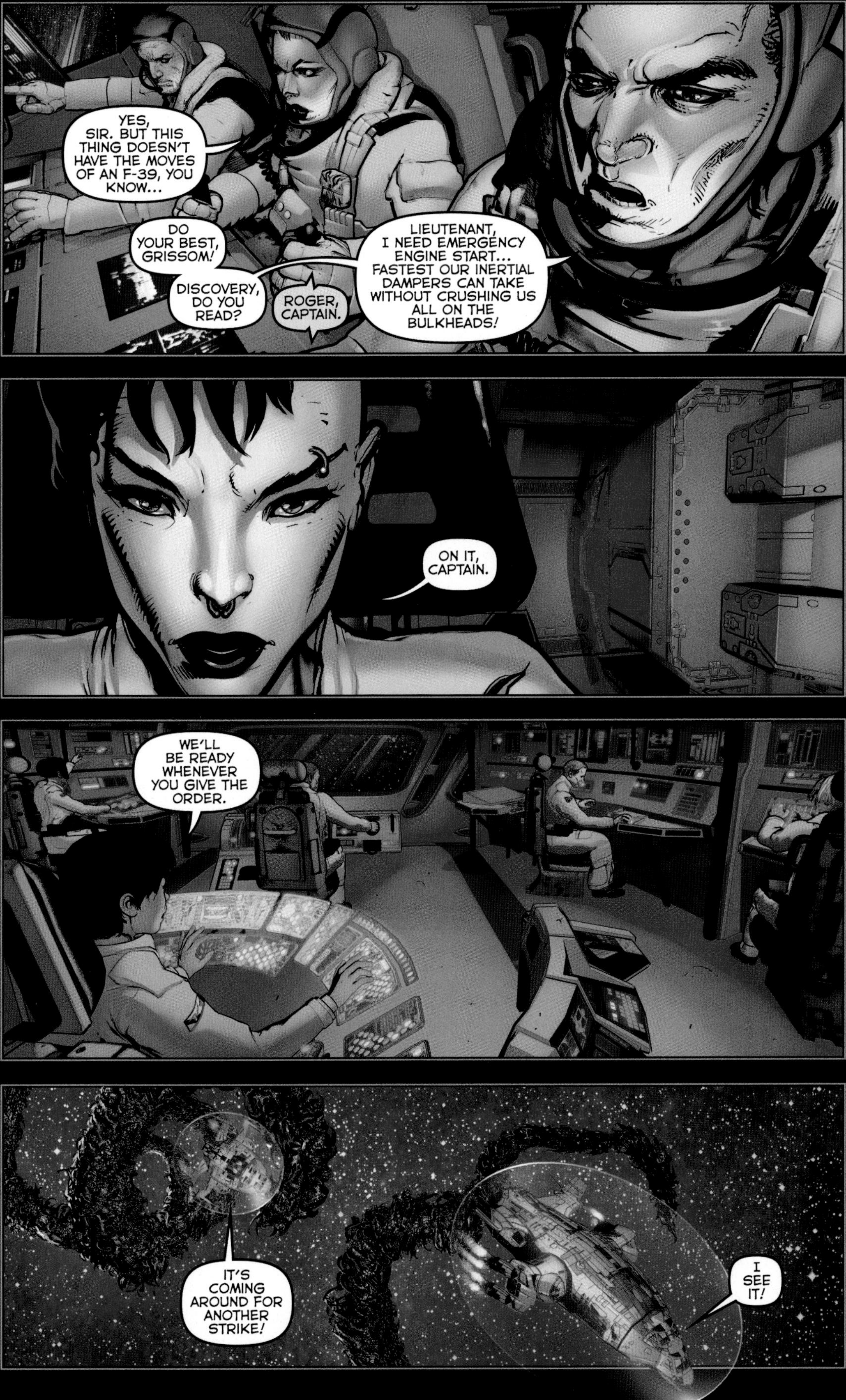
YES, SIR. BUT THIS THING DOESN'T HAVE THE MOVES OF AN F-39, YOU KNOW...
DO YOUR BEST, GRISSOM!
DISCOVERY, DO YOU READ?
ROGER, CAPTAIN.
LIEUTENANT, I NEED EMERGENCY ENGINE START... FASTEST OUR INERTIAL DAMPERS CAN TAKE WITHOUT CRUSHING US ALL ON THE BULKHEADS!
ON IT, CAPTAIN.
WE'LL BE READY WHENEVER YOU GIVE THE ORDER.
IT'S COMING AROUND FOR ANOTHER STRIKE!
I SEE IT!

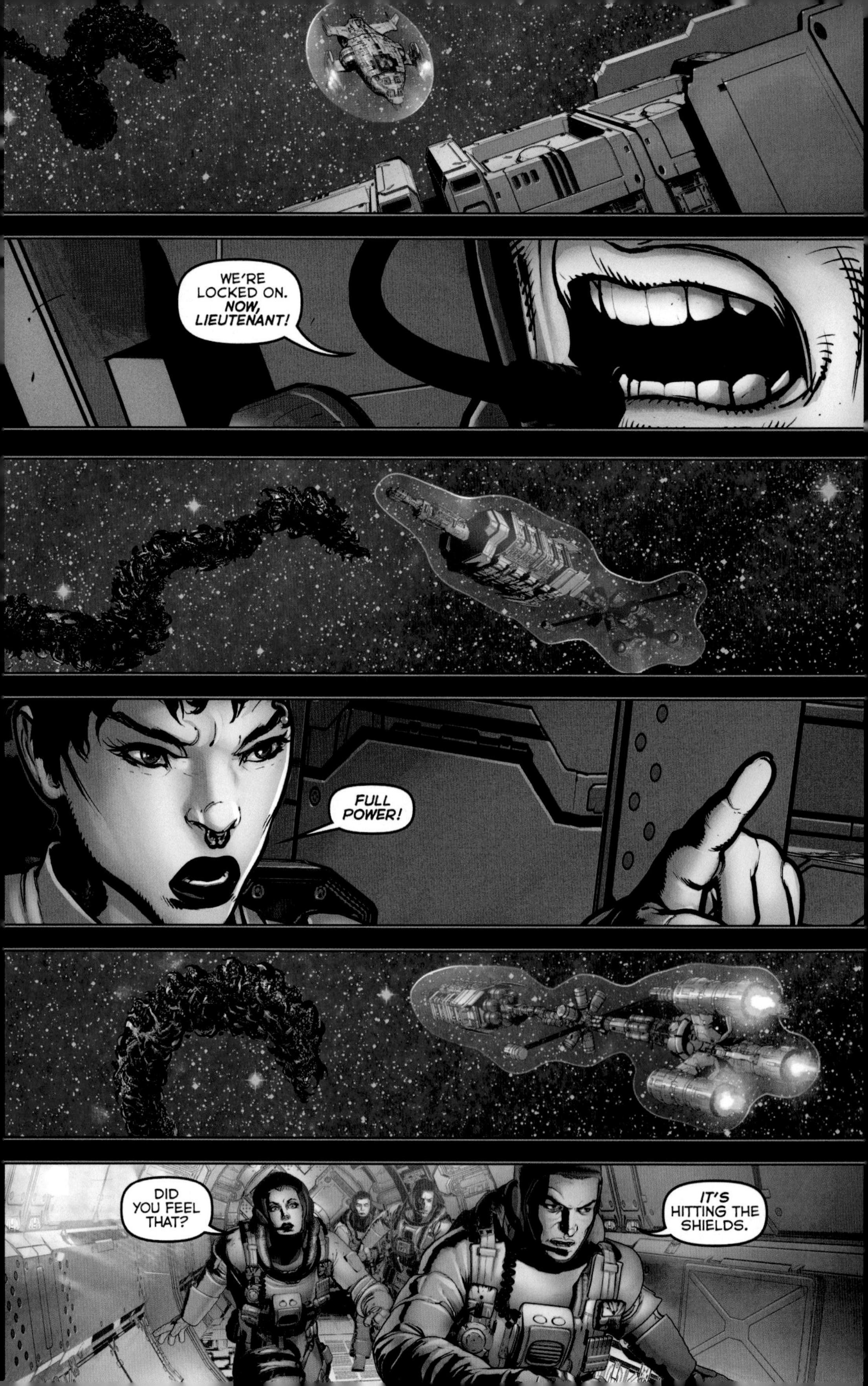
WE'RE LOCKED ON. *NOW, LIEUTENANT!*
FULL POWER!
DID YOU FEEL THAT?
IT'S HITTING THE SHIELDS.

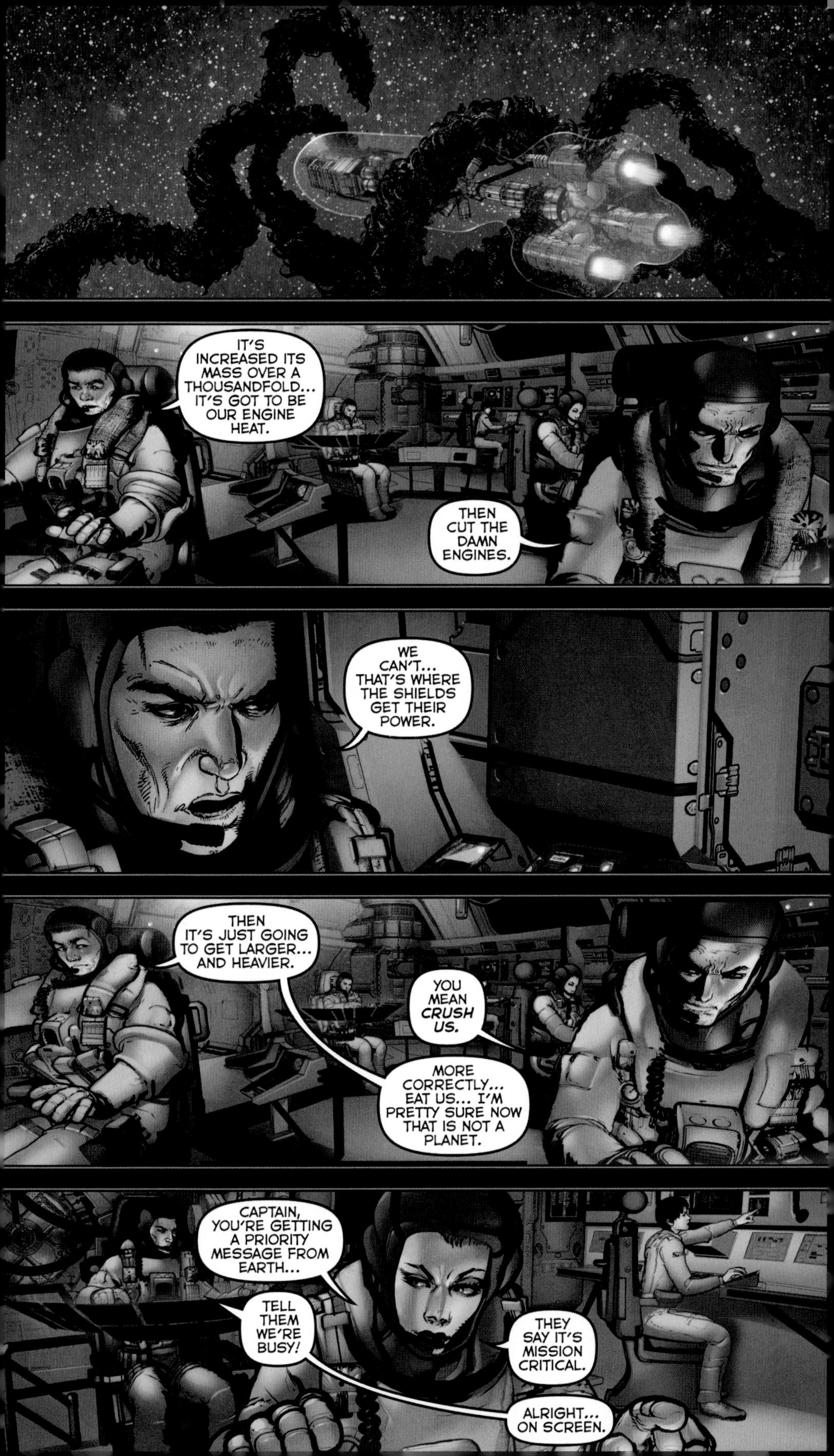
IT'S INCREASED ITS MASS OVER A THOUSANDFOLD... IT'S GOT TO BE OUR ENGINE HEAT.
THEN CUT THE DAMN ENGINES.
WE CAN'T... THAT'S WHERE THE SHIELDS GET THEIR POWER.
THEN IT'S JUST GOING TO GET LARGER... AND HEAVIER.
YOU MEAN *CRUSH* US.
MORE CORRECTLY... EAT US... I'M PRETTY SURE NOW THAT IS NOT A PLANET.
CAPTAIN, YOU'RE GETTING A PRIORITY MESSAGE FROM EARTH...
TELL THEM WE'RE BUSY!
THEY SAY IT'S MISSION CRITICAL.
ALRIGHT... ON SCREEN.

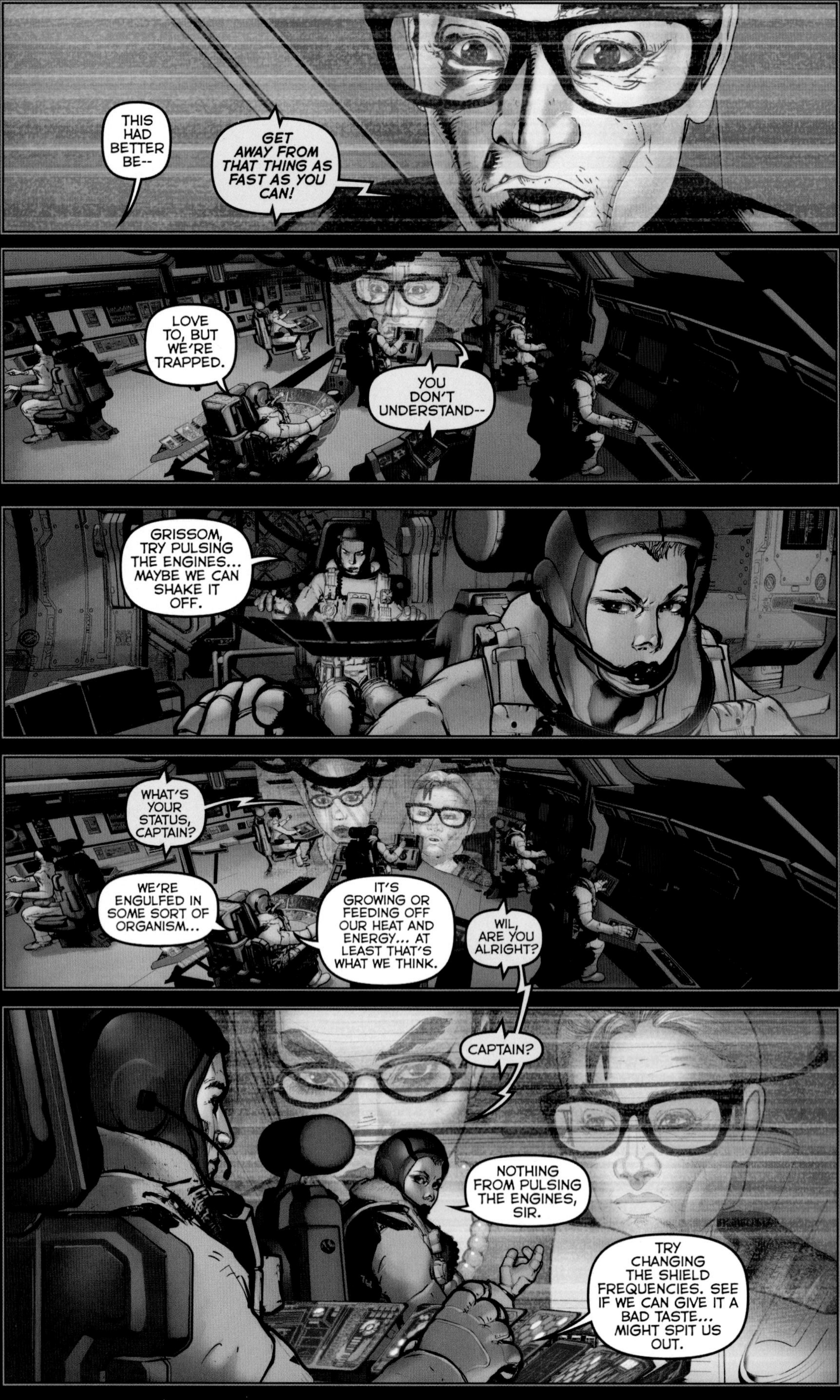
THIS HAD BETTER BE--
GET AWAY FROM THAT THING AS FAST AS YOU CAN!
LOVE TO, BUT WE'RE TRAPPED.
YOU DON'T UNDERSTAND--
GRISSOM, TRY PULSING THE ENGINES... MAYBE WE CAN SHAKE IT OFF.
WHAT'S YOUR STATUS, CAPTAIN?
WE'RE ENGULFED IN SOME SORT OF ORGANISM...
IT'S GROWING OR FEEDING OFF OUR HEAT AND ENERGY... AT LEAST THAT'S WHAT WE THINK.
WIL, ARE YOU ALRIGHT?
CAPTAIN?
NOTHING FROM PULSING THE ENGINES, SIR.
TRY CHANGING THE SHIELD FREQUENCIES. SEE IF WE CAN GIVE IT A BAD TASTE... MIGHT SPIT US OUT.

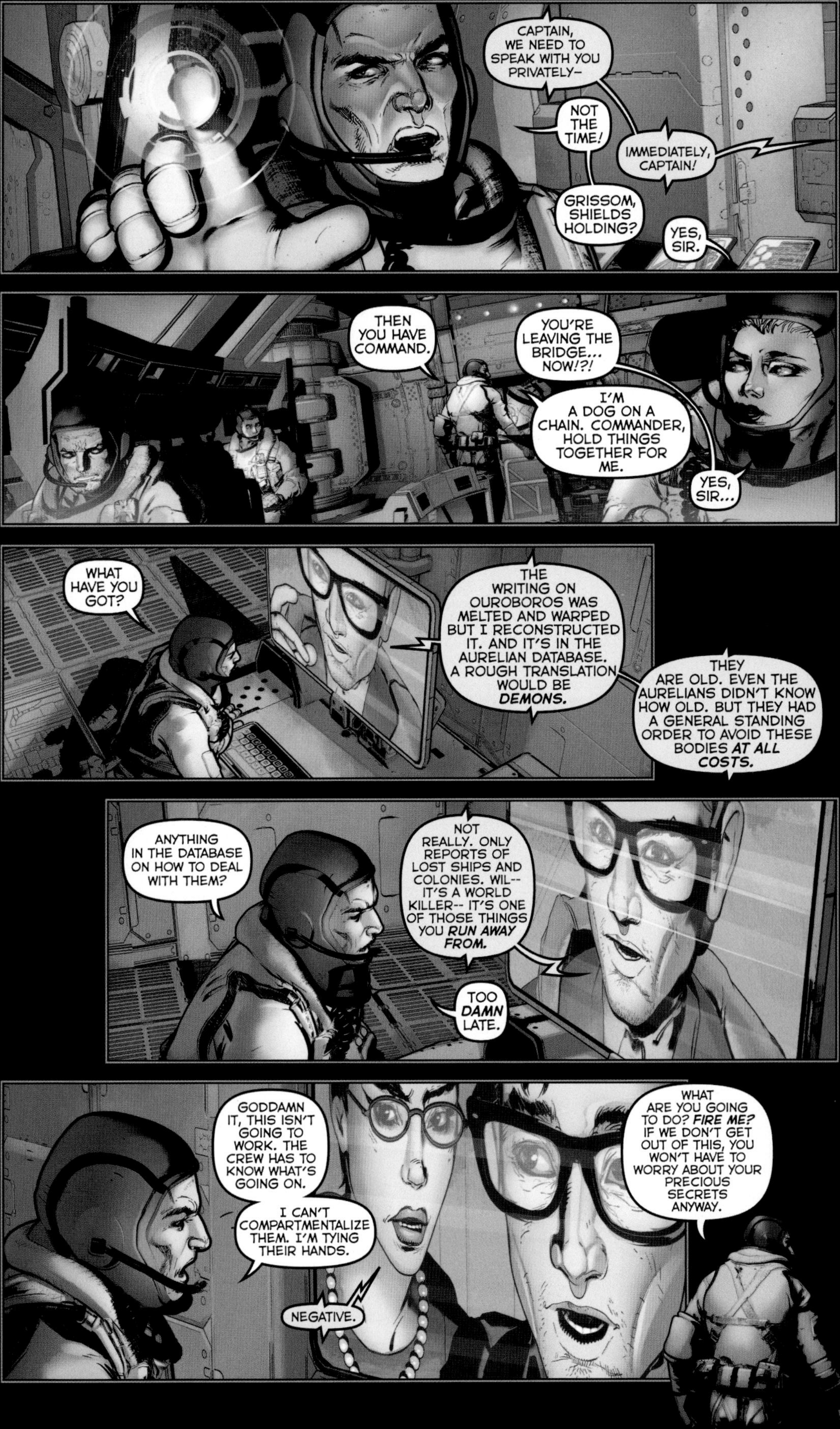
CAPTAIN, WE NEED TO SPEAK WITH YOU PRIVATELY–
NOT THE TIME!
IMMEDIATELY, CAPTAIN!
GRISSOM, SHIELDS HOLDING?
YES, SIR.
THEN YOU HAVE COMMAND.
YOU'RE LEAVING THE BRIDGE... NOW!?!
I'M A DOG ON A CHAIN. COMMANDER, HOLD THINGS TOGETHER FOR ME.
YES, SIR...
WHAT HAVE YOU GOT?
THE WRITING ON OUROBOROS WAS MELTED AND WARPED BUT I RECONSTRUCTED IT. AND IT'S IN THE AURELIAN DATABASE. A ROUGH TRANSLATION WOULD BE DEMONS.
THEY ARE OLD. EVEN THE AURELIANS DIDN'T KNOW HOW OLD. BUT THEY HAD A GENERAL STANDING ORDER TO AVOID THESE BODIES AT ALL COSTS.
ANYTHING IN THE DATABASE ON HOW TO DEAL WITH THEM?
NOT REALLY. ONLY REPORTS OF LOST SHIPS AND COLONIES. WIL-- IT'S A WORLD KILLER-- IT'S ONE OF THOSE THINGS YOU RUN AWAY FROM.
TOO DAMN LATE.
GODDAMN IT, THIS ISN'T GOING TO WORK. THE CREW HAS TO KNOW WHAT'S GOING ON.
I CAN'T COMPARTMENTALIZE THEM. I'M TYING THEIR HANDS.
NEGATIVE.
WHAT ARE YOU GOING TO DO? FIRE ME? IF WE DON'T GET OUT OF THIS, YOU WON'T HAVE TO WORRY ABOUT YOUR PRECIOUS SECRETS ANYWAY.

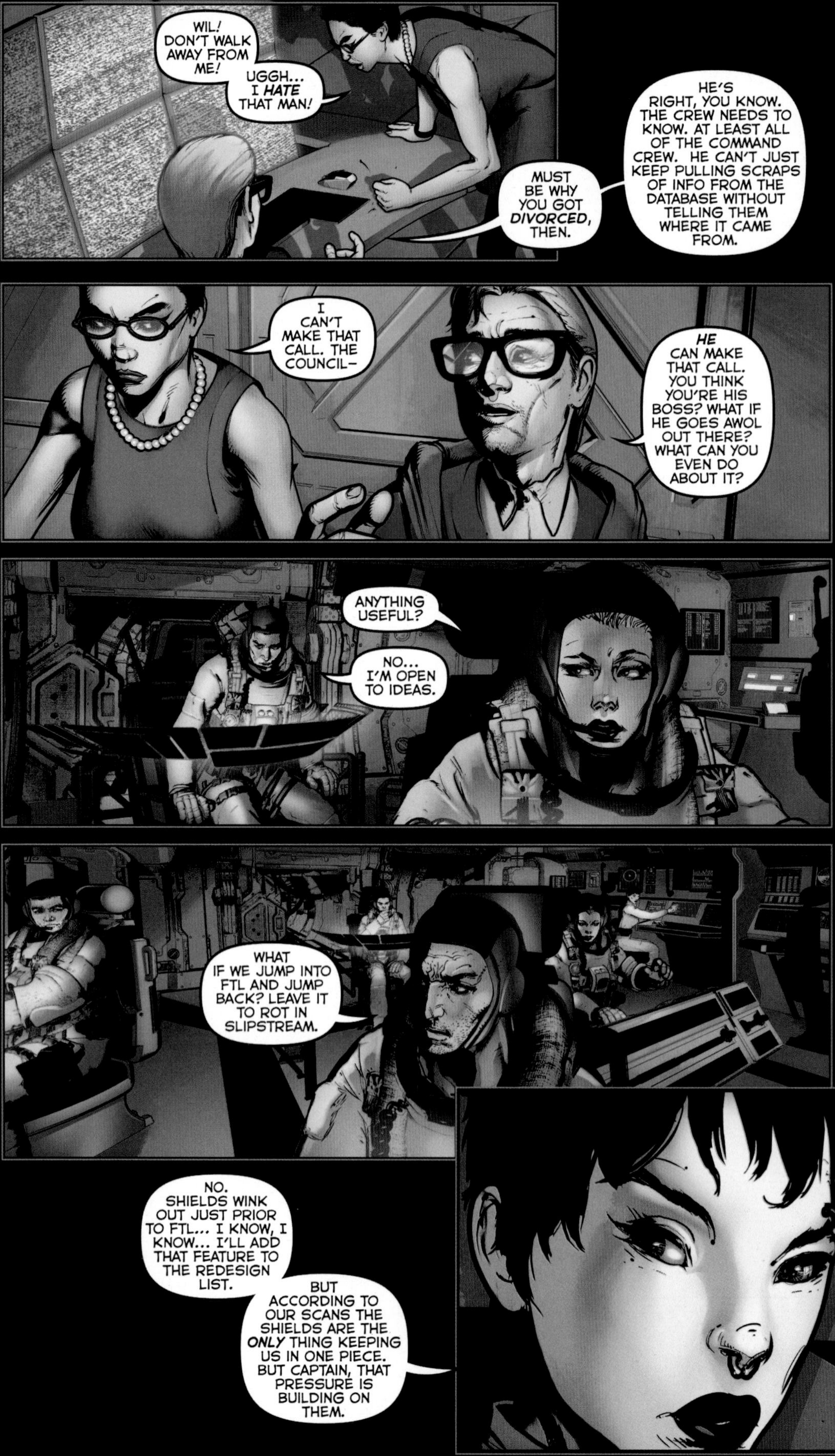
WIL! DON'T WALK AWAY FROM ME!
UGGH... I *HATE* THAT MAN!
MUST BE WHY YOU GOT *DIVORCED*, THEN.
HE'S RIGHT, YOU KNOW. THE CREW NEEDS TO KNOW. AT LEAST ALL OF THE COMMAND CREW. HE CAN'T JUST KEEP PULLING SCRAPS OF INFO FROM THE DATABASE WITHOUT TELLING THEM WHERE IT CAME FROM.
I CAN'T MAKE THAT CALL. THE COUNCIL–
HE CAN MAKE THAT CALL. YOU THINK YOU'RE HIS BOSS? WHAT IF HE GOES AWOL OUT THERE? WHAT CAN YOU EVEN DO ABOUT IT?
ANYTHING USEFUL?
NO... I'M OPEN TO IDEAS.
WHAT IF WE JUMP INTO FTL AND JUMP BACK? LEAVE IT TO ROT IN SLIPSTREAM.
NO. SHIELDS WINK OUT JUST PRIOR TO FTL... I KNOW, I KNOW... I'LL ADD THAT FEATURE TO THE REDESIGN LIST.
BUT ACCORDING TO OUR SCANS THE SHIELDS ARE THE *ONLY* THING KEEPING US IN ONE PIECE. BUT CAPTAIN, THAT PRESSURE IS BUILDING ON THEM.

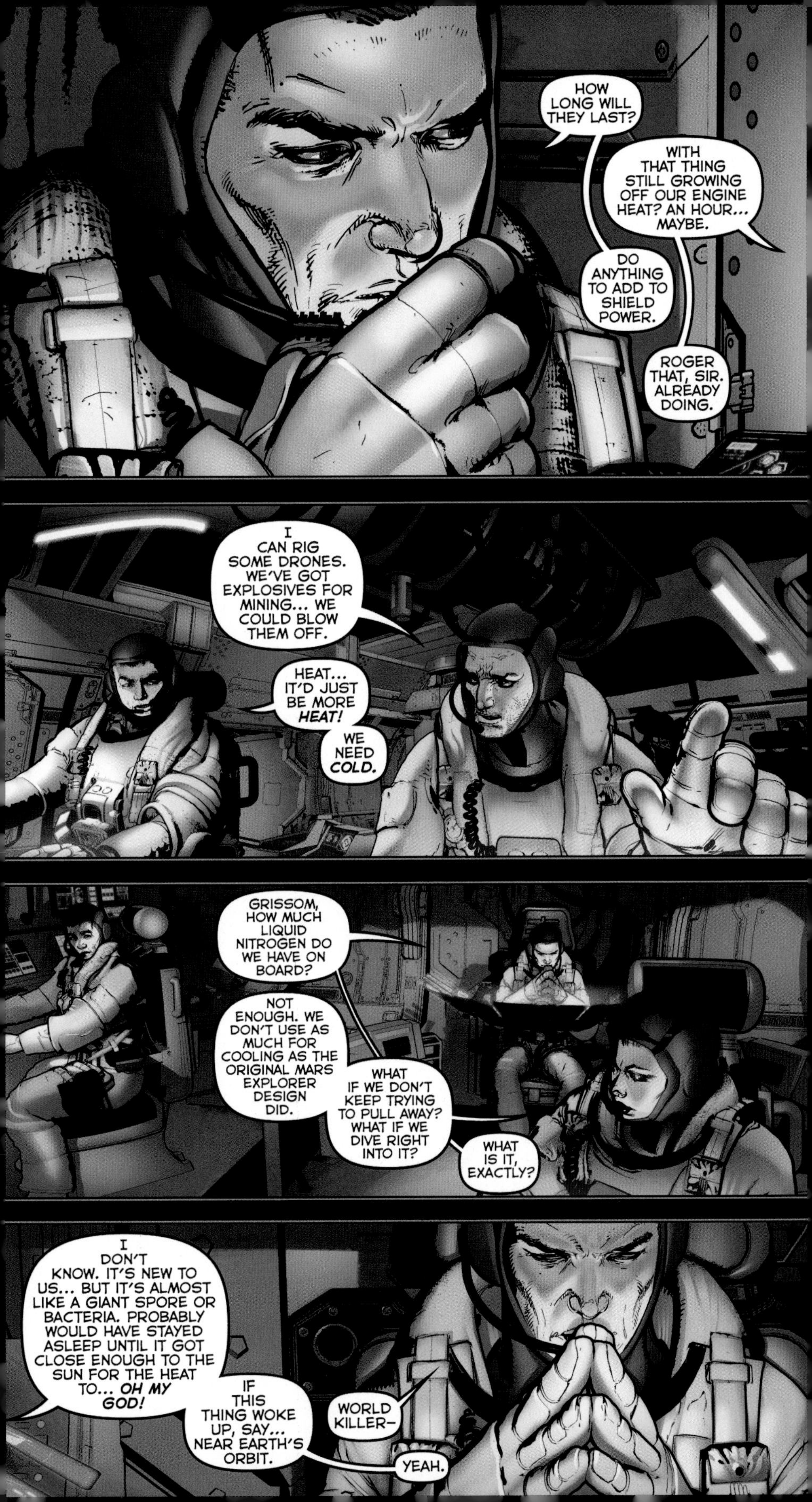
HOW LONG WILL THEY LAST?
WITH THAT THING STILL GROWING OFF OUR ENGINE HEAT? AN HOUR... MAYBE.
DO ANYTHING TO ADD TO SHIELD POWER.
ROGER THAT, SIR. ALREADY DOING.
I CAN RIG SOME DRONES. WE'VE GOT EXPLOSIVES FOR MINING... WE COULD BLOW THEM OFF.
HEAT... IT'D JUST BE MORE *HEAT!*
WE NEED *COLD.*
GRISSOM, HOW MUCH LIQUID NITROGEN DO WE HAVE ON BOARD?
NOT ENOUGH. WE DON'T USE AS MUCH FOR COOLING AS THE ORIGINAL MARS EXPLORER DESIGN DID.
WHAT IF WE DON'T KEEP TRYING TO PULL AWAY? WHAT IF WE DIVE RIGHT INTO IT?
WHAT IS IT, EXACTLY?
I DON'T KNOW. IT'S NEW TO US... BUT IT'S ALMOST LIKE A GIANT SPORE OR BACTERIA. PROBABLY WOULD HAVE STAYED ASLEEP UNTIL IT GOT CLOSE ENOUGH TO THE SUN FOR THE HEAT TO... *OH MY GOD!*
IF THIS THING WOKE UP, SAY... NEAR EARTH'S ORBIT.
WORLD KILLER–
YEAH.

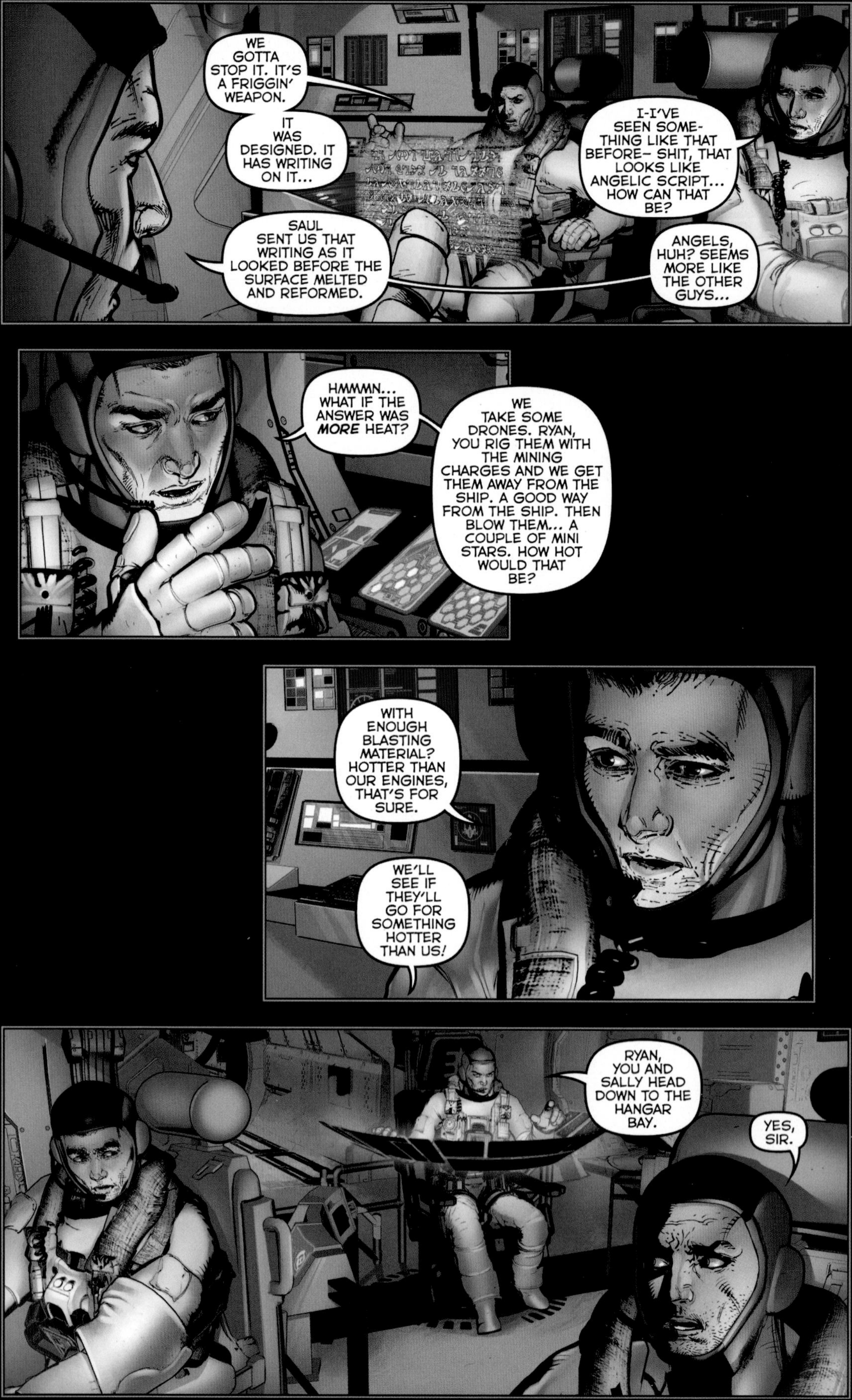
WE GOTTA STOP IT. IT'S A FRIGGIN' WEAPON.
IT WAS DESIGNED. IT HAS WRITING ON IT...
I-I'VE SEEN SOME-THING LIKE THAT BEFORE– SHIT, THAT LOOKS LIKE ANGELIC SCRIPT... HOW CAN THAT BE?
SAUL SENT US THAT WRITING AS IT LOOKED BEFORE THE SURFACE MELTED AND REFORMED.
ANGELS, HUH? SEEMS MORE LIKE THE OTHER GUYS...
HMMMN... WHAT IF THE ANSWER WAS *MORE* HEAT?
WE TAKE SOME DRONES. RYAN, YOU RIG THEM WITH THE MINING CHARGES AND WE GET THEM AWAY FROM THE SHIP. A GOOD WAY FROM THE SHIP. THEN BLOW THEM... A COUPLE OF MINI STARS. HOW HOT WOULD THAT BE?
WITH ENOUGH BLASTING MATERIAL? HOTTER THAN OUR ENGINES, THAT'S FOR SURE.
WE'LL SEE IF THEY'LL GO FOR SOMETHING HOTTER THAN US!
RYAN, YOU AND SALLY HEAD DOWN TO THE HANGAR BAY.
YES, SIR.

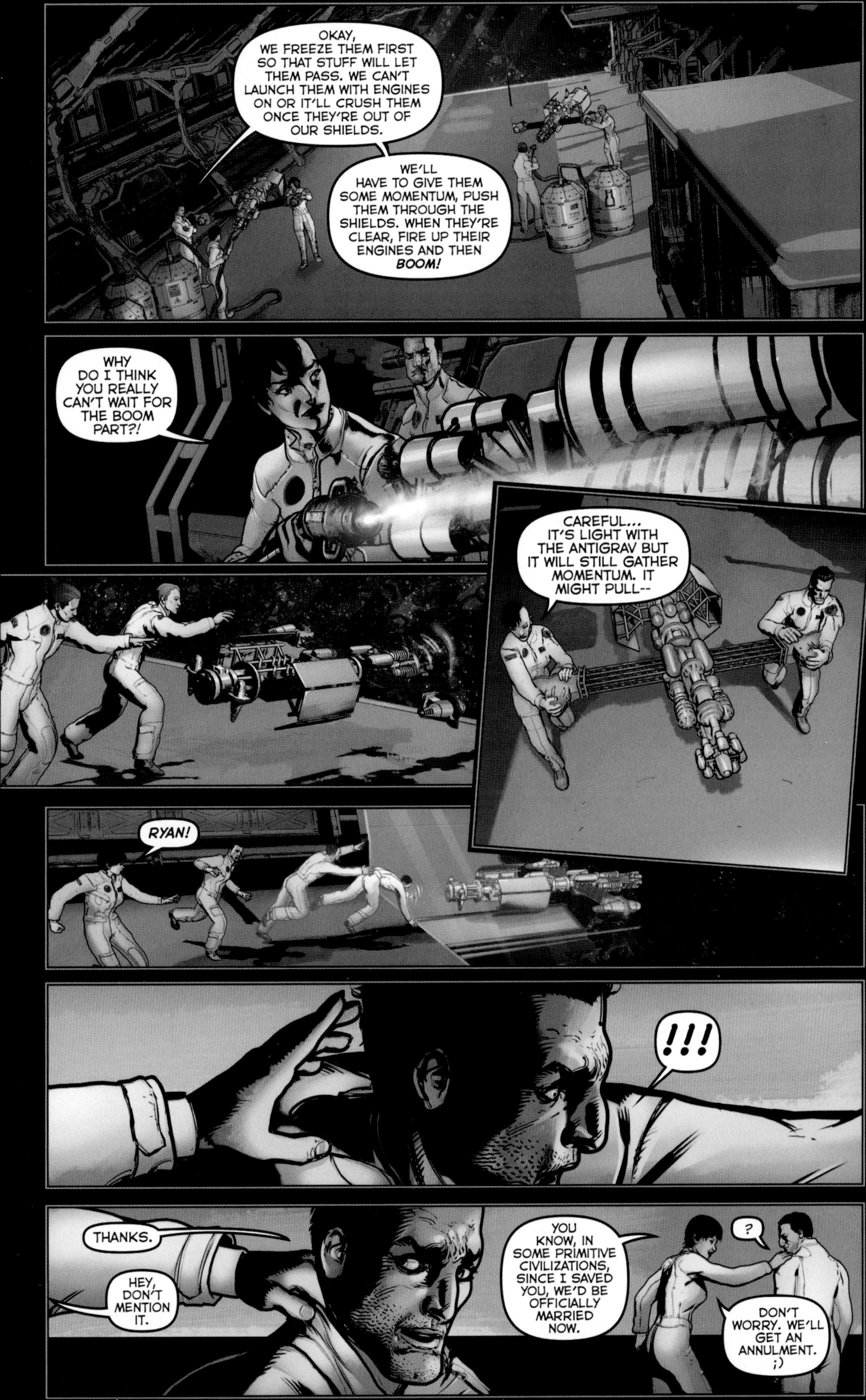
OKAY, WE FREEZE THEM FIRST SO THAT STUFF WILL LET THEM PASS. WE CAN'T LAUNCH THEM WITH ENGINES ON OR IT'LL CRUSH THEM ONCE THEY'RE OUT OF OUR SHIELDS.
WE'LL HAVE TO GIVE THEM SOME MOMENTUM, PUSH THEM THROUGH THE SHIELDS. WHEN THEY'RE CLEAR, FIRE UP THEIR ENGINES AND THEN *BOOM!*
WHY DO I THINK YOU REALLY CAN'T WAIT FOR THE BOOM PART?!
CAREFUL... IT'S LIGHT WITH THE ANTIGRAV BUT IT WILL STILL GATHER MOMENTUM. IT MIGHT PULL--
RYAN!
!!!
THANKS.
HEY, DON'T MENTION IT.
YOU KNOW, IN SOME PRIMITIVE CIVILIZATIONS, SINCE I SAVED YOU, WE'D BE OFFICIALLY MARRIED NOW.
?
DON'T WORRY. WE'LL GET AN ANNULMENT. ;)

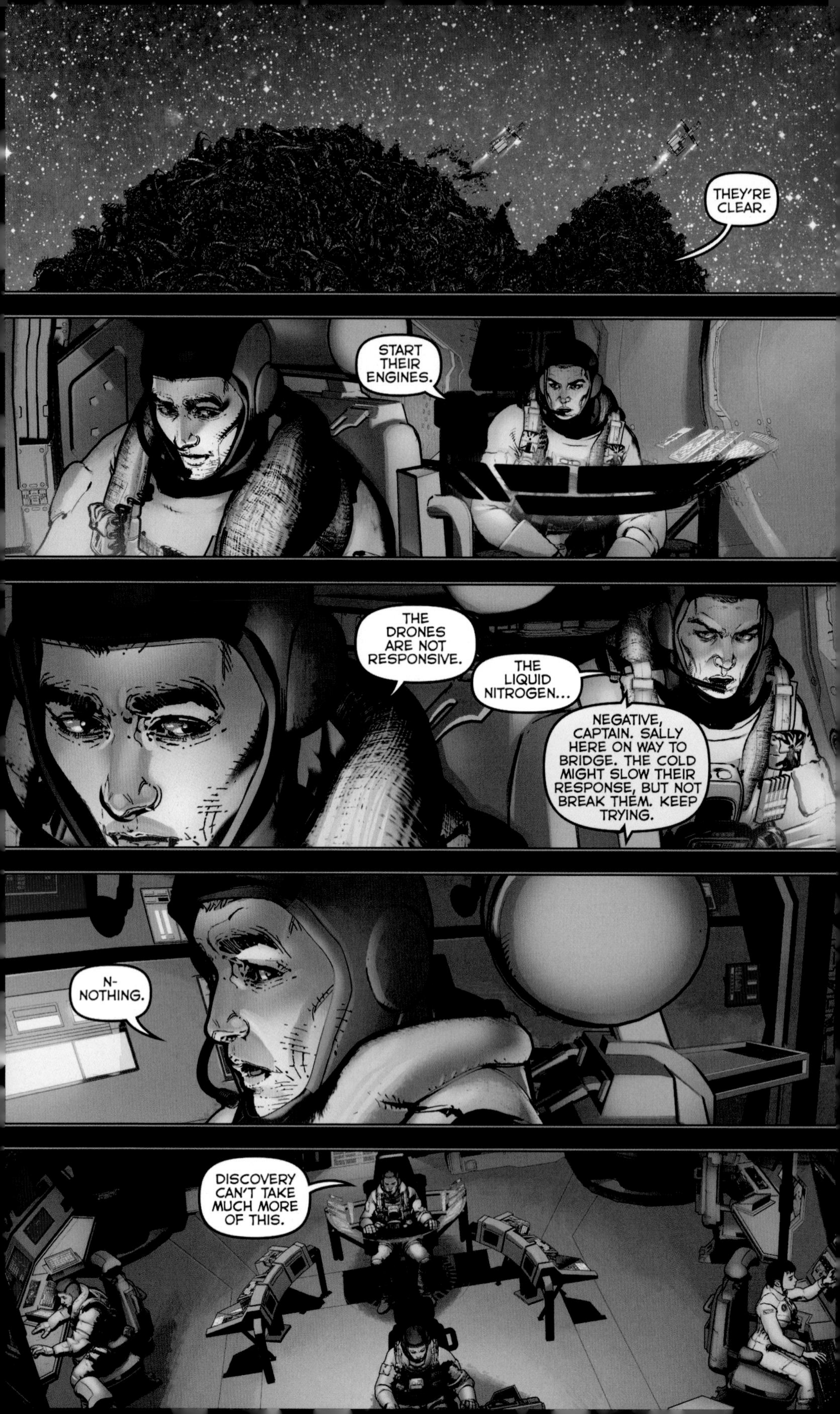
THEY'RE CLEAR.
START THEIR ENGINES.
THE DRONES ARE NOT RESPONSIVE.
THE LIQUID NITROGEN...
NEGATIVE, CAPTAIN. SALLY HERE ON WAY TO BRIDGE. THE COLD MIGHT SLOW THEIR RESPONSE, BUT NOT BREAK THEM. KEEP TRYING.
N- NOTHING.
DISCOVERY CAN'T TAKE MUCH MORE OF THIS.

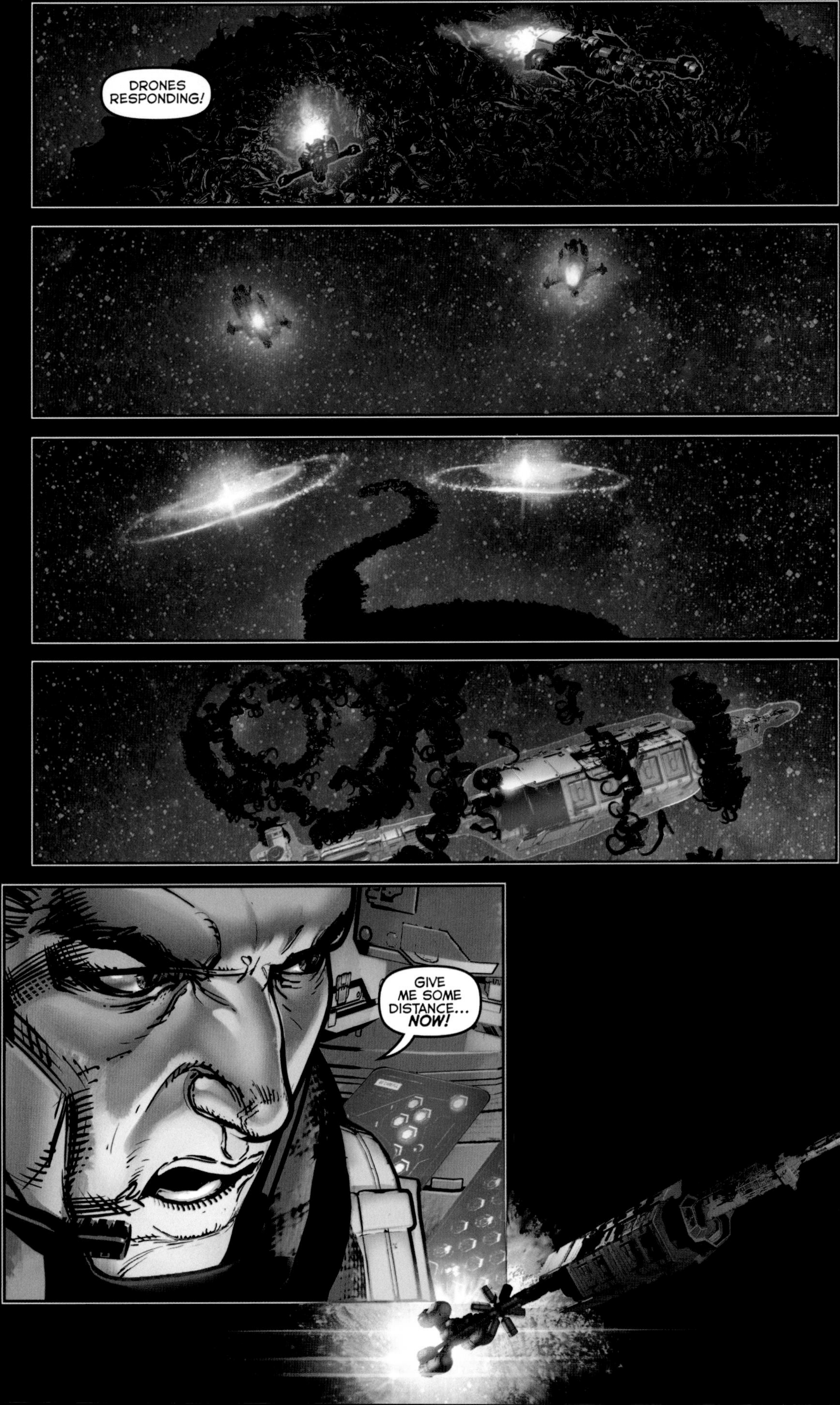
DRONES RESPONDING!
GIVE ME SOME DISTANCE... NOW!

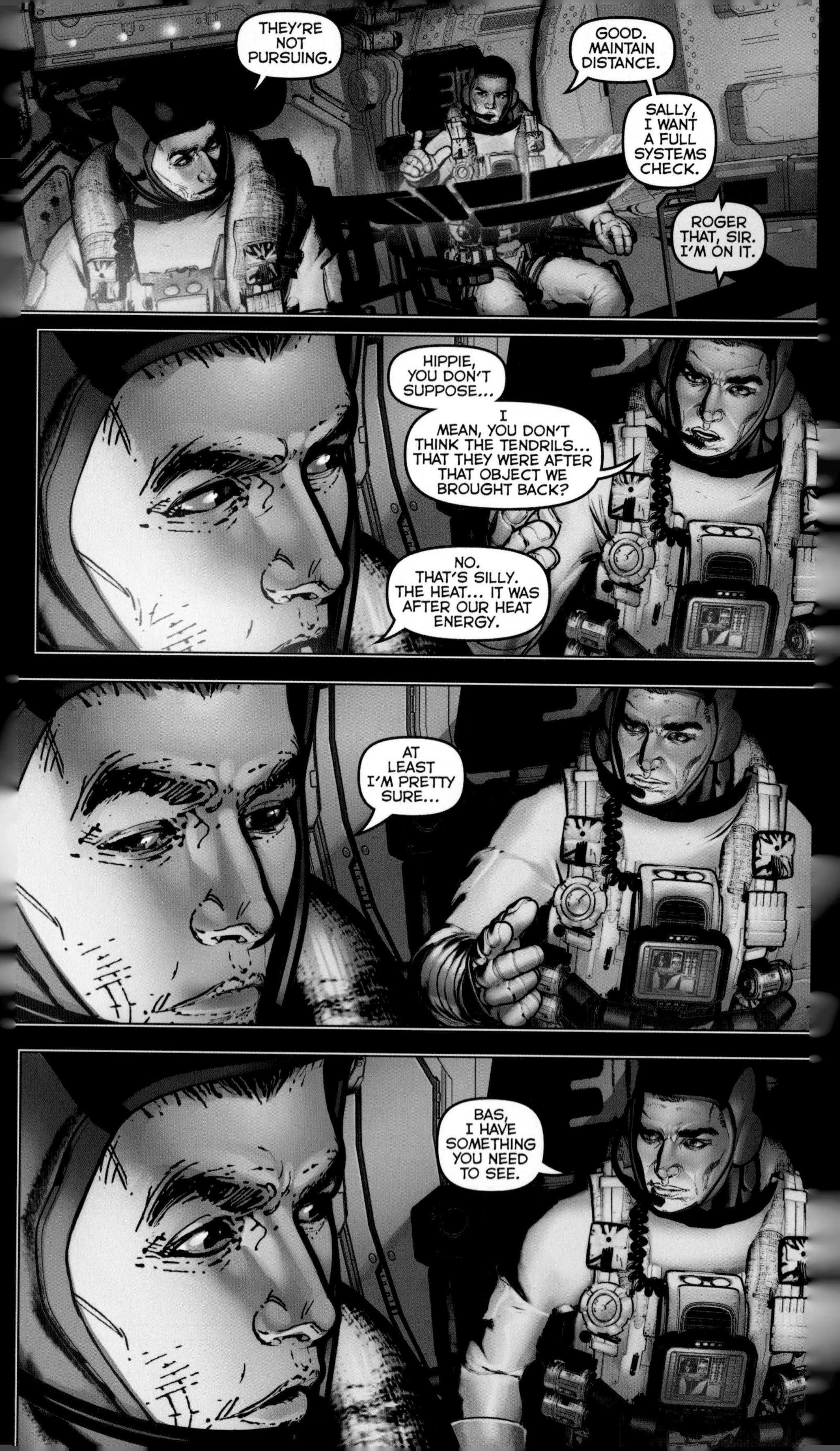
THEY'RE NOT PURSUING.
GOOD. MAINTAIN DISTANCE.
SALLY, I WANT A FULL SYSTEMS CHECK.
ROGER THAT, SIR. I'M ON IT.
HIPPIE, YOU DON'T SUPPOSE...
I MEAN, YOU DON'T THINK THE TENDRILS... THAT THEY WERE AFTER THAT OBJECT WE BROUGHT BACK?
NO. THAT'S SILLY. THE HEAT... IT WAS AFTER OUR HEAT ENERGY.
AT LEAST I'M PRETTY SURE...
BAS, I HAVE SOMETHING YOU NEED TO SEE.

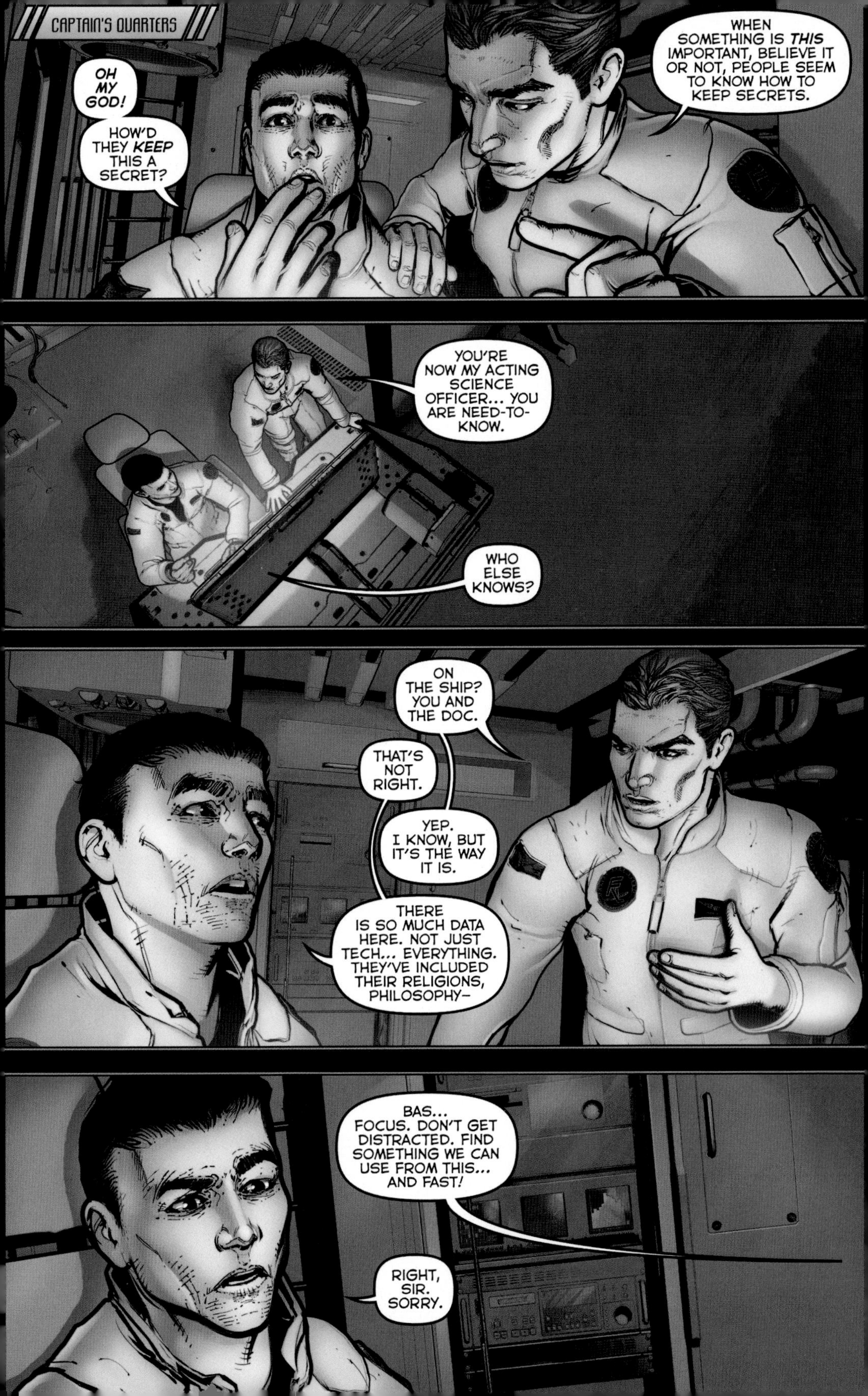
CAPTAIN'S QUARTERS
OH MY GOD!
HOW'D THEY KEEP THIS A SECRET?
WHEN SOMETHING IS THIS IMPORTANT, BELIEVE IT OR NOT, PEOPLE SEEM TO KNOW HOW TO KEEP SECRETS.
YOU'RE NOW MY ACTING SCIENCE OFFICER... YOU ARE NEED-TO-KNOW.
WHO ELSE KNOWS?
ON THE SHIP? YOU AND THE DOC.
THAT'S NOT RIGHT.
YEP. I KNOW, BUT IT'S THE WAY IT IS.
THERE IS SO MUCH DATA HERE. NOT JUST TECH... EVERYTHING. THEY'VE INCLUDED THEIR RELIGIONS, PHILOSOPHY–
BAS... FOCUS. DON'T GET DISTRACTED. FIND SOMETHING WE CAN USE FROM THIS... AND FAST!
RIGHT, SIR. SORRY.

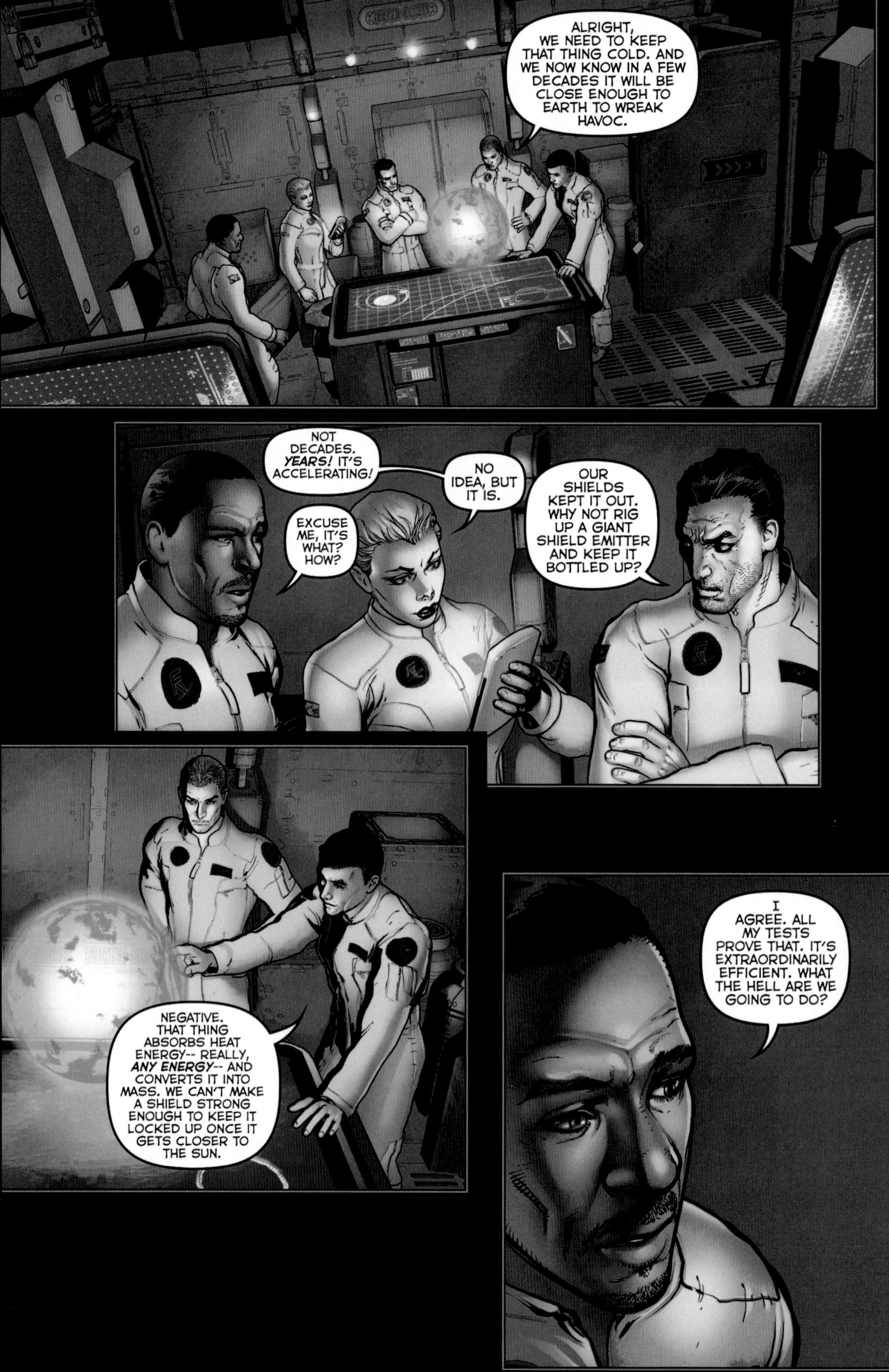
ALRIGHT, WE NEED TO KEEP THAT THING COLD. AND WE NOW KNOW IN A FEW DECADES IT WILL BE CLOSE ENOUGH TO EARTH TO WREAK HAVOC.
NOT DECADES. *YEARS!* IT'S ACCELERATING!
EXCUSE ME, IT'S WHAT? HOW?
NO IDEA, BUT IT IS.
OUR SHIELDS KEPT IT OUT. WHY NOT RIG UP A GIANT SHIELD EMITTER AND KEEP IT BOTTLED UP?
NEGATIVE. THAT THING ABSORBS HEAT ENERGY-- REALLY, *ANY ENERGY*-- AND CONVERTS IT INTO MASS. WE CAN'T MAKE A SHIELD STRONG ENOUGH TO KEEP IT LOCKED UP ONCE IT GETS CLOSER TO THE SUN.
I AGREE. ALL MY TESTS PROVE THAT. IT'S EXTRAORDINARILY EFFICIENT. WHAT THE HELL ARE WE GOING TO DO?

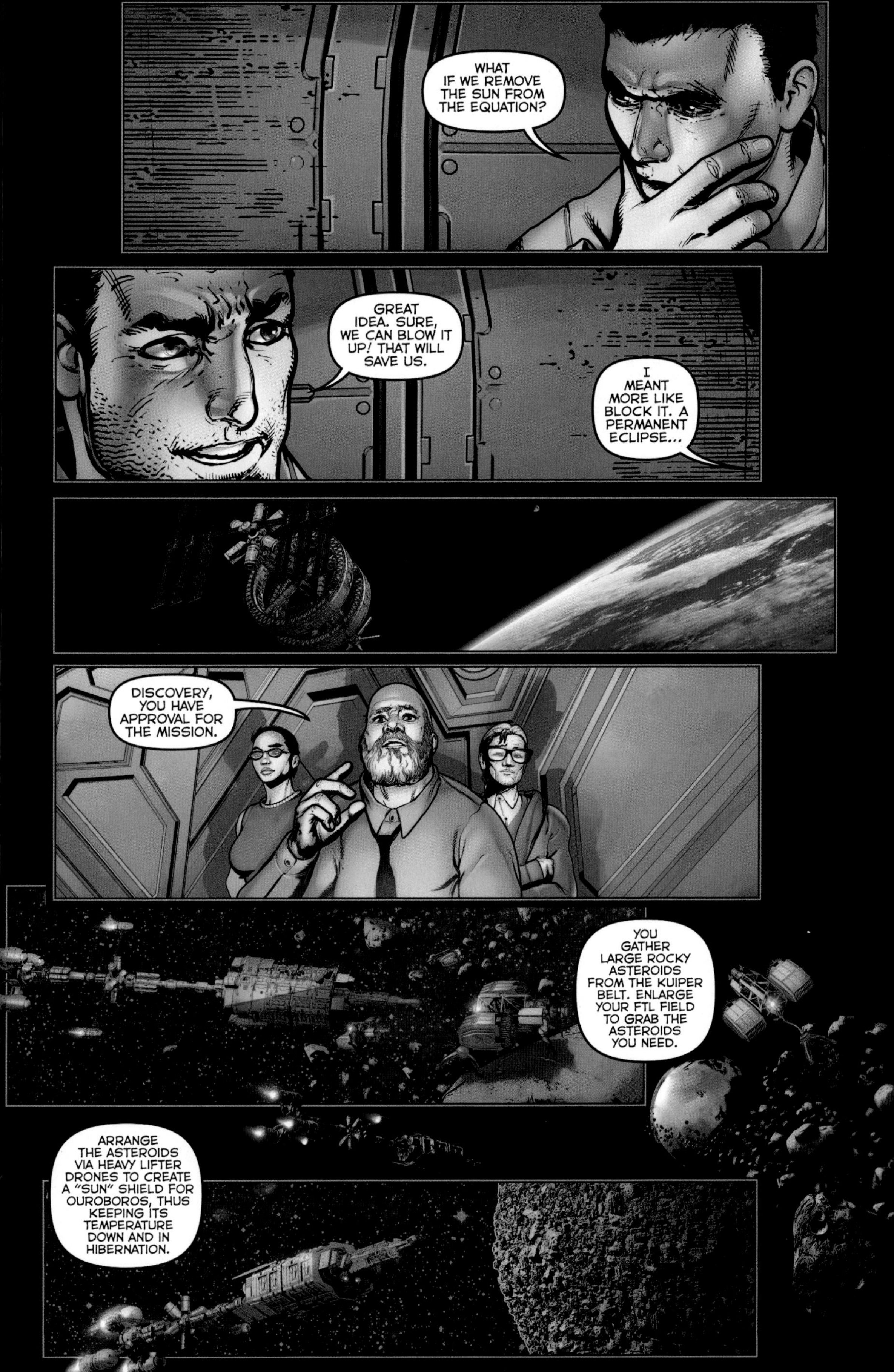
WHAT IF WE REMOVE THE SUN FROM THE EQUATION?
GREAT IDEA. SURE, WE CAN BLOW IT UP! THAT WILL SAVE US.
I MEANT MORE LIKE BLOCK IT. A PERMANENT ECLIPSE...
DISCOVERY, YOU HAVE APPROVAL FOR THE MISSION.
YOU GATHER LARGE ROCKY ASTEROIDS FROM THE KUIPER BELT. ENLARGE YOUR FTL FIELD TO GRAB THE ASTEROIDS YOU NEED.
ARRANGE THE ASTEROIDS VIA HEAVY LIFTER DRONES TO CREATE A "SUN" SHIELD FOR OUROBOROS, THUS KEEPING ITS TEMPERATURE DOWN AND IN HIBERNATION.

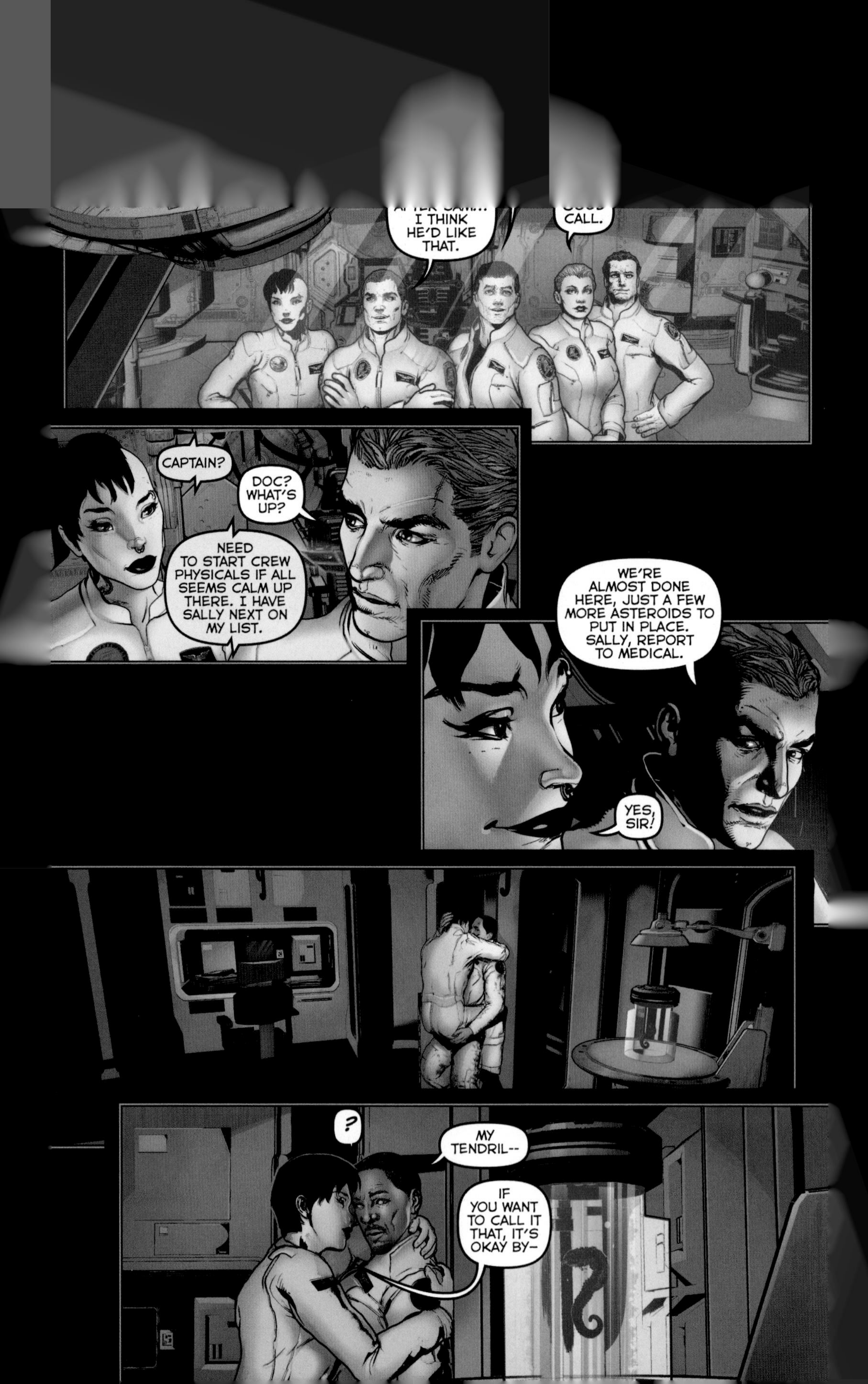
I THINK HE'D LIKE THAT.
CALL.
CAPTAIN?
DOC? WHAT'S UP?
NEED TO START CREW PHYSICALS IF ALL SEEMS CALM UP THERE. I HAVE SALLY NEXT ON MY LIST.
WE'RE ALMOST DONE HERE, JUST A FEW MORE ASTEROIDS TO PUT IN PLACE. SALLY, REPORT TO MEDICAL.
YES, SIR!
?
MY TENDRIL--
IF YOU WANT TO CALL IT THAT, IT'S OKAY BY–

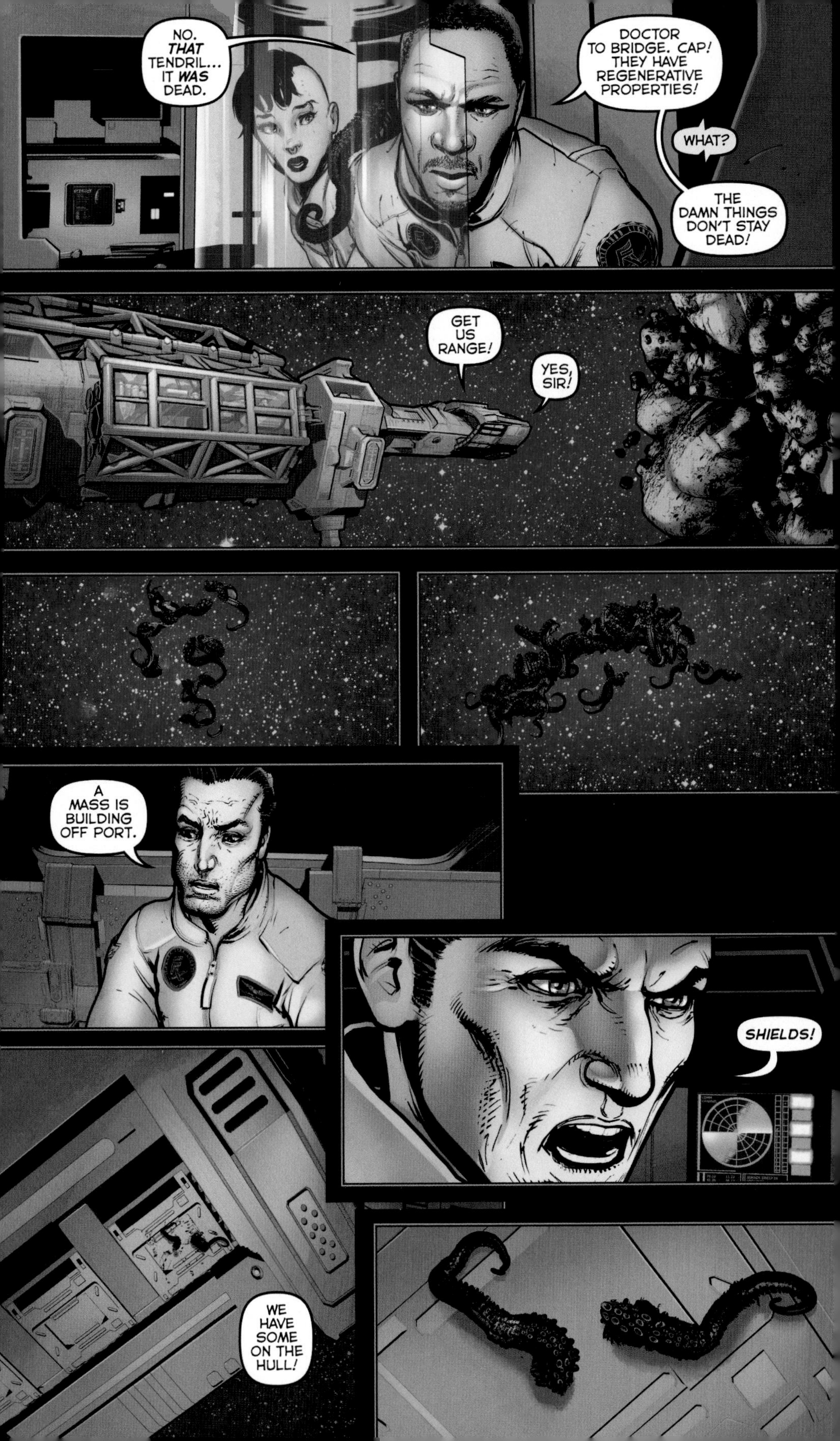
NO. *THAT* TENDRIL... IT *WAS* DEAD.
DOCTOR TO BRIDGE. CAP! THEY HAVE REGENERATIVE PROPERTIES!
WHAT?
THE DAMN THINGS DON'T STAY DEAD!
GET US RANGE!
YES, SIR!
A MASS IS BUILDING OFF PORT.
SHIELDS!
WE HAVE SOME ON THE HULL!

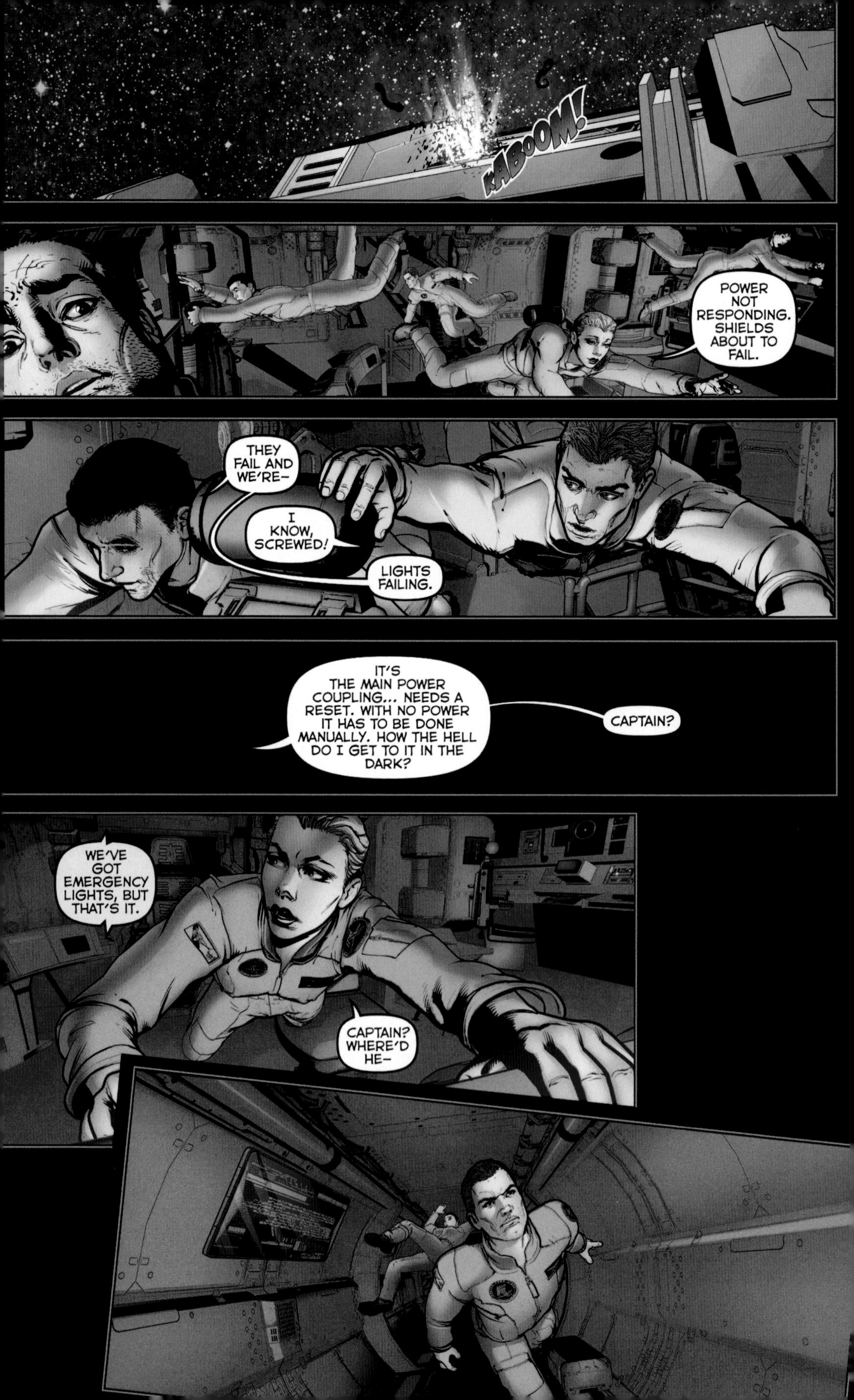
KABOOM!
POWER NOT RESPONDING. SHIELDS ABOUT TO FAIL.
THEY FAIL AND WE'RE–
I KNOW, SCREWED!
LIGHTS FAILING.
IT'S THE MAIN POWER COUPLING... NEEDS A RESET. WITH NO POWER IT HAS TO BE DONE MANUALLY. HOW THE HELL DO I GET TO IT IN THE DARK?
CAPTAIN?
WE'VE GOT EMERGENCY LIGHTS, BUT THAT'S IT.
CAPTAIN? WHERE'D HE–

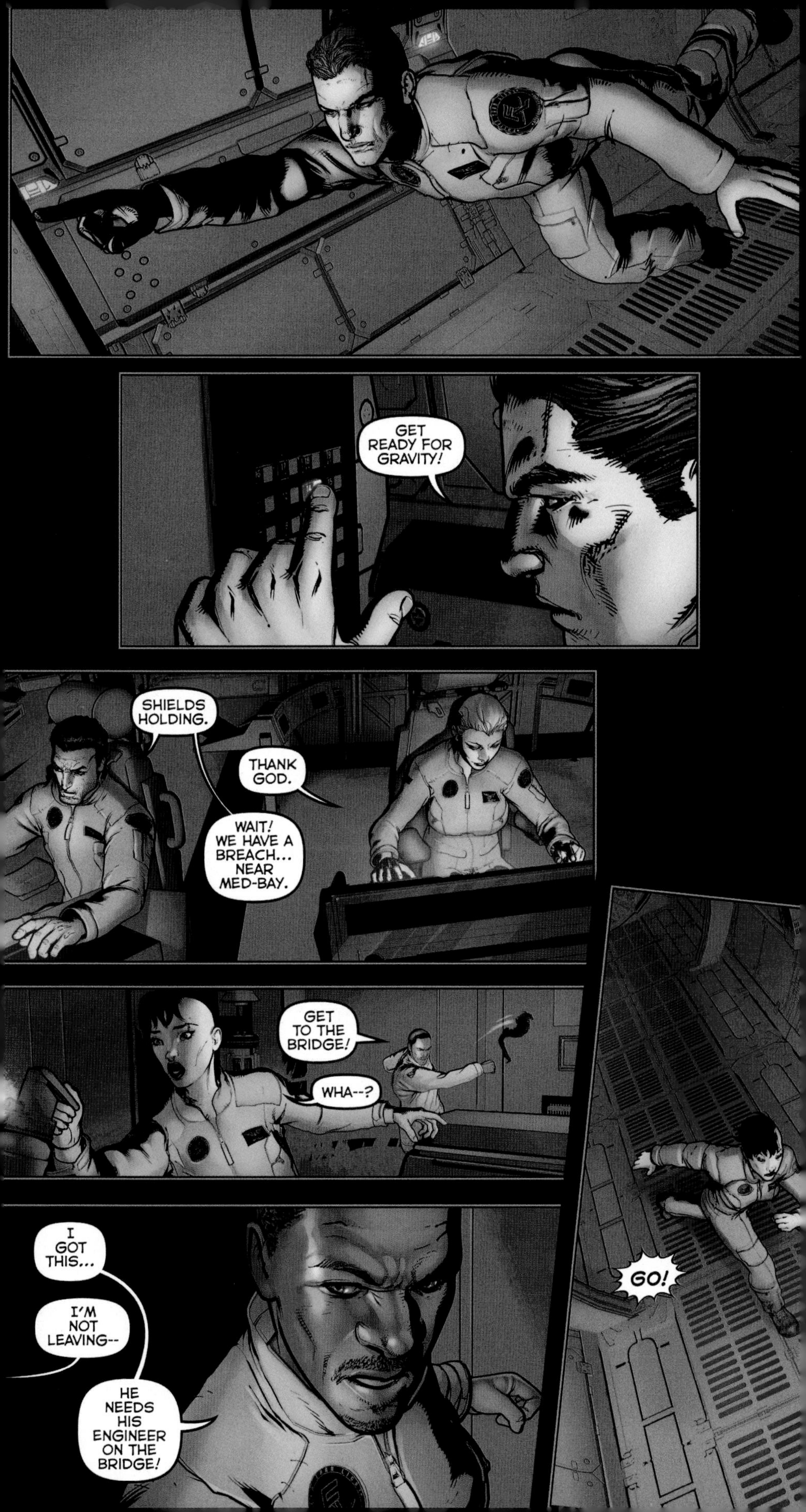
GET READY FOR GRAVITY!
SHIELDS HOLDING.
THANK GOD.
WAIT! WE HAVE A BREACH... NEAR MED-BAY.
GET TO THE BRIDGE!
WHA--?
I GOT THIS...
I'M NOT LEAVING--
HE NEEDS HIS ENGINEER ON THE BRIDGE!
GO!

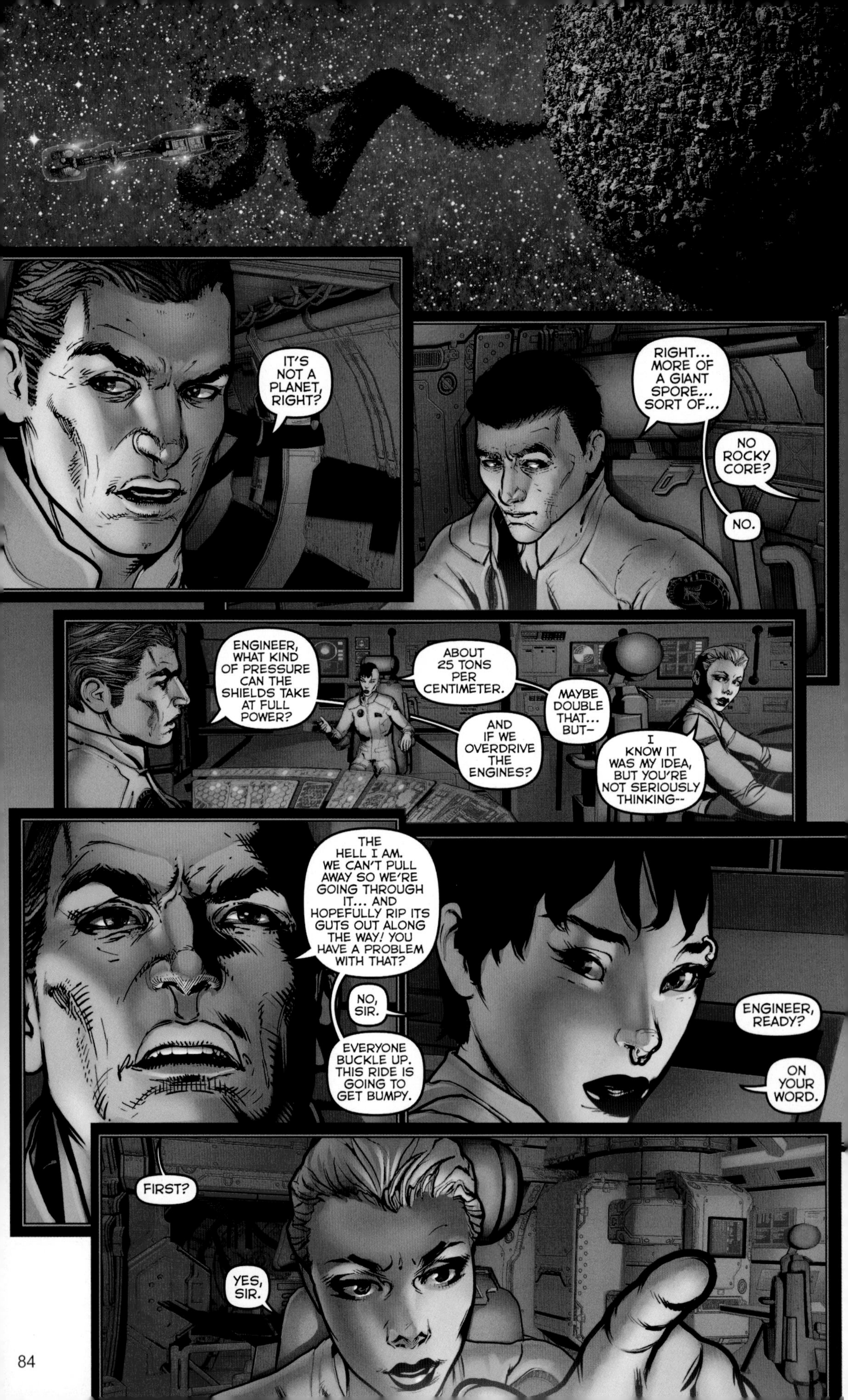

IT'S NOT A PLANET, RIGHT?
RIGHT... MORE OF A GIANT SPORE... SORT OF...
NO ROCKY CORE?
NO.
ENGINEER, WHAT KIND OF PRESSURE CAN THE SHIELDS TAKE AT FULL POWER?
ABOUT 25 TONS PER CENTIMETER.
AND IF WE OVERDRIVE THE ENGINES?
MAYBE DOUBLE THAT... BUT–
I KNOW IT WAS MY IDEA, BUT YOU'RE NOT SERIOUSLY THINKING--
THE HELL I AM. WE CAN'T PULL AWAY SO WE'RE GOING THROUGH IT... AND HOPEFULLY RIP ITS GUTS OUT ALONG THE WAY! YOU HAVE A PROBLEM WITH THAT?
NO, SIR.
EVERYONE BUCKLE UP. THIS RIDE IS GOING TO GET BUMPY.
ENGINEER, READY?
ON YOUR WORD.
FIRST?
YES, SIR.

ENGINES TO FULL.

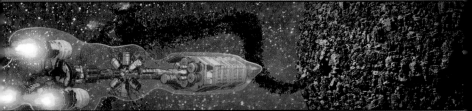

THEY'RE SOLIDIFYING ON THE SURFACE... IT'S REACTING!

MORE SPEED...

MORE SPEED!

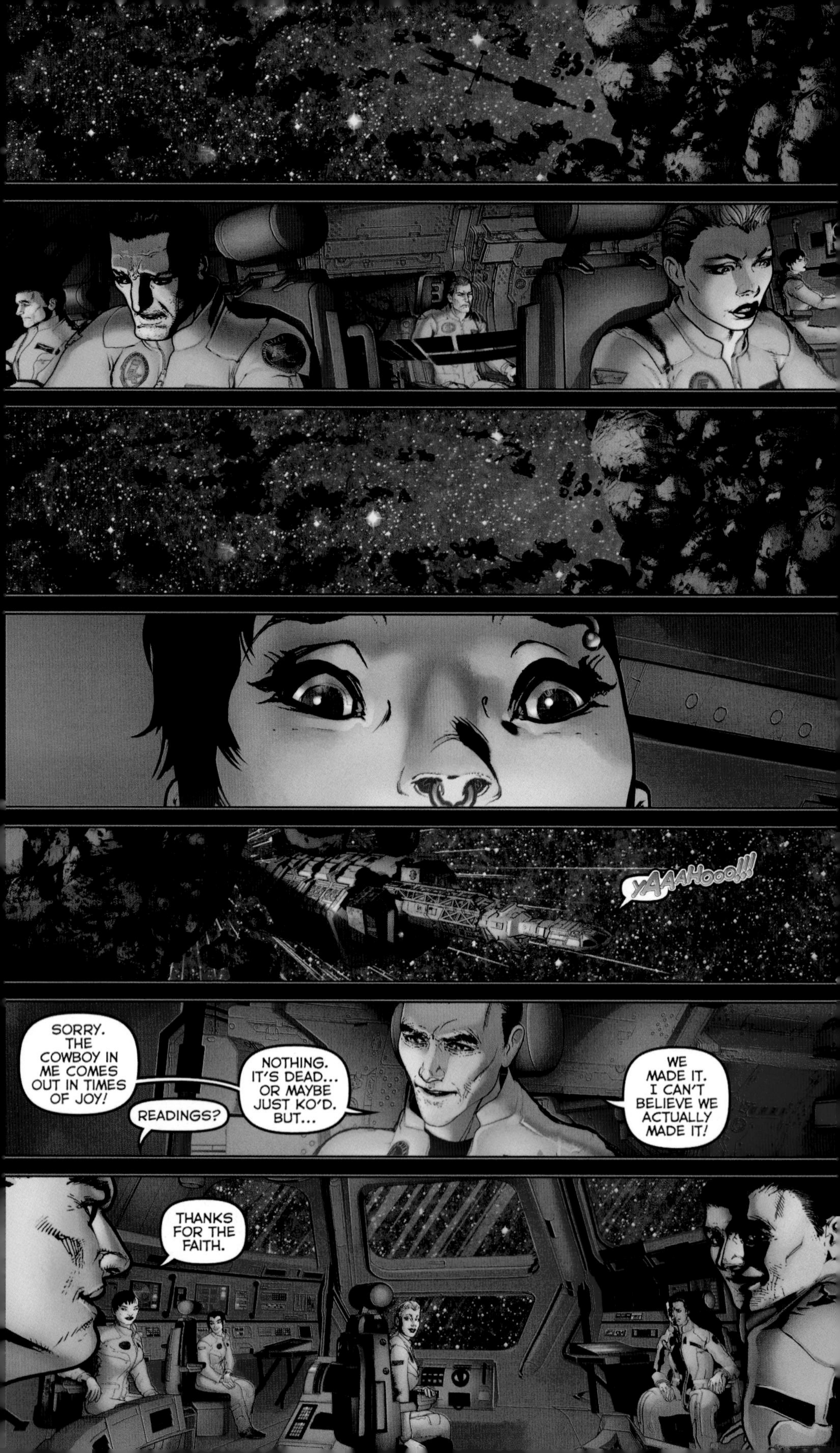
YAAAHOOO!!!
SORRY. THE COWBOY IN ME COMES OUT IN TIMES OF JOY!
READINGS?
NOTHING. IT'S DEAD... OR MAYBE JUST KO'D. BUT...
WE MADE IT. I CAN'T BELIEVE WE ACTUALLY MADE IT!
THANKS FOR THE FAITH.

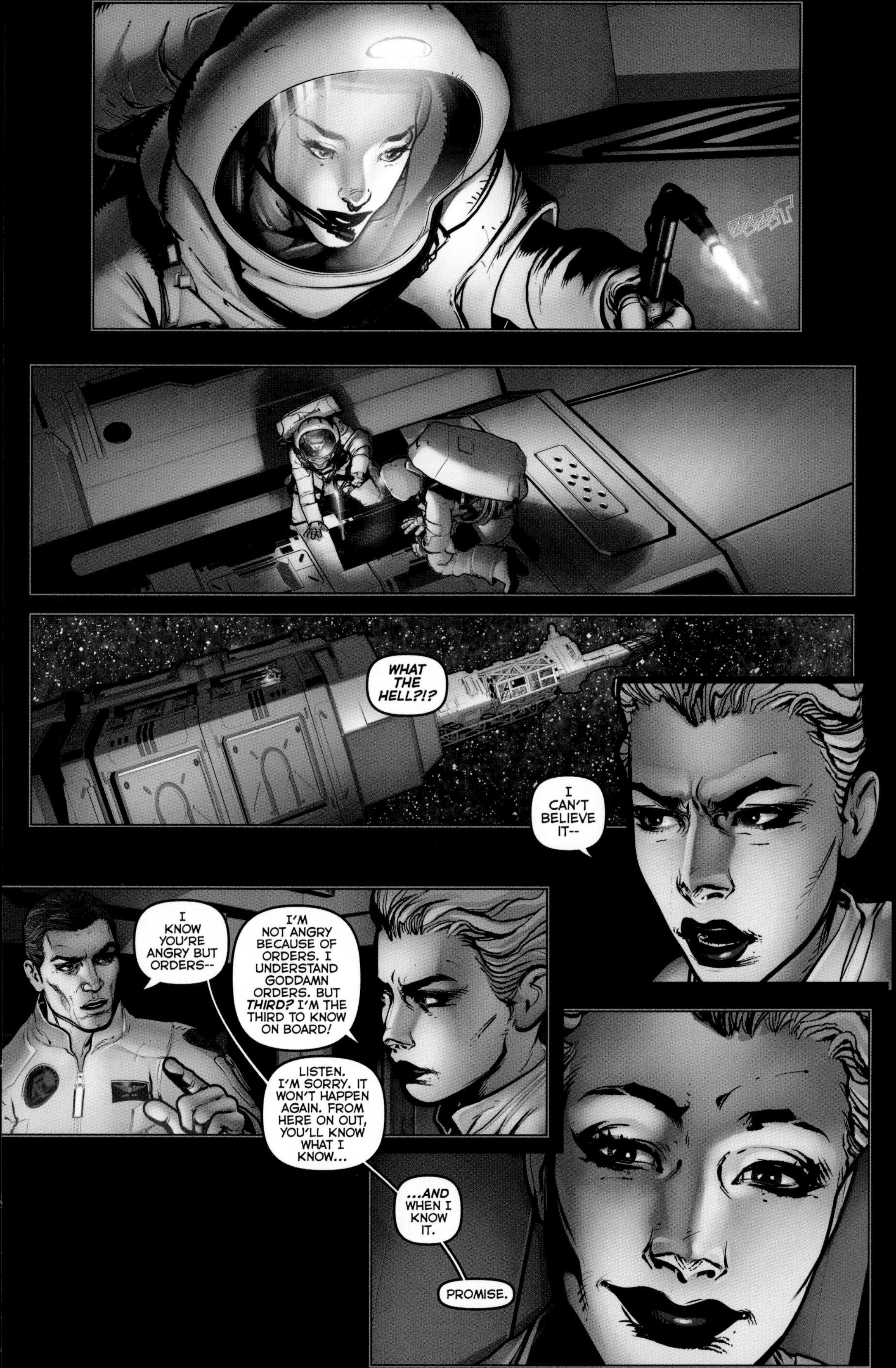
ZZZZT
WHAT THE HELL?!?
I CAN'T BELIEVE IT--
I KNOW YOU'RE ANGRY BUT ORDERS--
I'M NOT ANGRY BECAUSE OF ORDERS. I UNDERSTAND GODDAMN ORDERS. BUT *THIRD?* I'M THE THIRD TO KNOW ON BOARD!
LISTEN. I'M SORRY. IT WON'T HAPPEN AGAIN. FROM HERE ON OUT, YOU'LL KNOW WHAT I KNOW...
...*AND* WHEN I KNOW IT.
PROMISE.

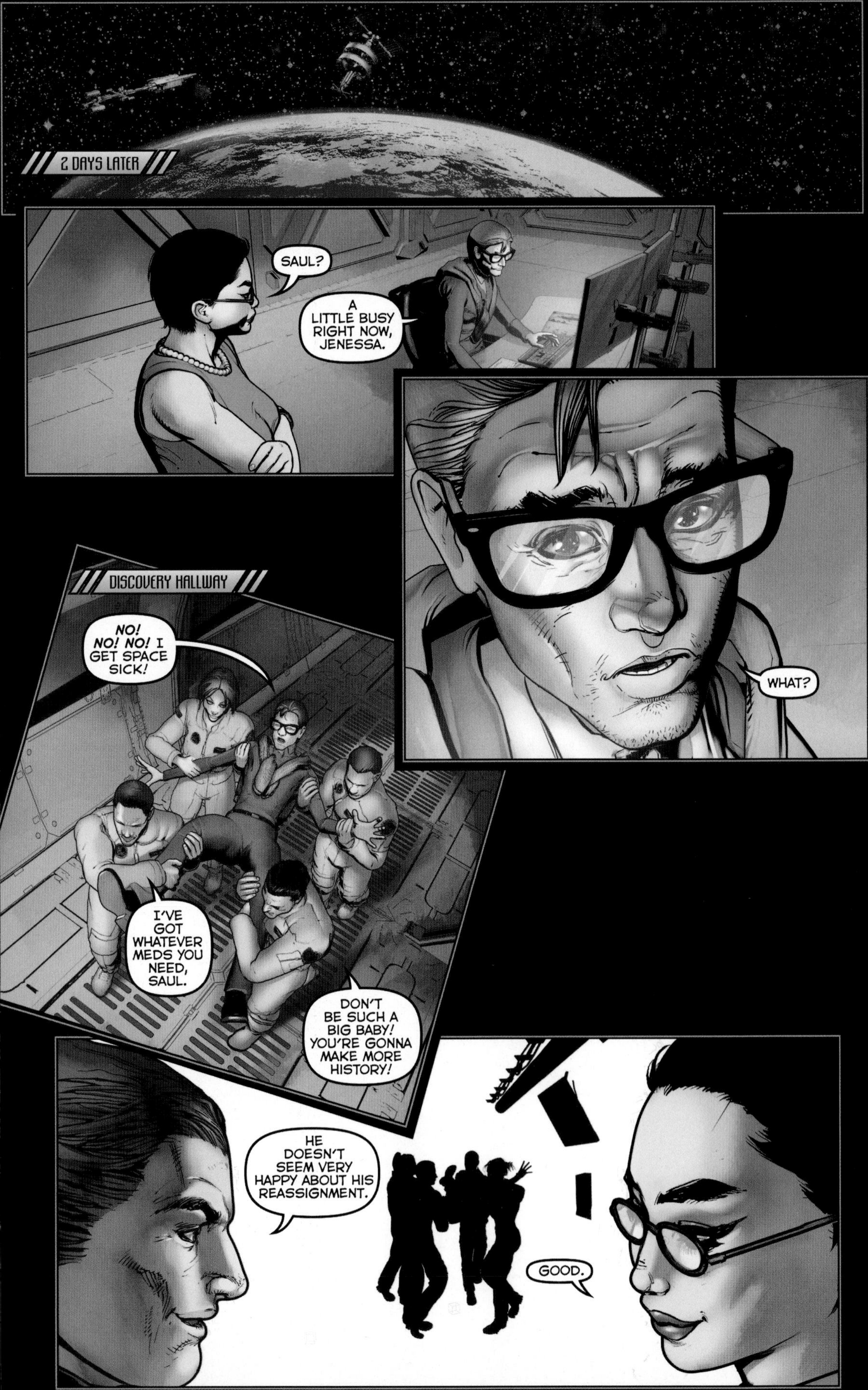
2 DAYS LATER
SAUL?
A LITTLE BUSY RIGHT NOW, JENESSA.
WHAT?
DISCOVERY HALLWAY
NO! NO! NO! I GET SPACE SICK!
I'VE GOT WHATEVER MEDS YOU NEED, SAUL.
DON'T BE SUCH A BIG BABY! YOU'RE GONNA MAKE MORE HISTORY!
HE DOESN'T SEEM VERY HAPPY ABOUT HIS REASSIGNMENT.
GOOD.

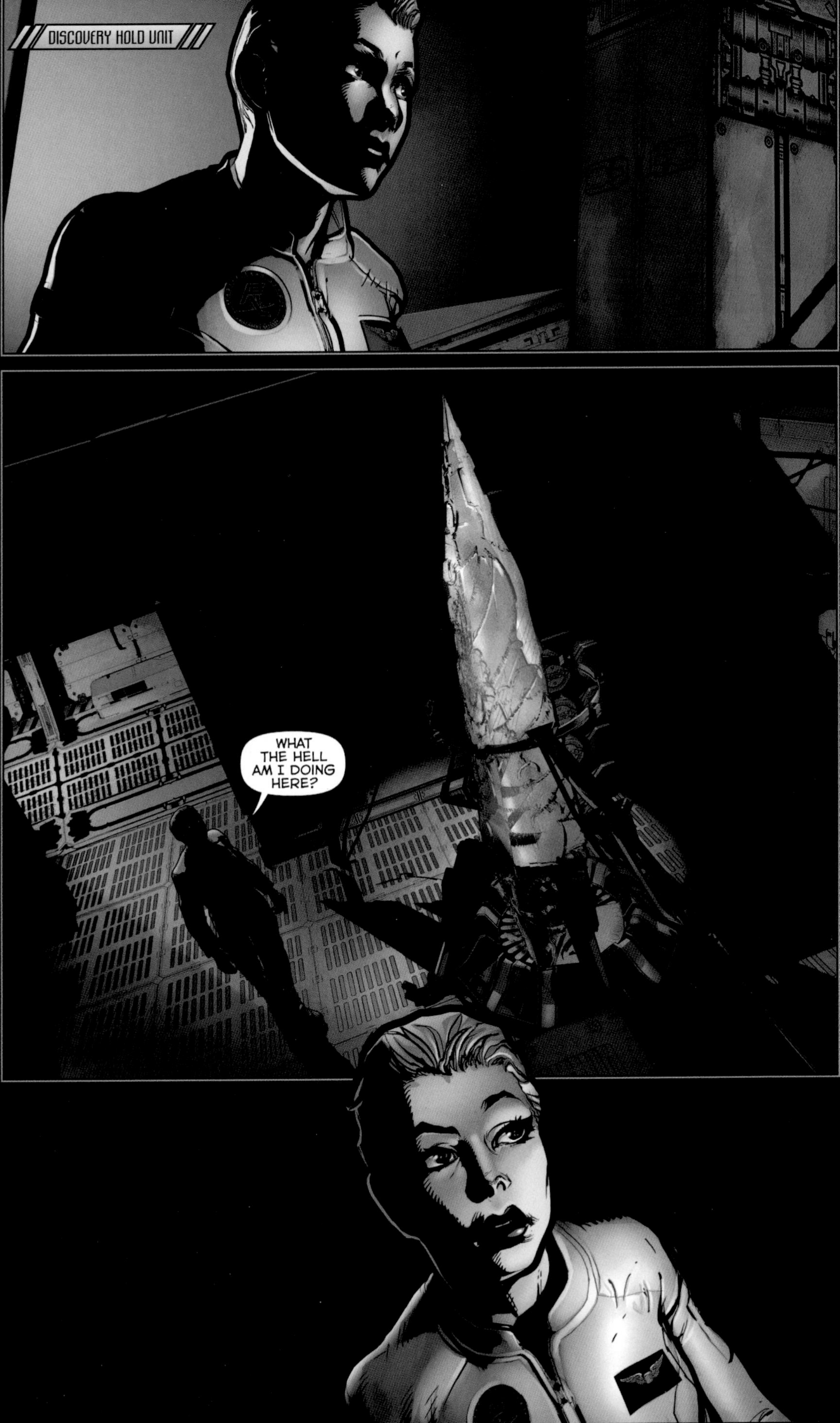
DISCOVERY HOLD UNIT
WHAT THE HELL AM I DOING HERE?

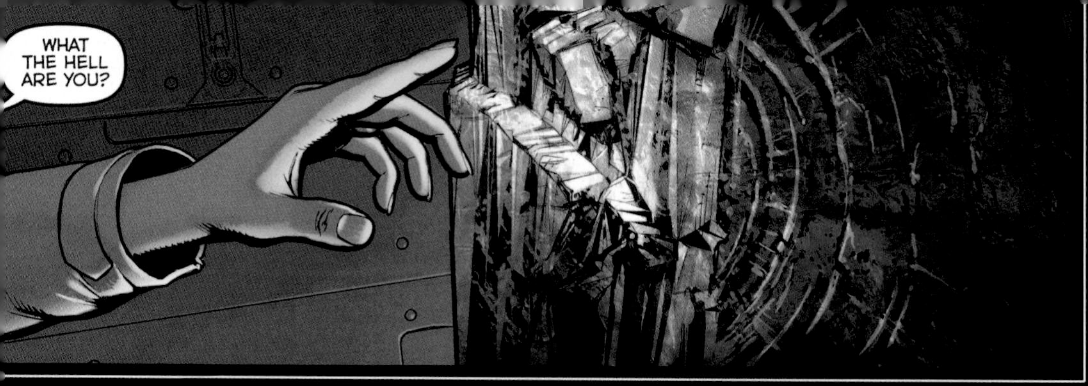
WHAT THE HELL ARE YOU?

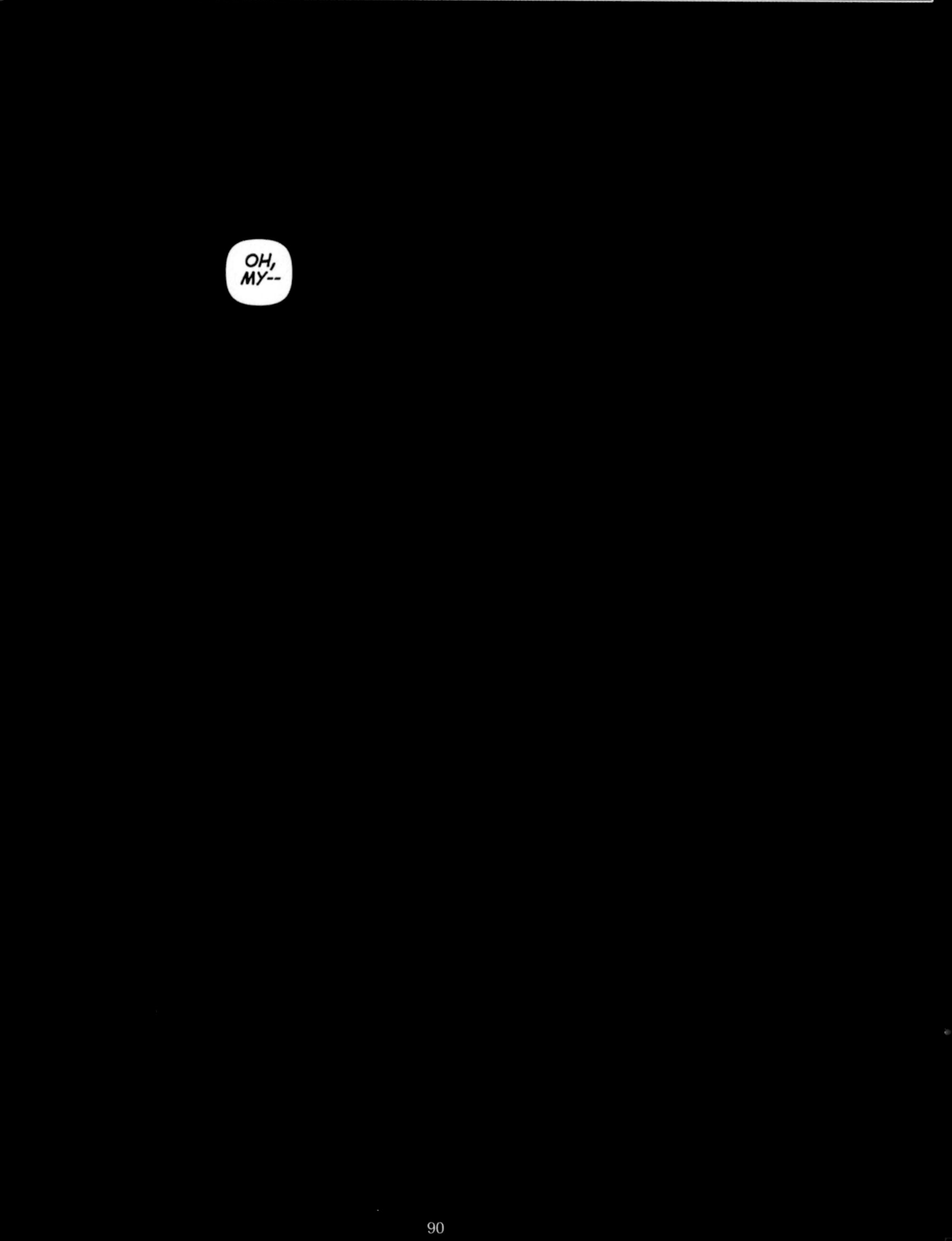
OH, MY--

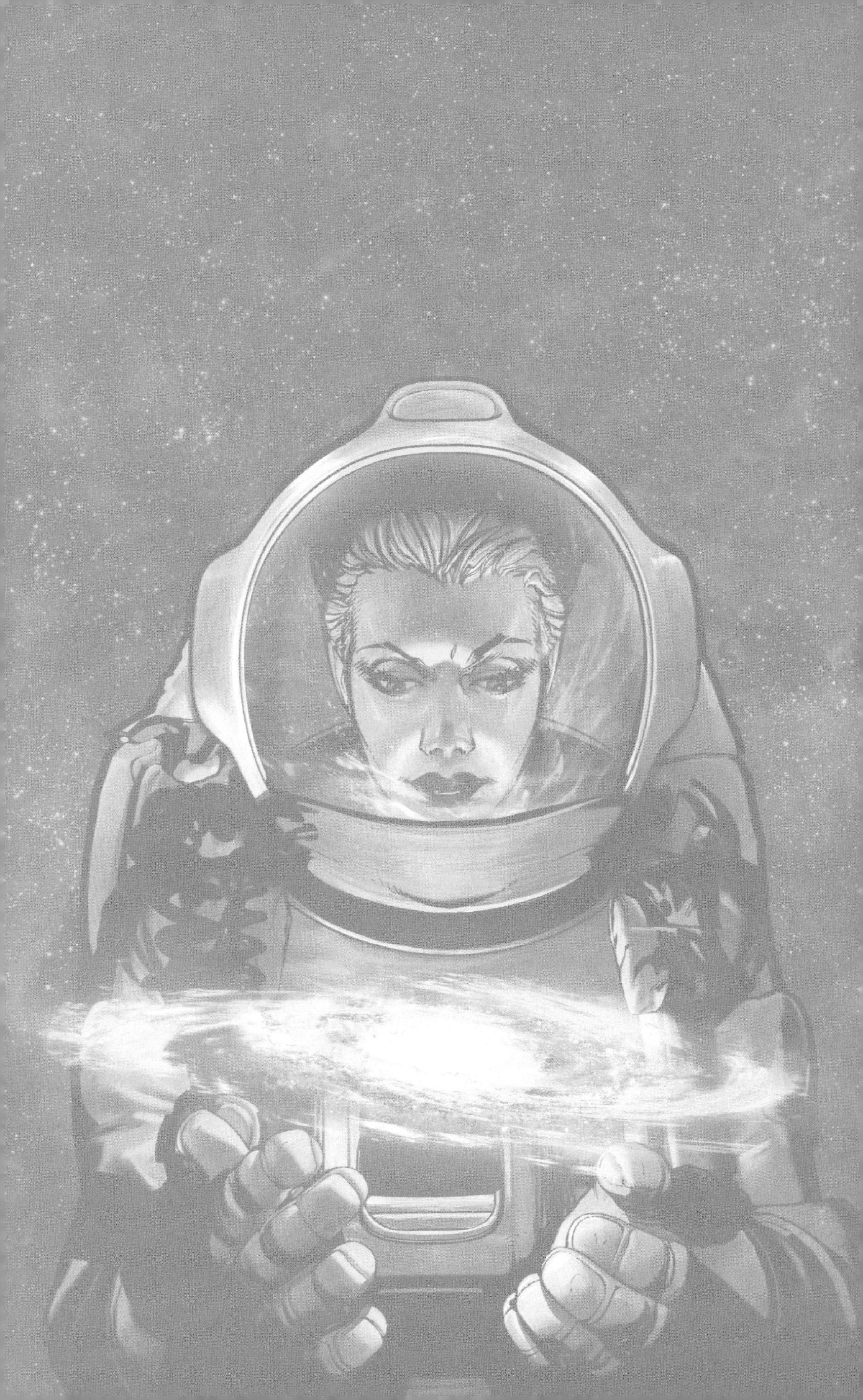

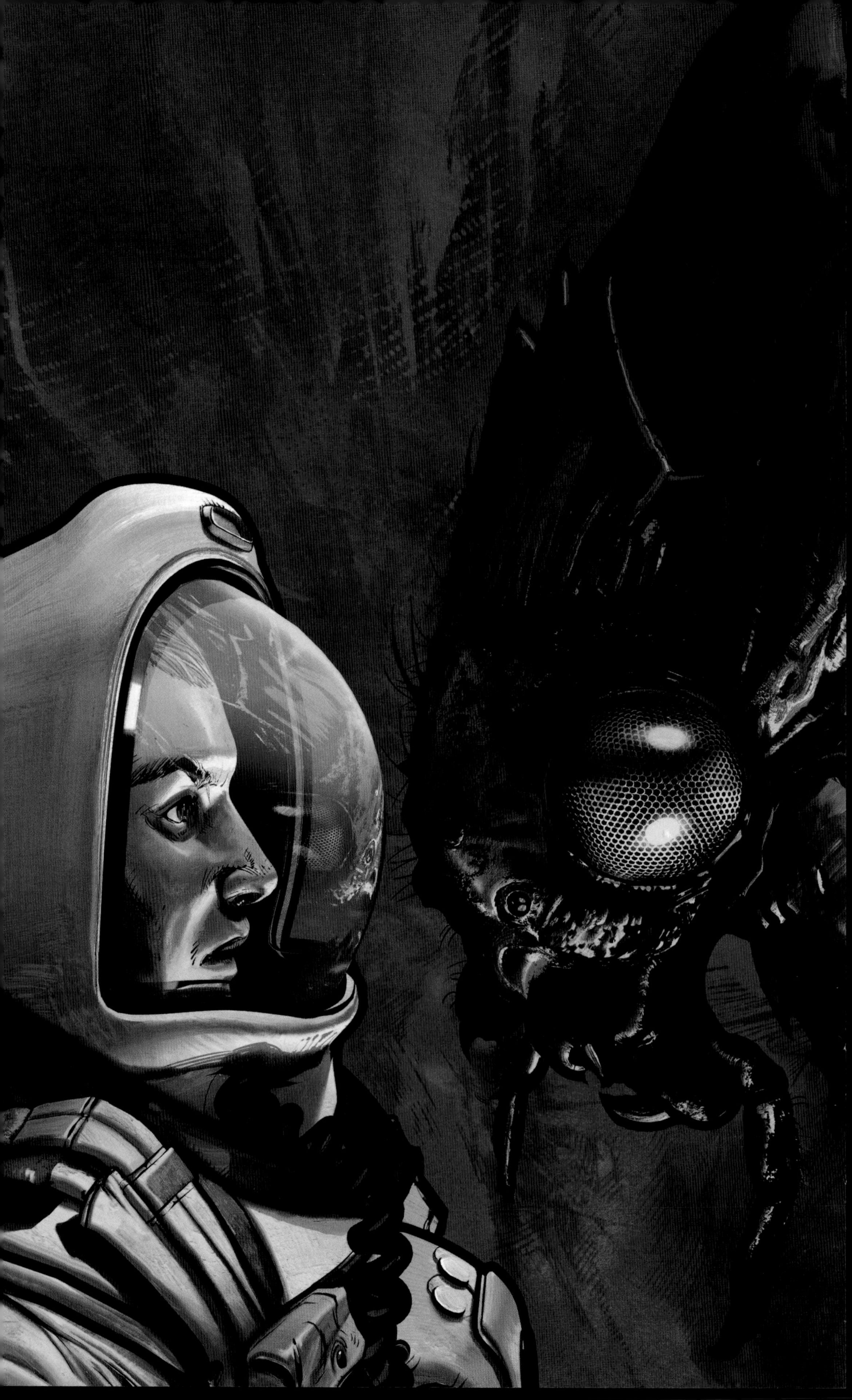

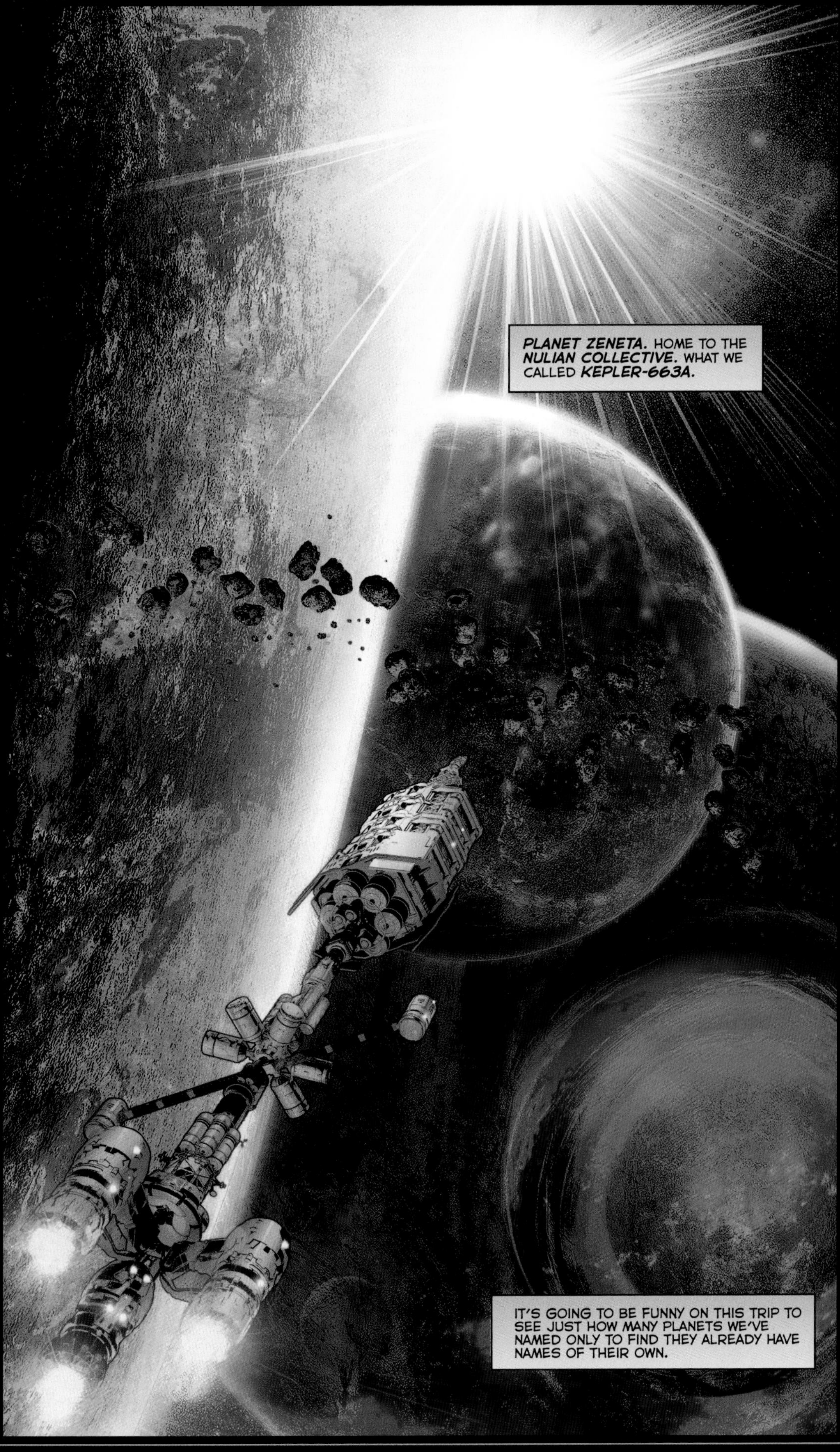
PLANET ZENETA. HOME TO THE NULIAN COLLECTIVE. WHAT WE CALLED KEPLER-663A.
IT'S GOING TO BE FUNNY ON THIS TRIP TO SEE JUST HOW MANY PLANETS WE'VE NAMED ONLY TO FIND THEY ALREADY HAVE NAMES OF THEIR OWN.

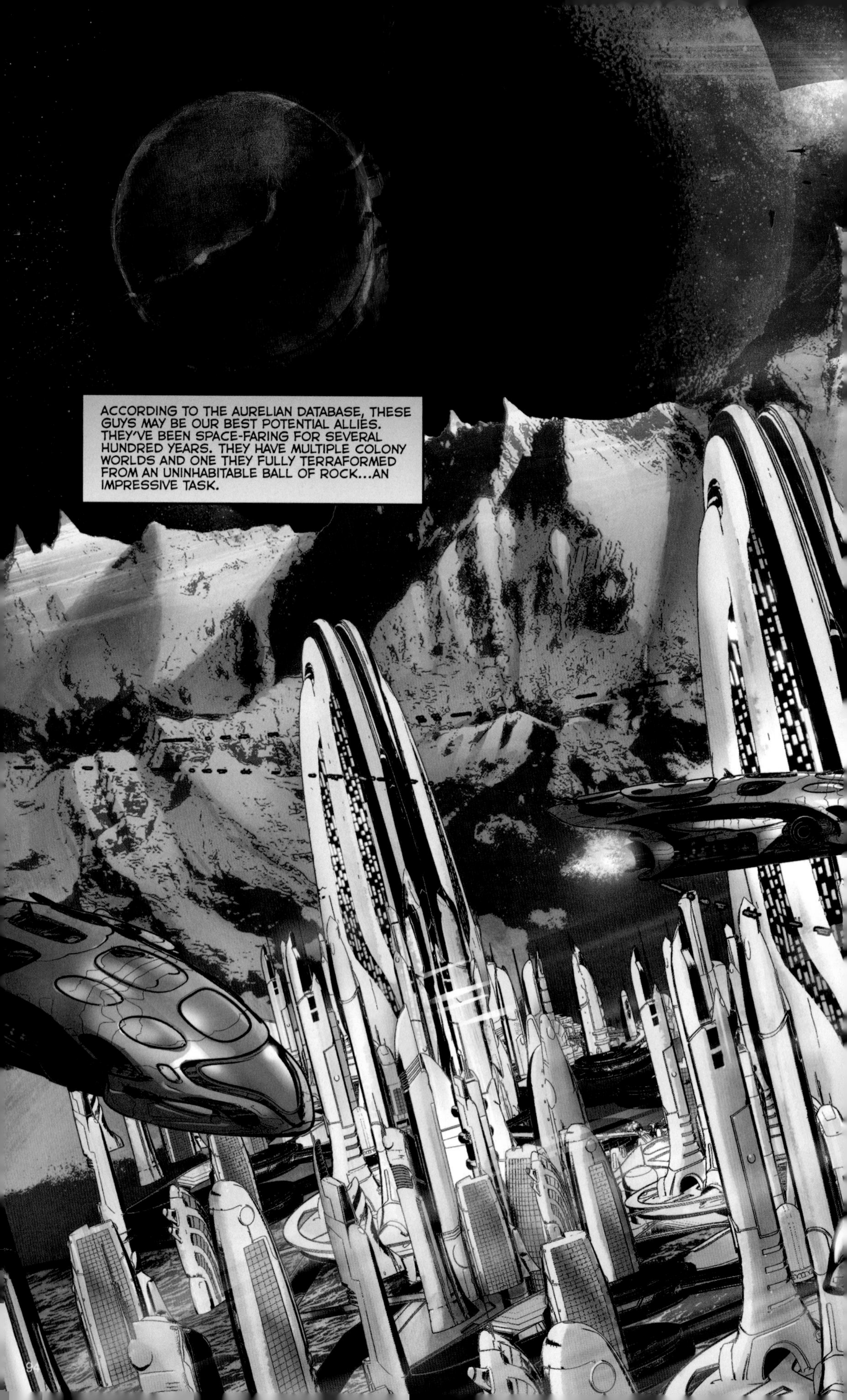
ACCORDING TO THE AURELIAN DATABASE, THESE GUYS MAY BE OUR BEST POTENTIAL ALLIES. THEY'VE BEEN SPACE-FARING FOR SEVERAL HUNDRED YEARS. THEY HAVE MULTIPLE COLONY WORLDS AND ONE THEY FULLY TERRAFORMED FROM AN UNINHABITABLE BALL OF ROCK...AN IMPRESSIVE TASK.

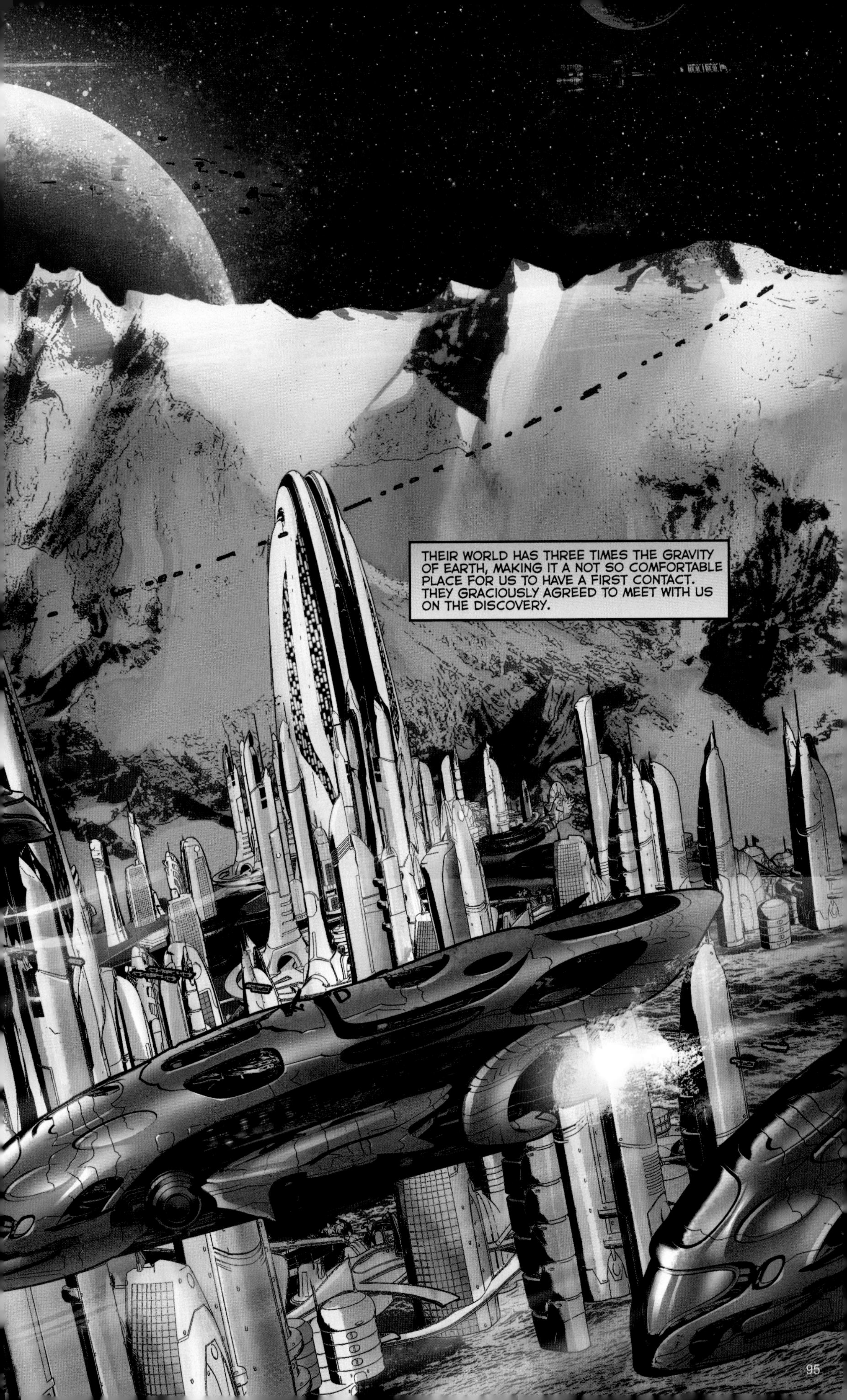
THEIR WORLD HAS THREE TIMES THE GRAVITY OF EARTH, MAKING IT A NOT SO COMFORTABLE PLACE FOR US TO HAVE A FIRST CONTACT. THEY GRACIOUSLY AGREED TO MEET WITH US ON THE DISCOVERY.

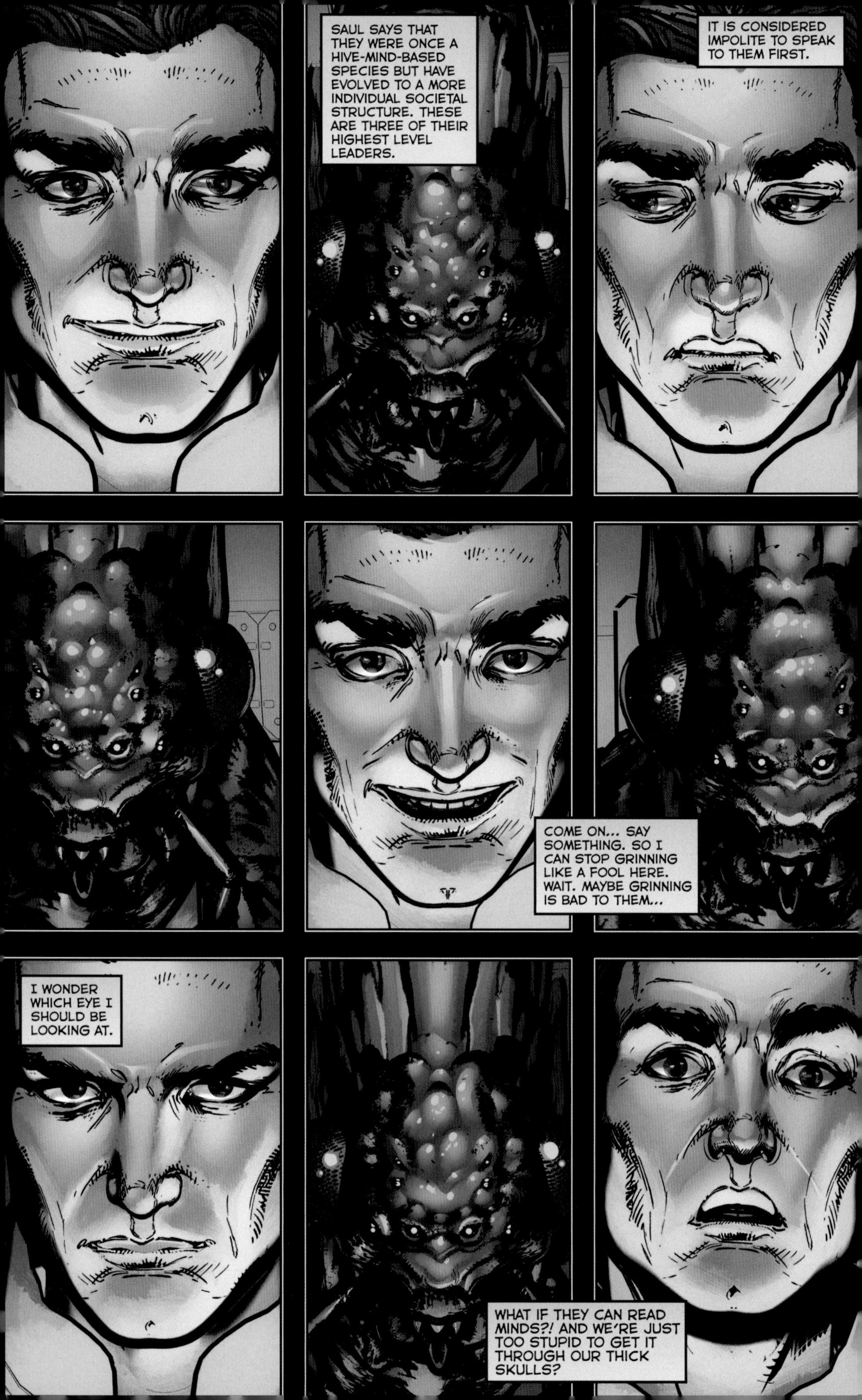

SAUL SAYS THAT THEY WERE ONCE A HIVE-MIND-BASED SPECIES BUT HAVE EVOLVED TO A MORE INDIVIDUAL SOCIETAL STRUCTURE. THESE ARE THREE OF THEIR HIGHEST LEVEL LEADERS.
IT IS CONSIDERED IMPOLITE TO SPEAK TO THEM FIRST.
COME ON... SAY SOMETHING. SO I CAN STOP GRINNING LIKE A FOOL HERE. WAIT. MAYBE GRINNING IS BAD TO THEM...
I WONDER WHICH EYE I SHOULD BE LOOKING AT.
WHAT IF THEY CAN READ MINDS?! AND WE'RE JUST TOO STUPID TO GET IT THROUGH OUR THICK SKULLS?

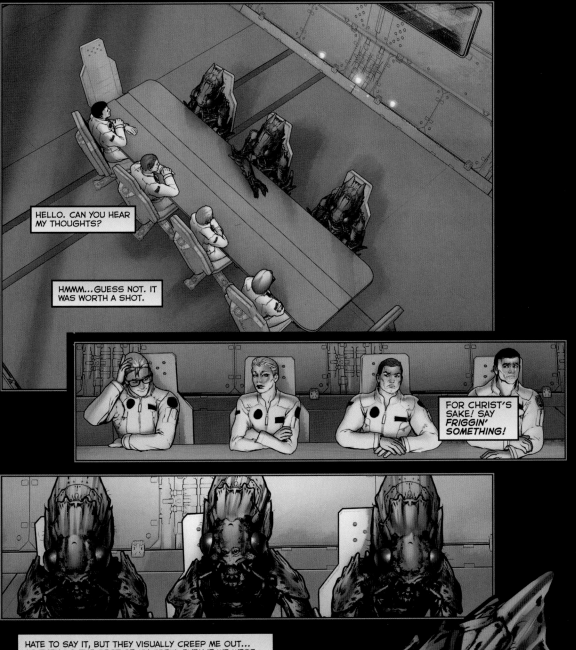

HELLO. CAN YOU HEAR MY THOUGHTS?

HMMM...GUESS NOT. IT WAS WORTH A SHOT.

FOR CHRIST'S SAKE! SAY *FRIGGIN'* SOMETHING!

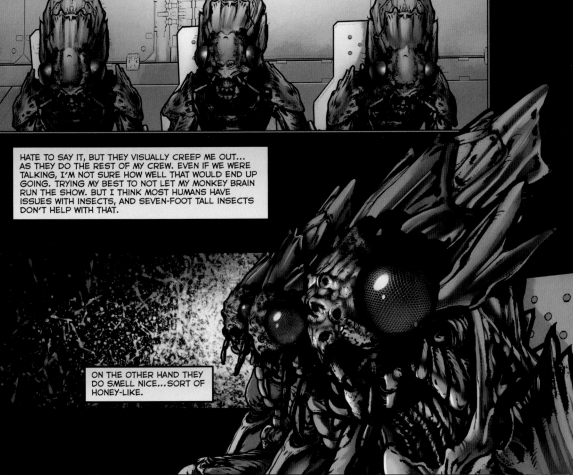

HATE TO SAY IT, BUT THEY VISUALLY CREEP ME OUT... AS THEY DO THE REST OF MY CREW. EVEN IF WE WERE TALKING, I'M NOT SURE HOW WELL THAT WOULD END UP GOING. TRYING MY BEST TO NOT LET MY MONKEY BRAIN RUN THE SHOW. BUT I THINK MOST HUMANS HAVE ISSUES WITH INSECTS, AND SEVEN-FOOT TALL INSECTS DON'T HELP WITH THAT.

ON THE OTHER HAND THEY DO SMELL NICE...SORT OF HONEY-LIKE.

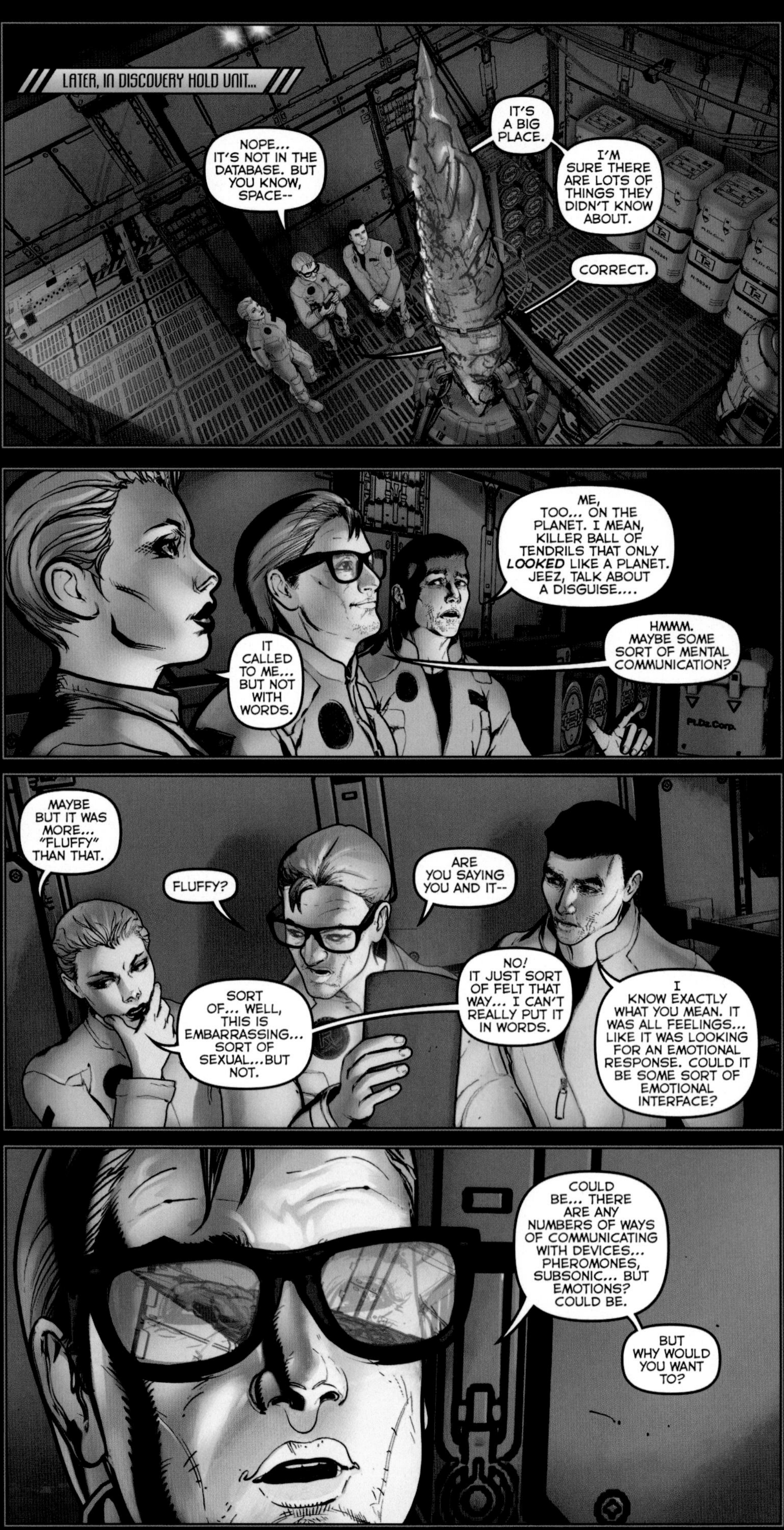
LATER, IN DISCOVERY HOLD UNIT...
NOPE... IT'S NOT IN THE DATABASE. BUT YOU KNOW, SPACE--
IT'S A BIG PLACE.
I'M SURE THERE ARE LOTS OF THINGS THEY DIDN'T KNOW ABOUT.
CORRECT.
ME, TOO... ON THE PLANET. I MEAN, KILLER BALL OF TENDRILS THAT ONLY LOOKED LIKE A PLANET. JEEZ, TALK ABOUT A DISGUISE....
IT CALLED TO ME... BUT NOT WITH WORDS.
HMMM. MAYBE SOME SORT OF MENTAL COMMUNICATION?
MAYBE BUT IT WAS MORE... "FLUFFY" THAN THAT.
FLUFFY?
ARE YOU SAYING YOU AND IT--
SORT OF... WELL, THIS IS EMBARRASSING... SORT OF SEXUAL...BUT NOT.
NO! IT JUST SORT OF FELT THAT WAY... I CAN'T REALLY PUT IT IN WORDS.
I KNOW EXACTLY WHAT YOU MEAN. IT WAS ALL FEELINGS... LIKE IT WAS LOOKING FOR AN EMOTIONAL RESPONSE. COULD IT BE SOME SORT OF EMOTIONAL INTERFACE?
COULD BE... THERE ARE ANY NUMBERS OF WAYS OF COMMUNICATING WITH DEVICES... PHEROMONES, SUBSONIC... BUT EMOTIONS? COULD BE.
BUT WHY WOULD YOU WANT TO?

THERE. MY LAST PUBLIC LOG ENTRY DONE. IT'S NOW GRISSOM'S PROBLEM... I NEVER KNEW WHAT TO SAY IN THOSE, ANYWAY.

SIR, RYAN HERE. SORRY TO DISTURB YOU, BUT WE'RE BEING HAILED.

WE NEAR ANY POPULATED WORLDS?

NO, SIR.

THEN A VOICE IN THE WILDERNESS.

SIR?

I'LL BE RIGHT THERE.

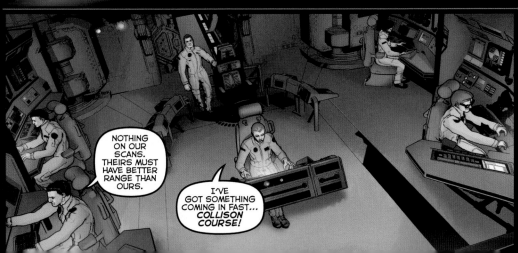

NOTHING ON OUR SCANS. THEIRS MUST HAVE BETTER RANGE THAN OURS.

I'VE GOT SOMETHING COMING IN FAST... COLLISON COURSE!

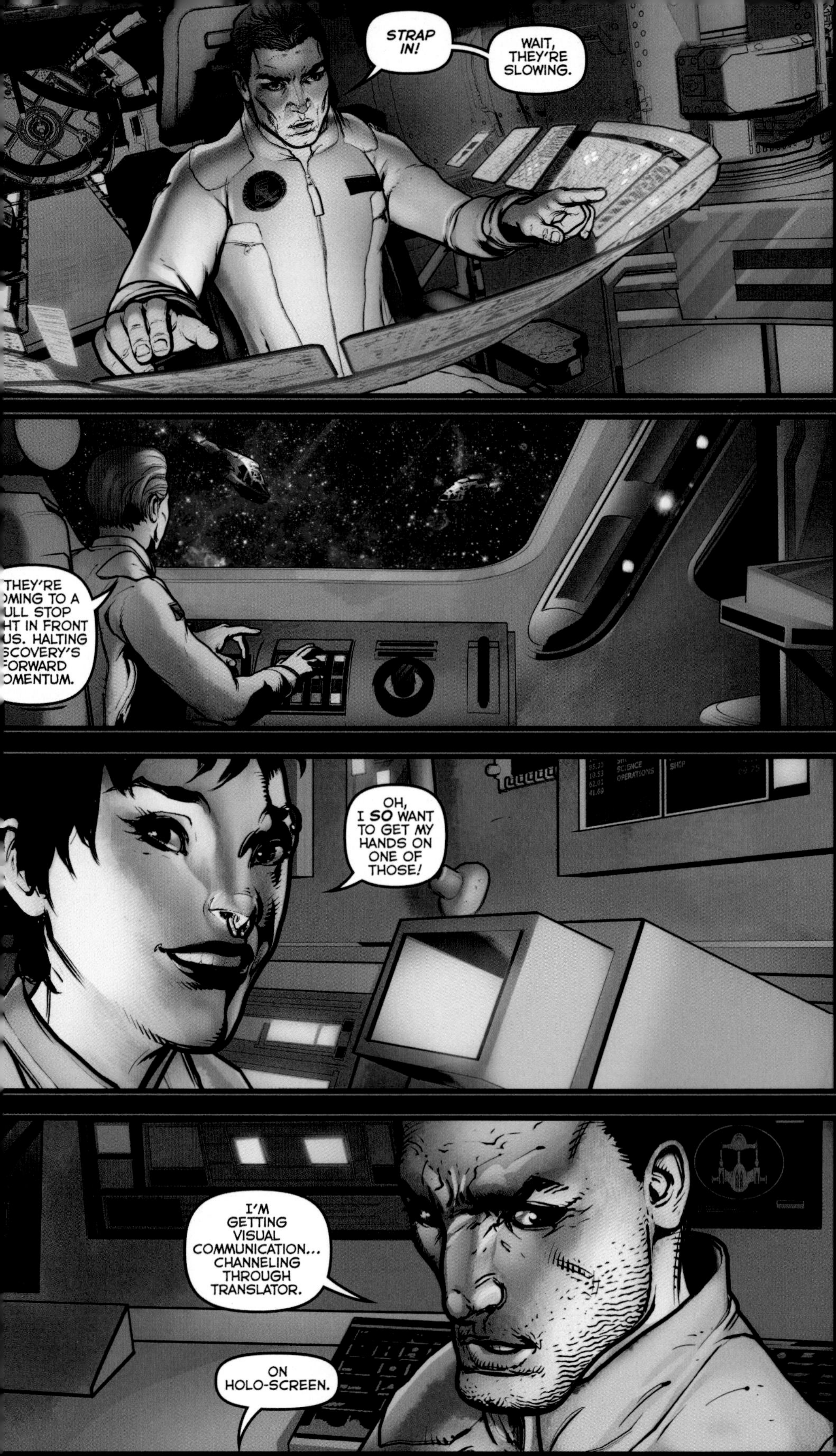

STRAP IN!
WAIT, THEY'RE SLOWING.
THEY'RE OMING TO A ULL STOP HT IN FRONT US. HALTING SCOVERY'S FORWARD OMENTUM.
OH, I **SO** WANT TO GET MY HANDS ON ONE OF THOSE!
I'M GETTING VISUAL COMMUNICATION... CHANNELING THROUGH TRANSLATOR.
ON HOLO-SCREEN.

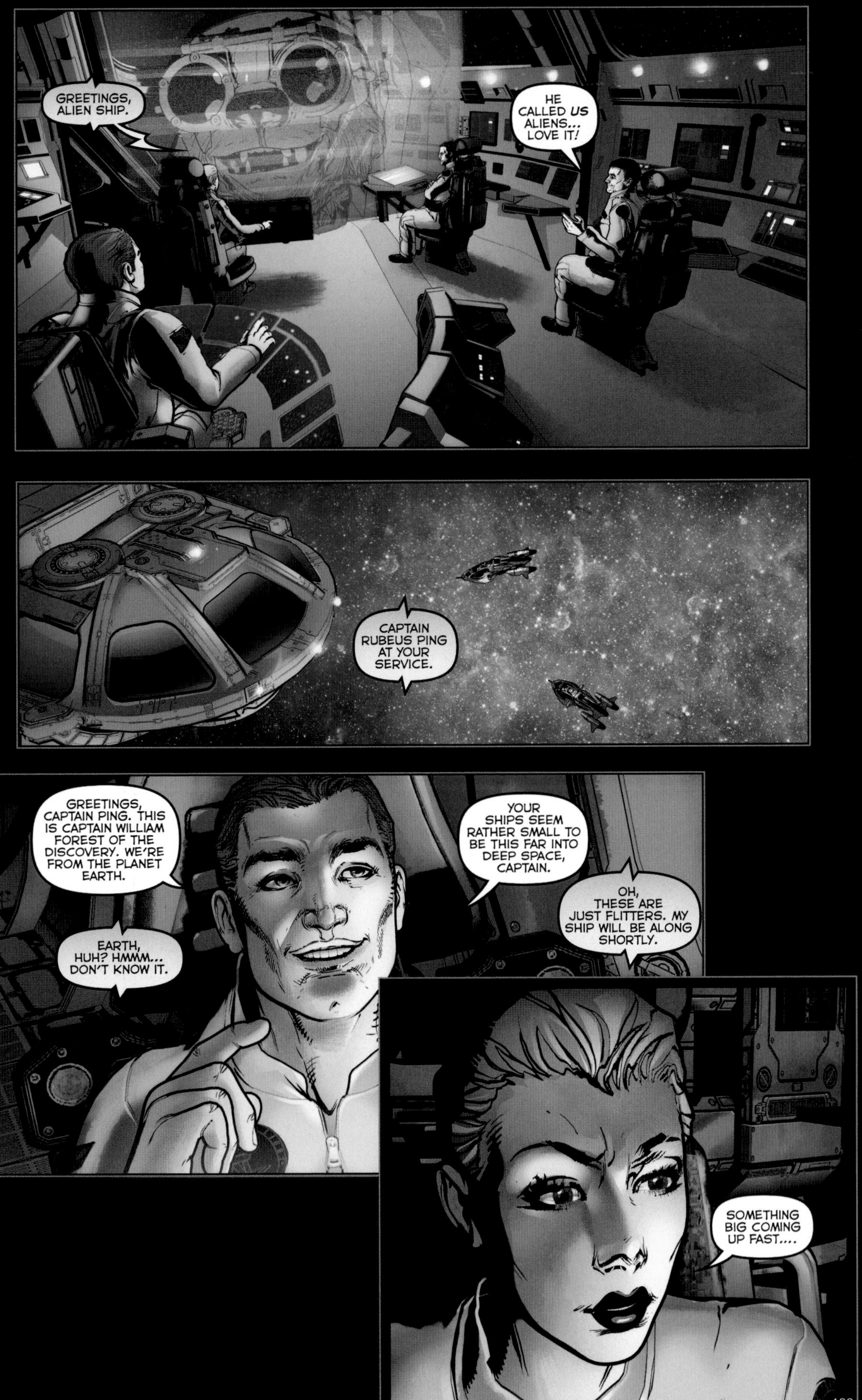
GREETINGS, ALIEN SHIP.
HE CALLED *US* ALIENS... LOVE IT!
CAPTAIN RUBEUS PING AT YOUR SERVICE.
GREETINGS, CAPTAIN PING. THIS IS CAPTAIN WILLIAM FOREST OF THE DISCOVERY. WE'RE FROM THE PLANET EARTH.
EARTH, HUH? HMMM... DON'T KNOW IT.
YOUR SHIPS SEEM RATHER SMALL TO BE THIS FAR INTO DEEP SPACE, CAPTAIN.
OH, THESE ARE JUST FLITTERS. MY SHIP WILL BE ALONG SHORTLY.
SOMETHING BIG COMING UP FAST....

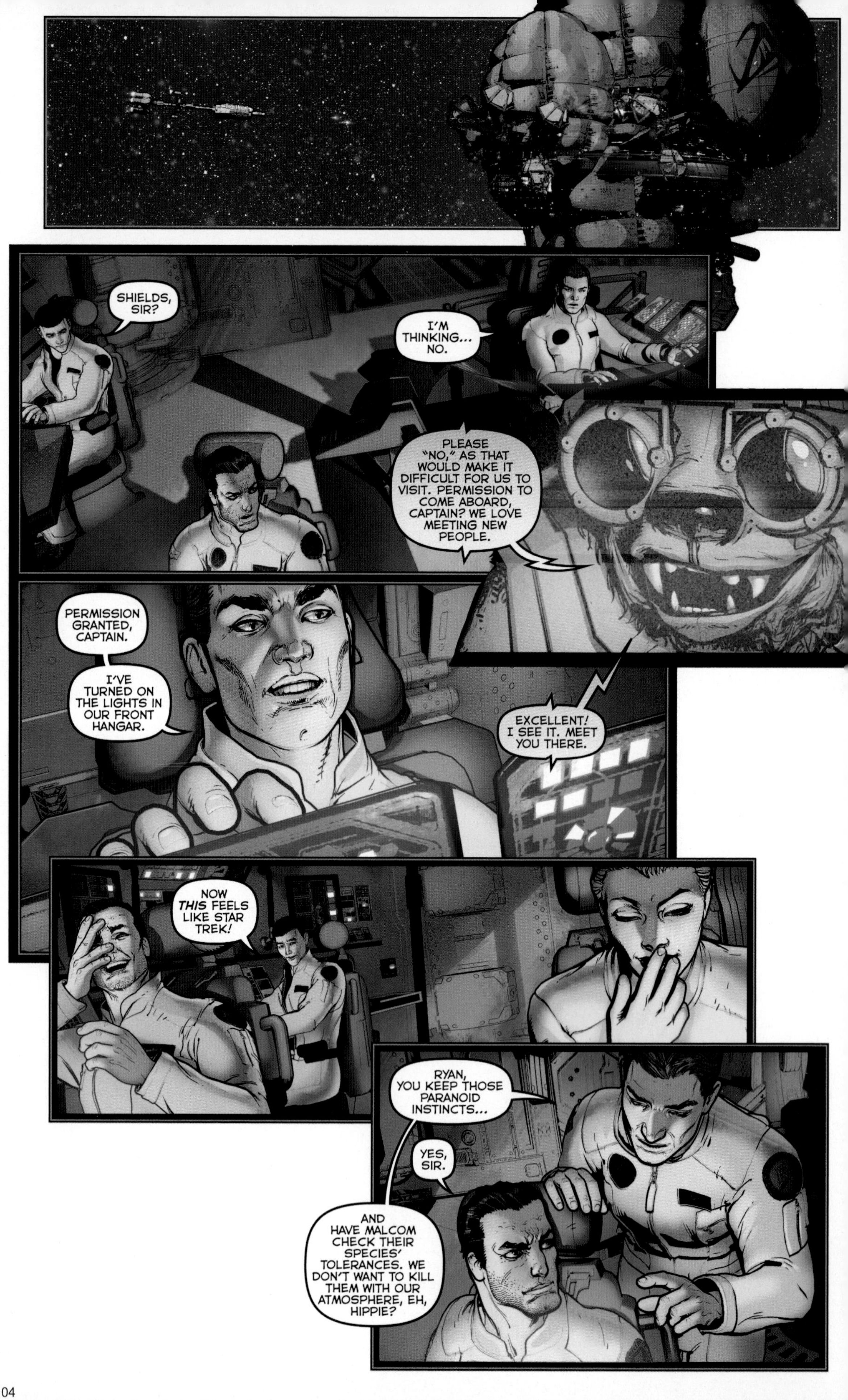

SHIELDS, SIR?
I'M THINKING... NO.
PLEASE "NO," AS THAT WOULD MAKE IT DIFFICULT FOR US TO VISIT. PERMISSION TO COME ABOARD, CAPTAIN? WE LOVE MEETING NEW PEOPLE.
PERMISSION GRANTED, CAPTAIN.
I'VE TURNED ON THE LIGHTS IN OUR FRONT HANGAR.
EXCELLENT! I SEE IT. MEET YOU THERE.
NOW *THIS* FEELS LIKE STAR TREK!
RYAN, YOU KEEP THOSE PARANOID INSTINCTS...
YES, SIR.
AND HAVE MALCOM CHECK THEIR SPECIES' TOLERANCES. WE DON'T WANT TO KILL THEM WITH OUR ATMOSPHERE, EH, HIPPIE?

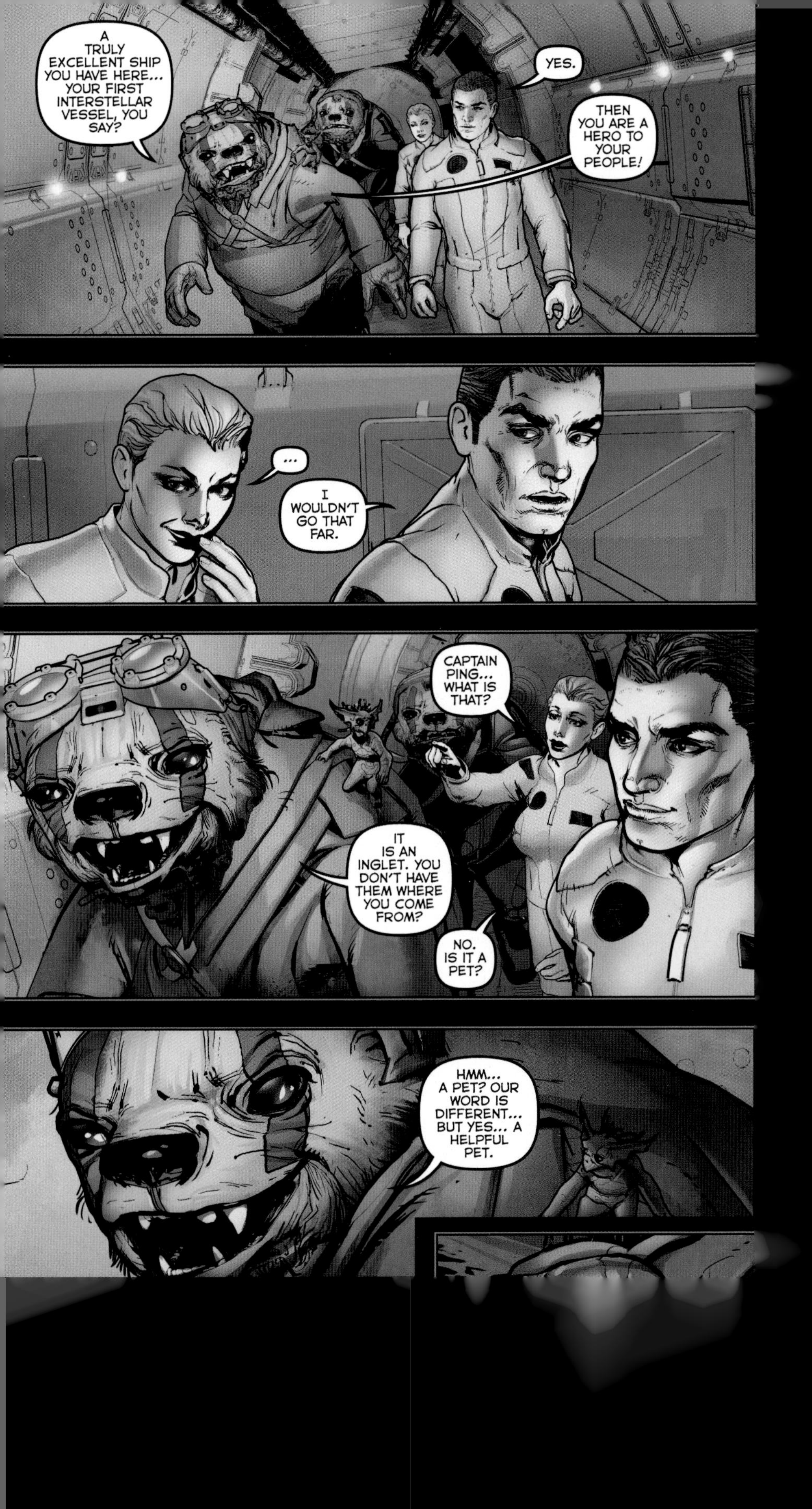
A TRULY EXCELLENT SHIP YOU HAVE HERE... YOUR FIRST INTERSTELLAR VESSEL, YOU SAY?
YES.
THEN YOU ARE A HERO TO YOUR PEOPLE!
...
I WOULDN'T GO THAT FAR.
CAPTAIN PING... WHAT IS THAT?
IT IS AN INGLET. YOU DON'T HAVE THEM WHERE YOU COME FROM?
NO. IS IT A PET?
HMM... A PET? OUR WORD IS DIFFERENT... BUT YES... A HELPFUL PET.

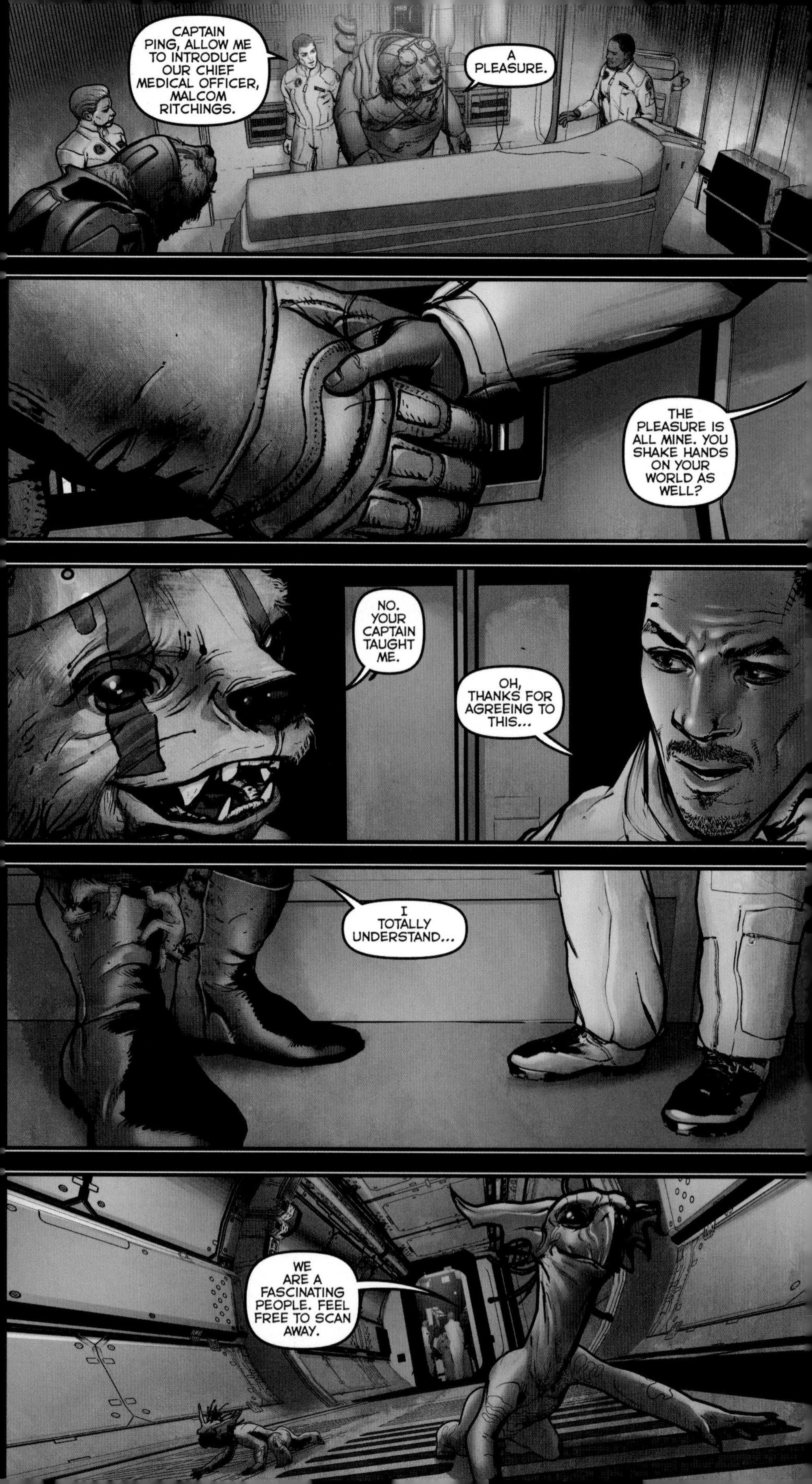
CAPTAIN PING, ALLOW ME TO INTRODUCE OUR CHIEF MEDICAL OFFICER, MALCOM RITCHINGS.
A PLEASURE.
THE PLEASURE IS ALL MINE. YOU SHAKE HANDS ON YOUR WORLD AS WELL?
NO. YOUR CAPTAIN TAUGHT ME.
OH, THANKS FOR AGREEING TO THIS...
I TOTALLY UNDERSTAND...
WE ARE A FASCINATING PEOPLE. FEEL FREE TO SCAN AWAY.

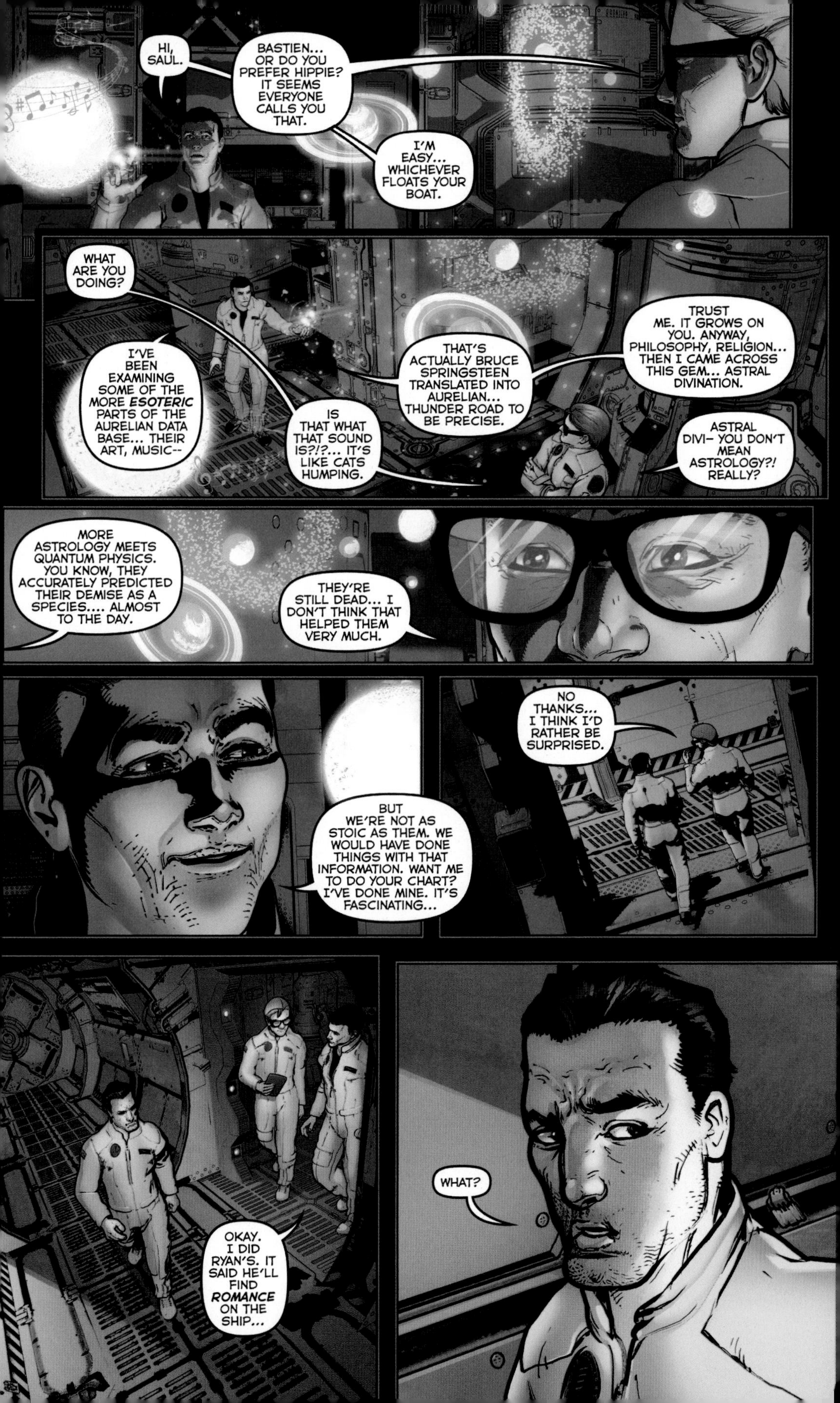
HI, SAUL.
BASTIEN... OR DO YOU PREFER HIPPIE? IT SEEMS EVERYONE CALLS YOU THAT.
I'M EASY... WHICHEVER FLOATS YOUR BOAT.
WHAT ARE YOU DOING?
I'VE BEEN EXAMINING SOME OF THE MORE ESOTERIC PARTS OF THE AURELIAN DATA BASE... THEIR ART, MUSIC--
IS THAT WHAT THAT SOUND IS?!?... IT'S LIKE CATS HUMPING.
THAT'S ACTUALLY BRUCE SPRINGSTEEN TRANSLATED INTO AURELIAN... THUNDER ROAD TO BE PRECISE.
TRUST ME. IT GROWS ON YOU. ANYWAY, PHILOSOPHY, RELIGION... THEN I CAME ACROSS THIS GEM... ASTRAL DIVINATION.
ASTRAL DIVI- YOU DON'T MEAN ASTROLOGY?! REALLY?
MORE ASTROLOGY MEETS QUANTUM PHYSICS. YOU KNOW, THEY ACCURATELY PREDICTED THEIR DEMISE AS A SPECIES.... ALMOST TO THE DAY.
THEY'RE STILL DEAD... I DON'T THINK THAT HELPED THEM VERY MUCH.
BUT WE'RE NOT AS STOIC AS THEM. WE WOULD HAVE DONE THINGS WITH THAT INFORMATION. WANT ME TO DO YOUR CHART? I'VE DONE MINE. IT'S FASCINATING...
NO THANKS... I THINK I'D RATHER BE SURPRISED.
OKAY. I DID RYAN'S. IT SAID HE'LL FIND ROMANCE ON THE SHIP...
WHAT?

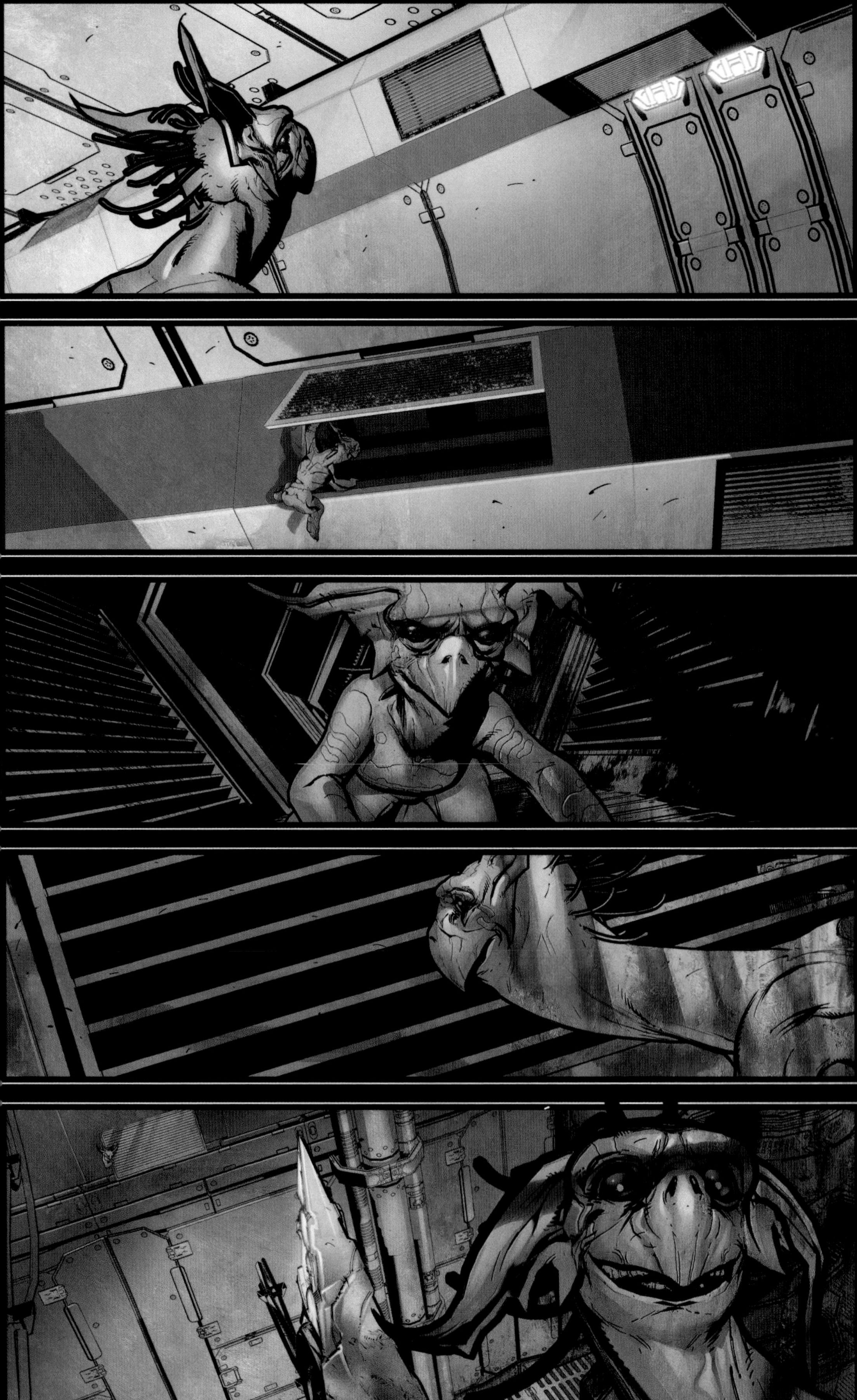

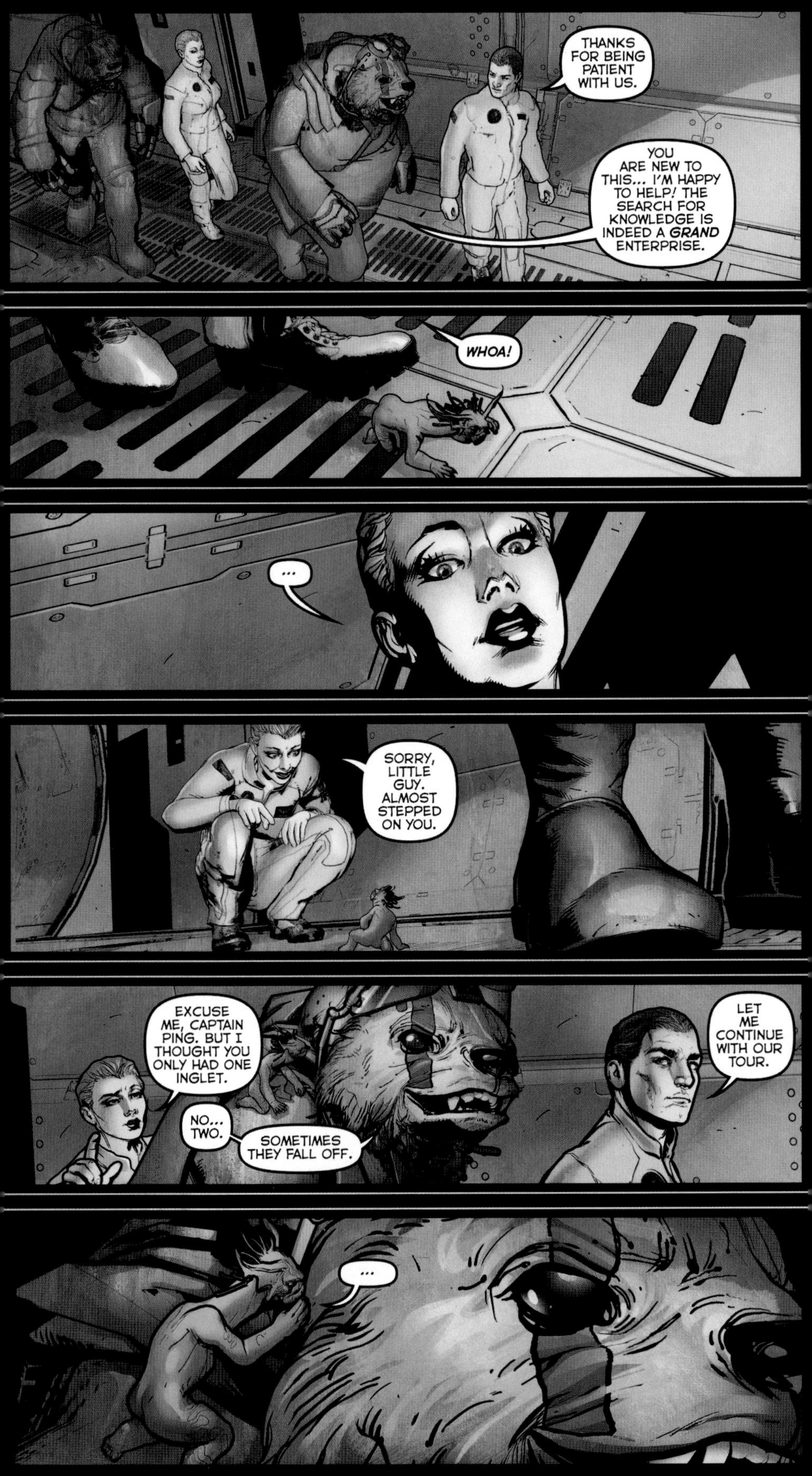
THANKS FOR BEING PATIENT WITH US.
YOU ARE NEW TO THIS... I'M HAPPY TO HELP! THE SEARCH FOR KNOWLEDGE IS INDEED A *GRAND* ENTERPRISE.
WHOA!
...
SORRY, LITTLE GUY. ALMOST STEPPED ON YOU.
EXCUSE ME, CAPTAIN PING. BUT I THOUGHT YOU ONLY HAD ONE INGLET.
NO... TWO.
SOMETIMES THEY FALL OFF.
LET ME CONTINUE WITH OUR TOUR.
...

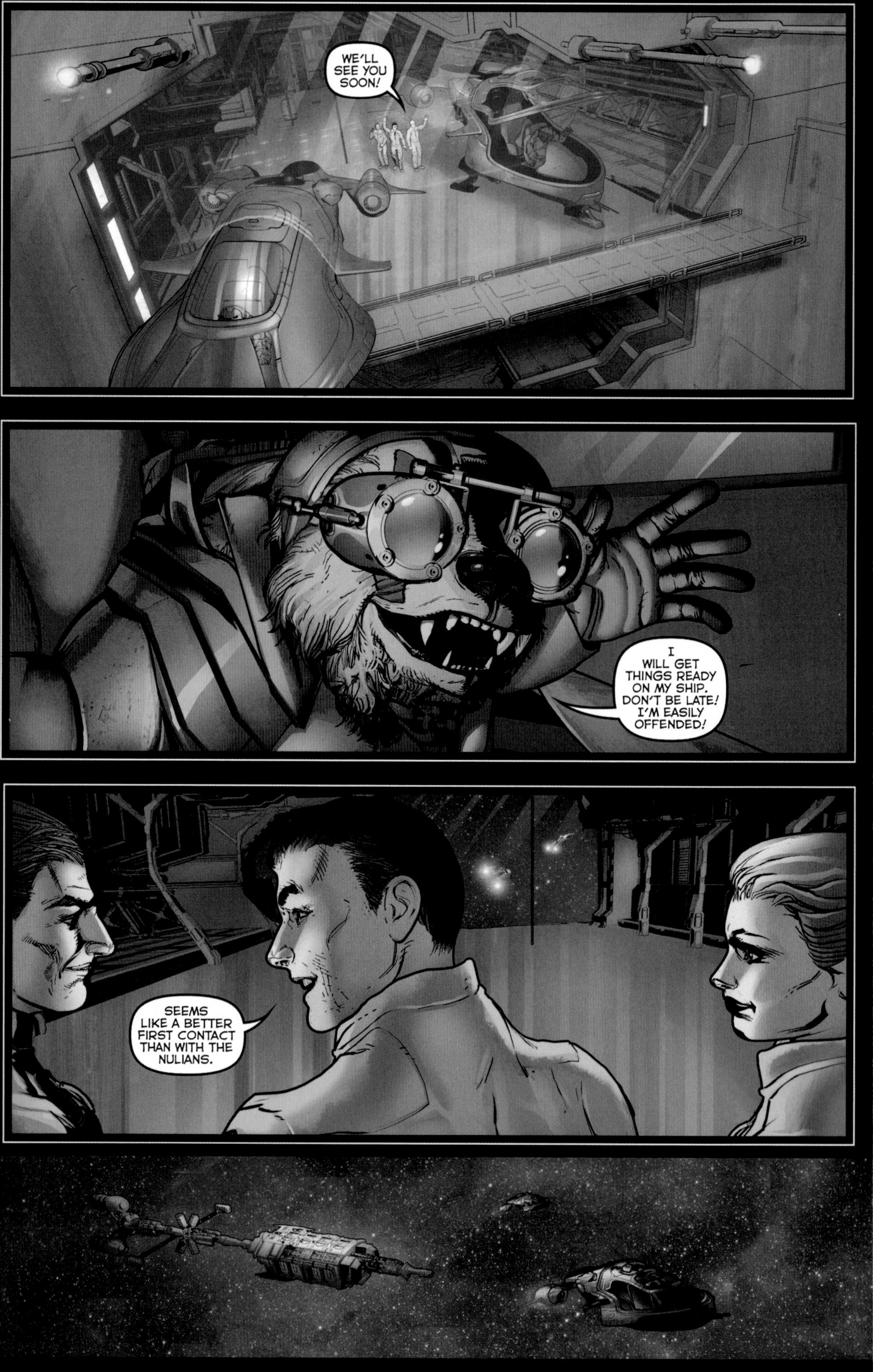
WE'LL SEE YOU SOON!
I WILL GET THINGS READY ON MY SHIP. DON'T BE LATE! I'M EASILY OFFENDED!
SEEMS LIKE A BETTER FIRST CONTACT THAN WITH THE NULIANS.

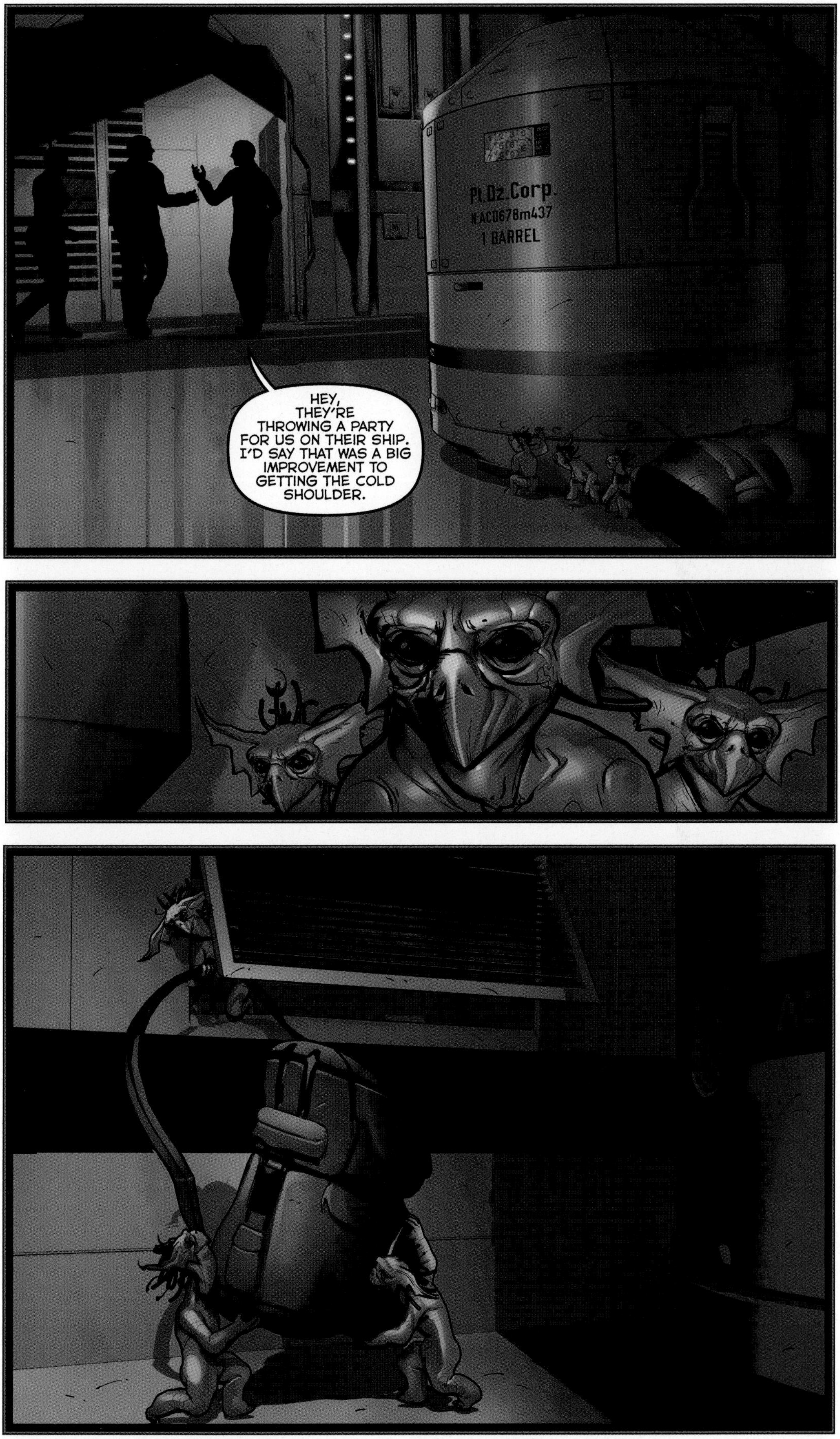
Pt.Dz.Corp.
N:AC0678m437
1 BARREL
HEY, THEY'RE THROWING A PARTY FOR US ON THEIR SHIP. I'D SAY THAT WAS A BIG IMPROVEMENT TO GETTING THE COLD SHOULDER.

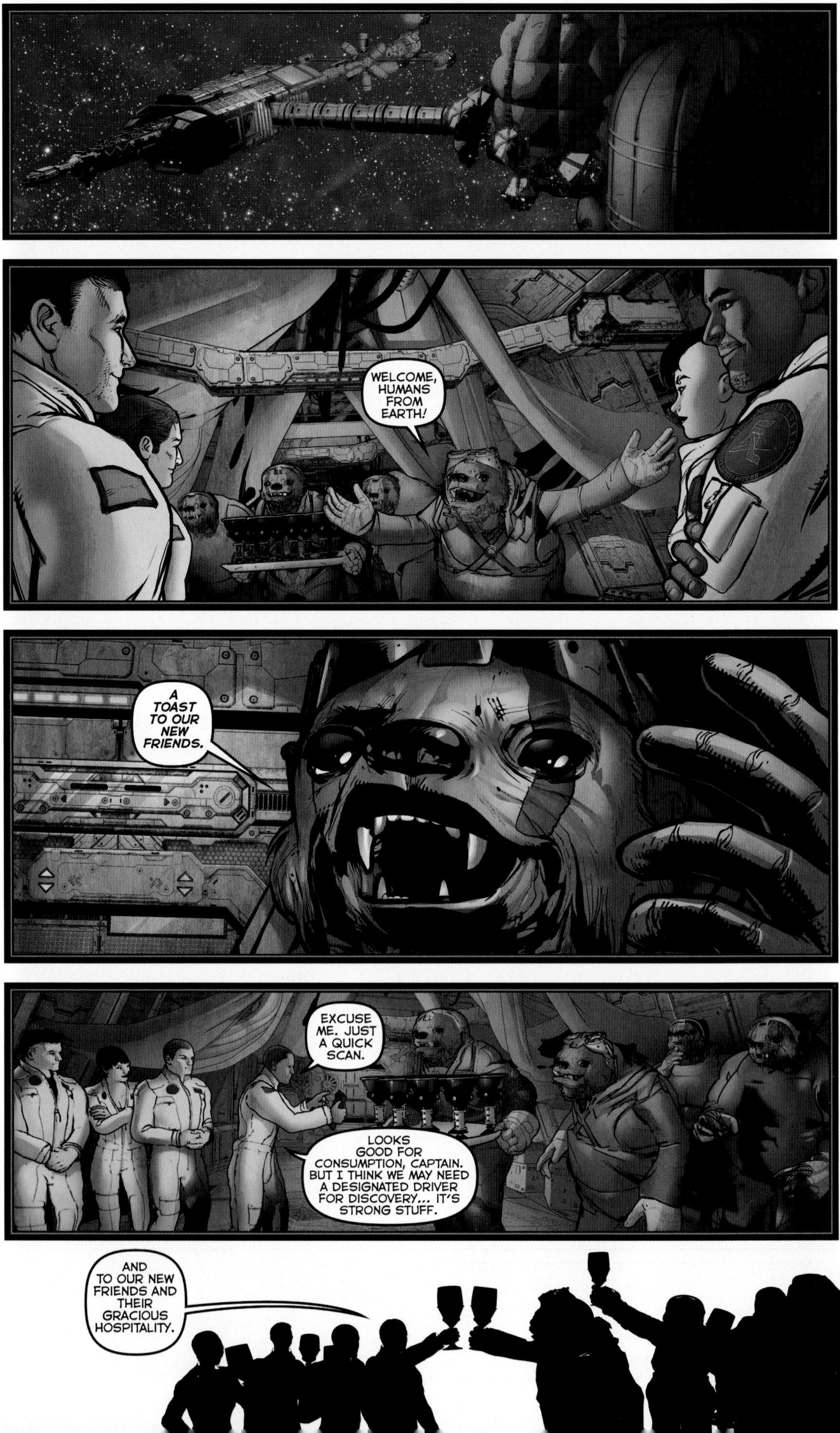
WELCOME, HUMANS FROM EARTH!
A TOAST TO OUR NEW FRIENDS.
EXCUSE ME. JUST A QUICK SCAN.
LOOKS GOOD FOR CONSUMPTION, CAPTAIN. BUT I THINK WE MAY NEED A DESIGNATED DRIVER FOR DISCOVERY... IT'S STRONG STUFF.
AND TO OUR NEW FRIENDS AND THEIR GRACIOUS HOSPITALITY.

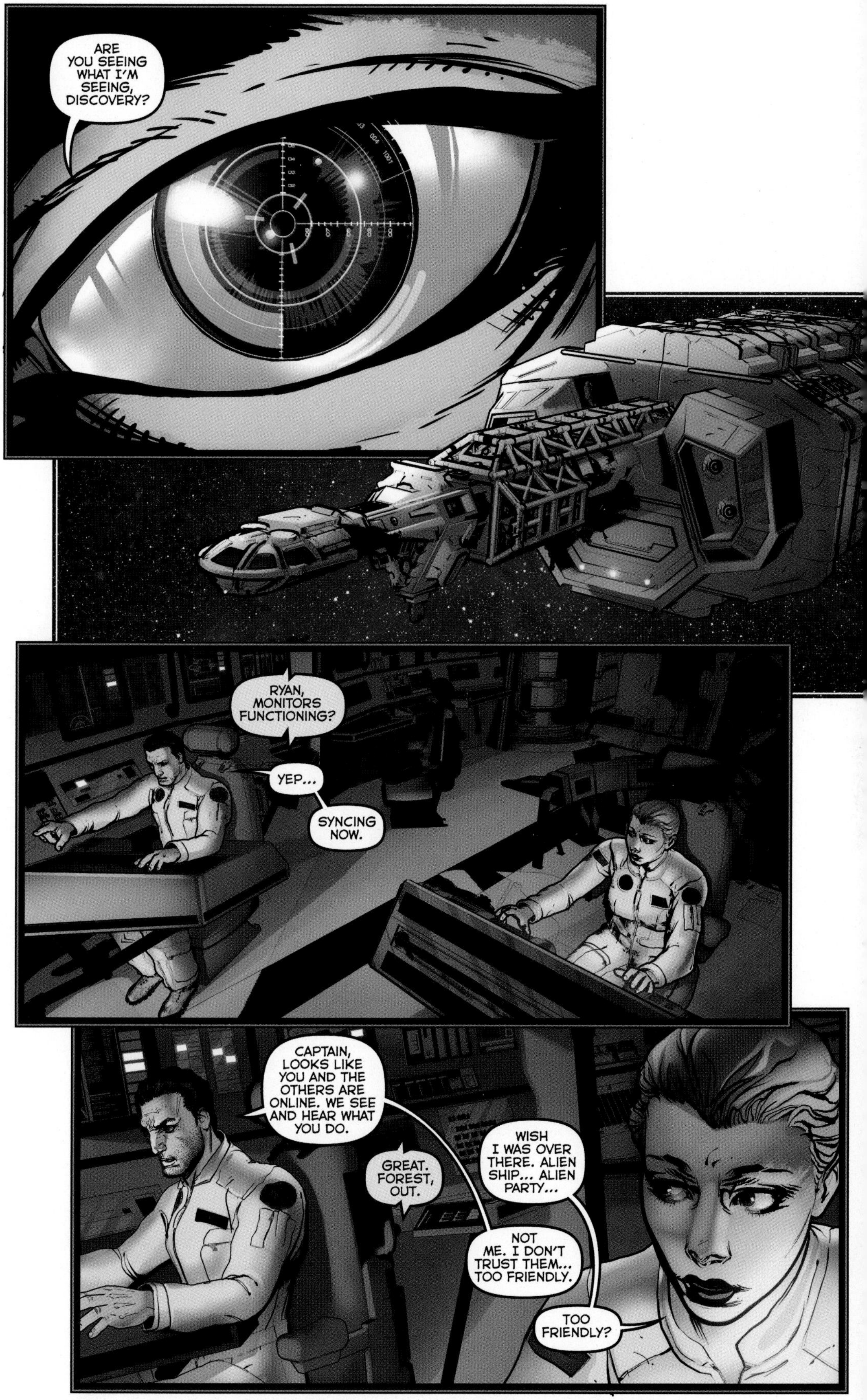
ARE YOU SEEING WHAT I'M SEEING, DISCOVERY?
RYAN, MONITORS FUNCTIONING?
YEP...
SYNCING NOW.
CAPTAIN, LOOKS LIKE YOU AND THE OTHERS ARE ONLINE. WE SEE AND HEAR WHAT YOU DO.
GREAT. FOREST, OUT.
WISH I WAS OVER THERE. ALIEN SHIP... ALIEN PARTY...
NOT ME. I DON'T TRUST THEM... TOO FRIENDLY.
TOO FRIENDLY?

INTERFACE, UP.

YEAH... LIKE IN A USED CAR DEALER SORT OF WAY. I JUST KNOW THEY'RE GONNA TRY AND SELL US SOMETHING BROKEN.

YOU'RE A SUSPICIOUS S.O.B., RYAN.

FOREST, WILLIAM
P.O.V.
REC

...

RITCHINGS, MALCOM
P.O.V.
REC

HOW'S THE SIGNAL QUALITY?

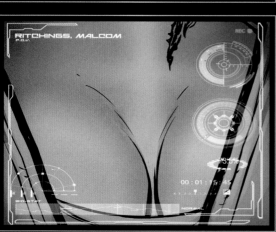

RITCHINGS, MALCOM
P.O.V.
REC

GREAT... THE MONITORS ARE WORKING... REALLY GREAT.

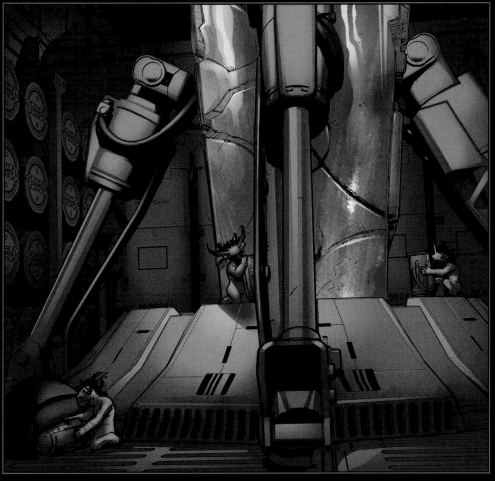

Beep
Beep
Beep

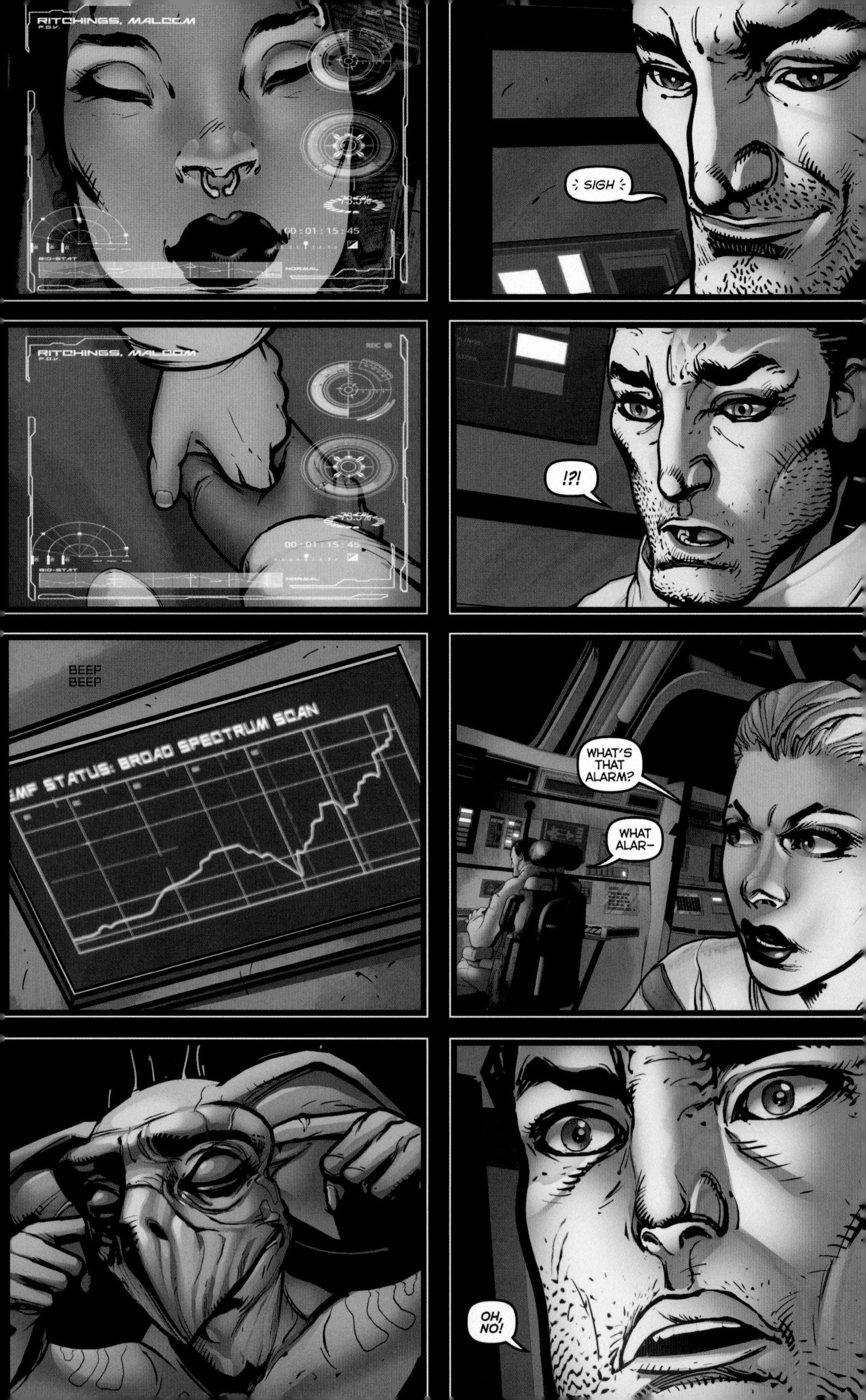
RITCHINGS, MALCOM
P.O.V.
73.5%
00:01:15:45
BIO-STAT
NORMAL
SIGH
RITCHINGS, MALCOM
P.O.V.
00:01:15:45
BIO-STAT
NORMAL
!?!
BEEP
BEEP
EMF STATUS: BROAD SPECTRUM SCAN
WHAT'S THAT ALARM?
WHAT ALAR–
OH, NO!

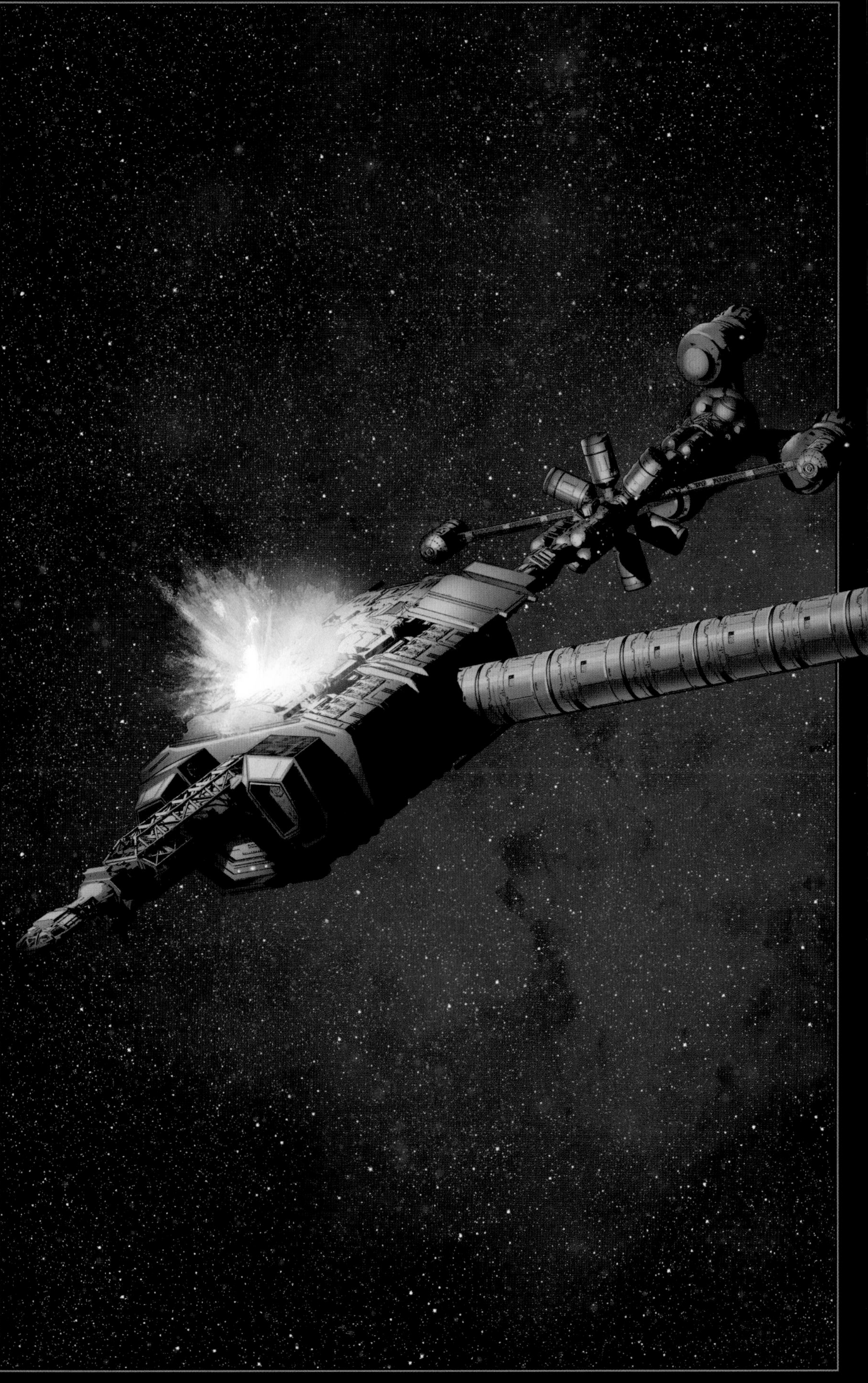

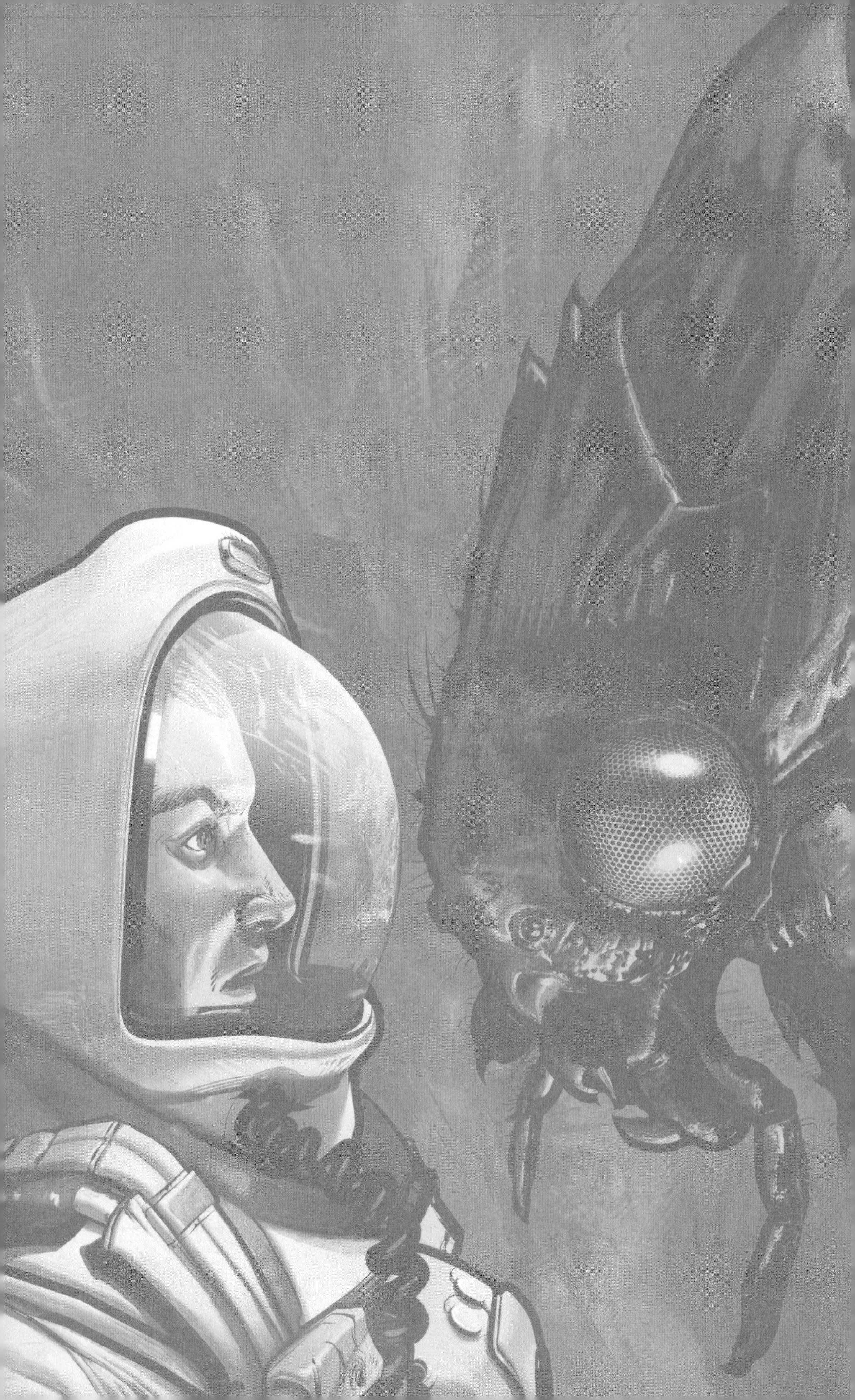

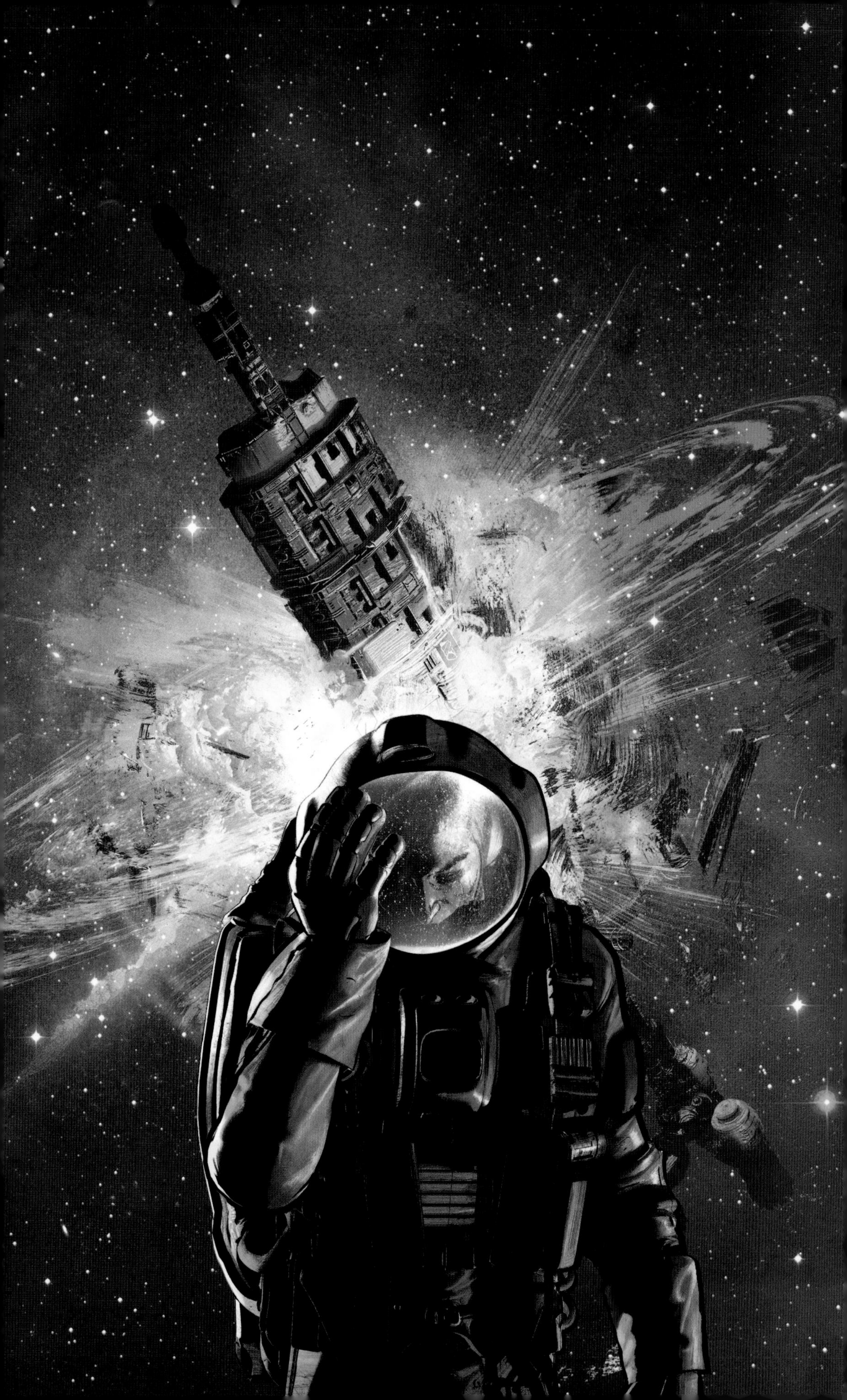

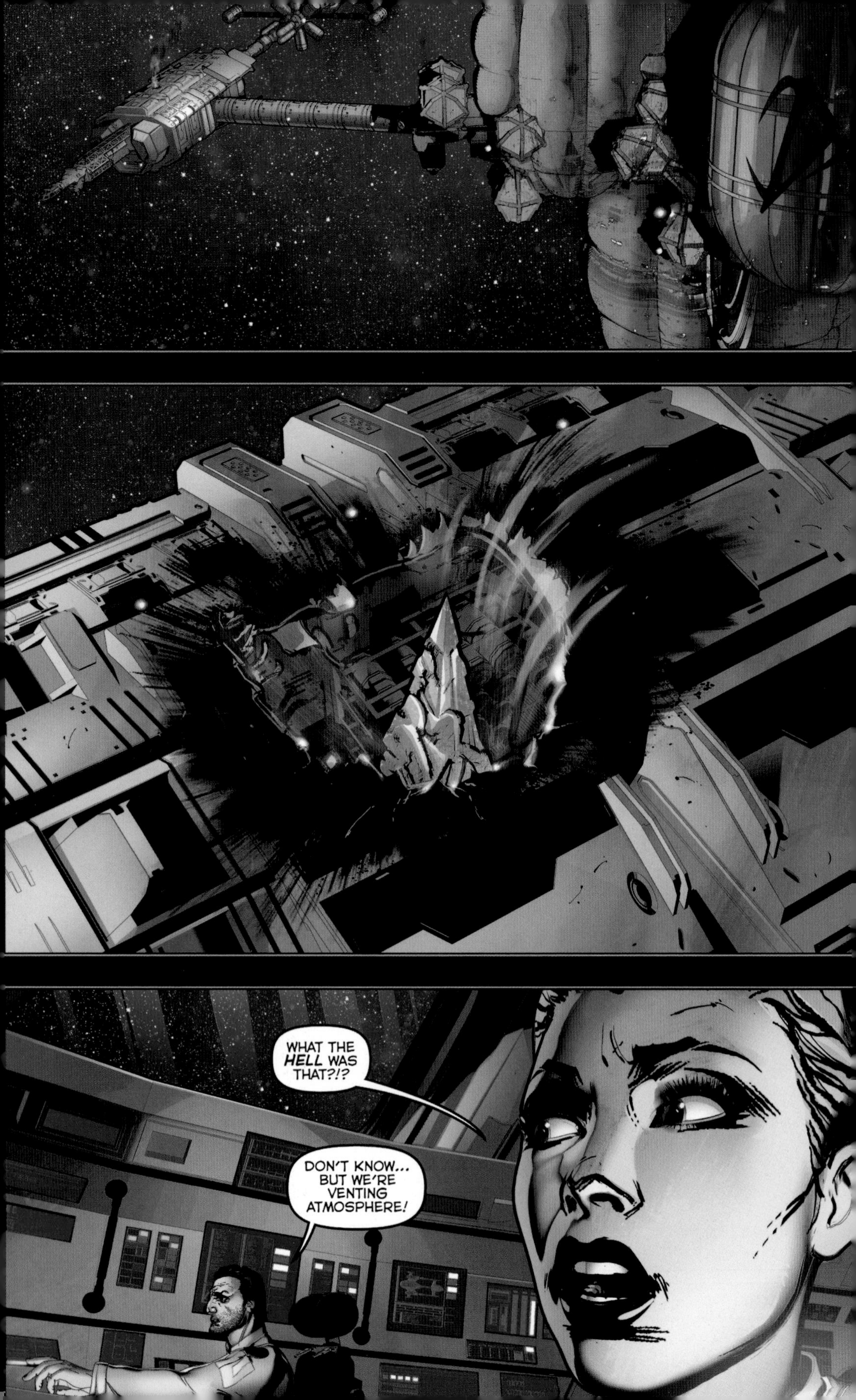
WHAT THE HELL WAS THAT?!?
DON'T KNOW... BUT WE'RE VENTING ATMOSPHERE!

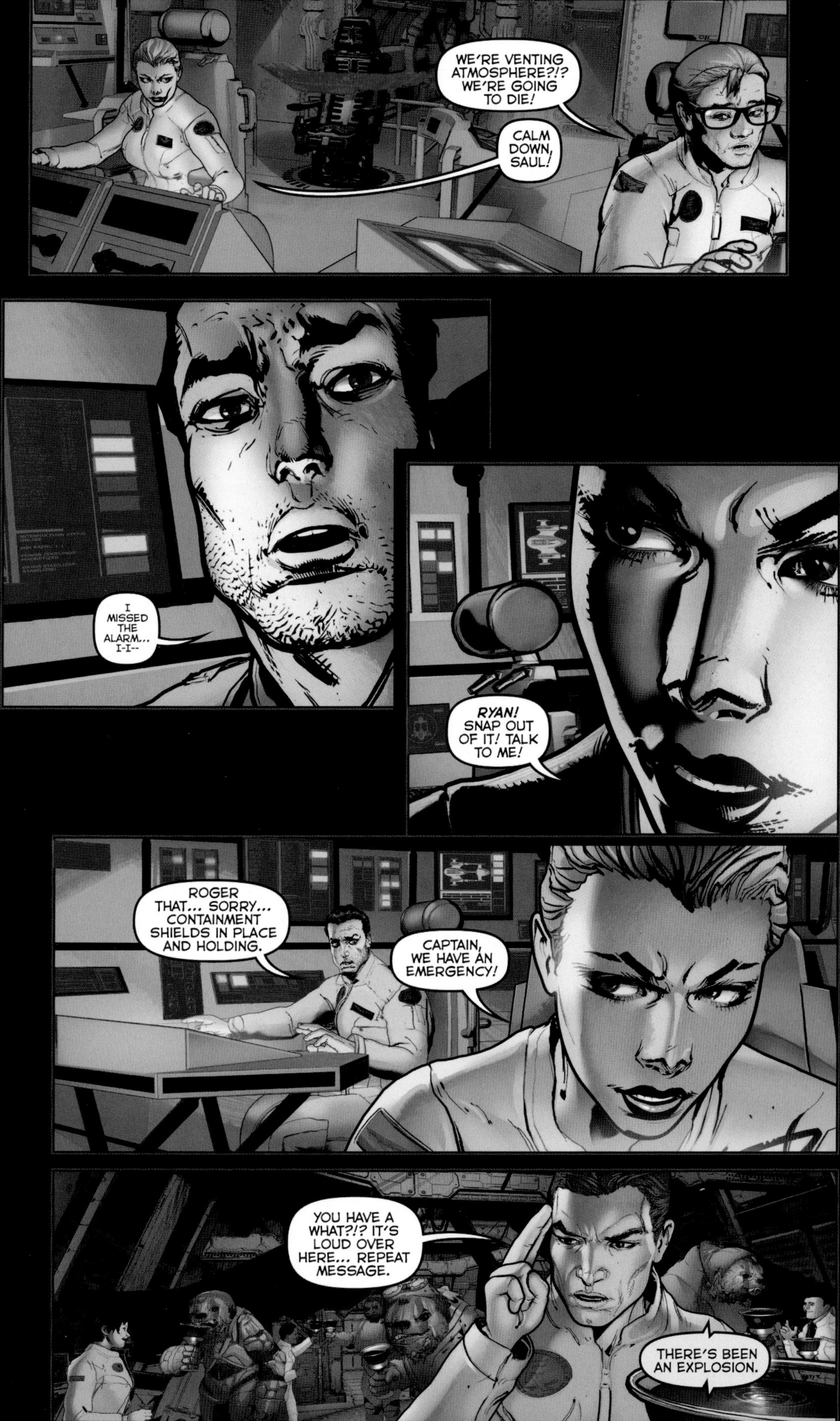
WE'RE VENTING ATMOSPHERE?!? WE'RE GOING TO DIE!
CALM DOWN, SAUL!
I MISSED THE ALARM... I-I--
RYAN! SNAP OUT OF IT! TALK TO ME!
ROGER THAT... SORRY... CONTAINMENT SHIELDS IN PLACE AND HOLDING.
CAPTAIN, WE HAVE AN EMERGENCY!
YOU HAVE A WHAT?!? IT'S LOUD OVER HERE... REPEAT MESSAGE.
THERE'S BEEN AN EXPLOSION.

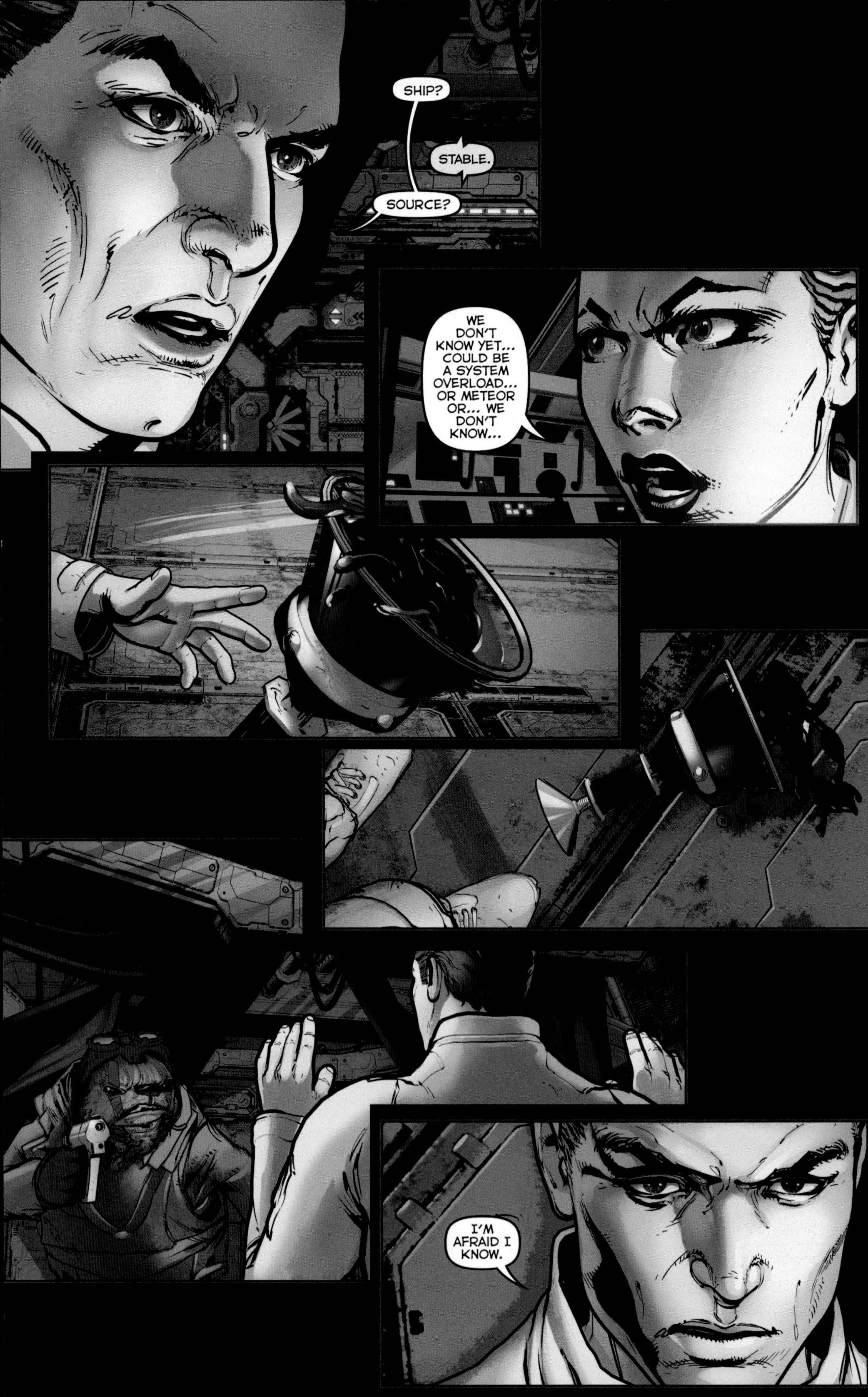
SHIP?
STABLE.
SOURCE?
WE DON'T KNOW YET... COULD BE A SYSTEM OVERLOAD... OR METEOR OR... WE DON'T KNOW...
I'M AFRAID I KNOW.

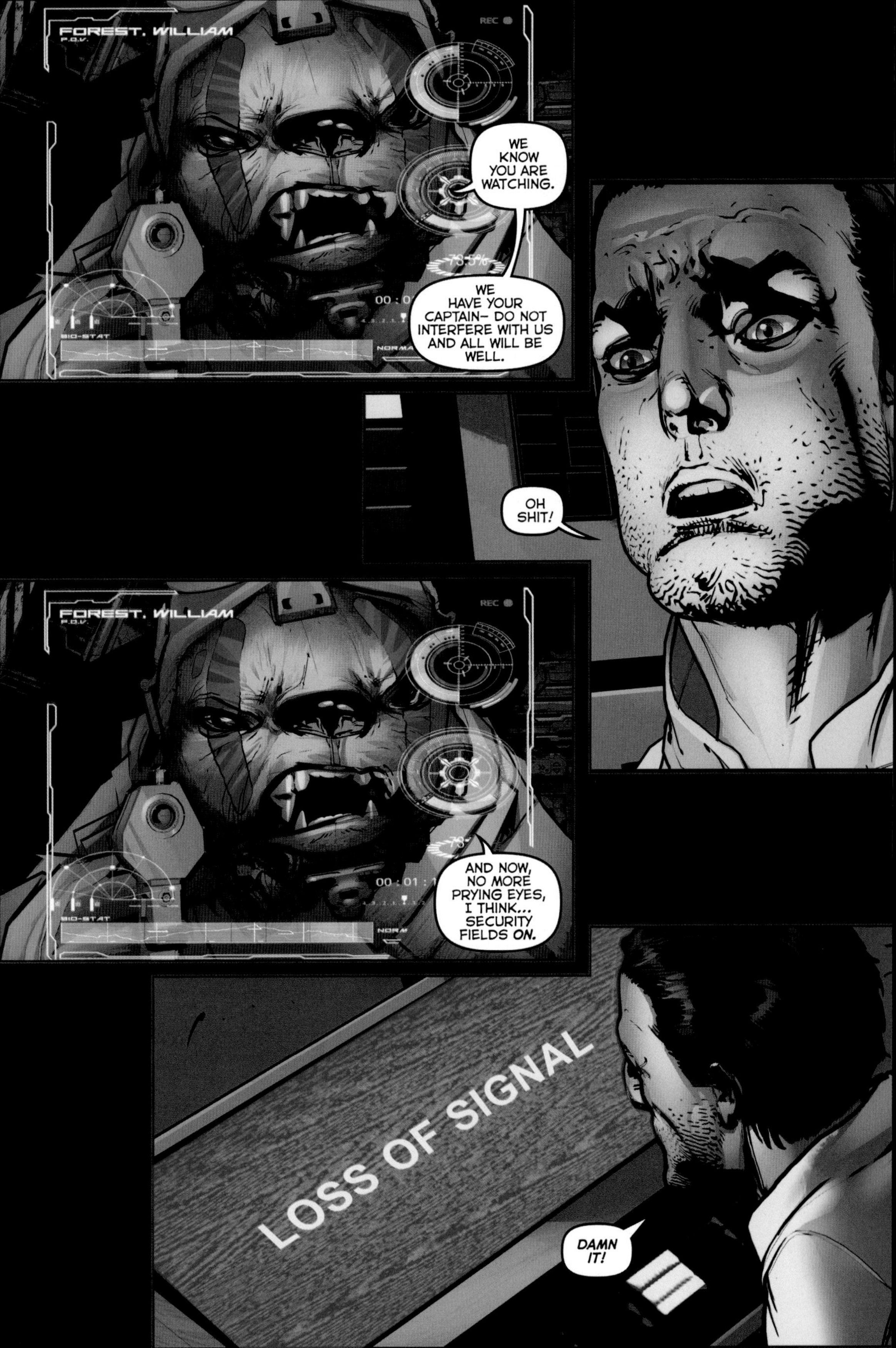
FOREST, WILLIAM
P.O.V.
REC
WE KNOW YOU ARE WATCHING.
WE HAVE YOUR CAPTAIN– DO NOT INTERFERE WITH US AND ALL WILL BE WELL.
BIO-STAT
OH SHIT!
FOREST, WILLIAM
P.O.V.
REC
AND NOW, NO MORE PRYING EYES, I THINK... SECURITY FIELDS *ON.*
BIO-STAT
LOSS OF SIGNAL
DAMN IT!

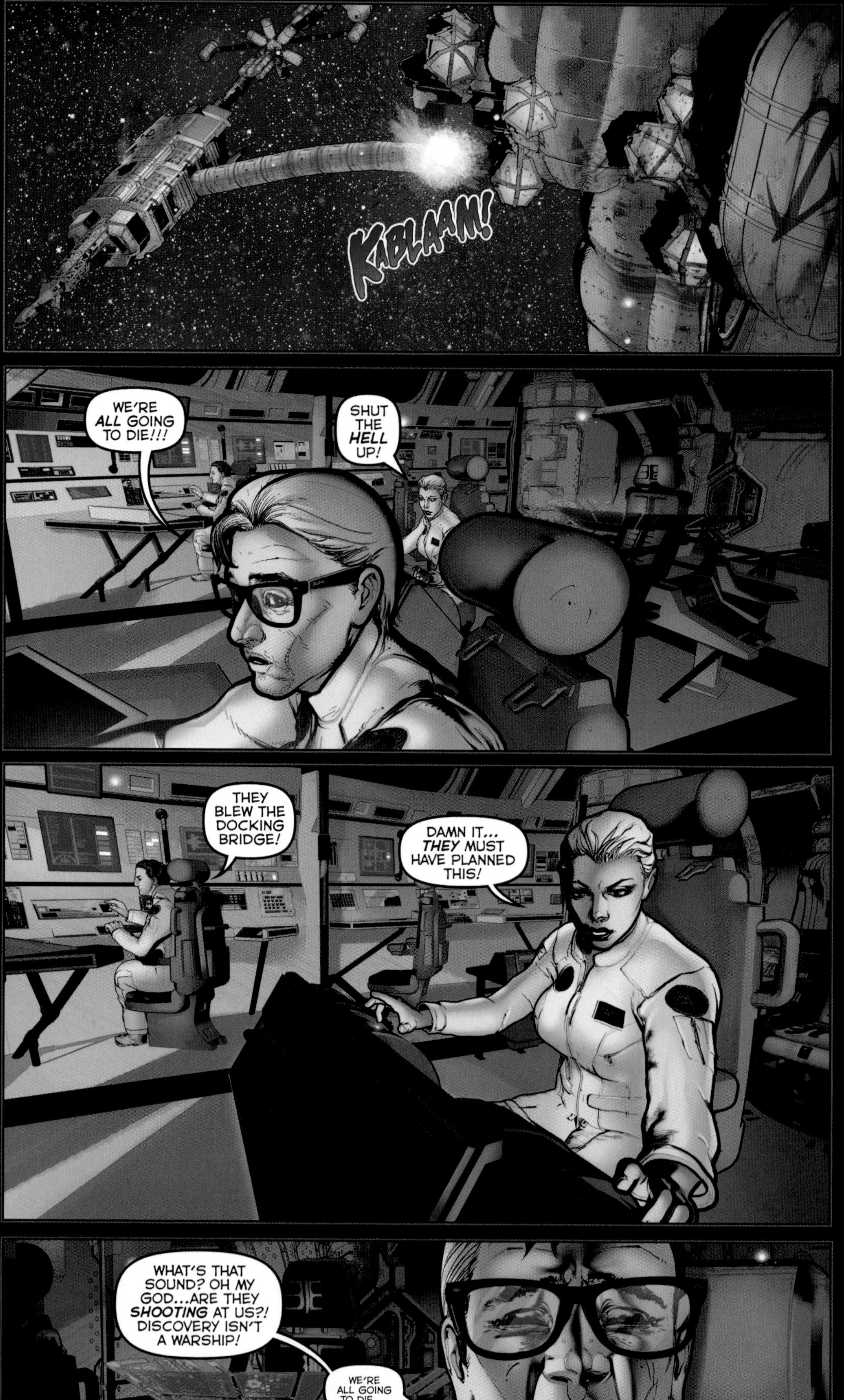
KABLAAM!
WE'RE ALL GOING TO DIE!!!
SHUT THE HELL UP!
THEY BLEW THE DOCKING BRIDGE!
DAMN IT... THEY MUST HAVE PLANNED THIS!
WHAT'S THAT SOUND? OH MY GOD...ARE THEY SHOOTING AT US?! DISCOVERY ISN'T A WARSHIP!
WE'RE ALL GOING TO DIE....

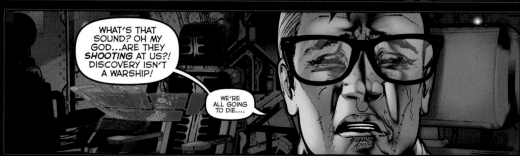

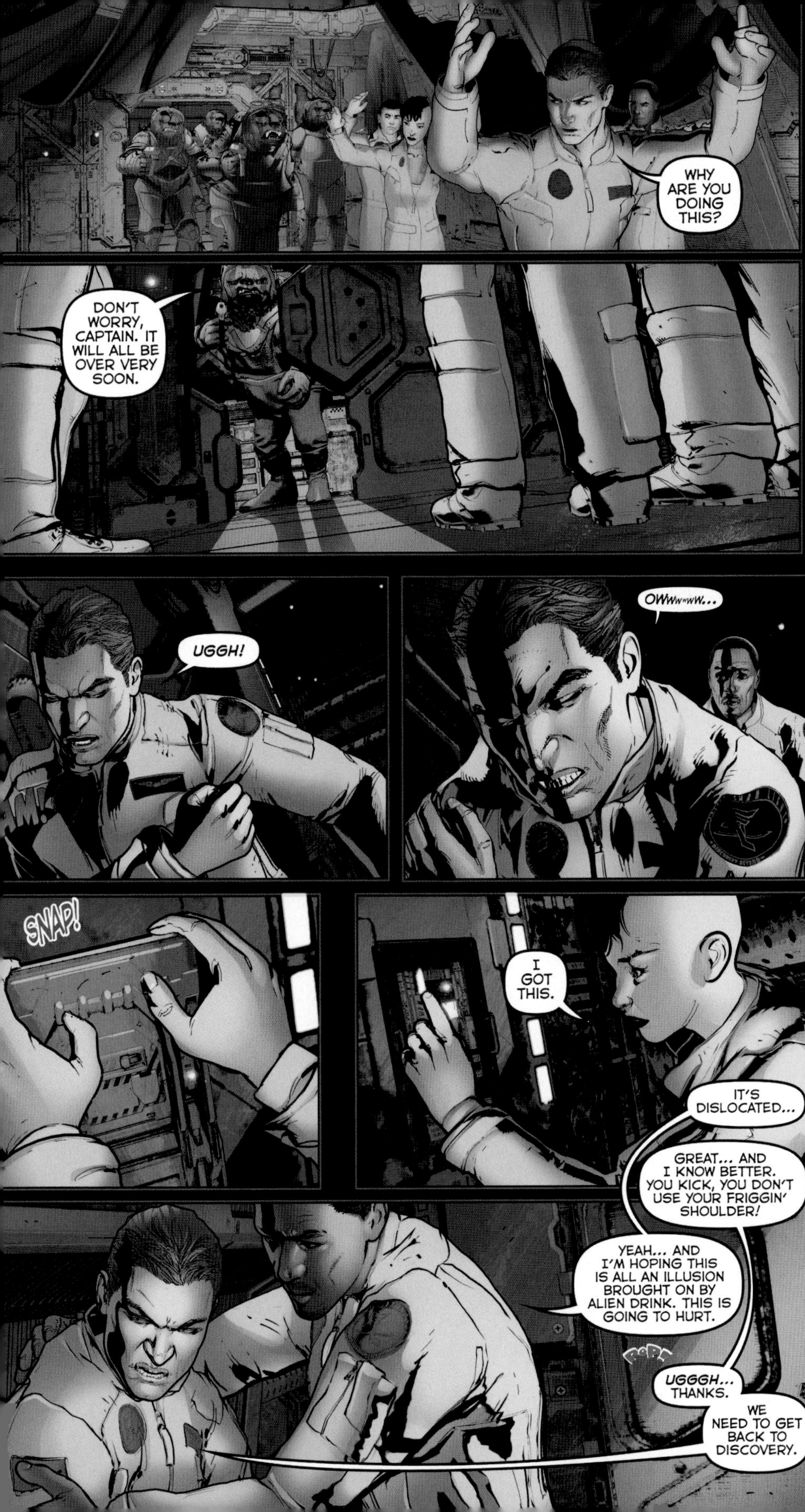
WHY ARE YOU DOING THIS?
DON'T WORRY, CAPTAIN. IT WILL ALL BE OVER VERY SOON.
UGGH!
OWWwwwW...
SNAP!
I GOT THIS.
IT'S DISLOCATED...
GREAT... AND I KNOW BETTER. YOU KICK, YOU DON'T USE YOUR FRIGGIN' SHOULDER!
YEAH... AND I'M HOPING THIS IS ALL AN ILLUSION BROUGHT ON BY ALIEN DRINK. THIS IS GOING TO HURT.
UGGGH... THANKS.
WE NEED TO GET BACK TO DISCOVERY.

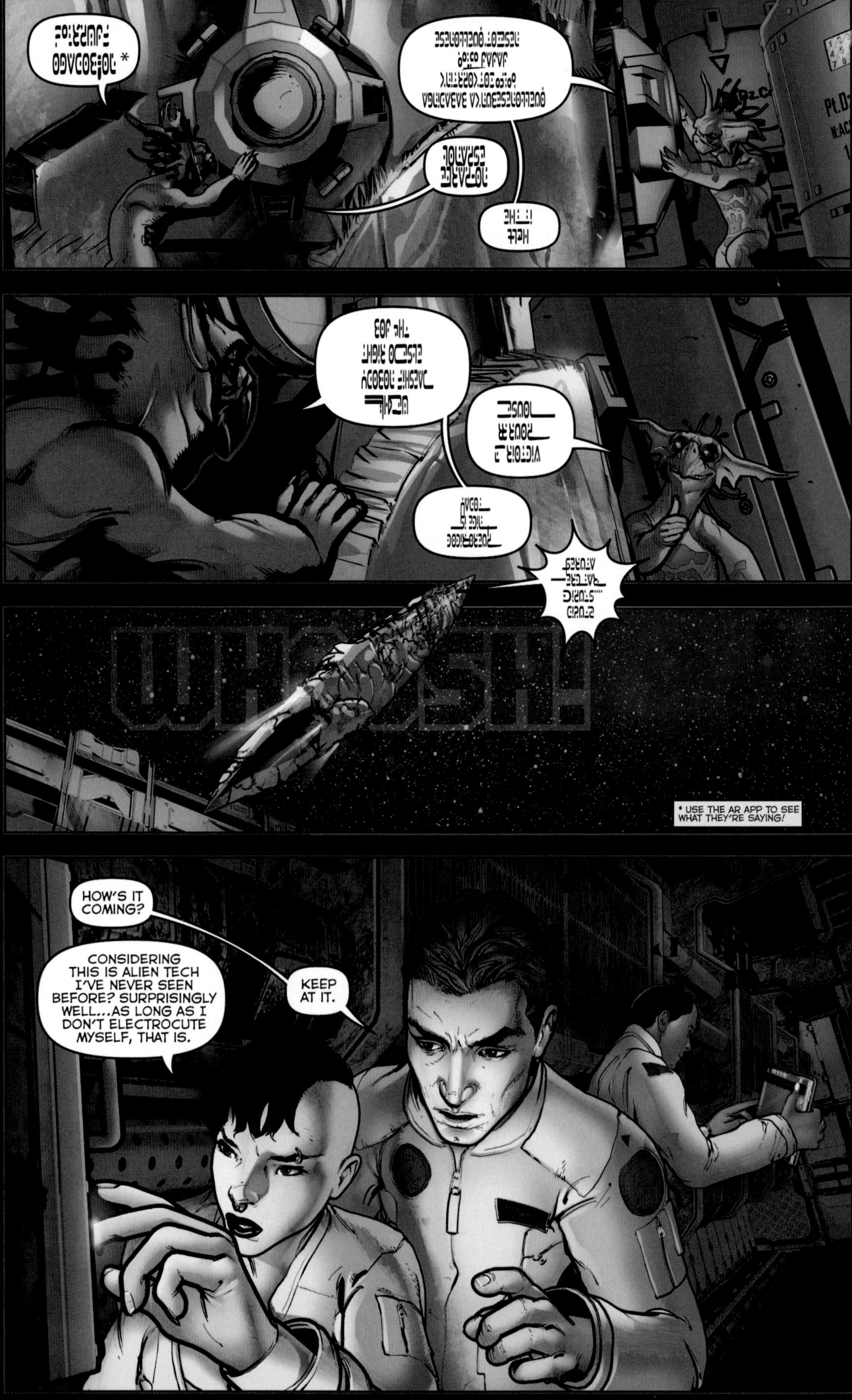
* USE THE AR APP TO SEE WHAT THEY'RE SAYING!
HOW'S IT COMING?
CONSIDERING THIS IS ALIEN TECH I'VE NEVER SEEN BEFORE? SURPRISINGLY WELL...AS LONG AS I DON'T ELECTROCUTE MYSELF, THAT IS.
KEEP AT IT.

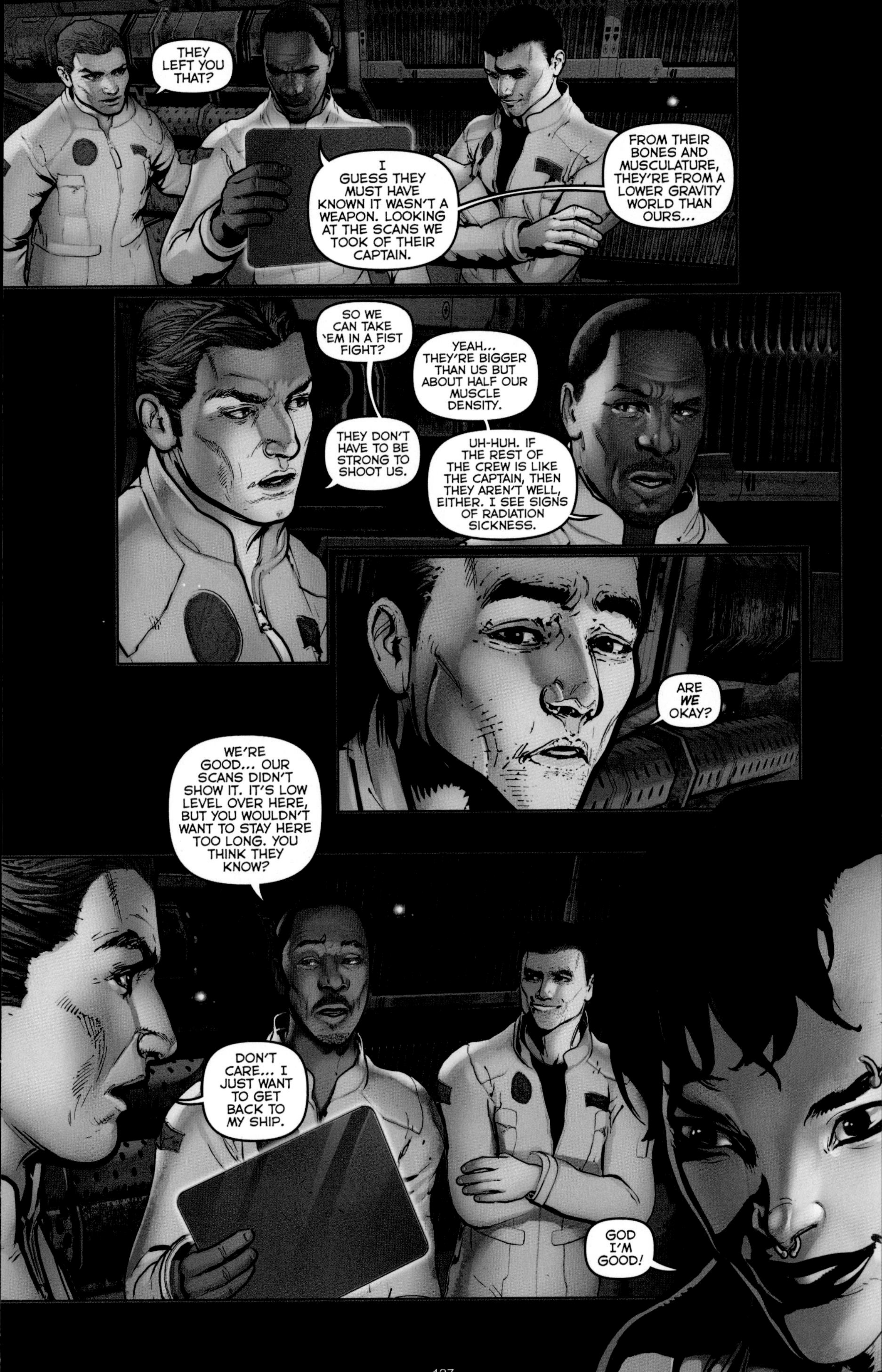
THEY LEFT YOU THAT?
I GUESS THEY MUST HAVE KNOWN IT WASN'T A WEAPON. LOOKING AT THE SCANS WE TOOK OF THEIR CAPTAIN.
FROM THEIR BONES AND MUSCULATURE, THEY'RE FROM A LOWER GRAVITY WORLD THAN OURS...
SO WE CAN TAKE 'EM IN A FIST FIGHT?
YEAH... THEY'RE BIGGER THAN US BUT ABOUT HALF OUR MUSCLE DENSITY.
THEY DON'T HAVE TO BE STRONG TO SHOOT US.
UH-HUH. IF THE REST OF THE CREW IS LIKE THE CAPTAIN, THEN THEY AREN'T WELL, EITHER. I SEE SIGNS OF RADIATION SICKNESS.
ARE *WE* OKAY?
WE'RE GOOD... OUR SCANS DIDN'T SHOW IT. IT'S LOW LEVEL OVER HERE, BUT YOU WOULDN'T WANT TO STAY HERE TOO LONG. YOU THINK THEY KNOW?
DON'T CARE... I JUST WANT TO GET BACK TO MY SHIP.
GOD I'M GOOD!

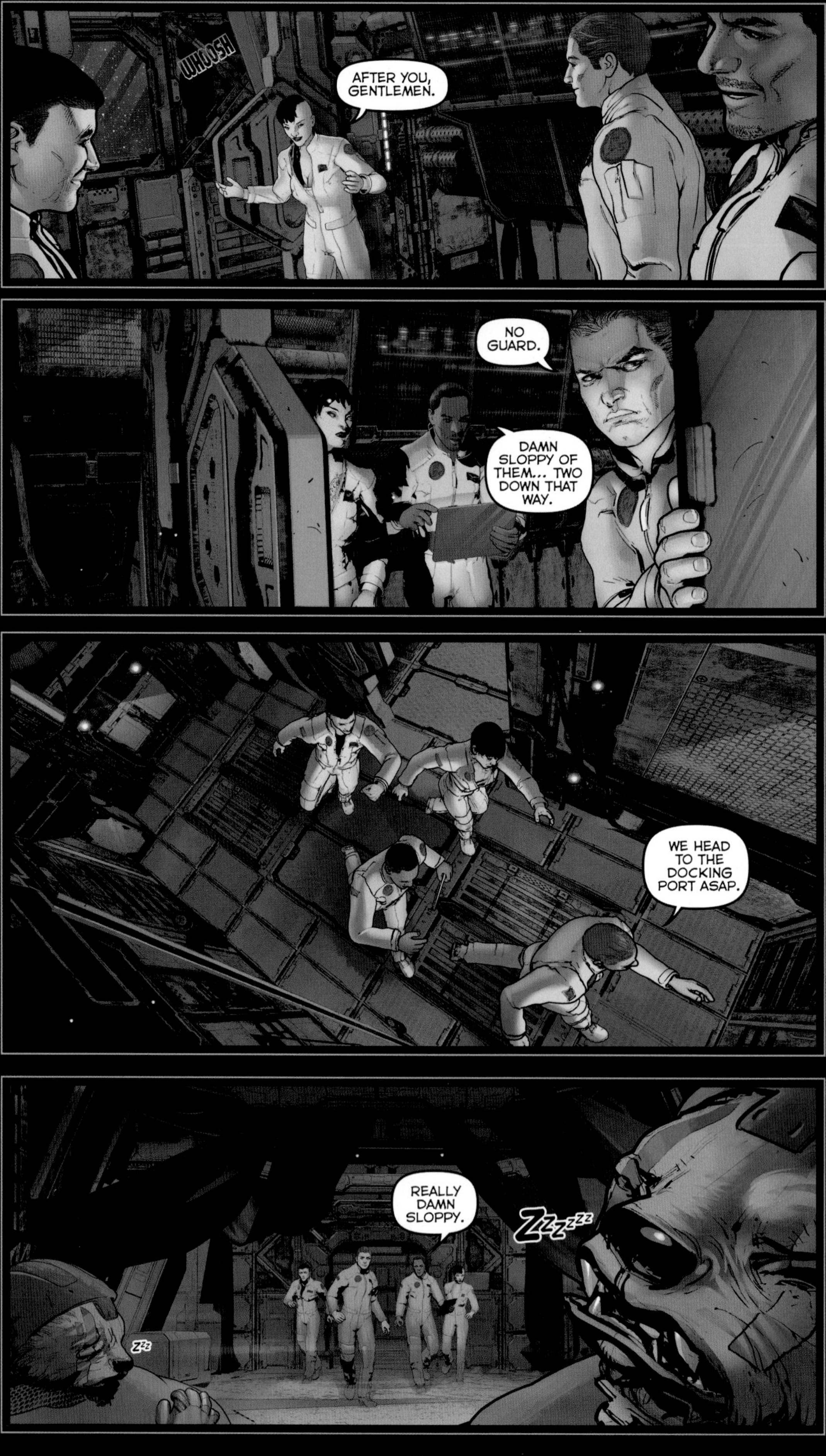
WHOOSH
AFTER YOU, GENTLEMEN.
NO GUARD.
DAMN SLOPPY OF THEM... TWO DOWN THAT WAY.
WE HEAD TO THE DOCKING PORT ASAP.
REALLY DAMN SLOPPY.
ZZzzzz
ZZz

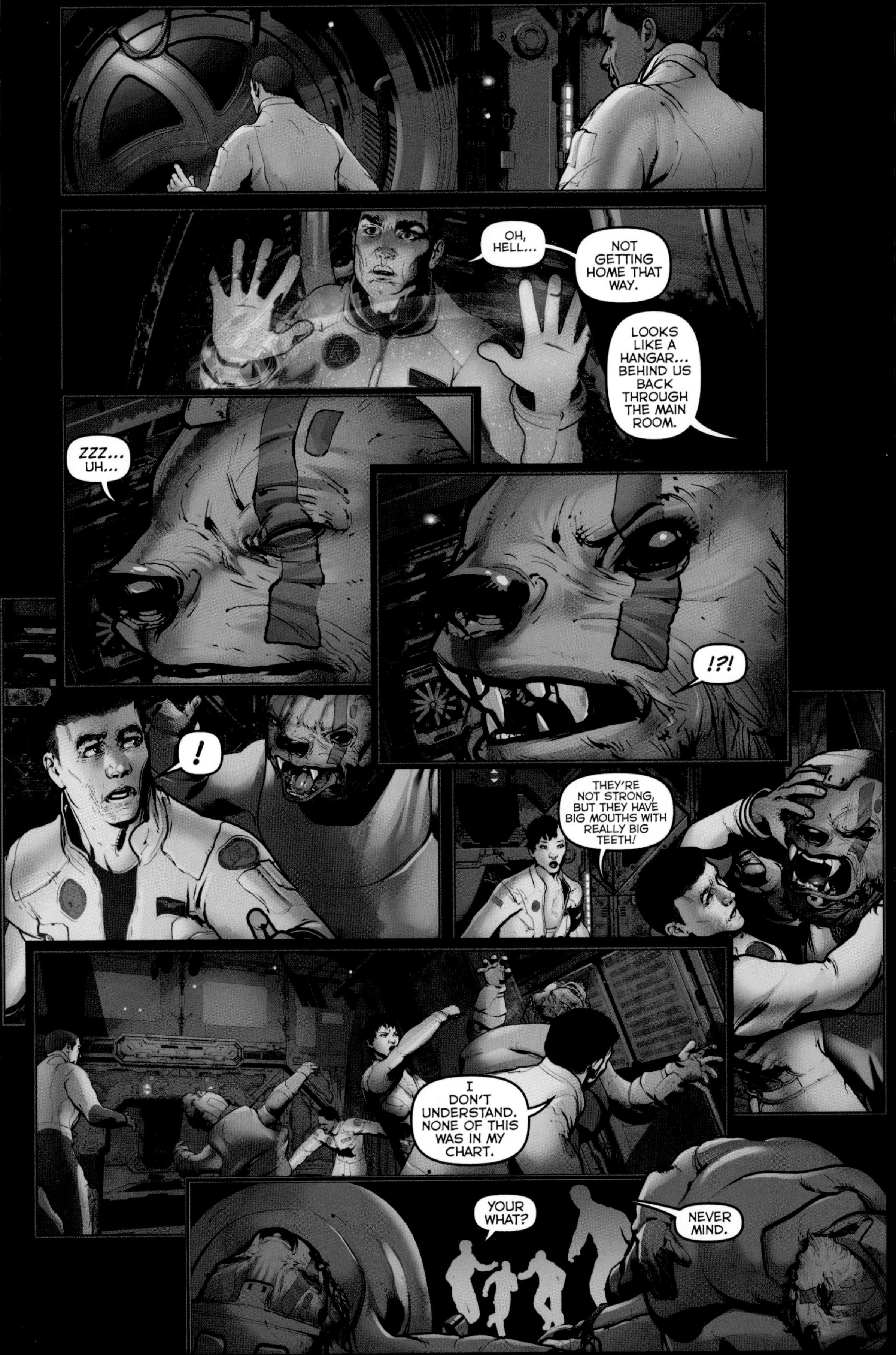
OH, HELL...
NOT GETTING HOME THAT WAY.
LOOKS LIKE A HANGAR... BEHIND US BACK THROUGH THE MAIN ROOM.
ZZZ... UH...
!?!
!
THEY'RE NOT STRONG, BUT THEY HAVE BIG MOUTHS WITH REALLY BIG TEETH!
I DON'T UNDERSTAND. NONE OF THIS WAS IN MY CHART.
YOUR WHAT?
NEVER MIND.

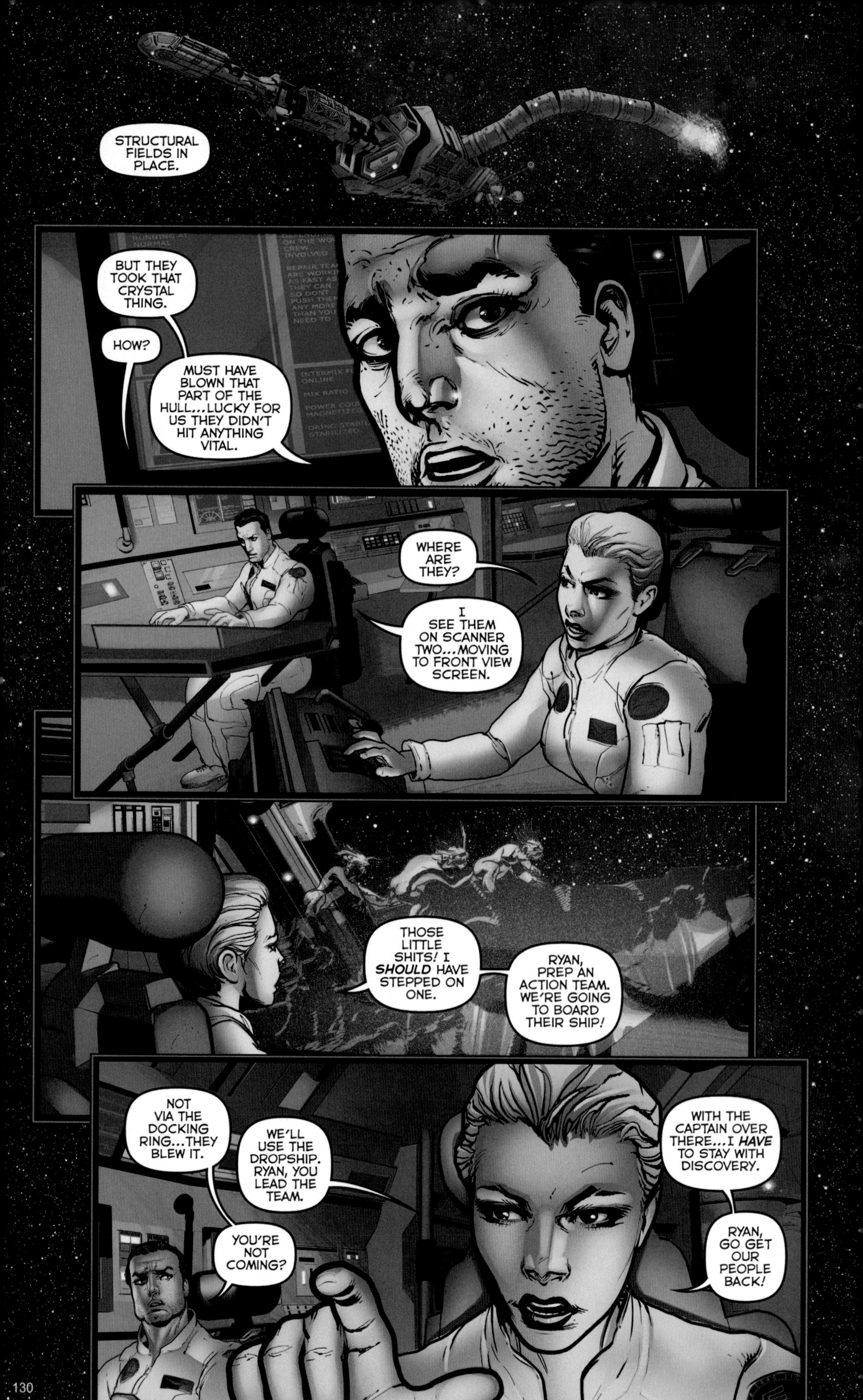
STRUCTURAL FIELDS IN PLACE.
BUT THEY TOOK THAT CRYSTAL THING.
HOW?
MUST HAVE BLOWN THAT PART OF THE HULL...LUCKY FOR US THEY DIDN'T HIT ANYTHING VITAL.
WHERE ARE THEY?
I SEE THEM ON SCANNER TWO...MOVING TO FRONT VIEW SCREEN.
THOSE LITTLE SHITS! I SHOULD HAVE STEPPED ON ONE.
RYAN, PREP AN ACTION TEAM. WE'RE GOING TO BOARD THEIR SHIP!
NOT VIA THE DOCKING RING...THEY BLEW IT.
WE'LL USE THE DROPSHIP. RYAN, YOU LEAD THE TEAM.
YOU'RE NOT COMING?
WITH THE CAPTAIN OVER THERE...I HAVE TO STAY WITH DISCOVERY.
RYAN, GO GET OUR PEOPLE BACK!

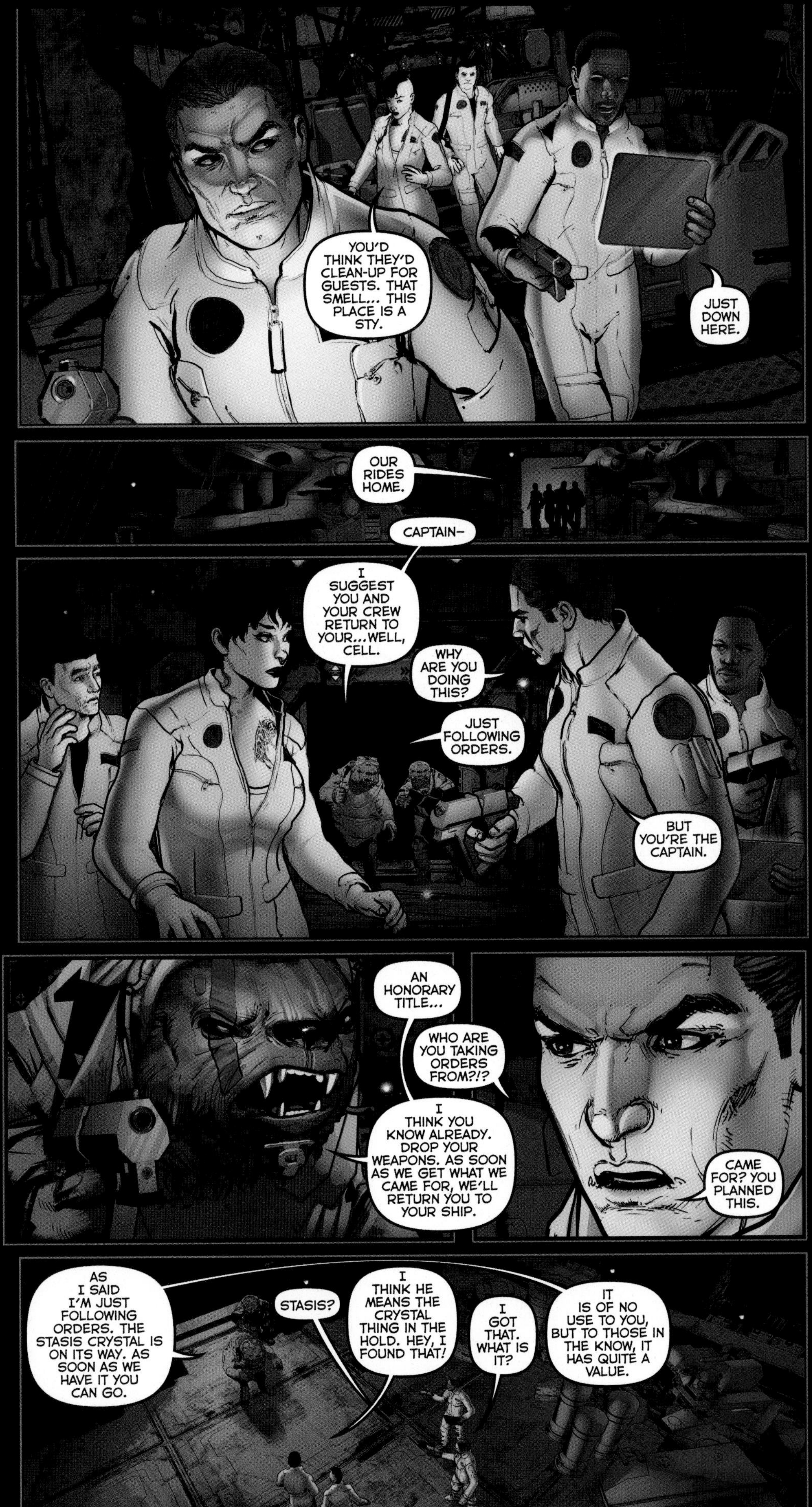
YOU'D THINK THEY'D CLEAN-UP FOR GUESTS. THAT SMELL... THIS PLACE IS A STY.
JUST DOWN HERE.
OUR RIDES HOME.
CAPTAIN—
I SUGGEST YOU AND YOUR CREW RETURN TO YOUR...WELL, CELL.
WHY ARE YOU DOING THIS?
JUST FOLLOWING ORDERS.
BUT YOU'RE THE CAPTAIN.
AN HONORARY TITLE...
WHO ARE YOU TAKING ORDERS FROM?!?
I THINK YOU KNOW ALREADY. DROP YOUR WEAPONS. AS SOON AS WE GET WHAT WE CAME FOR, WE'LL RETURN YOU TO YOUR SHIP.
CAME FOR? YOU PLANNED THIS.
AS I SAID I'M JUST FOLLOWING ORDERS. THE STASIS CRYSTAL IS ON ITS WAY. AS SOON AS WE HAVE IT YOU CAN GO.
STASIS?
I THINK HE MEANS THE CRYSTAL THING IN THE HOLD. HEY, I FOUND THAT!
I GOT THAT. WHAT IS IT?
IT IS OF NO USE TO YOU, BUT TO THOSE IN THE KNOW, IT HAS QUITE A VALUE.

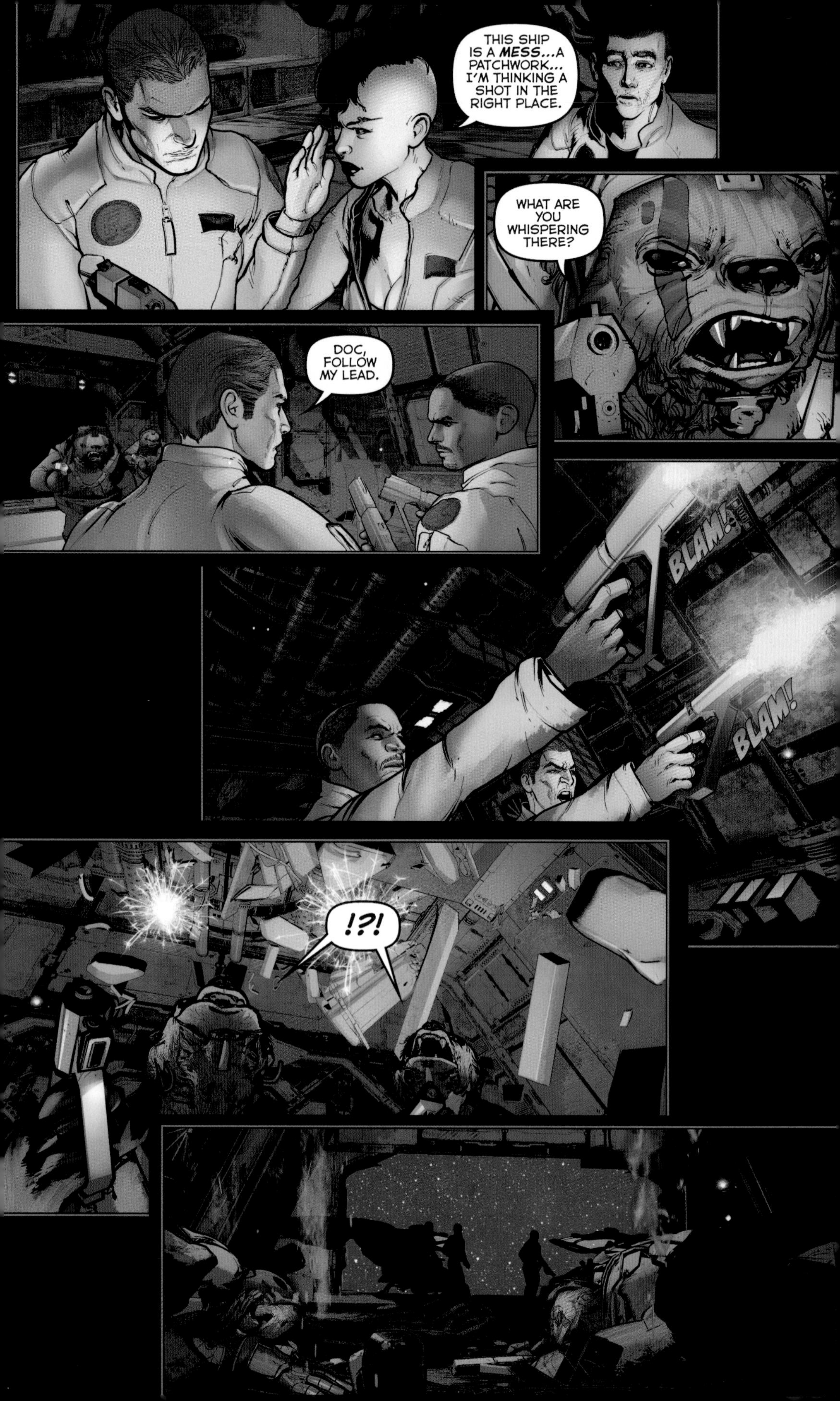
THIS SHIP IS A MESS...A PATCHWORK... I'M THINKING A SHOT IN THE RIGHT PLACE.
WHAT ARE YOU WHISPERING THERE?
DOC, FOLLOW MY LEAD.
BLAM!
BLAM!
!?!

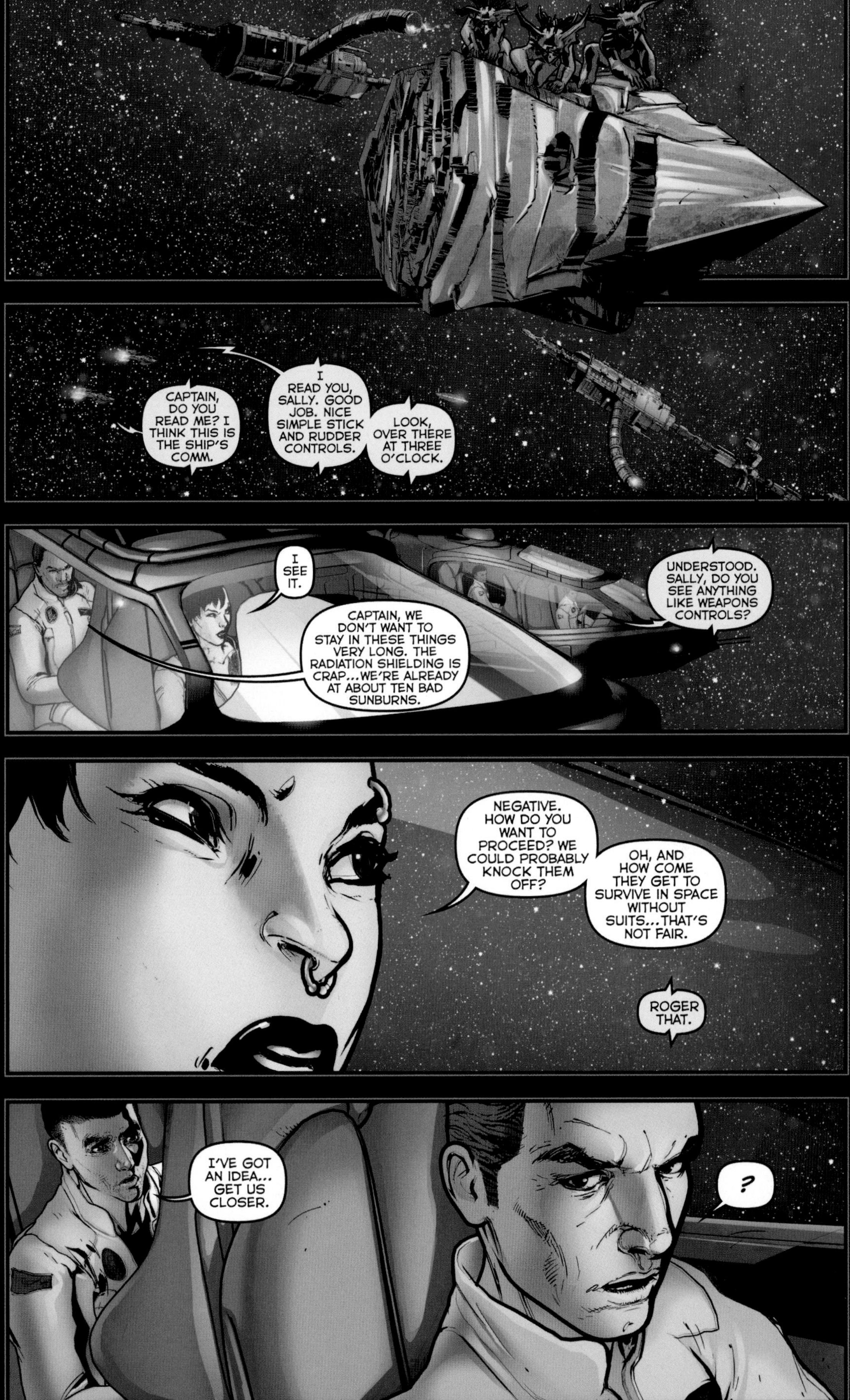
CAPTAIN, DO YOU READ ME? I THINK THIS IS THE SHIP'S COMM.
I READ YOU, SALLY. GOOD JOB. NICE SIMPLE STICK AND RUDDER CONTROLS.
LOOK, OVER THERE AT THREE O'CLOCK.
I SEE IT.
CAPTAIN, WE DON'T WANT TO STAY IN THESE THINGS VERY LONG. THE RADIATION SHIELDING IS CRAP...WE'RE ALREADY AT ABOUT TEN BAD SUNBURNS.
UNDERSTOOD. SALLY, DO YOU SEE ANYTHING LIKE WEAPONS CONTROLS?
NEGATIVE. HOW DO YOU WANT TO PROCEED? WE COULD PROBABLY KNOCK THEM OFF?
OH, AND HOW COME THEY GET TO SURVIVE IN SPACE WITHOUT SUITS...THAT'S NOT FAIR.
ROGER THAT.
I'VE GOT AN IDEA... GET US CLOSER.
?

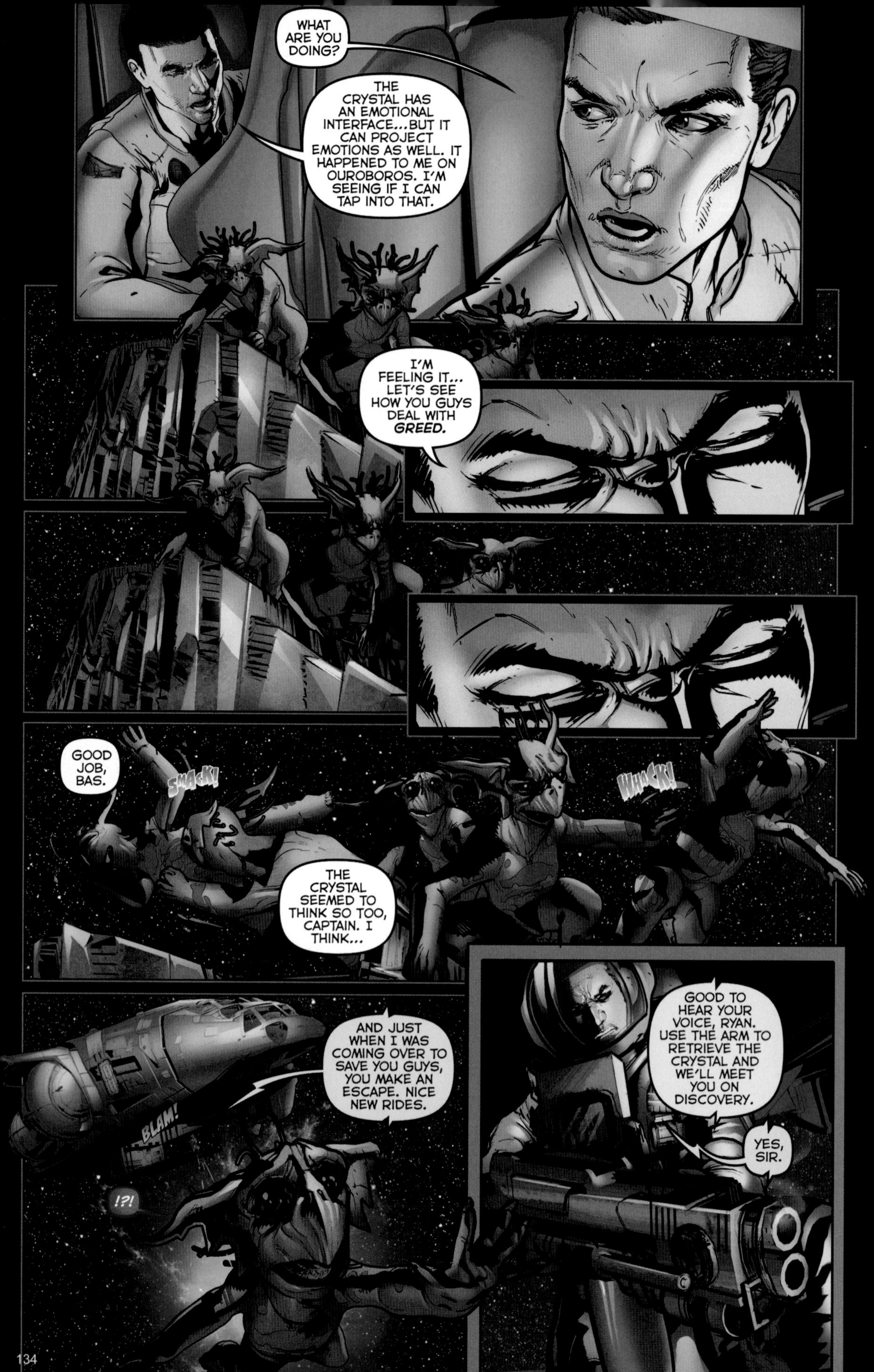
WHAT ARE YOU DOING?
THE CRYSTAL HAS AN EMOTIONAL INTERFACE...BUT IT CAN PROJECT EMOTIONS AS WELL. IT HAPPENED TO ME ON OUROBOROS. I'M SEEING IF I CAN TAP INTO THAT.
I'M FEELING IT... LET'S SEE HOW YOU GUYS DEAL WITH *GREED.*
GOOD JOB, BAS.
SMACK!
WHACK!
THE CRYSTAL SEEMED TO THINK SO TOO, CAPTAIN. I THINK...
AND JUST WHEN I WAS COMING OVER TO SAVE YOU GUYS, YOU MAKE AN ESCAPE. NICE NEW RIDES.
BLAM!
!?!
GOOD TO HEAR YOUR VOICE, RYAN. USE THE ARM TO RETRIEVE THE CRYSTAL AND WE'LL MEET YOU ON DISCOVERY.
YES, SIR.

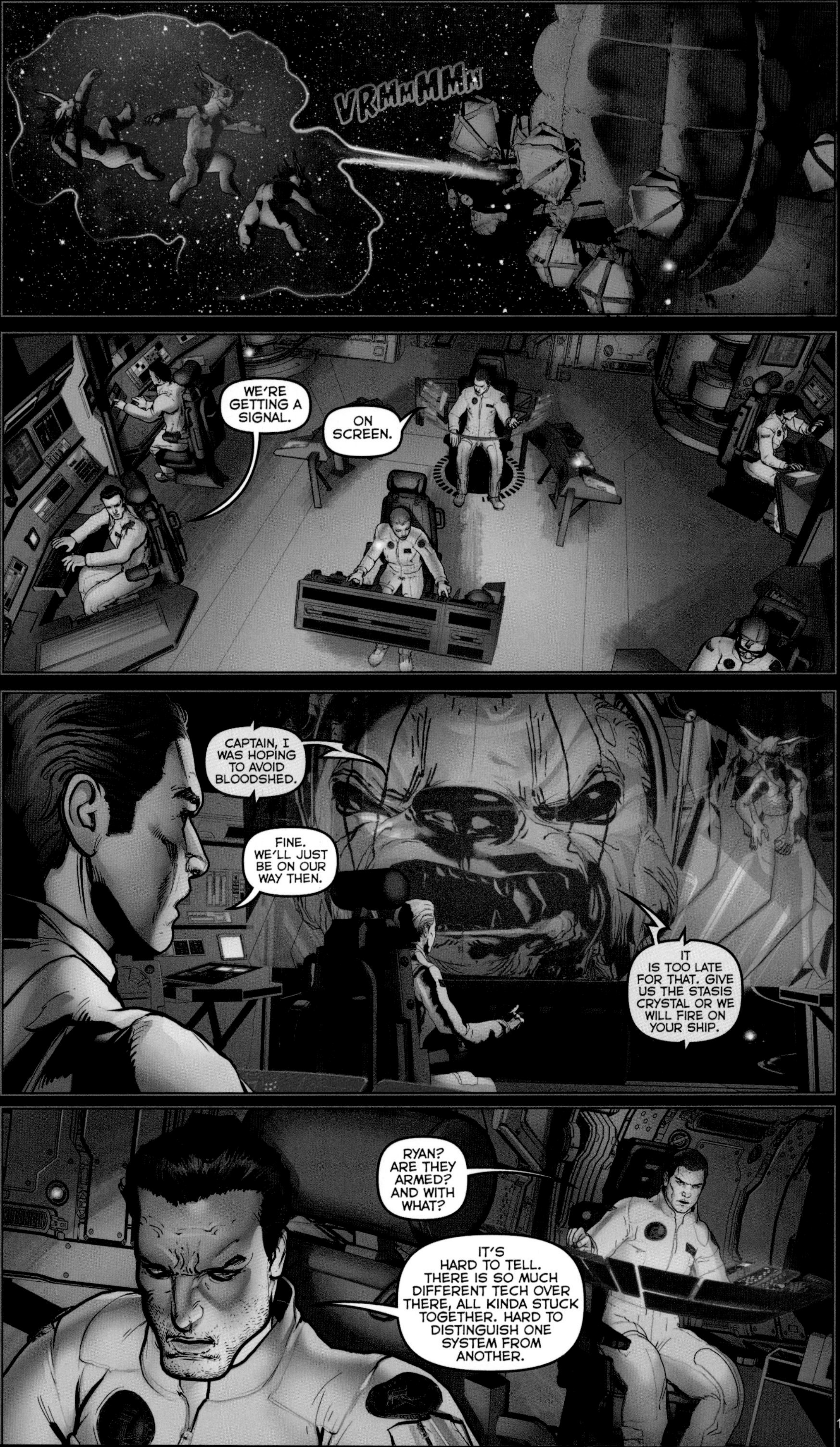
VRMMMMM
WE'RE GETTING A SIGNAL.
ON SCREEN.
CAPTAIN, I WAS HOPING TO AVOID BLOODSHED.
FINE. WE'LL JUST BE ON OUR WAY THEN.
IT IS TOO LATE FOR THAT. GIVE US THE STASIS CRYSTAL OR WE WILL FIRE ON YOUR SHIP.
RYAN? ARE THEY ARMED? AND WITH WHAT?
IT'S HARD TO TELL. THERE IS SO MUCH DIFFERENT TECH OVER THERE, ALL KINDA STUCK TOGETHER. HARD TO DISTINGUISH ONE SYSTEM FROM ANOTHER.

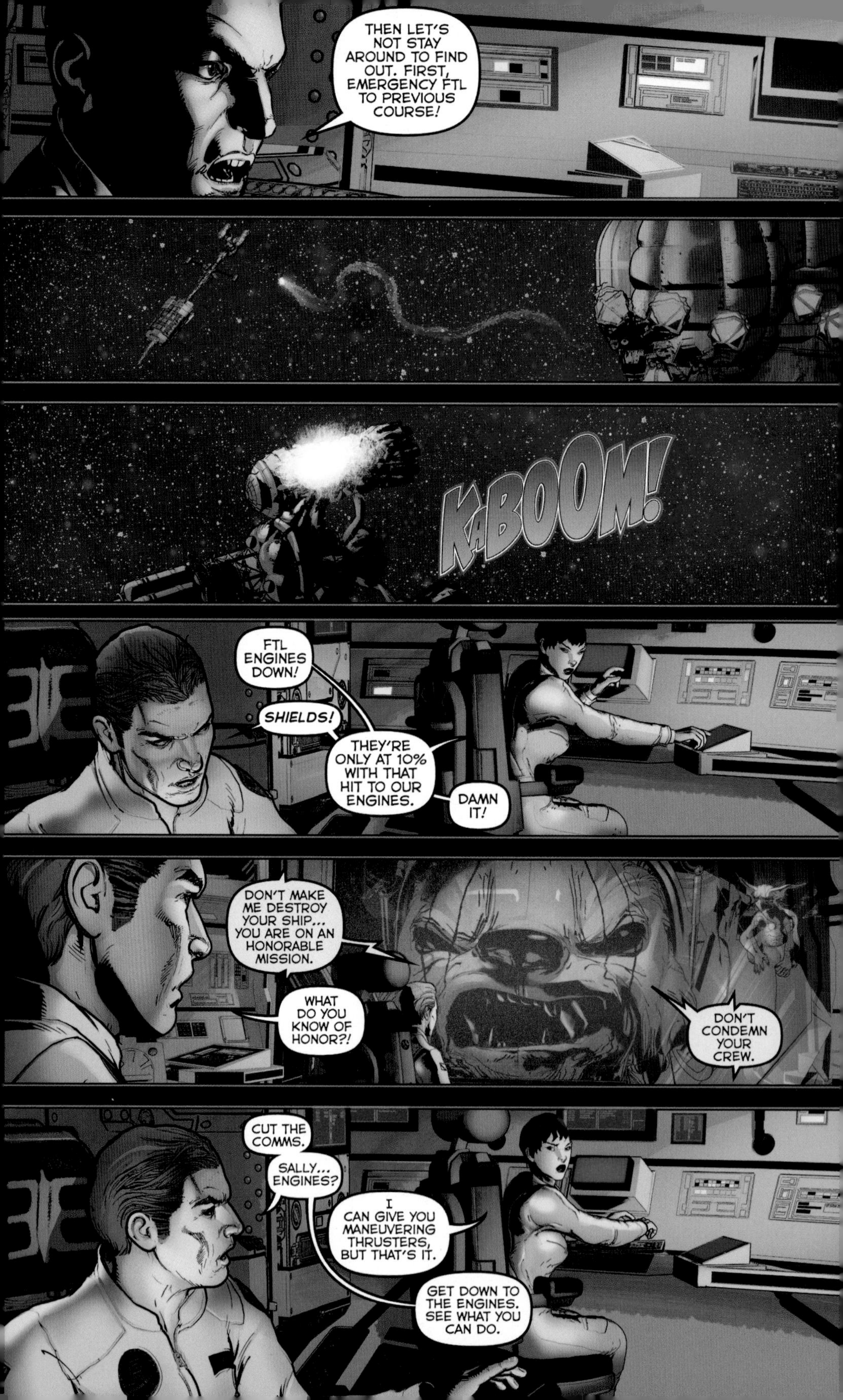
THEN LET'S NOT STAY AROUND TO FIND OUT. FIRST, EMERGENCY FTL TO PREVIOUS COURSE!
KABOOM!
FTL ENGINES DOWN!
SHIELDS!
THEY'RE ONLY AT 10% WITH THAT HIT TO OUR ENGINES.
DAMN IT!
DON'T MAKE ME DESTROY YOUR SHIP... YOU ARE ON AN HONORABLE MISSION.
WHAT DO YOU KNOW OF HONOR?!
DON'T CONDEMN YOUR CREW.
CUT THE COMMS.
SALLY... ENGINES?
I CAN GIVE YOU MANEUVERING THRUSTERS, BUT THAT'S IT.
GET DOWN TO THE ENGINES. SEE WHAT YOU CAN DO.

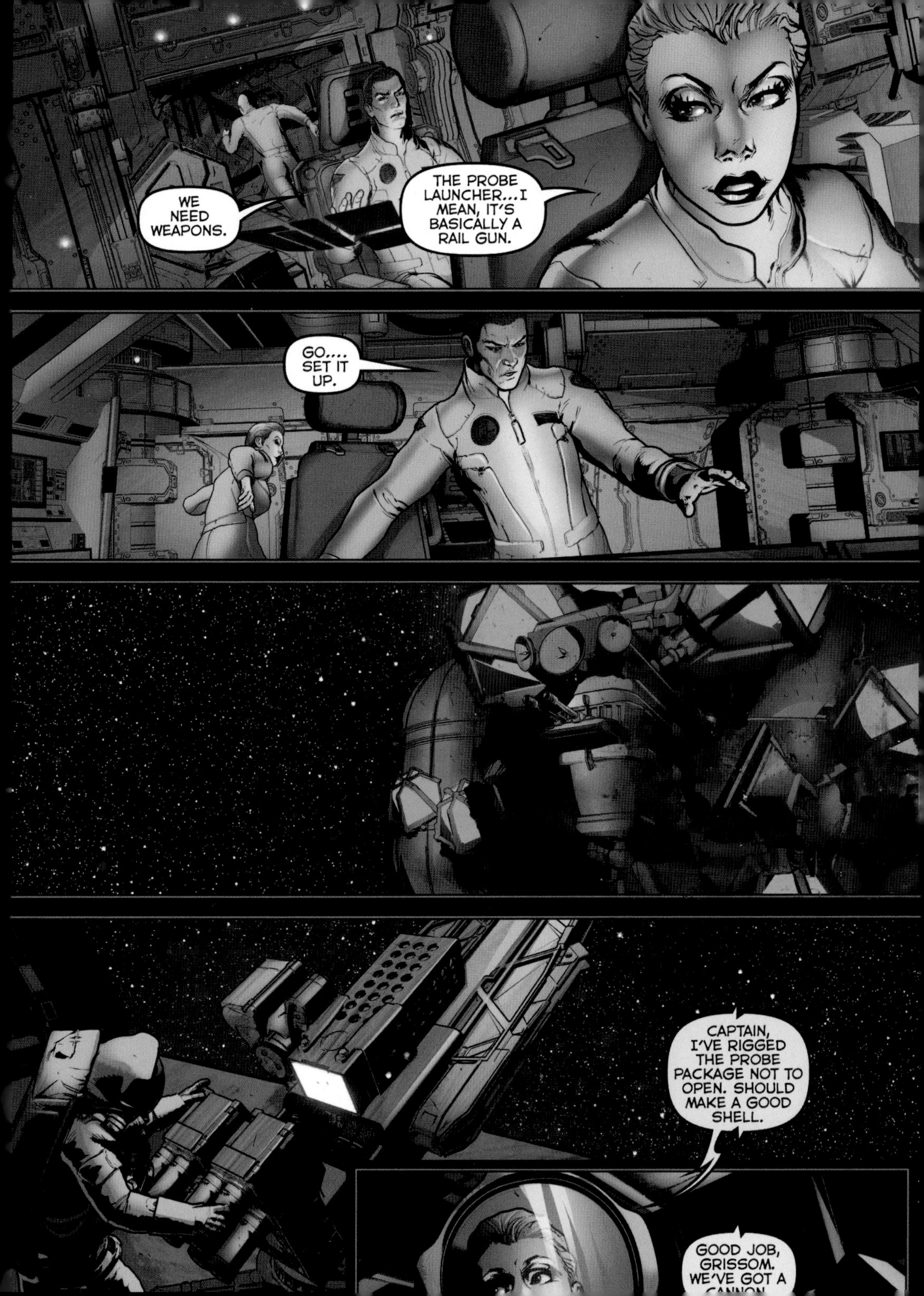
WE NEED WEAPONS.
THE PROBE LAUNCHER...I MEAN, IT'S BASICALLY A RAIL GUN.
GO.... SET IT UP.
CAPTAIN, I'VE RIGGED THE PROBE PACKAGE NOT TO OPEN. SHOULD MAKE A GOOD SHELL.
GOOD JOB, GRISSOM. WE'VE GOT A

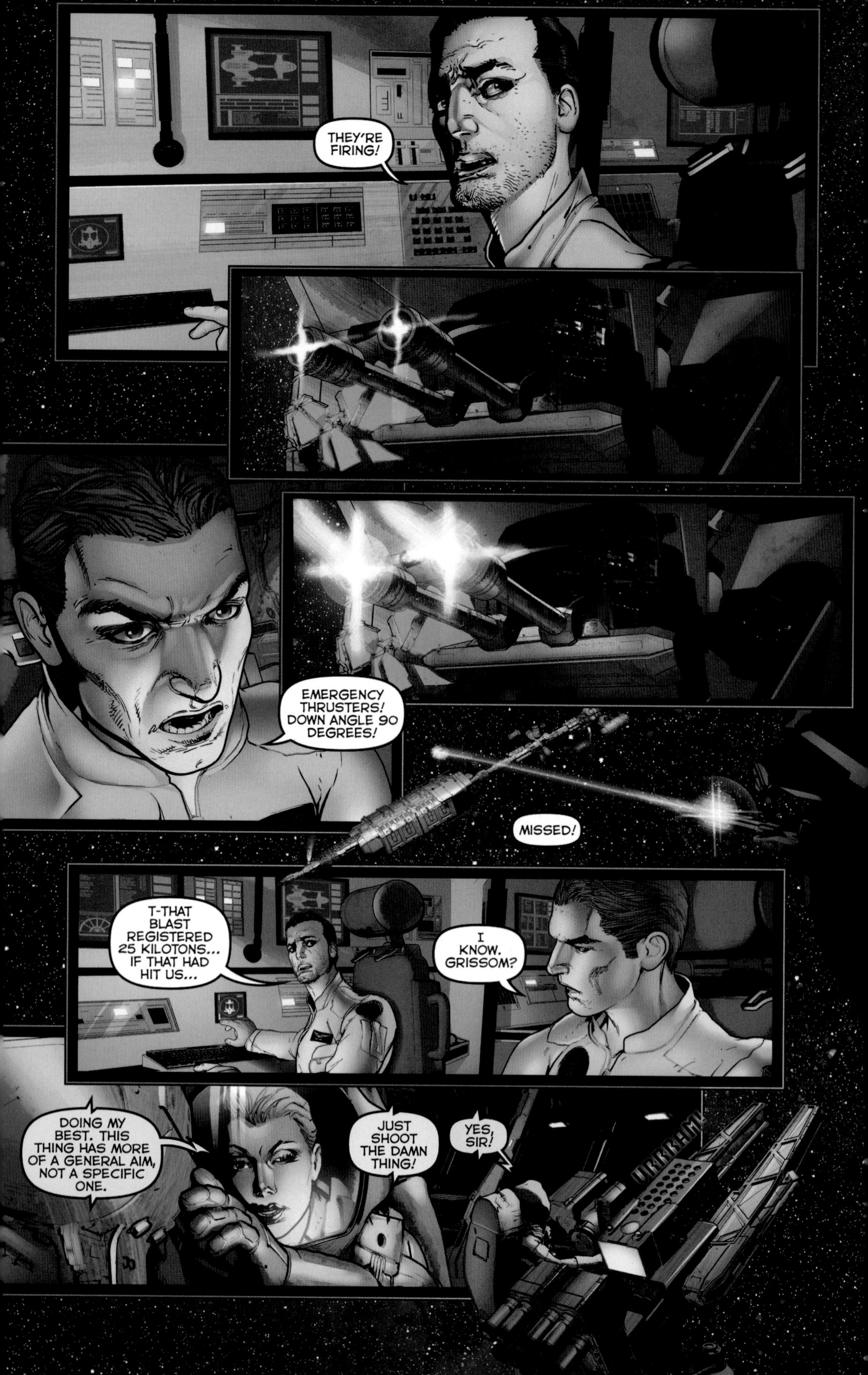
THEY'RE FIRING!
EMERGENCY THRUSTERS! DOWN ANGLE 90 DEGREES!
MISSED!
T-THAT BLAST REGISTERED 25 KILOTONS... IF THAT HAD HIT US...
I KNOW. GRISSOM?
DOING MY BEST. THIS THING HAS MORE OF A GENERAL AIM, NOT A SPECIFIC ONE.
JUST SHOOT THE DAMN THING!
YES, SIR!

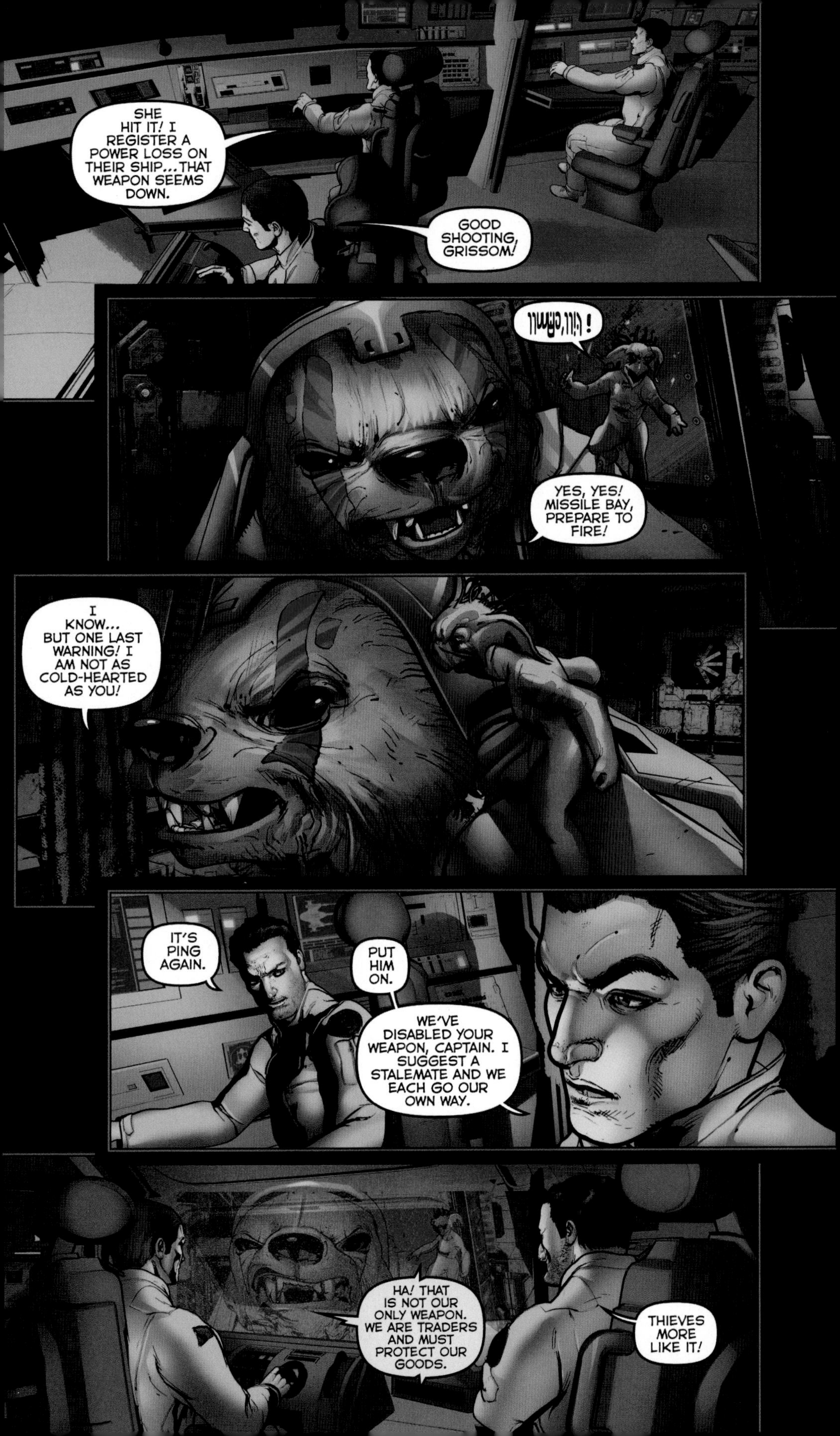
SHE HIT IT! I REGISTER A POWER LOSS ON THEIR SHIP...THAT WEAPON SEEMS DOWN.
GOOD SHOOTING, GRISSOM!
YES, YES! MISSILE BAY, PREPARE TO FIRE!
I KNOW... BUT ONE LAST WARNING! I AM NOT AS COLD-HEARTED AS YOU!
IT'S PING AGAIN.
PUT HIM ON.
WE'VE DISABLED YOUR WEAPON, CAPTAIN. I SUGGEST A STALEMATE AND WE EACH GO OUR OWN WAY.
HA! THAT IS NOT OUR ONLY WEAPON. WE ARE TRADERS AND MUST PROTECT OUR GOODS.
THIEVES MORE LIKE IT!

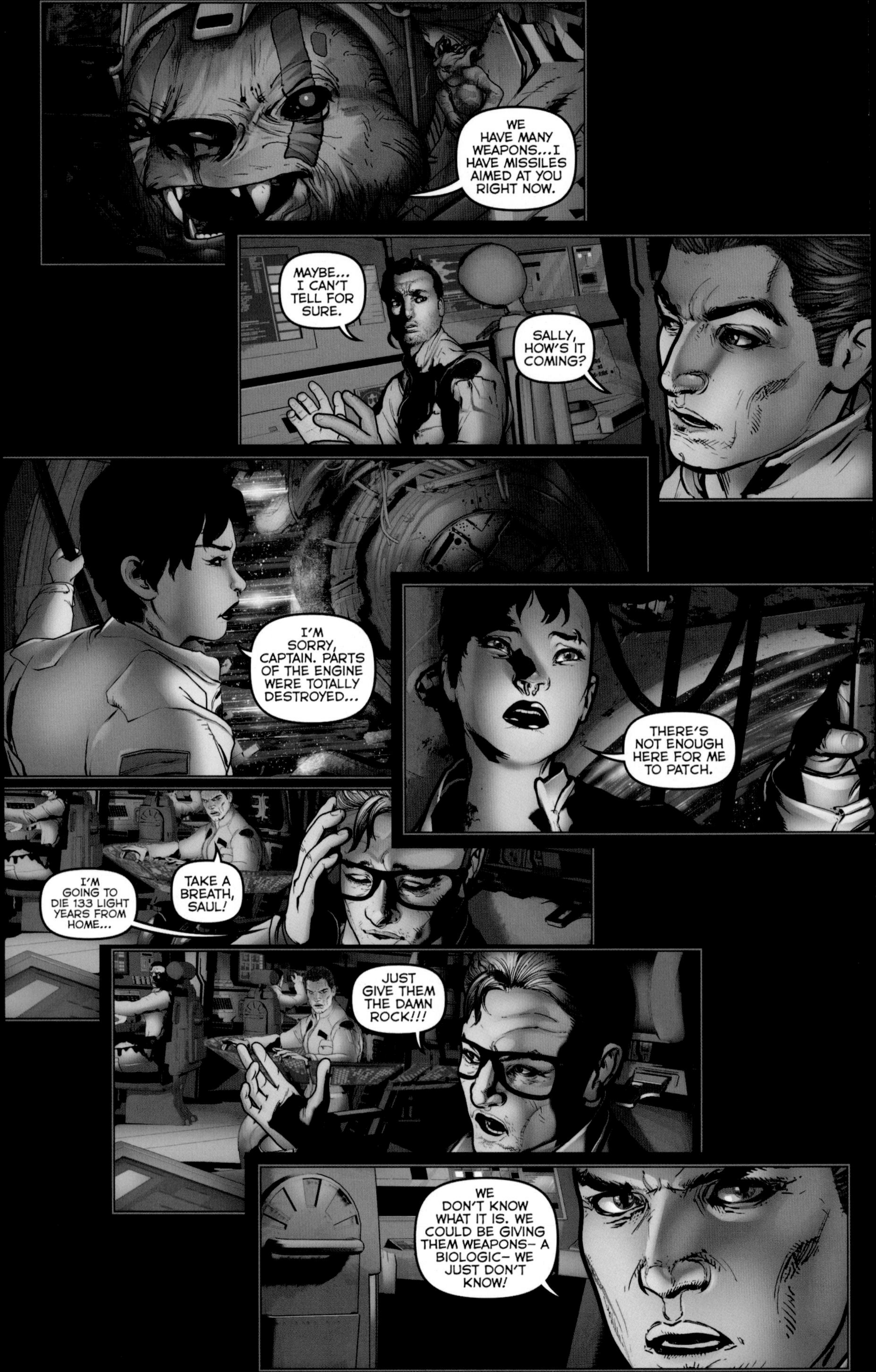
WE HAVE MANY WEAPONS...I HAVE MISSILES AIMED AT YOU RIGHT NOW.
MAYBE... I CAN'T TELL FOR SURE.
SALLY, HOW'S IT COMING?
I'M SORRY, CAPTAIN. PARTS OF THE ENGINE WERE TOTALLY DESTROYED...
THERE'S NOT ENOUGH HERE FOR ME TO PATCH.
I'M GOING TO DIE 133 LIGHT YEARS FROM HOME...
TAKE A BREATH, SAUL!
JUST GIVE THEM THE DAMN ROCK!!!
WE DON'T KNOW WHAT IT IS. WE COULD BE GIVING THEM WEAPONS– A BIOLOGIC– WE JUST DON'T KNOW!

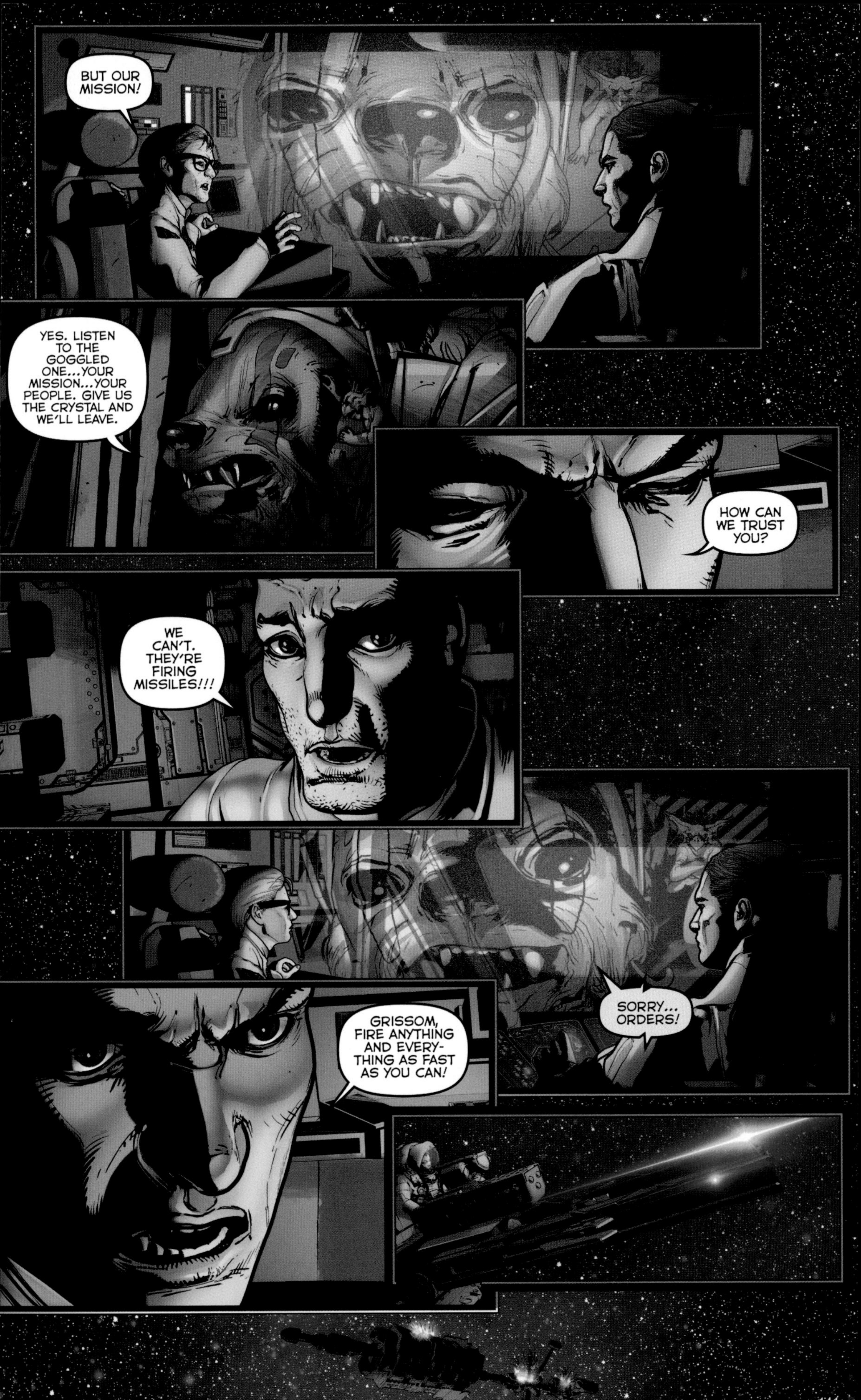
BUT OUR MISSION!
YES. LISTEN TO THE GOGGLED ONE...YOUR MISSION...YOUR PEOPLE. GIVE US THE CRYSTAL AND WE'LL LEAVE.
HOW CAN WE TRUST YOU?
WE CAN'T. THEY'RE FIRING MISSILES!!!
SORRY... ORDERS!
GRISSOM, FIRE ANYTHING AND EVERY-THING AS FAST AS YOU CAN!

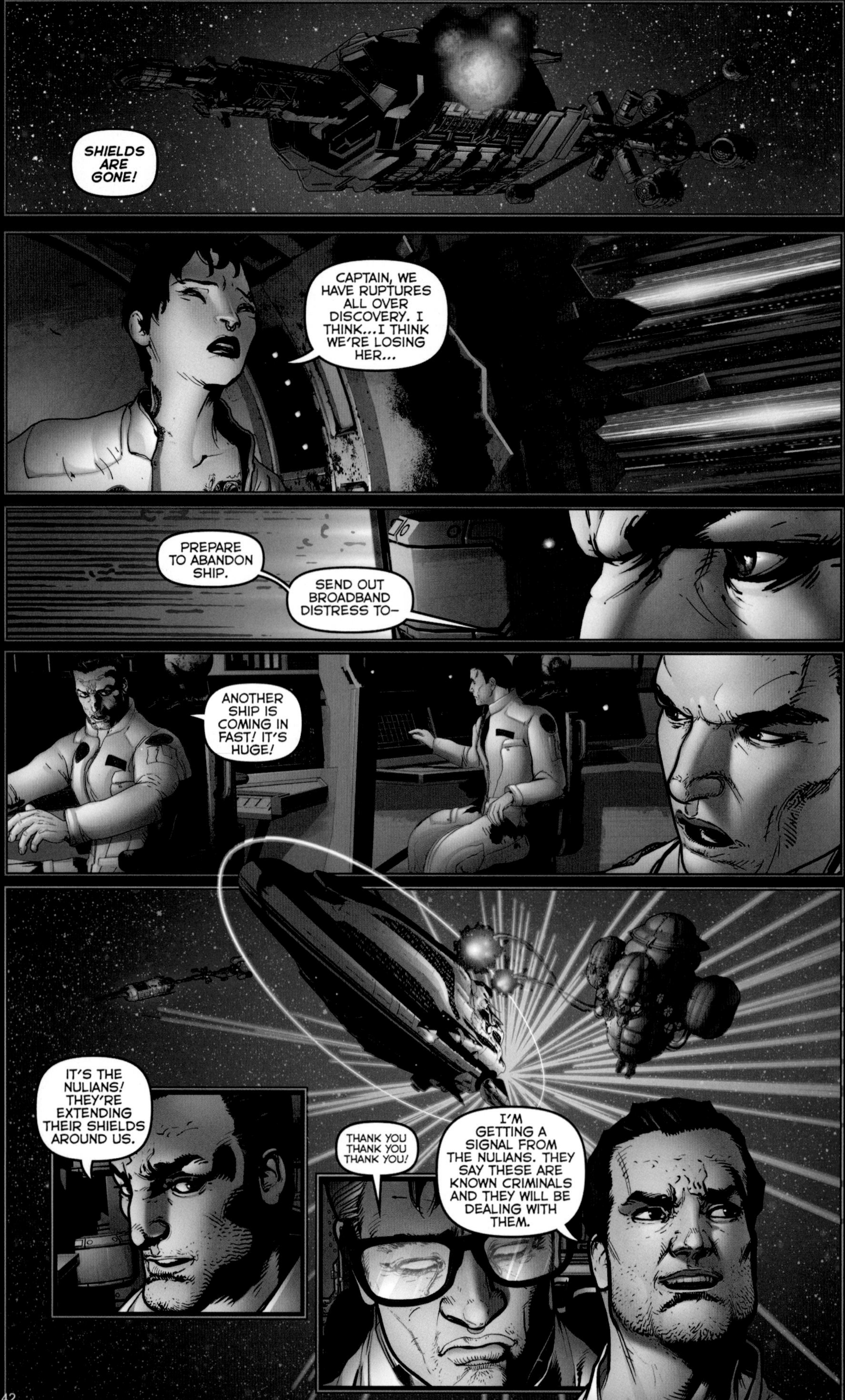
SHIELDS ARE GONE!
CAPTAIN, WE HAVE RUPTURES ALL OVER DISCOVERY. I THINK...I THINK WE'RE LOSING HER...
PREPARE TO ABANDON SHIP.
SEND OUT BROADBAND DISTRESS TO–
ANOTHER SHIP IS COMING IN FAST! IT'S HUGE!
IT'S THE NULIANS! THEY'RE EXTENDING THEIR SHIELDS AROUND US.
THANK YOU THANK YOU THANK YOU!
I'M GETTING A SIGNAL FROM THE NULIANS. THEY SAY THESE ARE KNOWN CRIMINALS AND THEY WILL BE DEALING WITH THEM.

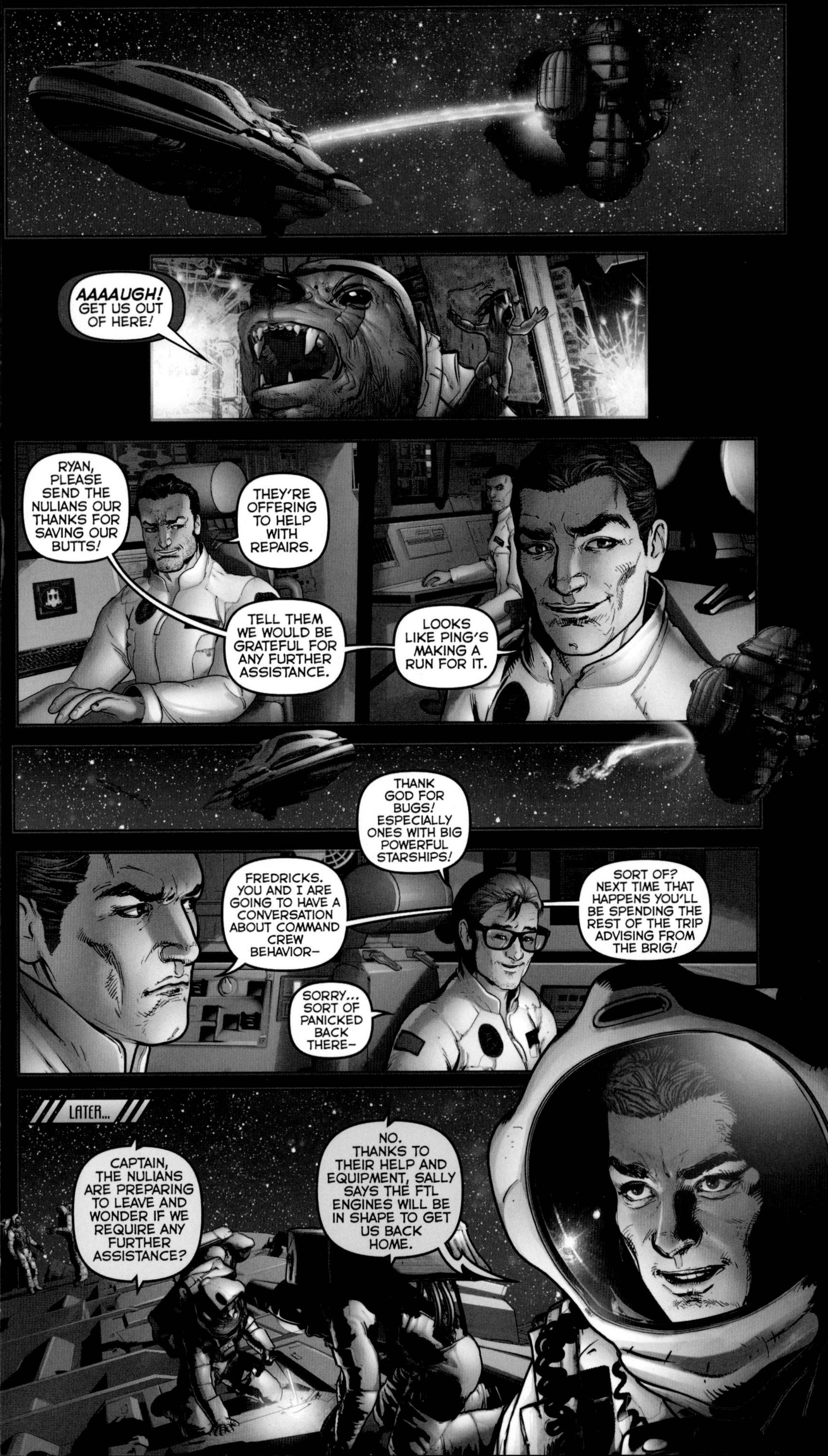
AAAAUGH! GET US OUT OF HERE!
RYAN, PLEASE SEND THE NULIANS OUR THANKS FOR SAVING OUR BUTTS!
THEY'RE OFFERING TO HELP WITH REPAIRS.
TELL THEM WE WOULD BE GRATEFUL FOR ANY FURTHER ASSISTANCE.
LOOKS LIKE PING'S MAKING A RUN FOR IT.
THANK GOD FOR BUGS! ESPECIALLY ONES WITH BIG POWERFUL STARSHIPS!
FREDRICKS. YOU AND I ARE GOING TO HAVE A CONVERSATION ABOUT COMMAND CREW BEHAVIOR–
SORRY... SORT OF PANICKED BACK THERE–
SORT OF? NEXT TIME THAT HAPPENS YOU'LL BE SPENDING THE REST OF THE TRIP ADVISING FROM THE BRIG!
LATER...
CAPTAIN, THE NULIANS ARE PREPARING TO LEAVE AND WONDER IF WE REQUIRE ANY FURTHER ASSISTANCE?
NO. THANKS TO THEIR HELP AND EQUIPMENT, SALLY SAYS THE FTL ENGINES WILL BE IN SHAPE TO GET US BACK HOME.

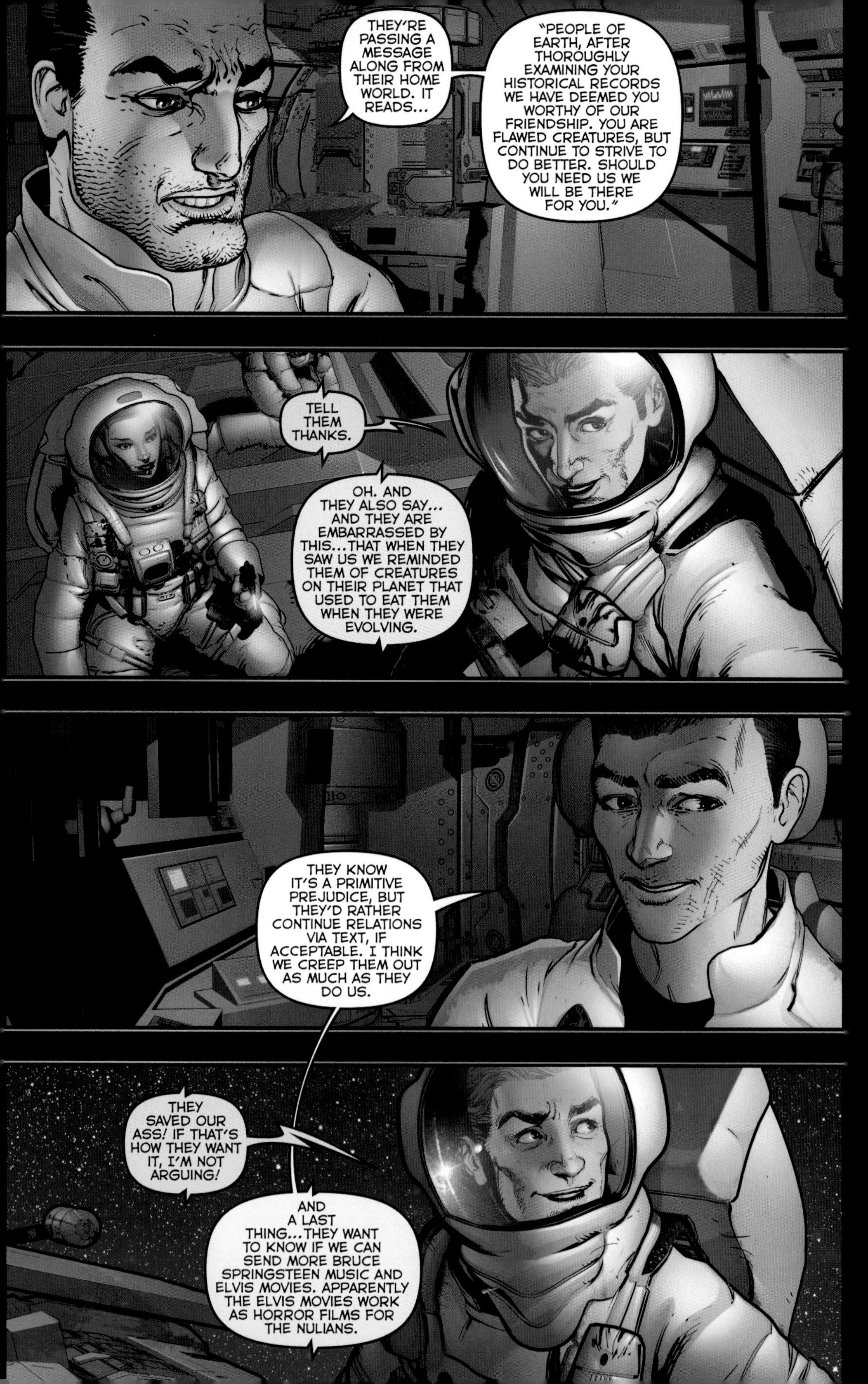
THEY'RE PASSING A MESSAGE ALONG FROM THEIR HOME WORLD. IT READS...
"PEOPLE OF EARTH, AFTER THOROUGHLY EXAMINING YOUR HISTORICAL RECORDS WE HAVE DEEMED YOU WORTHY OF OUR FRIENDSHIP. YOU ARE FLAWED CREATURES, BUT CONTINUE TO STRIVE TO DO BETTER. SHOULD YOU NEED US WE WILL BE THERE FOR YOU."
TELL THEM THANKS.
OH. AND THEY ALSO SAY... AND THEY ARE EMBARRASSED BY THIS...THAT WHEN THEY SAW US WE REMINDED THEM OF CREATURES ON THEIR PLANET THAT USED TO EAT THEM WHEN THEY WERE EVOLVING.
THEY KNOW IT'S A PRIMITIVE PREJUDICE, BUT THEY'D RATHER CONTINUE RELATIONS VIA TEXT, IF ACCEPTABLE. I THINK WE CREEP THEM OUT AS MUCH AS THEY DO US.
THEY SAVED OUR ASS! IF THAT'S HOW THEY WANT IT, I'M NOT ARGUING!
AND A LAST THING...THEY WANT TO KNOW IF WE CAN SEND MORE BRUCE SPRINGSTEEN MUSIC AND ELVIS MOVIES. APPARENTLY THE ELVIS MOVIES WORK AS HORROR FILMS FOR THE NULIANS.

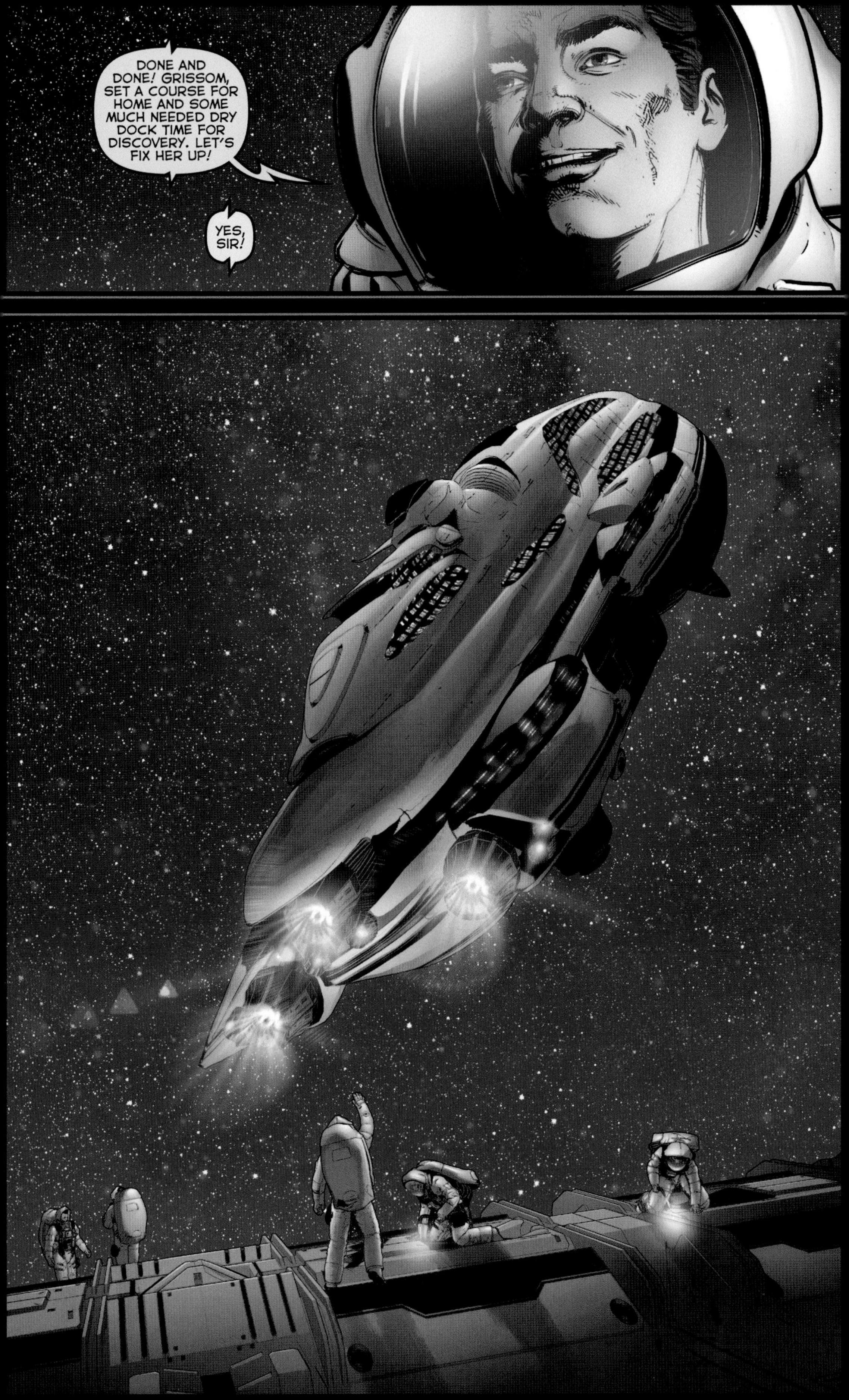
DONE AND DONE! GRISSOM, SET A COURSE FOR HOME AND SOME MUCH NEEDED DRY DOCK TIME FOR DISCOVERY. LET'S FIX HER UP!
YES, SIR!

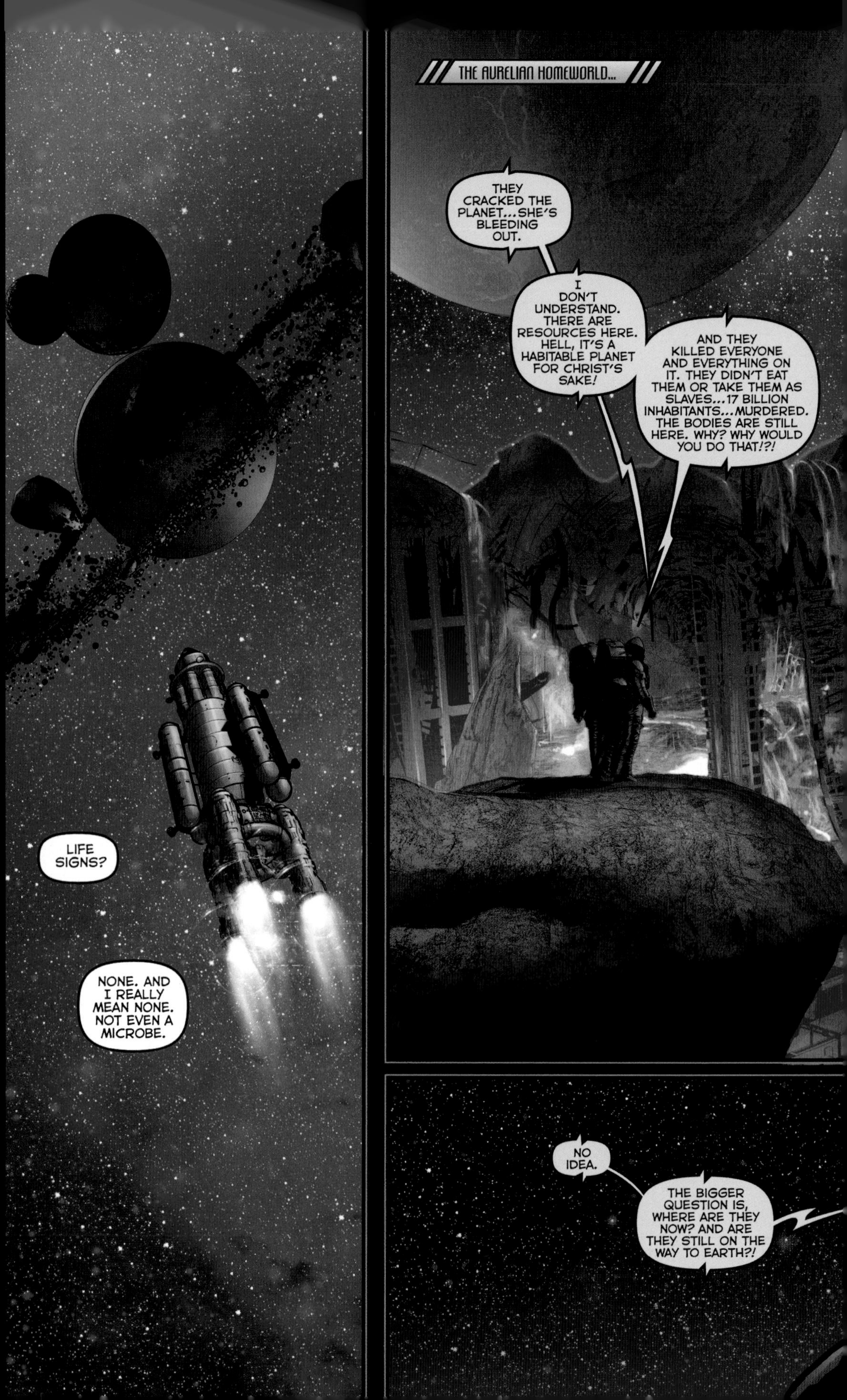
LIFE SIGNS?
NONE. AND I REALLY MEAN NONE. NOT EVEN A MICROBE.
THE AURELIAN HOMEWORLD...
THEY CRACKED THE PLANET...SHE'S BLEEDING OUT.
I DON'T UNDERSTAND. THERE ARE RESOURCES HERE. HELL, IT'S A HABITABLE PLANET FOR CHRIST'S SAKE!
AND THEY KILLED EVERYONE AND EVERYTHING ON IT. THEY DIDN'T EAT THEM OR TAKE THEM AS SLAVES...17 BILLION INHABITANTS...MURDERED. THE BODIES ARE STILL HERE. WHY? WHY WOULD YOU DO THAT!?!
NO IDEA.
THE BIGGER QUESTION IS, WHERE ARE THEY NOW? AND ARE THEY STILL ON THE WAY TO EARTH?!

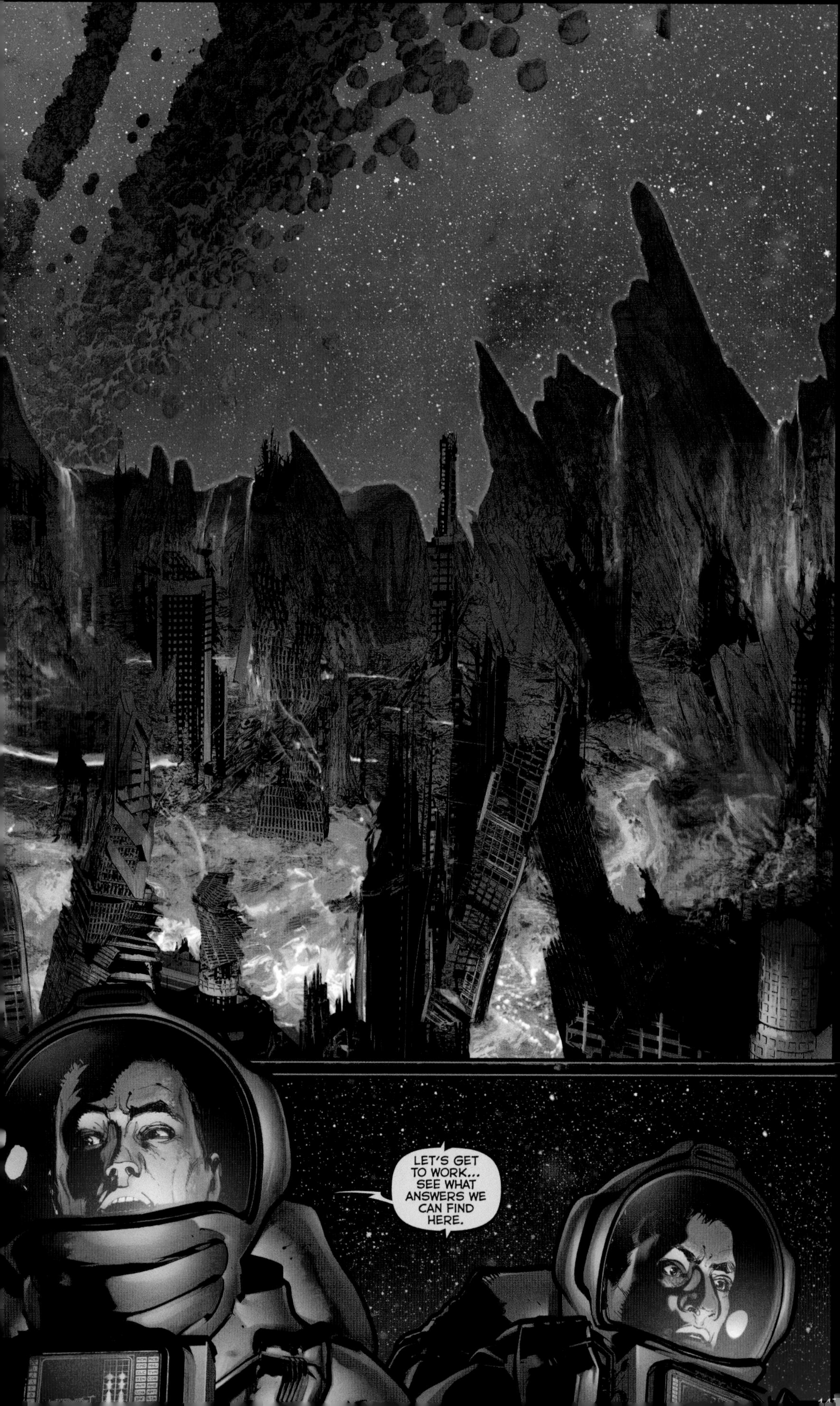
LET'S GET TO WORK... SEE WHAT ANSWERS WE CAN FIND HERE.

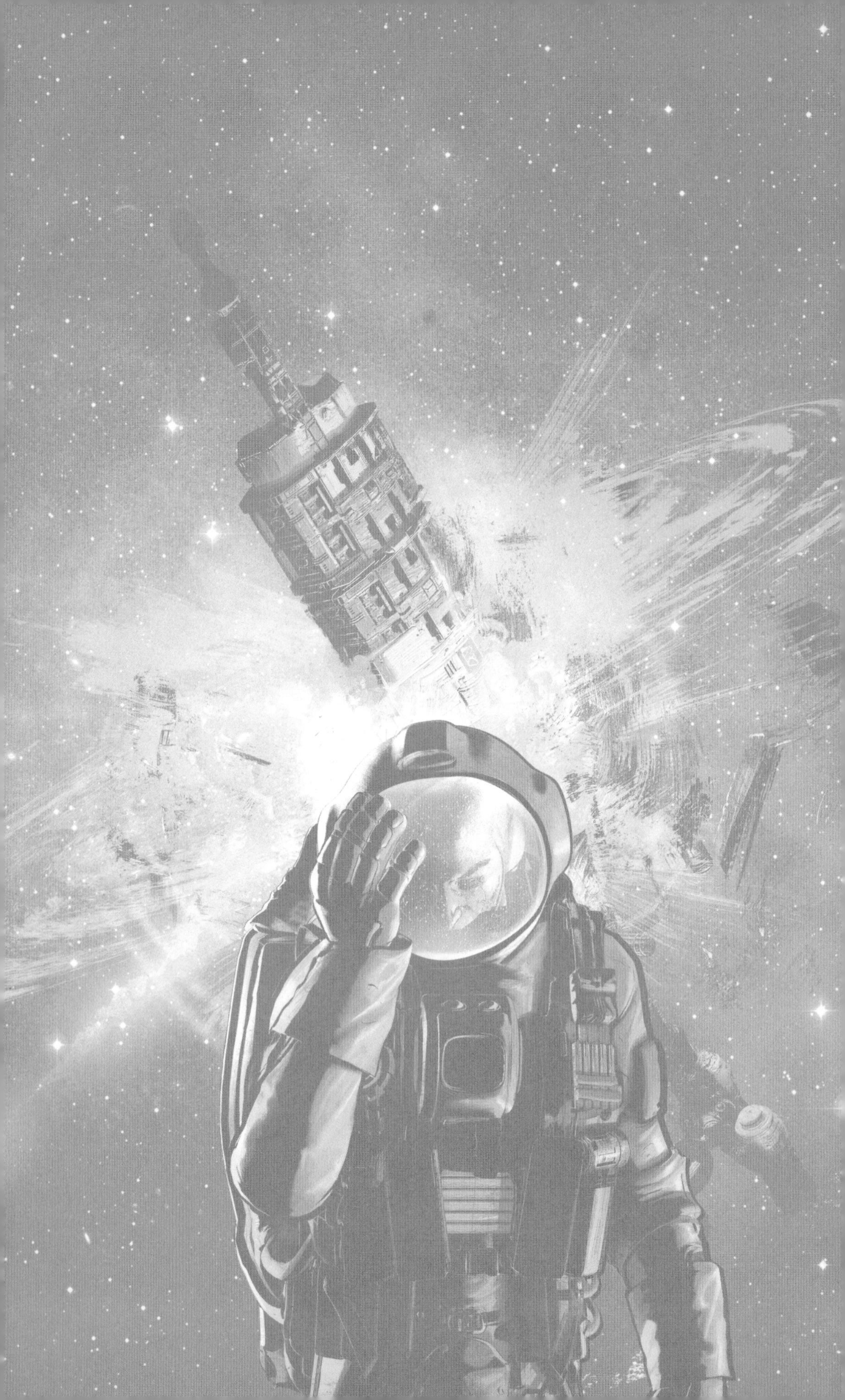

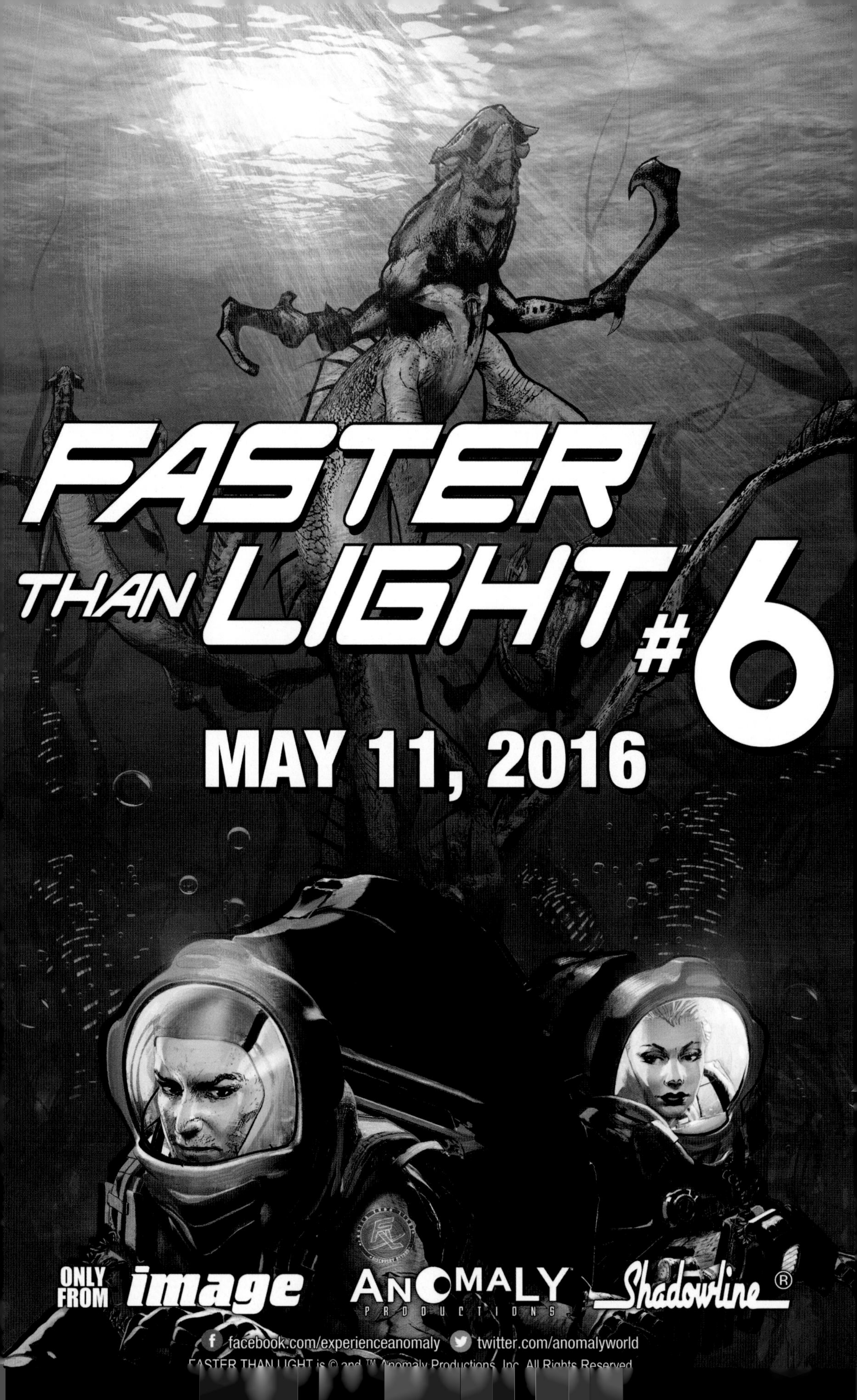

FASTER THAN LIGHT™ #6
MAY 11, 2016
ONLY FROM image
ANOMALY PRODUCTIONS
Shadowline®
facebook.com/experienceanomaly
twitter.com/anomalyworld
FASTER THAN LIGHT is © and ™ Anomaly Productions, Inc. All Rights Reserved.

THIS is diversity! Graphic Novels For the Discriminating Reader

HORROR

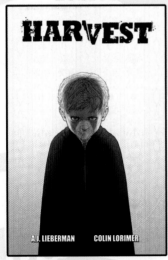

HARVEST
A.J. LIEBERMAN
COLIN LORIMER

HUMOR

XENOHOLICS

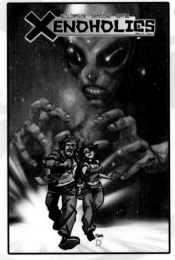

HISTORICAL FICTION

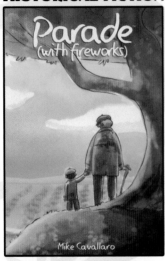

Parade
(with fireworks)
Mike Cavallaro

SUPER-HERO

THE MANTLE
ED BRISSON
BRIAN LEVEL
JORDAN BOYD
VOLUME ONE

SCIENCE-FICTION

HABERLIN VAN DYKE HEMP
FASTER THAN LIGHT
VOLUME ONE

ADULT CONTENT

BOMB QUEEN
DELUXE EDITION
VOLUME ONE
Jimmie Robinson

Follow ShadowlineComics on f and t

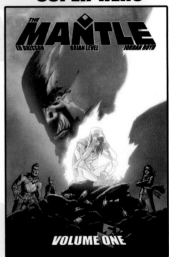

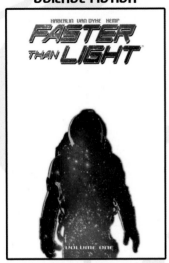

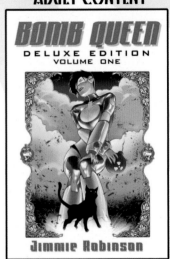

A Book For Every Reader...A Book For Every Taste!

DRAMA

indy

AUTO-BIO

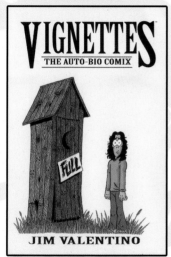

KID FRIENDLY

FANTASY

CRIME

Only from image® Shadowline®